"Buried bene[...]
Night, Deadly N[...]
lack - a uniqu[...], and thus cult film status."
MATTHEW ROZSA, *Salon.com*

"His personal psychodrama which keeps us
engaged with what is as much a human tragedy
as a succession of sensational thrills."
ANTON BITEL, *Little White Lies*

"Smart exploitation filmmaking."
RICHARD CORLISS, *TIME Magazine*

"Worth revisiting every December."
PATRICK CAVANAUGH, *The Wolfman Cometh*

"An exploitative surgical strike on its era's
hollow feelings of holiday cheer by way of a broadside
attack against both Christian conservatism and
the perpetual misery machine of Catholicism."
NICK ROGERS, *Midwest Film Journal*

"Puts the axe back in Xmas."
ROB ALDAM, *Backseat Mafia*

"Honestly, if you're a horror fan, *Silent Night, Deadly Night*
should be an essential part of your Christmas rotation."
PATRICK KING, *Cultured Vultures*

beneath the blood-soaked Santa suit, "Silent Night" has something a lot of slasher films ... identity, and thus cult-film statu...

SILENT NIGHT, DEADLY NIGHT

He knows
when you've
been naughty.™

by
Armando Muñoz

Based on the screenplay by
Michael Hickey

Foreword by
Scott Schneid & Dennis Whitehead

TITAN BOOKS

Silent Night, Deadly Night
Print edition ISBN: 9781803362649
E-book edition ISBN: 9781803362687

Published by Titan Books
A division of Titan Publishing Group Ltd
144 Southwark Street, London SE1 0UP
www.titanbooks.com

First edition: October 2025
10 9 8 7 6 5 4 3 2 1

This is a work of fiction. All of the characters, organizations, and events portrayed in this novel are either products of the author's imagination or are used fictitiously. Any resemblance to actual persons, living or dead (except for satirical purposes), is entirely coincidental.

A CIP catalogue record for this title is available from the British Library.

EU RP (for authorities only)
eucomply OÜ, Pärnu mnt. 139b-14, 11317 Tallinn, Estonia
hello@eucompliancepartner.com, +3375690241

Designed and typeset in Minion Pro by Richard Mason.

Printed and bound by CPI Group (UK) Ltd, Croydon, CR0 4YY.

For Santa Claus

FOREWORD

Scott Schneid & Dennis Whitehead

The oft-used phrase *"This isn't your father's…"* – car, computer, fill in the blank – applies oh-so-well to author Armando Muñoz' novelization of the screenplay for our cult classic SILENT NIGHT, DEADLY NIGHT. We've wanted to do a book based on Michael Hickey's lean-mean screenplay for quite some time, and can proudly say good things come to those who wait (in this case, pairing Armando, an accomplished horror novelist and fan of the film, with the right material). The result… a long overdue novelization of our holiday slasher that sure as hell AIN'T your father's SNDN.

To novelize or not to novelize, that was the initial question. What's the point of doing one if you're just going to faithfully rehash the movie script, character for character, scene for scene, subplot for subplot. No, Armando had something more devilish in mind, and we let him loose, taking the reader on a ride into the subterranean depths of emotional depravity. Whose, you might ask? Well, our lead characters of course: Billy, Mother Superior, Grandpa, Sister Margaret and others.

Remember, SNDN was made in 1984, a very conservative time in America. And while it shocked many upon its release – *"Santa Claus as a psycho killer...? How dare you?!"* – that was then and this is now. So while a good story is both timeless and universal (and we always thought SNDN was a very good story), the zeitgeist of the '80s limited just how deep we could explore the impact that violence and repression can have on a human being. Yes, Billy impaled Denise on reindeer antlers and Mother Superior took pleasure whipping her charges with a leather belt, but Armando wanted more. Much, much more. More dysfunctional behavior, more psychological underbelly, more ugliness – ideas and story points that we could never have woven into the '84 film unless we wanted nobody to see it... no studio to release it.

So, who is Armando Muñoz and why did we hire him? Well, we were introduced to Armando by the ever-energetic documentary filmmaker Anthony Masi, founder of Beyond Killer Games (formerly Stop The Killer Games), a company that makes slasher board games from '80s horror films (including SNDN), and now novelizations of same. Anthony, an admirer of Armando's work, thought he'd be great to do the adaptation, and set up a lunch for the four of us. Prior to getting together, we'd read a couple of Armando's early horror novels and really dug his writing. Growing up in a conservative Nevada town, he harbored an aversion to both the church and the moral majority, feeling them to be "an oppressive force in American culture during the 1980s." And although the movie didn't make it to his little berg in its initial theatrical run, Armando saw it on VHS two years later, beginning a decades-long love affair with all things SNDN. During the course of our 2-plus hours with Armando, we encouraged him to expand on Michael's original screenplay, to deepen what was already there, add new characters and kills as he saw fit. We gave him free rein to explore, confident that he would deliver something very special.

The novel format allows a writer to dig deep. Armando has done that here and we hope you love it. We also know that some of you may find it abhorrent, disgusting or just plain in baaaaad taste. If you're in the latter camp, you would have been in good company back in 1984. Those that picketed theaters playing the movie – yes, numerous folks actually did, protesting the vile, anti-family-values horror show splashed across neighborhood marquees – might have a cardiac arrest if they read the novelization today. We don't think you will. As a matter of fact, we agree with our writer, who told us that the first time he saw SNDN he thought it was a "refreshing middle finger to authority" and felt "those who protested its release back in the day were the offensive ones."

SILENT NIGHT, DEADLY NIGHT shocked and pissed off a whole lot of people in the year of our Lord nineteen-eighty-four. A fairly simple, straightforward story about a psychotic Santa Claus offing the naughty on Christmas Eve, it became an infamous pop culture phenomenon that has lived on through the decades. Now, almost forty years later, here comes the novelization, poised to again shock horror fans everywhere. While remaining faithful to the original story, author Muñoz has added new characters, new plot elements, and more mayhem. So, like Armando, who prefers his entertainment on the "naughty" side, let's celebrate that he has given us another holiday tradition we can revel in:

Silent Night, Deadly Night: The Novel

Let the reading begin!

Scott Schneid & Dennis Whitehead
Co-Executive Producers – SILENT NIGHT, DEADLY NIGHT
LOS ANGELES, CALIFORNIA
NOVEMBER 2023

You've made it through Halloween,
now try and survive
Christmas.

CHAPTER 1

In Christmas Joy, the holiday season was never-ending.

The town was nestled in a deep Utah valley between rolling hills and expansive rock formations. Through the extended winter season, which lasted from October until March or April when the thaw finally arrived, the quaint township of Christmas Joy was a winter wonderland blanketed with snow. A white Christmas was guaranteed, and a white New Year, and a white Valentine's Day most likely. White Easters weren't uncommon. Easter egg hunting in the snow was an added treat.

Mormon settlers landed in the valley in 1849. The founders' decision to make it a holiday town was strictly financial. A holiday would be an easy point of civic pride, and create a yearly windfall as the season approached, whichever season was chosen.

The town could have been Thanksgiving Falls and filled the land with turkey farms. Or maybe Easterburg, where they held the biggest annual Easter egg hunt in the state. But with their coffers firmly in mind, the founders settled on Christmas Joy. Christmas was the biggest cash grab holiday of them all with presents all but mandatory. And the windfall could be attributed to the baby Jesus, bless his thrifty little heart.

The date Christmas Joy was officially established was December 24, 1854. The founder who chose the town name was Randall Hart, a literature lover who adored *The Night Before Christmas*. At the founders' yearly Christmas parties, Randall was known to stage a highly theatrical reading of the poem, sitting high upon a stool while reading by the light of a candlestick.

Another suggested name, Santa Town, was luckily passed over. What a public relations disaster that would have been later in the next century.

Starting in 1914, a yearly Christmas Market was established on all weekends in December. Held at the city park and town square, this became a celebratory civic hub of commerce during the holiday season. There was only one year, 1951, when no Christmas Market was held, as that month brought the state's heaviest snowfall of the century.

The Christmas Rejoice Presbyterian Church opened in 1906, and quickly became the community's favored house of worship. The church house was striking, with a steeply slanted southern roof that featured many stained-glass mosaics. Somehow the windows never broke from the weight of the heavy snowfall, and that was considered by many to be some kind of miracle. The building sat above fifteen wide steps, which helped keep the church house above snow level most of the time. The high point of this impressive structure was not a cross, but a dazzling, sparkling Star of Bethlehem. This guiding star of faith could be seen from every corner of town.

The town's Catholic church, the Conception of Saint Mary Church, was rather modest in comparison to the Presbyterian Church. Attendance was low during the winter months, as the church never had an adequate heating system. Nobody could hear the sermons over the rattling radiators that gave off an unpleasant electrical smell and no discernible heat. People joked you had to be cold-blooded to go there. Preaching blue lips issued forth a chilly mist.

While the congregation at the Conception of Saint Mary Church was meager, the Catholic church had a heavy presence in the community due to Saint Mary's Home for Orphaned Children, a sprawling brick fortress on the outskirts of town. The orphanage housed forty or more orphans most of the time.

Unlike the rest of the town, the orphanage exhibited no holiday pride, and there were zero decorations during the holiday season. This resistance was not the edict of the orphanage alone. The Catholic Church held considerable resistance to the modern marketing of Christmas with toy sales and Santa Claus, so much so that some spoke about this holiday war like a grudge match – the Catholic Church vs. Santa Claus.

Perhaps the Catholics recognized the pagan traditions incorporated into the modern holiday. The Holy Day of Obligation was obligation enough, with mandatory attendance at one of the triduum of Masses - the Angels' Mass at midnight, the Shepard's Mass at dawn, or the King's Mass on

Christmas Day. There was no Santa's Mass, as some deacons were wont to point out.

Despite their steadfast adherence to doctrine, Saint Mary's Home for Orphaned Children would have a major part to play in the evolution of Santa Claus in the late twentieth century. So infamous would their part be that the whole nation would learn of the events that transpired there over the years, culminating in many acts that would shock the world.

The orphanage would become the new North Pole of Naughtiness.

If Christmas Joy had a holiday industry, it was provided by the flora. The town advertised year-round all the holiday plants native to the area, including Evergreen Pines, firs, poinsettias, and that suck face flora most preferred by holiday horndogs, mistletoe. The demand for Christmas trees over the holidays was high as people from across the state made a yearly pilgrimage to Christmas Joy to get one, giving them bragging rights.

As the 1970s arrived, the plant business that made the most greenbacks was Mistletoe Farms. The expansive plant nursery located on the outskirts of town was owned and operated by Dolores Cliff, a lumberjack-dressed lesbian whose moxie was matched only by the size of her mullet. Mean kids often taunted her over her manly looks, driving by Mistletoe Farms shouting out her nickname, Mr. Camel Toe. In response, she would grab the belt loops of her jeans and hitch her pants high to show it off. She wore her camel toe with the same pride she wore her hair.

One pugnacious teen once wandered into her nursery taunting, "Hey Mr. Camel Toe! Who's your wife, Mrs. Claus!?"

The bully's hounding laughter turned to a high-pitched yelp of terror when she charged at him with a double-bladed tree-chopping axe, chasing him all the way to the edge of her lot.

"You want to be a eunuch!? I'll give you a camel toe!" Dolores shouted with conviction.

This happened one week before Christmas, when Mistletoe Farms was doing peak business. Her sales increased as word got around, and a new nickname was born – Lezzy Borden.

When the holiday season rolled around in 1971, Christmas Joy was suffering a depression of sorts. This crisis was not economic, but spiritual. The population was at a high of 29,480.

The Vietnam War had been going on far too long, beamed nightly into homes on the evening news. On this year, forty-three favored sons of Christmas Joy were absent, spending their holiday in that hopeless, war-torn region overseas. As families sat by the fire and ate Christmas pudding (thirteen ingredients to represent Jesus and his twelve disciples), the G.I.s in the swampy, hot jungles were lucky to have blood pudding (two ingredients: rice and pig's blood) for the holiday.

Less than one dozen of this year's local servicemen would ever make it back to Christmas Joy alive, shell-shocked and far removed from the holiday spirit. Good will toward men did not apply on those distant battlefields which followed the young men home within their heads.

The Love Generation was well represented in town since the late 1960s, but this winter many of them were heartbroken. Jim Morrison had died that summer, closing those doors of perception behind him, and following so close behind the losses of Jimi Hendrix and Janis Joplin, their trip had turned bad. Youth saw little hope for the future.

The seasonal weather was unusually mild this year, following an unexpected Indian summer. Some modest snowfall still dusted the hills, but there was little snow left in town. To many it just didn't look like Christmas. Rigid traditionalists thought the holiday would be ruined because their Christmas wasn't white enough.

There was one public event that December that would have people talking well into the next year. The Little Miss Christmas Cutie Pageant was a tradition since 1963, established in part to lift the spirits of the town during another depressed holiday season, due to the November assassination of President John F. Kennedy. The pageant was held at the Christmas Joy Community Center, the largest indoor gathering spot in town. Attendance had steadily grown each year, until spectators were packed to the rafters.

The contestants were local girls between the ages of eight and twelve, doing their best with their awkward stage walking to imitate Shirley Temple in cutesy Christmas couture. The top prizes for Little Miss Christmas Cutie were a sash, a trophy, a crown that had a large star in the front which looked like a Christmas tree topper, and a $100 gift certificate for Ira's Toys, the town's most popular toy store located on

Main Street just two blocks from the park.

Nobody in attendance that year was prepared for the debut of little Denise Delaney.

This stage stealing five-year-old had the audience enraptured from the moment she strutted out in her holly adorned halter top, short skirt made of tinsel, and belt spotted with sleigh bells. The youngest contestant to ever enter the contest, she was also the most mature. Rather than imitate Shirley Temple, she went full Marilyn Monroe, and she had the blonde hair and artificial mole to match.

Those who found Denise scandalous would call the girl a slut who took after her mother. Sandra Delaney would certainly win an adult Christmas Cutie pageant if the town had one. Denise's reputation was established at that pageant and would only grow over time.

Denise won the title of Little Miss Christmas Cutie 1971 to great applause. When given the microphone after she was crowned, she bragged.

"My booty is a cutie!" Denise exclaimed as she wiggled her bottom for all to see. Each shake produced a pronounced jingle from her sleigh bell belt. The audience responded with thunderous laughter, and a few highly inappropriate catcalls and wagging tongues.

Denise knew what the audience wanted and served it to them, blowing kisses, winking, and shaking her behind. "Jingle booty! Jingle booty!" Denise added, and the reaction nearly blew the roof off the joint.

The Shirley Temples were not at all happy with the

mini-Marilyn in their midst. They were fully ignored, many of them bawling their eyes out from the side of the stage.

The town would be reciting Denise's catchphrases and shaking their jingle booties for many seasons.

There was another homegrown export that holiday season that would go beyond local lingo and become a part of the nation's holiday tradition for thousands, if not millions. It started with a song.

Mary Songbird was the stage name for a young local folk singer who debuted during the Summer of Love. She modeled herself after Joan Baez, singing peace songs while playing an acoustic guitar, and two years later she would see Joan perform live as the closing act for the first night at Woodstock. That was the best night of her life.

By 1971, peace was no longer selling, and living in Christmas Joy brought few performing opportunities. Taking local pride to heart, Mary recorded an original Christmas album in her home studio called Christmas Joy Carols. For the first time, she billed herself as Merry Songbird.

The first single, titled "Santa's Watching", was released on the day after Thanksgiving, 1971, and got played on a few radio stations in Utah. The catchy holiday carol quickly became the number one requested track of the day, and Merry became a seasonal success.

It was a shame that for many locals, the song "Santa's Watching" would bring a chill instead of cheer. The song was the top single on Utah's radio stations on Christmas Eve, the night of Santa's terrible, shocking rampage.

"Santa's watching, Santa's waiting.
Christmas Eve is slowly fading.
Can you hear him in the night?
Close your door, turn out the light.

Santa's watching, Santa's creeping.
Now you're nodding, now you're sleeping.
Were you good for mom and dad?
Santa knows if you've been bad.

There might be a treat for you in Santa's bag of toys,
But Christmas won't be fun and games
for naughty girls and boys.

Santa's watching, Santa's waiting.
Everybody's celebrating.
Did you do your best this year?
Too late now, 'cause SANTA'S HERE."

Christmas Joy appeared to be the quintessential small American town, festive with holiday jingles and carols carried on the crisp winter breeze. The town wished to embody the holiday in every shape, sound, and sensation. If the town had a flavor, it would be the biting sweetness of a peppermint candy cane.

But these holiday staples were a woefully thin blanket

that covered an ominous underbelly of hidden abuses and collective town sin.

On the surface, the town existed in a perpetual haze of good cheer and morality. But there was a rot beneath the syrupy holiday sweetness, a cavity capable of great pain, causing irreversible damage. Denial allowed the rot to spread unchecked.

For the many who were depressed during the holiday season, they were stuck in a town where that season had no end.

Christmas Joy was not the puritanical Christian paradise it purported to be, and no amount of holiday decorations draped excessively over the community could hide the truth. One major tragedy had the potential to forever turn the clock back to medieval times and ancient blood rites.

On December 24, 1971, Christmas Joy's social contract with the holiday would unravel with the speed of a dry Christmas tree going up in flames.

It would be a silent night, deadly night.

CHAPTER 2

The cold and barren Utah landscape seemed starkly undressed for Christmas Eve, Jim Chapman thought. The massive mountains in the distance were thoroughly snow-topped, and the surrounding perky hills had a modest covering, like a sheer negligee. But the valley floor they were driving through was about as bare as a stripper's shaved crotch.

Jim smirked at the thought, then caught himself. Dirty thoughts while driving was the norm to keep him alert during particularly long jaunts, and he endured a considerable amount of those. As an accountant, he frequently had to travel across the state doing the books for several businesses. He couldn't get too excited by driving sex fantasies now, because he was carrying his whole family in their Chevrolet Kingswood station wagon for this Christmas Eve excursion.

The sky was a heavy gray, keeping full daylight at a distance while adding drabness to the unremarkable scenery. Last Christmas Eve this drive had been perilous, with active blizzard conditions and patches of black ice on the asphalt.

The station wagon had fishtailed and nearly sent them into a snowbank on the side of the road. His wife Ellie screamed so loud it nearly made his ears bleed. She also reminded him of that frightening near miss as they set off on today's journey, as though that ice had been his fault.

The family was silent now. Ellie sat beside him with their almost one-year-old son Ricky on her lap. The baby was awake but quiet. Perhaps he was lulled into a stupor by the rattling car and the constant stream of Christmas music on the AM radio.

They could consider the silence a Christmas miracle. Like most parents of young ones, quiet time was a rarity. They'd been operating on limited sleep for five years, which made them frequently grouchy and easy to irritate, especially with each other.

He glanced at his wife and saw her looking with a contented smile at the scenery outside the windows. All his gripes were swept aside. It was Christmas Eve, and he'd be remiss if he didn't count his blessings, starting with his wife. With her bosom boosted by motherhood, she wore a tight blue button up sweater over her pink blouse. Despite their depressing destination, she'd put on considerable makeup, with striking eyeshadow, rouge on her cheeks, and candy red lipstick. Her blonde hair was styled ala America's Sweetheart Cybill Shepherd.

No doubt about it, he had the most bangable wife on the block, if not in all of Christmas Joy. Not that there'd been much banging since little Ricky's arrival.

Both of their boys were blessings. While he'd never say so to Ellie, he was proudest to have two male children, because he found them to be the superior sex. His mindset was conditioned by his upbringing. The youngest of four brothers, his single parent household was run by his strict disciplinarian father Harold. His mother had died not long after his birth, so he had no memory or sense of her. She'd died tragically young at thirty-four by natural causes. Jim never had reason to question his dad about her passing. Maybe he should have.

Ricky was acting the angel now, but that was typically not the case. His other son, five-year-old Billy, was exceptionally well-behaved. Billy was that rare anomaly – a thoughtful child who resisted the urge to chatter incessantly and move about restlessly.

Billy was occupied by a book on the back seat. When Jim was five, he'd had no interest in reading, nor had he at ten. He wouldn't pick up a periodical with written words for fun until he discovered *Playboy* when he was in middle school. Those magazines he only looked at for the pictures.

His family was his greatest blessing. It was good to recognize this while he had them around, or before he got soft in the head and could no longer remember or appreciate them. That terrible fate he might be genetically predisposed toward if he took after his father.

Each day was a gift, and you never knew when you'd received your last one.

The song on the radio ended, a jazzy instrumental of 'Silent Night'. Interesting that even without voices he heard the words in his head. They were quite fertile lyrics, with virgin, mother, and child representing the whole reproductive journey of life.

Jim gave his wife a glance, and she wore a grin of holiday contentment. She turned her eyes his way and flashed a loving smile. His excitement rose, and if he got any hotter, he might have to crack his driver's window and get a blast of freezing air. Maybe it wouldn't be such a silent night tonight after all if they could get the bedsprings squeaking. If the boys woke, they could blame the noise on Santa's sleigh.

The announcer on the radio launched into his station identification.

"This is KSCZ radio wishing you the joy of the season. The weather looks good for Santa Claus tonight with a full moon and a starry sky to help him find his way. The temperature right now here in Bartlesville, twenty-one degrees, brrrr! Well, let's listen to 'Christmas Fever'."

There was nobody inside the station wagon with a greater case of Christmas fever than Billy. He was at that perfect age when Christmas was the most mysterious and magical night of the year.

Every seasonal sensation entranced him. The lights and colors and sparkly things. The decorations, the Christmas tree, and the bounty of gift-wrapped presents beneath it. The tastes of peppermint candy, crispy peanut brittle, and the delicious marvel of a gingerbread house. Last Christmas as he ate his first gingerbread house with enthusiasm, he pictured himself like the terrifying Abominable Snowman from *Rudolph the Red-Nosed Reindeer*, which he'd just seen for the first time broadcast on television.

Last week he'd caught his second airing of *Rudolph the Red-Nosed Reindeer*, with some wailing interruptions from his baby brother. He still found the Abominable Snowman frightful, but the beast was kind of adorable too – after all his sharp teeth had been wrenched out of their sockets.

Most exciting for Billy were the rituals of Christmas Eve, culminating in the arrival of Santa Claus.

Today, his parents let him open one present early. The illustrated hardcover picture book in his hands was that gift (strategically chosen to keep him occupied for today's road trip).

This volume was a bit worn around the edges and well read. Though the tag said "From: Santa", his mom told him the book had been originally given to her by her mother when she was Billy's age, and it was now a family heirloom for him to take care of and pass down to his kids. He didn't know what an heirloom was, nor did he understand what his book had to do with hair.

The book was *The Night Before Christmas* by Chester C. Moore. From the glossy front cover to the back, every page was packed with colorful artwork. The most frequent drawings were of Santa Claus. This was no surprise, as the poem's original title was *A Visit From St. Nicholas*.

The first images showed Santa running his toy workshop.

He employed elves in pointy hats to wield saw and hammer and paintbrush, creating building blocks and toy cars and rocking horses. They were all well fed with angel and star-shaped cookies baked and served by Mrs. Claus. Santa must have been eating a lot of her cookies, to judge by his chubby cheeks and round belly.

Once the titular date arrived, Santa filled his magic red sack with presents for all the kids in the world. Then he put the bulging bag into the back of his sleigh and lined up his flying reindeer. They had cool names like Dasher and Prancer and Dopey and Bashful (he often got Santa's reindeer and the Seven Dwarfs mixed up). He was left wondering where Rudolph was. His favorite, red-nosed reindeer was nowhere to be found in the book's pages.

He was eager to make sense of the mythology, because like most legends it was messy and full of competing accounts.

Into the night sky Santa's sleigh took flight, passing over snowy hills and soaring over homes. Billy assumed every family had a house like his, with a front yard, driveway, garage, and backyard with playground equipment. Homes like the ones drawn in the book, with their expansive rooftops used as landing strips for Santa's reindeer and sleigh.

Santa's next feat mystified him the most, and that was his route of entry into the house, through the chimney. He saw Santa as very large with a gift sack just as wide, while the chimney seemed to be a rather skinny passageway. The logical conclusion he made was that Santa stretched himself and his sack out to fit through, like he was made of rubber.

Once inside the living room, Santa distributed his gifts, placing sweets and smaller offerings into the stockings hanging from the mantle over the fireplace, and arranging the bigger presents beneath the Christmas tree. This gift-giving helped him work up a big appetite, which was why milk and cookies were left out for him.

With his delivery made and snacks consumed, Santa placed a finger aside his nose and nodded, and that was all it took for him to slip back up the chimney.

Billy believed that every kid received presents. Gifts were not conditional to good behavior in this book's account of the legend.

Santa's story was easy to understand through the pictures. When it came to reading the whole text of the poem, he was not yet capable. He did recognize individual words throughout. He knew *Christmas*. He knew St. Nick was another name for Santa – the name Santa Claus did not appear in the book once. Other words he was able to discern were *mouse*, *mamma*, *sleigh*, *reindeer*, *toys*, *elf*, and *merry*. He also knew both *belly* and *jelly*, and the way they were placed so close to each other made him giggle. The word *creature* he also recognized, but he didn't like that word much because it gave him the creepers.

There was a joy he found in recognizing words. Understanding brought him pride. He'd met children who had no interest in reading, or outright loathed it. Those were the kids he tended not to like much.

Billy looked through the side window. While he didn't

know if the dark clouds would deliver rain or snow, he knew it was late in the day, and it would soon turn fully black above those clouds. The night before Christmas was coming, but he wasn't going to be back when it arrived.

Worry gripped him. What if their house was at the start of Santa's journey and they weren't home? They hadn't left out any milk or cookies, and the Christmas tree lights were off. Would Santa bypass their house if he wasn't snug in his bed?

His interest in Santa was so great, he wanted to stay awake so when he heard the clatter of hooves overhead, he could slip out of bed, head down the stairs, and see the jolly jelly belly in person. He wanted to meet the legend. Witness the magic. Hand him a cookie, cautiously, like when he fed large animals at the zoo.

"Mom?" Billy asked, revealing two missing front teeth. He'd been losing his teeth lately, though by more pleasant means than the Abominable Snowman.

Ellie looked over the seat and Billy continued. "What time is it?"

Ellie checked the clock on the dashboard. "It's almost 4:30, honey. We're gonna be at grandpas pretty soon."

Jim gave Ellie an appreciative smile, knowing she was being careful with her words for Billy's sake. Referring to this jaunt as visiting grandpa made it sound so traditional, and it was a tradition because they made this trip every Christmas Eve. It would be more depressing to say they were visiting grandpa's hospital. In some of her more heated moments, she'd referred to the place as *that mental ward*.

In Ellie's lap, Ricky was not disturbed by the intrusion of voices. The baby drooled heavily over his pouty lower lip.

The questions Billy had about the book and Santa nagged at him.

"Mom?"

"Yes, Billy?"

"What time does Santa Claus come?"

Ellie found her son's question endearing. The book had worked its magic. There would likely come a time soon when classmates would ruin the illusion for him, so she hoped he enjoyed believing the legend while it lasted. She'd had the myth ruined by a bully cousin before she was six years old and that influenced her feelings about him for life. She never liked him.

"Not until everyone's asleep in bed," Ellie answered.

Billy knew that bedtime came soon after dinner. Maybe they would let him stay up late to see the magic man in action. He firmly believed the fantastic images presented in the storybook would occur in his living room tonight.

"Can't I stay up and see him?"

Ellie smirked at his suggestion. He really was enamored with the legend. With luck he'd listen to her and not try to sneak out of bed that night, only to ruin the legend for himself by seeing who was really putting the presents under their tree. They would not be dressing as Mr. and Mrs. Claus, but they would snack on the milk and cookies left out. She exchanged a grin with Jim.

"I wouldn't do that if I were you," Ellie replied. "It's

naughty to stay up past your bedtime. Santa Claus doesn't bring presents to naughty children."

Billy never wanted to engage in naughty behavior. He prided himself on being a very good boy, the best boy possible, most of the time. It'd be terrible if all his good behavior was for nothing. The next question he asked in a pouty voice.

"What if we don't get home by my bedtime?"

"We will, hon, don't worry." Ellie looked over her shoulder at Billy reassuringly. "Santa Claus is going to bring you a big surprise tonight. You just wait and see." She gave him a knowing smile. Billy tried to return the gesture, but his smile was hesitant.

The big surprise was a bounty of gifts, more than he'd ever received before. While they'd gotten him the Snoopy Astronaut so many kids wanted, there were many additional gifts she thought would reward his curiosity and eager to learn nature. These included an Etch-A-Sketch and a Lite-Brite board. Jim had been pushing to get him some Nerf Balls, something athletic, but her successful argument was they didn't need balls flying around when there was a newborn in the house. And no Operation either. Not only would the buzzer test her patience, but it would also trigger the baby to tears and terrify Billy.

She'd noticed that Billy was an exceptionally sensitive child. That summer they'd taken the boys to a matinee of *Willy Wonka & the Chocolate Factory*. While most children in the audience watched with wonder, Billy was often frightened, and he asked if they could leave midway through. The boy reached terrified tears during Wonka's hallucinogenic boat ride, while the baby watched with wide eyes.

The type of rough play and toys that most young boys liked held little interest for Billy. As a mother who didn't want to see her son break a leg in football practice or take up a lethal hobby like firearms, Ellie considered his aversion to violence a good thing.

Billy had an interest in books before he fully understood them. In this respect Billy took after her, as she'd been an early reader before becoming a full-fledged book worm. If Billy wanted to explore his imagination rather than engage in fisticuffs, she would support him, even if such sensitivities gave her husband reservations.

They were spoiling Billy, Jim told her on more than one occasion, but she saw nothing wrong with that. They both experienced deep nostalgia as they re-lived the Christmas experience from the position of providers, while seeing the magic again through their child's eyes. They were financially stable in an unstable period – the U.S. dollar had been devalued just the past week for the second time in history – and if they had the means, they wanted to deliver a Christmas to remember.

Billy was really hoping he'd get a Snoopy Astronaut. He hoped he didn't get a G.I. Joe figure, which all the boys were interested in. Why would he want a drab green stick of angry plastic when he could have an awesome toy animal like a spotted beagle or brown bear?

Billy wished for many things, but his greatest wish on the night before Christmas was to see Santa in person.

It would be an absolute shock when he did.

Billy looked out the side window again in anticipation of the coming night, searching the sky for Santa's sleigh and the flying legend himself.

He never got his Snoopy Astronaut, Etch-A-Sketch, or Lite-Brite that year, or any other. He would also never read *The Night Before Christmas* again.

CHAPTER 3

The Utah Mental Facility was a state-run institution located on the outskirts of Bartlesville. The Chapmans' arrival time was 4:45 p.m. Ellie hoped they could be back on the road within an hour and back home ninety minutes after that.

The institution sat at the end of a dead-end road with the hills at its back. The street was lined with a long white picket fence and canopied with the bare branches of hickory trees. It would almost be a quaint, picturesque scene if not for the ominous nature of the structure at the end of the road. The ugly brick building and parking lot were encircled by a high wire fence. The building had been built the prior century, and it looked like it had never been given a single renovation.

There was one solitary, sun-bleached Christmas wreath hanging from the outer fence, flapping in the crisp wind, battered from riding out decades of harsh winters. The sad wreath looked like it'd been around since the original Christmas.

The Visitor Parking area was nearly empty, and they

pulled into a spot close to the building. The turnout was no surprise; who wanted to celebrate the holiday in a dreary old castle such as this? Ellie certainly had no interest in being there and regarded this visit as a marital obligation.

Ellie hated Jim's father Harold. She'd met him two years before he was admitted to the Utah Mental Facility. His condition was rapid onset dementia. He'd assaulted an employee of his company, ripping a whole handful of long hair out of her head. At least the woman fought back, kneeing Harold in the nuts so hard the left one burst. When the police processed Harold for the assault, the woman's hair was found in his underpants.

Ellie hated not only Harold, but his family business that Jim was an accountant for. In the mid-1960s, Harold opened his first strip club in Utah, named Honkers. His claim in the press was that his "gentlemen's club" was located near a popular turnpike and saw a lot of truckers who liked to honk when they drove by. Ellie saw the lie in this, because the truckers who frequented Honkers were most definitely not gentlemen, and the name of the joint was an obvious reference to breasts.

Within no time, Honkers began to pop up throughout Utah, the Midwest, and the Bible Belt, where residents prided themselves on their wholesomeness. When the early 1970s arrived, the chain pushed the boundaries of decency by going from topless to bottomless entertainment. Many joked that Honkers could change their name to Beavers.

Harold had a legendary habit of honking his dancers.

He'd grab their breasts and squeeze twice while going "honk-honk!" It was almost expected by every dancer who had the displeasure of meeting him.

The first time Ellie was alone in a room with Harold, he did it to her. Her immediate response was a resounding slap. She was his son's future wife, and it was imperative he learn right away to never do that again.

"He honked me," she told Jim that night once the visit was over.

He suppressed a chuckle. "Well, can you blame him?"

Jim slept on the couch that night. From that day on he would be ever so careful how he handled his wife's breasts in bed. He even stopped using the name Honkers around the house, referring to it only as *the company*. Ellie informed him that at no point in the future was she to be left alone in Harold's company.

Though she had no interest in seeing Harold for Christmas or any other time of the year, this was the one annual allowance for it she would grant her husband. Jim's father was the only parent they had left. A few years after she went off to college, her parents had perished together in a car accident while coming home from Sunday services. On a mountain road, her father had dozed behind the wheel and sideswiped a tree, causing the car to overturn and burst into flames. Ever since, she'd had an understandable fear of dying on the road.

As for bringing Billy and Ricky along for the visit to a mental ward, Jim also won that argument. Even though

Harold had been in a non-speaking state for a couple years now, Jim thought it was best for his son to have the sense of a grandparent in his life.

While Ellie allowed this, she had a plan to speak with Billy years later about what kind of man his grandfather really was, one who would place his hands upon his daughter-in-law. Harold would not get away with a clean legacy.

"We're here," Jim announced as he turned off the car. Ellie could offer no additional words of encouragement. She would be gritting her teeth this entire visit. She just wanted to be home doing holiday things in their holiday house, and it was her belief that Jim kept up this seasonal visit to keep on his old man's good side and not get excised from his will. In that concern, she was complicit.

"Grandpa!" Billy announced with enthusiasm to see a man he barely knew. His memory of the quiet man in the hospital was faint, because these visits were brief, and there was little to remember about him. What he had was an innate love for the man because he was family.

He was a very good boy in that regard.

Harold Chapman didn't give a fuck for his family, or anyone else for that matter. At seventy-four ornery years of age, he was finally all out of fucks. And he didn't give a holly jolly shit that it was Christmastime either.

He was wearing a reddish-brown robe over his blue pajamas, which along with his slippers was what he wore most days. There were no longer suits in his closet. He no longer got dressed up for anyone.

His face was perpetually unshaven, with a scraggly gray beard. His eyebrows were like giant hairy caterpillars over his eyes. He cultivated the furry sprouts that came out of his ears and nostrils, which frequently carried the ripe fruit of food and boogers. Sometimes dingleberries made their way into his facial fur by design. He enjoyed watching others lose their appetites eating around him.

With his fuzzy white face and reddish robe, all he needed was a longer beard, red stocking cap, and about a hundred more pounds on his frame and he would look like Santa Claus. They were simpatico, as he had also a life-long habit of trying to get others to sit on his lap.

The diagnosis of his dementia was premature, he believed. When he attacked that stripper at Honkers, he was in full control of his actions. He could become increasingly nasty to the human race, but hey, it wasn't his fault. Some might say his accelerating misanthropy was itself a condition of dementia, but he believed he suffered from nothing more than a perpetual raging case of asshole-ism.

All he had to do was sit on his ass and drool all day, hell, he wanted to do that anyway. You could have others do your laundry, make your meals, feed you by hand, or even wipe your ass, and you could be a jerk about it. All he had to do was soil himself on occasion and play dumb.

He had more than enough money that he could have spent his twilight years in style in a high-end retirement home. The dark and dank Utah Mental Facility was more his cranky style. There would be fewer eyes upon him, less oversight of his misdeeds, and nobody who would give a shit about him either.

While everyone thought he was checking out of life, he was not without ambition. Harold wanted nothing less than to establish the greatest reign of perverse terror to ever occur within the cold institutional walls. After three years of residence there, he had fully achieved his aim.

Harold's disruptions were directed at patients and staff alike. Most didn't know they were being fucked with, and many blamed their confusion on their own untrustworthy brains. Harold was a kleptomaniac, but he didn't keep possession of the things he stole. The personal belongings of others would disappear in the garbage, or missing clothing would be found in unflushed toilets. People would not get their garments back once they marinated with a floater.

Sometimes stolen items were left in the possession of somebody else, so they got the blame. The general chaos and mistrust these switcheroos created was a constant source of entertainment, especially if the patients came to blows. Most amusing was when the dentures of patients were switched in the middle of the night, something that made them spitting mad.

When he was in a giving mood, he would leave unexpected presents of bodily waste. It thrilled him to wet somebody else's bed. Others might find feces tucked under their pillow at night. If he was feeling especially generous, he might wipe shit on somebody's upper lip as they slept. Staff were also recipients of his fecal follies, when they found files that had done double duty as toilet paper, or *double doody* as he thought of it.

Much of Harold's mischief occurred at night. He was an insomniac, and the staff was less observant during those hours. Lack of sleep made him more irritable, his preferred state of operation.

All the women got honked, and that included the nurses. Some of the larger men got honked too if their boobs were big enough. Asses got honked. Balls got honked. Patients were honked in their sleep.

His pajamas were loose, so they were easy to shed. He was a mad streaker. During his nocturnal naked journeys, he'd find someone to give a willie wake up call, tapping or slapping some sleeper's face with his johnson. Startled out of sleep, they would awake to a terrible trouser snake dangling in their face. Even worse was when they saw a soiled moon. Their terror gave him a thrill.

Sometimes in the dead of night, he would whisper obscene sexual fantasies in the ears of sleeping victims. He could, in fact, speak just fine. He just didn't care to unless he was speaking absolute filth.

Lately he'd taken to adding *tails* to his streaking sessions, unexpected items hanging out of his butthole. Sometimes it was a stolen article of clothing, namely panties. Other times it was personal items like a hairbrush (the handle fit perfectly), and sometimes even food items.

Recently, haggard Ms. Haggerty had complained to an

orderly that Harold was prancing down the hallway naked with a celery stick sticking out of his ass. When the orderly found him sitting in the Recreation Room with a blank look on his face, he was fully clothed and eating a celery stick. The orderly dismissed Ms. Haggerty's wild story, but he did wonder where Harold got the peanut butter his celery had been dipped in.

Harold was not erect when he paraded around buck naked. He'd lost the ability to get hard ages ago. And yet, when he found himself perversely excited, he still had the ability to drip a copious amount. His escapades often left pecker tracks. One janitor thought there was a snail infestation due to all the slimy trails he found, and snail poison was spread around to curb the nonexistent invasion. The slime trails increased.

Then came the pictures. Nobody knew who got him the Polaroid camera, or how he continued to get cartridges of film (it was his son Phillip, who knew exactly what kind of mischief his father had in mind). His budding attempts at photography could all be labeled obscene, consisting mostly of shots of his limp noodle or hiney hole. These pictures tended to be found in the pockets of patients and purses of nurses. Worse were the Polaroids he took of his bowel movements, which he liked to leak, so to speak, during mealtime. The worst Polaroids were the unsuspecting nudes of sleeping or sedated residents. Sometimes he let the victims have them, so they knew their privacy had been violated.

Then there was Nurse Terry. Unlike his other targets of

torment, she had the ability to resurrect his dead dick, which made her some kind of angel. He couldn't just schedule an appointment to get time with her, so he took to hurting himself to secure her care. Much to his surprise he liked hurting himself, it gave him a thrill he was otherwise lacking. Then he got more creative. He stuck a toothpick through his nipple so Nurse Terry would have to extract it. After she tended to his nipple, he honked hers.

Elevating his game, knowing Nurse Terry would have to strip him to treat him, he stabbed his scrotum with a dinner fork. She learned this was no accident, as genital mutilation became a common occurrence for Harold while she was working.

Though Harold felt he had a grip on his impulses, he was not a doctor, and he had misdiagnosed himself. He was well into early stages of dementia, and his rapid onset of sadomasochism and sadism were clarion signs that late-stage dementia was moving in.

He was beginning to forget things, like names and dates or what he ate yesterday. Today, however, was not the typical Friday night with *The Don Rickles Show* airing on CBS on the Recreation Room television. He'd actually been looking forward to this date all week.

Every Christmas Eve he received an insincere visit from his least favorite, pussy-whipped son Jim. Inevitably, he'd bring that bossy bitch wife of his and their pouty brat, make that brats. The bitch – he couldn't remember her name – had been carrying so much baby weight last year it was a miracle her water hadn't burst on the asylum floor. Her tits had been pleasingly swollen, and he had to resist asking her if they were full of eggnog.

Harold believed Jim and his spawn came every night before Christmas to be included in his will. Harold was a major asshole for a reason, and he didn't trust anyone who wanted to visit him. Jim was in for a big surprise when his pops kicked the bucket.

This year, Harold was going to have fun with Billy. Something about that boy irritated him greatly. With his timid eyes and pouty lips, Billy struck him as a sissy. Perceiving him an easy target, he wanted to give the little creampuff something to pout about. If he tried hard enough, maybe he could make the boy pee his pants.

Harold wanted to ruin everyone's Christmas.

Dr. Conrad met the Chapmans in the Waiting Room and led them into a different hallway than they were accustomed.

"I've had your father brought to the Recreation Room." To grant them privacy on this special day, the Recreation Room was reserved for the Chapmans for an hour. What Dr. Conrad didn't mention was they were the only family to visit a patient today.

The family followed the doctor side-by-side. Billy was in the middle, with each parent holding his hand. Ellie's other arm cradled Ricky and a blanket. She appeared uncomfortably weighted down, but she would have been uneasy in this place no matter what. Institutions like this made her apprehensive for no reason other than she never wanted to end up in one.

Something else brought a grimace to her face. The air was bad in this cold corridor, almost like it was one long toilet stall. Luckily, she only had to endure these conditions for a handful of minutes and then they would be out. It was difficult to think of those who had to work in a place like this, and worse for those institutionalized here.

Jim's father was deteriorating quickly and wouldn't be around much longer, she thought with only a modicum of relief. But what if he lived to one-hundred, and their only memories of Christmas Eve was this cruel place, devoid of color or cheer or hope? That wasn't fair to them, and it was especially unfair to their children, who deserved to be at home where their world was merry and bright.

"Is this the long way? I don't remember it being this far," Ellie said, unable to hide her irritation.

"We had a pipe break in the hall. We need to cut through Ward A first," Dr. Conrad answered.

I'm smelling a broken sewage pipe, Ellie thought, and her nose crinkled as her stomach rolled.

"Right this way," Dr. Conrad said and stopped at a security door that he unlocked. Ellie saw the sign that indicated they were entering WARD A.

Ellie wanted to turn around with the boys and wait in the car, but the door closed and clicked as it locked behind them. They were trapped, only she knew that wasn't true. There was another door at the end of this corridor with an EXIT sign over it, and Dr. Conrad had the key.

All they had to do was cross the long corridor filled with wandering, mumbling patients with vacant eyes. Their hospital gowns whispered along with their slippers on the stone floor. A few moaned and whined, others raged at unseen others, one cried like a baby. Few patients seemed to notice the new arrivals. There were two orderlies in there with them, one stationed at each door.

Ellie couldn't believe the number of patients held in this slender holding pen, without any chairs to sit. It seemed cruel to her. She was unaware this had to do with the temporary closure of the Recreation Room. Ward A became the patients' milling area for the hour. Unbeknownst to Ellie, Dr. Conrad was a customer in high standing at the nearest Honkers, and he often favored the exalted owner of his favorite joint with preferential treatment.

With these lost souls wandering around her, Ellie had a terribly disturbing vision. Would Jim suffer the same malady of mind later in life and end up in his father's quarters here at the Utah Mental Facility? That question led her to an even more diabolical thought.

Might dementia skip a generation like other hereditary conditions? Would Billy be the one to lose his mind and end up institutionalized?

Encircled by the mentally disturbed and clutching her sons, Ellie swore to herself that she and the boys would never enter the Utah Mental Facility again.

Billy stared dumbfounded at the funny, strange people wandering around. Little Ricky really had no reaction to anything in front of him except for hunger for his mamma's milk.

"Stay close to me," Dr. Conrad said, and he began to cross the corridor.

"Stay close," Ellie repeated with a stern look at Billy. He couldn't get any closer to his parents if he tried, as he was sandwiched tightly between them with his hands held.

As the family unit crossed the hall, patients recognized others in their midst, and excitement began to build. Chatter and laughter and a "cock-a-doodle-do" grew louder. The visitors were people magnets now, and everyone wanted to involve them in their delusions.

A pudgy bald man with an animated face swooped in before Billy.

"Are you my monkey?"

Billy had no answer for that, and his eyes opened wide with alarm. This was starting to feel like a scary ride to him, like Willy Wonka's terrifying boat ride down the chocolate river.

"Out of the way," Dr. Conrad ordered his charges.

Most stepped aside to allow the visitors passage, except for a tall, grizzled old woman who stepped near the family. Her sunken, beady eyes were homed in on Billy. When she spoke, it was a shriek.

"Agh! There he is! That's him!"

To Billy, the woman looked like a witch. Her screech and attention gave him a guilty feeling. He wondered what he'd done that was bad.

The witch pointed an arthritically twisted finger at Billy, and he thought it looked like a gnarled claw.

"Catch him, doctor! Throw him in the locked room! He's the guilty one!"

Now Billy was certain he was the guilty one, and he worried the doctor would do as the woman ordered. He didn't want to go to the locked room for Christmas.

The witch was now right before him, swooping in. An orderly rushed over and restrained her, allowing the visitors to pass. Billy heard her scream behind him.

"Guilty! Guilty! Guilty!"

The accusations turned into a horrible, rattling cough. This sound was so alarming Billy glanced back.

Still restrained, the old woman leaned forward and spit blood onto the floor.

Billy was greatly relieved when the doctor unlocked the door and led them out of Ward A.

Little did he know he had just crossed the threshold to greater terror.

CHAPTER 4

The old man sat motionless in the wooden chair with his unfocused eyes trained upon some undiscernible smudge on the linoleum floor. There were more comfortable looking padded chairs in the room, but maybe his back needed the hard wooden support of this seat, Jim thought. His father's face looked more weathered than he'd ever seen it. Harold's eyes had never looked so lost.

Jim could see his father sitting directly before him, but looking more closely, he couldn't see the man at all within this human shell.

It was truly heartbreaking to see his father in such a vulnerable, weakened state. He and Ellie didn't bother to take a seat, instead they crouched closely before him. Harold gave not even the slightest hint that he knew anyone was there. His state was near comatose.

Jim spoke in slow, measured sentences. "Dad? Can you hear me? It's me, Dad. Jimmy."

Even though it didn't appear his dad could see him, he

wore a forced grin as he spoke. Billy stood beside his father, three generations of Chapmans all within feet of each other. Billy wore no false expression, his confusion as he looked at his grandpa nakedly apparent.

Ellie put on the false smile her husband wore. "Dad? It's Ellie."

Harold gave no look of recognition to the woman in front of him. She was able to hold her smile for all of four seconds. Though she didn't care for Harold, she understood it must be devastating for her husband to see his father in such a state.

When Ellie continued, her voice could not conceal her irritation. "We have Billy here and little Ricky too. We all came to wish you a Merry Christmas."

If he'd had an urgency of bowels, Harold would have shitted his pants right then, so they'd have to marinate in the hot stink.

The uncomfortable silence was broken by Billy.

"Why doesn't grandpa say something?"

Ellie gave Billy a stern look.

"He doesn't hear us, honey. He doesn't even know we're here."

I can hear just fine, bitch, Harold thought. He considered them the stupid ones, because they were all fooled.

"Then what did we come for?" Billy asked with confusion.

"Billy," Ellie snapped severely. "Shhh."

His mom's quick shushing confused him further. She'd just told him grandpa couldn't hear them.

"He's gotten so much worse," Jim said despairingly.

Dr. Conrad stepped forward to interrupt the family's pity party.

"I have your father's records, Mr. Chapman. We can review them in my office."

Jim and Ellie looked at each other and nodded. Jim stood as Ellie reached out to touch Billy's hand reassuringly.

"Come on, hon."

"Why not leave the older child here? We can talk more freely," Dr. Conrad said.

Ellie and Jim consulted with a look. Jim shrugged, while Ellie just wanted to get through this uncomfortable business as quickly as possible.

"Wait right here, okay, honey? Daddy and I are going to be right back," Ellie said in a reassuring voice that did not ease Billy's discomfort.

Billy cast an uncertain look at his grandpa, who stared ahead intensely at nothing.

"Don't worry. Grandpa's not gonna hurt you," Ellie said and followed with a hollow chuckle that got a "goo" and drooly burp out of Ricky. "We'll be back in a jiff."

Ellie flashed Jim a hesitant look, and they followed Dr. Conrad to the door. Had they looked back, they would have seen how timid Billy was to be left alone. Usually when left in the company of his elders, he felt watched over. That was not the case now.

Dr. Conrad led Ellie, Jim, and Ricky out. There was a click as the door locked. There was no orderly on duty. Due to the holiday, the facility was working with a skeleton staff.

Unlike the cacophony in Ward A, the Recreation Room was eerily silent.

Billy looked nervously around the room, trying to avoid sight of the old man he knew only as Grandpa. This was the only room in the facility with Christmas decorations, garlands and ornaments around the windows and tissue paper honeycomb Christmas trees and red bells overhead.

Billy stood beside the chair in the exact spot his parents left him. Curiosity got the better of him, and his eyes drifted to Grandpa.

Grandpa stared straight ahead with blank eyes, barely blinking.

Billy stared uneasily at Grandpa.

Grandpa didn't move a muscle, then his eyes darted to the side to look at him.

Billy's eyes widened with surprise.

"Grandpa?"

Now Grandpa's muscles did move, the ones that turned his mouth upward into a grin. His lips pulled open, revealing his pearly whites, though they were not so white now that he was within knocking distance of the pearly gates. There was awareness in his eyes.

"Mom!" Billy called out, eager to share this miracle.

Grandpa's arm shot off the chair's armrest and clutched Billy by the upper arm, uncomfortably tight.

"Shhhh! Quiet!" Grandpa hissed.

Because he was taught to respect his elders, Billy kept quiet.

Grandpa's introductory smile vanished. "What do you

want her for? She can't help you. Nobody can."

Billy didn't like the way Grandpa's face scrunched up and grimaced at him. The way his big hairy eyebrows arched over his beady, watery eyes seemed angry. He didn't know why Grandpa would be upset with him.

Billy's apprehension was plainly visible upon his face. Grandpa liked that fearful look on him.

"You scared, ain't ya?" Grandpa asked, and Billy nodded. "You should be."

Billy was plenty scared now. His response to fright was to freeze.

Grandpa's straining face was changing color before Billy's eyes, turning redder like his blood was rising to the surface. He was also breathing heavily. When words came out, they were delivered with intensity, as though each one took effort to get out.

"Christmas Eve is the scariest damn night of the year. I'd be scared too if I was you."

Grandpa's uncomfortable grip on Billy's arm tightened further. Now Grandpa was leaning toward him, and when he opened his mouth, it smelled rotten. Though his delivery was intense, there was notable glee.

"You know what happens on Christmas Eve, don't ya?"

Billy nervously nodded yes. He was afraid of giving the wrong answer.

"Do you know all about… Santa Claus?" Grandpa asked.

Billy was relieved, because he did know about Santa Claus, and he nodded. He'd just looked at the book on him.

"He brings presents to all good boys and girls," Billy informed him with pride.

Grandpa laughed, but there was no humor in it. "Hehe-heeee." The malicious grin became a sneer of disgust. "Your daddy told you that, didn't he?"

Billy nodded affirmative.

"Well, I tell you something," Grandpa said, and now he appeared to be crying, whether in pain or joy was not apparent. "Santa Claus only brings presents to them that's been good all year. To the ones that ain't done nothing naughty. Naughty!"

Harold gave another pained grimace, as he was grinding his teeth and biting the insides of his cheeks until they bled. He gulped down the blood. His eyes narrowed into accusatory slits of judgment.

"All the other ones, all the naughty ones, he punishes."

Billy recoiled as the final word was spit from Grandpa's mouth.

Grandpa tilted his head questioningly at Billy, like he had his number. Billy mistook Grandpa's insanity for authority.

"What about you, boy? You been good all year?"

Grandpa was looking at Billy so intensely the boy knew he would be caught if he lied. He wanted to be good, for Grandpa, for Santa, and for his parents most of all. And he prided himself on being very polite. Most of the time.

But last month there'd been a day at the park where two bully boys, Perry and Spencer, dared him to pull one of Tammy Berger's pigtails. Most of the kids teased Tammy because of her face full of freckles and bright red hair. Billy accepted the dare, snuck up behind Tammy, pulled her pigtail, and laughed. But he pulled too hard, and it hurt her, and her ribbon unfastened so the hair came loose. Worst of all, Tammy really liked him, so his pigtail yank made her cry.

Billy hadn't been a good boy all year, after all, and he couldn't lie about it, because that would be naughty. Nor was lying in his nature. He shook his head no.

Grandpa nodded with glee, almost like he was glad Billy would get in trouble. Tears escaped from his eyes.

"You see Santa Claus tonight, you better run boy! You better run for your life!"

This horrible news was delivered with so much venom Billy could feel spittle upon his face. Grandpa let him go so he could fall back into his chair, wracked with laughter over Billy's misfortune. "Tee-hee-hee-hee-hee-hee-hee!"

Billy was mortified by Grandpa's warning. He didn't doubt it as fact. This was nothing like the storybook he read on the car ride here. *The Night Before Christmas* and his mom had it all wrong. Mom told him to be a good boy to get gifts, but she hadn't said a thing about punishment. That omission made him lose trust in his mother.

But how could she know that Santa Claus was coming to punish him tonight? She thought he was a good boy, because he'd never told her what he did in the park that day. Maybe not telling his mother what he'd done was also naughty.

He'd been a bad pigtail yanker this year. That meant Santa Claus was coming tonight to punish him, and if Grandpa said to run for your life, the conclusion was that punishment meant death. The night before Christmas brought lethal judgment from the sky above, to strike down bad boys like him with a bolt of lightning.

Grandpa wasn't just laughing for effect. The boy's terror was palpable, and he found it fucking hilarious. The little shit would be traumatized about Santa Claus for life! This was even better than telling him that Santa didn't exist. The boy's corruption was as delicious as a hot toddy spiked with bourbon by the crackling fire on Christmas Eve.

Grandpa's laughing fit was interrupted by a click from the door unlocking. Grandpa's eyes snapped that way.

Ellie, Ricky, and Jim returned with Dr. Conrad, who was holding Harold's medical file.

"Time to go home, Billy," Jim announced as he stepped up. This time Ellie stayed a few steps away from Harold. She didn't want to be in honking distance. Little Ricky honked her instead.

Harold sat in the exact position of stupor he'd held when the adults left the room. Billy was relieved Grandpa had that vacant look again.

Jim crouched at his father's knee. If anyone looked closely enough, they would have seen the fresh tear marks on Harold's cheeks, but nobody noticed, not even his most loving son. It was easier for people to not see him even when he was right in front of their faces. To see him was to acknowledge the grim realities of life, where they were all headed but wished to deny. Especially on Christmas.

"Dad, we have to go now. We'll come back and see you soon."

Bullshit, Harold thought behind his vacant stare. He knew Jim's clan only appeared once a year, and that was one appearance too many.

"Come on, son," Jim said to Billy, and he stood up. Ellie couldn't get out of there fast enough, and she marched to the door patting Ricky.

Billy watched his parents' departure as he hesitated beside Grandpa. He turned to the old man, who no longer seemed to notice him.

The boy moved in close, placing his hands on the old man's shoulder and speaking into his ear.

"I'll be good from now on. I promise!"

Billy ran off after his parents.

The boy totally believed the threat. Harold hoped Billy would lie in terror under the covers all night, unable to sleep as he waited for Santa's punishment.

There was something about Billy he liked, he had to admit. There was a spark in this boy he hoped to ignite like the pilot light on a stove. He'd given up on his son Jim long ago. At this point, the only way he'd gain respect for Jim is if he strangled Ellie and left her out in the desert like he'd done with his own wife Lilyan. She probably made a better dinner for the vultures than she ever made for him at home.

In the case of the Chapmans, insanity would indeed skip a generation.

Twilight had fallen by the time the Chapmans got back on the road home. Jim drove, heavy hearted about his limited interaction with his father. The terrible thing was, Harold would only deteriorate further. At some point, his father would be bed ridden and no longer able to sit in that wooden chair, and soon after he'd be in a wooden coffin. Then this Christmas Eve ritual on the road would be no more.

Ellie relaxed in the passenger seat, her head resting back against her headrest. That horrible business at the sanitarium was behind her, and she wouldn't have to see that terrible man for another year. This annual visit had become such a downer she'd begun to dread Christmas Eve as a result. But that would be no more.

The stress she'd felt inside the facility today was the snapping of her last straw, or in this case, candy cane. She and the boys would stay at home while Jim visited his male chauvinist pig of a father in the future.

Now she could think of Christmas things like carolers and baking cookies and placing presents under the tree. Within no time she'd lulled herself into a pleasant doze. Ricky was strapped into the baby seat beside Billy. The baby was dozing like his mother.

Billy sat in disturbed silence. All he could think about was the threat in store tonight. He didn't even want to go home or go to sleep now. He might never wake up.

He thought of those familiar song lyrics, *"He sees you when you're sleeping, he knows when you're awake."* Santa's punishment would come either way. *"He knows if you've been bad or good, so be good for goodness sake."*

Otherwise, Santa Claus would kill you. The song reinforced Grandpa's warning.

The storybook he'd received that day no longer felt honest. *The Night Before Christmas* didn't warn of Santa's punishment for naughty kids. The book didn't tell him to run for his life. It didn't tell the whole story, or the most important part. He pushed the book further away from him on the seat.

"Mommy, were you ever naughty when you were little?" Billy asked.

Though her eyes were closed, Ellie heard Billy's question. She remembered the time she gave her first handjob to a boy at summer camp, and the time she fucked the whole offensive line of the college football team. Yep, she'd been naughty alright, and a grin spread across her face.

"Mmmm, once or twice," Ellie said, though that was a fib. She'd had a reputation for being naughty all the time.

"Did Santa Claus ever punish you?" Billy asked.

Ellie snapped out of her fond memories and her eyes opened. She looked back at Billy with concern.

"Where did you get an idea like that, hon?"

"Grandpa," Billy answered.

Ellie looked at her son with astonishment. Jim appeared uncertain behind the wheel.

"Grandpa?" Jim asked doubtfully.

"Grandpa said Santa Claus was gonna punish me," Billy whined with worry.

Ellie looked at Jim with concern, and he shared a look of doubt.

"You think dad could have talked to him?" Jim asked her. Normally he would be apt to believe Billy, but to believe this would reveal an uncomfortable truth. If dad really did speak to his grandson, it meant he'd purposely ignored his own son.

"I don't see why Billy would lie," Ellie said, inclined to believe her son in this instance. "Maybe we should call Dr. Conrad."

Now that he had his parents' attention, Billy's fear came out as a shout. Normally he wouldn't raise his voice like this, because he'd been scolded before for being too loud and waking his baby brother, but his emotion was so high he couldn't help it.

"I don't want him to come! I'm scared!"

"Of who, honey?" Ellie asked with rising concern.

"Santa Claus!" Billy shouted with unbridled terror.

Ellie replied authoritatively. "Honey, there's nothing to be scared of."

Billy was seized with desperation. It was already dark, and tonight he was a target.

"Grandpa said Santa Claus was gonna punish me!"

Billy's idea was ridiculous, Ellie thought. What kid held this much fear of Santa Claus, every child's favorite myth? This terror over Santa was just too much. Also, she didn't like being shouted at by a child who'd been taught better than that.

"Billy, calm down," she said sternly. "Grandpa's nothing but a crazy old fool."

With her last word, she looked accusingly at Jim, because she wanted him to hear her feelings about his old man. Her anger at Billy and her husband was entirely misplaced, she understood, because she was most angry with herself.

Now she understood the severity of the mistake she'd made today, beyond agreeing to bring the boys along for this visit without a second thought. For years she would not allow herself to be left alone in the company of Harold, but today, at Dr. Conrad's request, she'd left Billy alone with him. The old man had appeared catatonic to them, but apparently, he had lucid moments too, and he used that lucidity to do what he did best, harass and terrorize.

Never would she and the boys see that old man again if she could help it.

Jim didn't argue against Ellie's insult of his father because she wasn't wrong about him.

Billy's reaction to his mother's words was severe. For the first time, he spoke to her in a scolding, threatening tone, starting with a gasp of offense.

"Mommy! You shouldn't have said that. It's naughty to say bad things about old people. Santa Claus will punish you!" Billy said with chilling finality as he imitated Grandpa.

"I'll just have to take my chances on that, won't I?" Ellie snapped back, yet unaware she was justifying Billy's belief in what he'd told her about Santa.

Ellie turned away from Billy, finished with this conversation. At least the shouting hadn't sent Ricky into a crying fit. She hugged herself, even though the car heater was blasting.

Billy's warning of a vengeful Santa coming to punish her creeped her out more than she cared to admit.

Billy sat in the dark back seat consumed by the worry that he and his mom were targeted for death tonight. He gulped, his mouth dry, and looked out his side window into the night sky, fearful he would see Santa's sleigh flying in.

He hoped Santa Claus was far, far away on the other side of the world.

As Billy was nervously watching the skies, Santa Claus was pulling in before the All-Nite Gas & Food Fort. This flashy rest stop was the only gas station on the road between Christmas Joy and Bartlesville, a nest of lights within a vast pool of darkness. Tonight, the outpost was like a ghost town, timeless and lawless as the Old West.

Instead of a red sleigh, Santa piloted a red 1971 Chevrolet Monte Carlo. This was by far the slickest ride on the road tonight, though from what Santa could see, there were no other cars out, at least not here in the boonies.

Santa didn't take a parking spot, even though all were empty. He pulled up alongside the building. The car door was not locked after he got out, as he needed a speedy getaway.

Santa carried his customary sack, but this one was empty. That would not be the case for long, as Santa was collecting presents tonight.

A grimy yellow streetlamp illuminated Santa from above, and from a distance, he must have cut an impressive silhouette with his oversized jacket and stocking cap. Up close in the harsh overhead light, he was the slimiest looking Santa anyone ever saw. His eyes danced with desperation and danger.

He was the Anti-Claus.

● ● ●

It was like any other night inside the All-Night Gas & Food Fort, it just felt much longer. There was a complete lack of customers. Levitt didn't mind the low traffic. He was the proprietor, and while he could have assigned the shift to somebody else, he didn't want to shell out extra holiday pay when he could save money and sit on his ass all night.

Typically, he could keep himself entertained, indulging in the best snacks, drinks, and fine reading material, including the XXX variety. Convenience store food was not healthy for long term sustenance, and Levitt showed that with about fifty pounds of excess weight. He was a middle-aged diabetes bomb waiting to go off.

Levitt stood by the register with the daily newspaper spread out on the counter. As he flipped the page a sales ad circular slipped out, for Ira's Toys in Christmas Joy. He thought there were too many sales ads cluttering the papers this time of year.

The radio was on, as it would be all night, but he couldn't find a station that played anything other than Christmas music. There wasn't a single holiday song he liked, let alone wanted to hear repeated every hour. Without any radio accompaniment he worried he would doze off, so he settled on a classical station. Even if the melodies were familiar, he didn't have to hear those dumb lyrics about some stupid snowman or dandy drummer boy.

Levitt was startled by the ringing bell that accompanied the opening door, and a strong gust of cold air swept Santa Claus into the store. Normally Levitt didn't flinch when the bell rang, but he hadn't seen a car enter the station at the gas pumps, nor had he heard a motor. Then again, this was Santa Claus, so maybe he flew in on his magic sleigh.

"Well, ho-ho-ho. I don't get enough of this shit on the radio, it has to come in my store now?" Levitt said in greeting.

Santa Claus replied with a chuckle, and Levitt gave him a look over. He appeared to be in his mid-fifties, though it was hard to tell beneath the bushy white hair and beard. A thick black belt cinched the jacket closed. He was more akin to a skeleton wearing a sleeping bag.

"What's the matter, you don't like Santa Claus?" Santa asked as he stepped up to the counter, grabbing three boxes of rolling papers off a shelf on his way there.

Levitt tried to peg Santa's accent, and it definitely wasn't North Pole. East Coast most likely, possibly Boston.

There was a strong whiff of booze on Santa's breath. That meant he was piloting his sleigh inebriated tonight. Santa Claus liked to party.

"Eh, it's good for business, bad for my stomach," Levitt replied as he rang up the rolling papers and put them into a brown paper bag. "A lot of phony sentiment, you know what I'm saying?" Once he said it, he realized that phony sentiment was Santa's bread and butter. Santa probably liked all that shit just fine.

The paper bag was set on the counter. "What charity are you with?" Levitt asked.

From inside his jacket, Santa Claus whipped out a Star Model B with his red-gloved hand and aimed the weapon at the proprietor.

Levitt lost his sarcastic tone in an instant. His full attention was on the black metal muzzle of the gun.

"What the hell you doin' that for?" Levitt inquired. Every word was crucial now. Some would be issued just to buy him time.

"I'm holding you up, asshole! Put the money in the bag." Santa placed his empty cloth sack on the counter.

"All right, all right." Levitt reached out to the register and opened the cash drawer, which sprang out with a jingle of change.

Levitt's hand slowly slipped down beneath the drawer. He spoke to keep Santa's eyes on his face.

"So, it's not all phony sentiment, is it?"

Beneath the register was Levitt's Smith & Wesson Model 15. His hand shook as he reached for it. The tremor was not a byproduct of fear, but rather a nervous symptom that had slowly developed over the past few years.

He'd drawn this gun twice over his thirteen years at the All-Nite Gas & Food Fort, and he'd filled those two thieves' bags too, their body bags. He'd long prided himself on being a fast draw.

"A lot of it's genuine greed." Levitt continued. His hand fumbled getting a good grip on his weapon. The safety was already off.

"All right, you!" Levitt shouted angrily as he whipped his handgun up, aiming at Santa.

Santa Claus pulled the trigger, and Levitt's stomach exploded red. The proprietor was knocked back off his feet, collapsing onto racks of potato chip bags. The shelves crashed down under the weight of him, and he hit the floor on his back.

The Ira's Toys ad circular on the floor was splashed with Levitt's blood.

"Stupid sonofabitch!" Santa Claus griped, and he reached over the counter, swiping bills out of the open register. Santa was going to have to fill his own sack tonight.

Levitt came back to awareness with hot lead searing in his belly. *I'm not as fast as I used to be,* he thought as he squirmed in agony. Then he realized his gun was still in his grip. Santa was busy rifling through the open register before him.

This was his chance. He was going to blow Santa's head off.

Levitt's shaky arm lifted the gun.

Santa saw the rising gun barrel, but he was faster on his trigger. A second slug tore into Levitt's belly. The proprietor's eyes bulged as his bloated tongue protruded from his mouth. The next deafening blast was also deadening as the bullet entered his forehead.

With the cash drawer cleared of a woefully small number of bills, Santa looked for anything else to stuff into his sack. Along with the rolling papers, he grabbed a large bottle of whiskey, a handful of lighters, a bag of pork rinds, beef jerky sticks, and a few adult magazines.

With his sack filled he stormed out of the convenience store counting the bills he stole. He stopped on the freezing outer threshold.

"Thirty-one bucks! Merry fucking Christmas!"

Santa Claus meant it too, the *fucking Christmas* part. He certainly looked like St. Nick, but if asked, he would call himself St. Mick.

Santa Claus was Mick Bottoms, a name he'd been teased about his whole life. Those who made fun got beat up and never did it again. Mick was an East Coast Irish street fighter, not from Boston as Levitt suspected, but from Baltimore. He lived on the lam, and the only reason he was in Utah for a spell was because he didn't have any warrants there, or so he thought.

Mick's last long-term residence was at the nightmarish Nevada State Prison in Carson City, where he'd just finished a ten-year stint for grand larceny, rape, and home invasion. On that last count, he was an awful lot like Santa Claus. Perhaps if he'd been wearing a Santa suit during the commission of those crimes, he'd have warranted a shorter sentence.

He'd been released from that hellhole one week ago.

First thing he did with his freedom was to hop on a Greyhound bus going east. He only made it one state over to Utah before he got off out of restlessness. A cheap motel room was secured in Millcreek, and that's where his bender began.

During his first visit to the local honky-tonk, he started a fight and was kicked out. A visit to a biker bar the next night went even worse, and he was lucky to get out with a serious ass kicking. There would be no hospital visit for what he suspected was a cracked rib.

While drunk in his motel room, he punched holes in the walls and broke the windows, marveling at how easy it was to bust through these vulnerable new walls around him. The motel manager called the cops, but he'd already fled by the time they arrived.

Hitching a ride in the back of a livestock truck, he headed further east crouched behind cow ass and jumped out in Bartlesville on Thursday, December 23. His first purchase was his Star Model B in an under the counter deal at a sketchy pawn shop. He also got a switchblade during the transaction. Now he had the means to acquire his next need, transportation.

The Chevrolet Monte Carlo was snagged that night outside a Woolworths near closing time. The make and model were a reward for his lucky timing. An older woman was behind the wheel, picking up her husband, who was the store Santa Claus. As St. Nick slipped into the front passenger seat, Mick shoved in after him with the gun to his fuzzy face. He ordered them to drive, fast, directing them deep into a back alley.

Before the engine was off, Mick shot St. Nick in the guts, and once Mrs. Nick started screaming, he pistol-whipped her, knocking her unconscious. St. Nick bled through the jacket, but the garment was so red you couldn't tell where the stains were. St. Mick pulled the body out of the car and stripped him of his suit. He stripped off his own clothes to put it on, and then he saw Mrs. Nick stirring behind the wheel.

Her clothes were easy to tear off. Like a rag doll, she offered no resistance. When he saw what Mrs. Nick looked like naked, she no longer turned him on. He was deflated.

St. Mick wrapped his hands around her neck and snapped it. There was no need to put her clothes back on, but they were gathered and thrown into the trunk with the nude corpses. The Santa suit was big for him, but it was effective camouflage during the holiday season. Nobody ever questioned where Santa was going at Christmastime. He was welcomed everywhere, into every home.

Following this double murder, he stopped at a liquor store, got a bottle of Jack Daniels, and chugged so much he passed out behind the wheel until Christmas Eve.

It wasn't until sundown that St. Mick split town, heading east to Christmas Joy. The old couple in the trunk had precious little cash in their wallets, so he was looking for an easy score. The All-Nite Gas & Food Fort just happened to be on his route, a perfectly isolated outpost to pillage. Another inadequate amount of cash was acquired.

At least he got some good snacks, another bottle of liquid fire, and some spank mags. He needed to make time for those soon, very soon, or else he might not be able to control himself from ravaging the next woman he crossed paths with.

A criminal mastermind he most certainly was not. Every crime he committed was the result of appetite and impulse.

He had no great plan in motion except to take and flee and see how far it got him.

St. Mick slipped behind the wheel and peeled out of the gas station.

Evil was often utterly banal, the result of ignorance and desperation. The notoriety that would come from Mick Bottoms' holiday crime spree could be attributed to the date most of it occurred. The events to come would be so depraved and diabolical it would become local legend and cause deadly repercussions for generations to come.

Trauma, like holidays, had a habit of becoming a recurring tradition.

CHAPTER  6

"This is Steve Carlson here at KLOX FM where the temperature this Christmas Eve is still holding in there at twenty-one degrees. Well, we hope Santa is dressed warm tonight, don't we?"

This was a rare moment of peace for the Chapmans. After the tense exchange between Ellie and Billy, it was a relief they were both sleeping. It'd been a dark day with Jim's father, and the disturbing twist of Harold's warning to Billy did not settle well with Jim at all.

He believed Billy, even though he didn't want to. It was too elaborate a fiction for his son to create. His father had a habit of sharing his bad behavior with others. Perhaps it was time to retire this yearly visit. His wife would surely applaud the decision.

His father was retreating in miles behind him, and best forgotten for now. He was with his closest family, on the way home to engage in Christmas traditions they would nostalgically recall for life.

Jim would cherish this silent night for as long as it lasted.

∮ ∮ ∮

Just past the fifteen-mile mark from Christmas Joy's city limits, the Chevrolet Monte Carlo blew a tire. Perhaps speeding and reckless driving played a part. The car swerved across lanes as it coasted to a stop on the icy road, ending up right over the center line.

St. Mick got out from behind the wheel, cursing up a storm. He kicked the ruined tire. He'd discarded the spare in the city alley, so he'd have enough room in the trunk to stash the bodies of naked Mr. and Mrs. Claus. Stuck in the worst possible place to attract cops, he had to wait for the assistance of a passerby.

That's when he met the acquaintance of Miss Candy Cane, and it was lust at first sight.

Miss Candy Cane was the December centerfold model for *Hot Lips,* the latest men's magazine on the market, and the most explicit. This curvy redhead wore nothing in her Christmas themed pictorial but a five-foot long candy cane that she straddled, licking it seductively. Her flesh was perfect, even with a staple through her coochie.

Santa had a hard candy cane in his pants, and he pulled down his trousers so he could beat off on the road with the centerfold spread over the hood. The cold was not a problem for him, in fact it aided in his excitement. During his long stays in the hole at the Nevada State Prison, a freezing space carved out of cold rock that served as sadistic solitary confinement, he did nothing but jerk off to pass the time and keep warm. The deep chill gave him a pelvic thrill.

In his horny mind's eye, he saw Miss Candy Cane on the hood of the car wrapped around that giant candy cane. He bet she tasted like peppermint everywhere.

"Santa's watching, Santa's waiting. Christmas Eve is slowly fading. Can you hear him in the night? Close your door, turn out the light."

Merry Songbird's holiday hit issued from the radio in the Chapmans' car. Though lulled into a nap, Billy's rest was not peaceful. The lyrics subconsciously nibbled at his unguarded gray matter, while Grandpa's Santa story had its claws deep within him.

"Santa's watching, Santa's creeping…"

Ellie stirred out of her doze with a smile upon her face. "How's it going, hon?" she asked, reaching out to touch Jim's arm tenderly.

"Got a way to go yet," Jim admitted, figuring they had thirty minutes until they got home. He reached over and stroked the back of her hair and had the fantasy of lowering her head into his lap to service him. Only if the boys were asleep, of course.

"Santa knows if you've been bad."

Ellie leaned forward in her seat, peering through the windshield.

"What's that?"

Jim looked at her longingly, lost in his erotic fantasy. "Hmmh?" he mumbled with a grin.

Ellie thought she saw something glint in the distance.

"Oh, I thought I saw something out there on the road."

Billy didn't hear her, dozing with his head rolled back against his seat.

Ellie's eyes caught a glint in the distance.

"There it is again, see?" Ellie said as she pointed through the windshield. As they followed a slight curve in the road, a car was revealed ahead sitting on the center line.

"There's something up there all right," Jim confirmed.

They saw there wasn't just a car in the middle of the road. Somebody was standing beside the trunk, waving their arms like railroad crossing guards.

St. Mick saw the Chapmans long before they saw him. Their headlights were on while his were off.

Their timing was shit, though. He was about a minute away from giving Miss Candy Cane a pearl necklace. He pulled up his red trousers. Miss Candy Cane was tossed into the open car door.

St. Mick popped the front hood to give the illusion of a breakdown. Then he walked to the rear of the car and began waving his arms to get the approaching car's attention.

How ironic it'd be if the other driver was speeding or not alert, mowing Santa down on the hard asphalt like he was a deer crossing the road. He could have checked the trunk for road flares, but that would require rearranging the two rotting bodies tangled in there. He'd take his chances, every move he made came with great risk now.

His gun was loaded and resting in his jacket pocket. He'd lost his chance to ejaculate, but his gun would get to shoot very soon.

"What would anyone be doing stopped out here in the..." Ellie began, and then chuckled. "Well, I'll be... Do you see what I see?" she asked excitedly.

Jim had to laugh. "He must be on his way to a party. You think we should wake up Billy?"

Billy was roused from his uneasy nap by his name. After rubbing his eyes, he looked ahead through the windshield. It took him a moment to comprehend what he was looking at, but once he did, his eyes opened wide, and his mouth dropped down in a gasp.

"Too late now, 'cause Santa's here."

Revealed in the bright headlights, Santa Claus stood in the road next to a stopped car, waving them down.

"Santa Claus!" Billy exclaimed with hair-raising urgency.

"Looks like you get to see him tonight after all, Billy," Jim said mirthfully, seeing this as a potentially magical moment for his son. He would have loved to experience a sight like this as a young boy.

"No daddy! I don't want to see him! Keep going! Don't stop!"

Ellie had been irritated by Billy's irrational fear of Santa Claus earlier. Now, the panic in his voice spread to her. His terror was so genuine, so palpable, she reacted as any mother would, with a fierce protective instinct. Her eyes darted between Billy and Jim with worry.

Jim slowed down as they came upon the stalled car, and Santa Claus walked towards their hood. Ellie was tempted to shout to Jim to just floor it and speed out of there, because this was a trap. She didn't want to give in to the terror, and she didn't want to wake Ricky, and then the opportunity for warning had passed because they were stopped. Jim rolled down his window.

Billy watched silently from the back seat with slack-jawed terror.

Santa Claus crouched before the open driver's window, and a grin was visible behind his bushy facial hair. Santa's face sent a chill through Ellie that was stronger than the frosty wind entering the open window.

"Need a ride, Santa Claus?" Jim asked jovially.

"Oh no, not exactly," Santa said.

Billy's terror was so great he could barely take a breath, his eyes open achingly wide. Santa was staring intensely at his mother. That scared him greatly because his mom had been naughty tonight too.

"What's the problem?" Jim asked.

"Oh, there's no problem, just some lousy luck. For you."

With alarm, Ellie saw Santa's right hand slide out of a jacket pocket. Revealed within the red glove was the black steel handle, followed by the shiny barrel of a gun.

With a click of the hammer, Santa Claus aimed the Star Model B directly at Jim's face.

"Jim! Go! Go!" Ellie shrieked. Little Ricky matched her with a wail of his own.

Jim didn't hesitate, slamming the gearshift into reverse and flooring the gas. The car lurched backwards with a squeal.

St. Mick turned with a sinister snarl. "Shit!" He aimed at the retreating car and fired twice. Two flowers of shattered glass bloomed on the windshield.

"No!" Ellie screamed.

Tires squealed as the station wagon suddenly veered right and backed up off the side of the road, plunging into a snowbank.

There was a moment of silence, and then Ricky's wails drifted out of the car.

With the car at a stop, Billy sat up in the tilted back seat. He wasn't fully sure what happened, but he feared his father was hurt from the gurgling sounds he was making. He also felt hot droplets on his face, unaware this was a smattering of his father's blood.

Looking out the side window, Billy saw Santa Claus lumbering their way.

Grandpa was right. Santa Claus was here to punish them because they'd been naughty. He never would have guessed that Santa would use a gun like the grizzled cowboys he frequently saw in old television westerns like The Rifleman.

Billy snapped into full flight mode, opening his side door. He crossed the asphalt, ducking down over the frozen embankment. There was a crop of winter stripped bushes he hid behind. The ground was terribly cold when he crouched down, and it froze his hands. His heavy breath appeared as frost in the air before him. He wasn't even wearing a jacket, and his mom got angry when he went out into the cold without a jacket.

His mom wasn't screaming now. He could see her sleeping in her seat with her head against the side window.

Through the bare branches, Billy watched Santa Claus close in on the car. Santa ran around the hood to the driver's side and yanked open the driver's door.

Jim fell out of the car and sprawled on the road face first. A good portion of his forehead was a caved in ruin of blood and bone. His cranium had taken both bullets above his eyes. Blood pulsed out of his head in waves, steaming as it spread over the frozen asphalt.

From Billy's vantage point, his father's arms were extended on the road his way, almost as if seeking his embrace. His eyes were wide open. Only this was different, he understood. The shooting victims in *The Rifleman* did not get to come back in the next episode.

Ricky continued to scream in the baby seat. Perhaps the baby felt the loss of his parent like another umbilical cord had been cut.

Ellie came back to awareness and the first thing she saw was the open driver's door. Jim wasn't behind the wheel. That's when she remembered the last thing she saw before her head hit the window. Jim had been backing up the car when his upper face exploded with blood.

With growing horror, Ellie leaned toward the empty seat

beside her. Blood dripped on her face from the gore that sprayed onto the roof of the car as Jim's head snapped back while his forehead erupted.

Leaning further, Ellie could see Jim sprawled on the road. She began screaming again. Billy and Ricky reacted with primal panic to the sound, how could they not? This was the worst thing a child could hear, and it clawed at their souls.

The scream was choked off as she remembered the one who shot her husband. That horrible Santa. She didn't see him ahead, nor did she see him through the shattered windshield or back window.

Ellie looked over her shoulder and saw Santa's grinning face leering at her against her side window. Her scream was ear-splitting. Santa wagged his tongue luridly at her.

The door was yanked open, and Santa lunged into the front seat as Ellie dove for the driver's door. Her arms were seized from behind and she was yanked back over the seat. Her screams became cries of helplessness and fear.

Billy's mouth was locked wide open with horror, frigid air freezing his lungs. He could barely breathe, though he understood his silence was keeping Santa Claus away from him. But his mother was screaming. So was Ricky. Would his baby brother get punished too?

St. Mick yanked the screaming woman out of the car and forced her down onto the asphalt on her back. From a distance he'd seen how succulent she was, a blonde with big tits – his favorite.

The great thing about being Santa Claus was you could do

and take anything you desired. Even a woman's vagina. He wondered how many of those he could stuff in Santa's sack.

St. Mick still had an erection from his rendezvous with Miss Candy Cane, and now he had a real woman to use it on. Ellie cried out when she felt the hot pressure of Santa's hard on through his trousers.

Hysterical, she slapped at Santa's chest and tried to squirm away, but she wasn't strong enough to get out from under him. He was going to take her right here, right now. Her cries and struggles did not turn him off, quite the opposite, it appeared. He was getting the reaction that excited him most.

As Santa tugged at her shirt and ripped it open, the little silver bells that circled the white wool cuffs at the end of his jacket jingled a disturbing holiday tune.

She wasn't wearing a bra, and her massive breasts were bare before him. Santa licked his lips and leaned down to grope them.

Ellie could not believe the nightmare of this sexual assault. She was going to be raped in front of her family. Would this maniac murder her when he finished so she couldn't identify him? What about her children?

Her fear was turning to anger. She slapped him and nearly knocked the costume beard off his face.

Santa Claus punched her, knocking her senseless.

"Never hit me!"

St. Mick removed something from a jacket pocket. With a snap, the switchblade revealed itself, pointed at the heavens above.

Billy was terrified by Santa and his scary looking knife. He was far too young to know anything about the birds and the bees, but he knew this was something forbidden, something adult, that he was witnessing. It was scary and traumatic, and it made his mommy cry.

These feelings were secondary to what Billy believed he was really watching. This was what happened to those that were naughty, just like Grandpa told him. This was punishment.

He'd loved Santa as dearly as a family member, until today. Now not only did he fear Santa, but he wished he could stop him, and hurt him back. But he was frozen to his spot. He looked down in horror momentarily, and then dared to look back up.

In a daze, Ellie realized her worst fear in life was coming true. She was about to die on the road, the terrible fate of her parents.

Santa Claus had the switchblade up against her neck now, and suddenly it was inside her neck, cutting all the way across. Blood gushed out of her gaping throat.

Billy saw his mommy was like his daddy now, unmoving and bleeding on the road.

Had all this happened because he'd been naughty this year? Could his parents' punishment have been avoided if he hadn't pulled Tammy Berger's pigtail? That seemed like the logical explanation to him. He promised himself right there that he would never pull a pigtail or be naughty ever again. If only he could take that pigtail yank back because he wanted his parents back. He was learning regret in the worst way possible.

St. Mick looked at the lifeless woman between his legs. She could no longer satisfy him like this. He stood up.

"Ho ho ho," he said to taunt the dead woman at his feet.

Santa staggered away from the body with his bloody switchblade in hand and aching candy cane in his pants. He saw the open back door to the car and remembered the small boy in the backseat when the family pulled up. The brat had gotten away.

Santa staggered to the center of the road, facing Billy's direction. The switchblade carved threatening arcs in the air as Santa looked side-to-side.

"Where are you, ya little bastard!?" Santa shouted in a slur that Billy knew from television was the voice of a drunk person.

Was Santa Claus drunk too?

Billy remained paralyzed in shock, a near catatonic state that worked to save his life. Unmoving, he could only watch as blood continued to pulse out of his daddy's head and his mommy's throat. His mind was like a delicate ornament hanging from a high branch on a Christmas tree that falls to the floor and explodes into dozens of jagged pieces.

It occurred to Billy that maybe it was better to step out from behind the bushes and submit to the punishment that he deserved. If his parents had endured it, so should he. His absolute shock would not allow movement and saved his life.

Ricky continued bawling, as if knowing he would never feed from his mother's breast again. From inside the car came a Christmas song on the radio, and it lulled the baby into a stupor.

A chorus of women, angels perhaps, sang together in righteous harmony. *"Little baby, sweet little baby, pretty little baby, sweet little baby. So so so so sweet…"*.

St. Mick had no time to waste chasing some little shit around. His immediate needs took precedence, getting money and getting the fuck out of there before any witnesses arrived. The man's wallet was collected from his back pocket and the woman's wallet from her purse.

He ducked into the front of the station wagon to pop open the trunk. This car looked stuck in the snowbank, and he didn't have time to dig it out. That damn baby was still crying, and he wanted to reach over the seat and punch it in the face, or better yet stick it with his switchblade, but he didn't have a single moment to waste on fun like that.

The trunk of the station wagon had exactly what he needed, a jack and a spare tire. He quickly got the flat changed on his Monte Carlo, and he rolled away from the scene of the crime.

St. Mick had already left a devastating trail of tragedy and horror in his wake this holiday season, but it was the final coup de grace of his killing spree that would cement him in the record books.

The first car to pull into the All-Nite Gas & Food Fort after St. Mick brought Officers Nero and Buckman. When they found Levitt, his body was still warm.

The chase was on. The Bartlesville police knew the car they

were looking for. There were customers inside Woolworths who saw the Santa abduction unfold through the Woolworth's windows when the car was jacked. Responding units were called in from Bartlesville and Christmas Joy.

When the first line of cop cars arrived at the scene with Billy's parents, they drove off without checking for survivors. The chase was more important to them. Billy watched them come and go from behind the bushes on the side of the road.

A high-speed shoot-out ensued on the frozen winter road. Officer Buckman was shot in the neck through the windshield, ending his life. Another police car travelling at high velocity had a front tire shot out, causing the car to slip sideways and flip, rolling repeatedly until it became a ball of flames. Officers Bishop and Boxell were roasted like chestnuts on an open fire.

A line of Christmas Joy police cruisers parked across all lanes just inside the city limits to stop the crook before he could infiltrate the town. Taking a swig off his latest bottle of liquid courage, St. Mick plowed right into the blockade.

In a cruel twist, the nearest pursuing cruiser did not stop in time, and St. Mick's Monte Carlo was crushed like an accordion. Officer Kincaid, on a blockade car's radio at the time, did not survive the impact, decapitated when his car door slammed against his neck.

The rear impact caused the Monte Carlo's trunk to burst open. Mr. Claus' body was crushed within the folding trunk while nude Mrs. Claus was launched straight up and out. The naked elderly cadaver landed atop the impacted, smoking hood of the police car, sitting upright and spread-eagle like a hood ornament from Hell.

St. Mick was not wearing his seat belt, and he was launched like a rocket through the windshield, along with his bottle and the nudie magazines littering the front seat. His stomach dragged against a massive shard of glass on the way out, tearing his belly wide open.

A grove of pine trees was where St. Mick landed. Hanging ten feet high in the branches, his intestines unraveled through his eviscerated stomach, draping the branches like garland. The ornaments around him were torn X-rated magazine pages stuck in the branches, the ripped centerfold of Miss Candy Cane with a branch through her navel. St. Mick was the human angel atop this blasphemous holiday tree.

Christmas was officially ruined.

CHAPTER 7

The number of dead from the Santa Claus rampage was ten, including the red-suited perp. While four of the dead were residents of neighboring Bartlesville, five were from Christmas Joy, where the final scene of carnage was spread. The Santa Claus Massacre was considered a Christmas Joy affair, though the town did not wish to lay claim to the notoriety.

Santa Claus as a local legend of fear was established. But only for a limited number of unlucky residents.

A remarkably successful coverup was enacted. Killer Santa could not become the murderous mascot for a Christmas town. The scale of this tragedy could level the entire community, economically and spiritually. The city government and police made a pact that very night to keep the costume of the killer secret. Mick Bottoms was reported as the killer, but he was a Baltimore boy, an out-of-town jailbird, best forgotten. The local newspaper was eager to comply, as they didn't want to lessen their circulation by scaring readers into moving away.

The crime scene photos were kept under lock and key,

and no photographic evidence of St. Mick was ever released. Inevitably, there were loose lips and rumor mongers among the survivors, witnesses, and their loved ones, but the legend of a killer Santa remained on the fringes, spoken in whispers.

It was as though the Santa suit had been given an unmarked grave in the woods. Killer Santa was now Christmas Joy's naughty little secret.

There would be punishment for this decision. This secret created repression and rot in those who knew. Captain Richards, who had been in his position for five years, was especially distraught. He'd never lost officers in the line of duty before, and he had to break the news to their families on Christmas. When he gave the eulogy at the funeral for the fallen officers, he broke down into uncontrollable, blubbering sobs while hunched over the podium. Before he was led away by consoling officers, he got a final statement out.

"God damn you, Santa Claus! God damn you!"

Within that horrible scene on the road on Christmas Eve, there were moments of grace and goodwill toward men, or in this case, child.

Officer Olly Barnes was the lone responding officer to stop by the station wagon after the car chase passed through. His role in this drama would be that of guardian angel.

Barnes was a two-year veteran of the Christmas Joy Police at twenty-four-years old. A young hothead he was not. He was the epitome of levelheaded and by the book, and some career cops might say that was to his detriment. Despite his seriousness and steadfast work ethic, other officers tended to not take the barrel-chested young man seriously.

Barnes was cursed with a funny face.

Perhaps it was the proximity of his small eyes, or his far from husky voice, or his bushy light brown hair and bushier moustache that had twirls at the end, or perhaps it was a combination of all these that made other officers deem him immature, not man enough for the job.

Even Barnes would admit his profession was an odd choice for him, and certainly not his first consideration. His initial dream job had been magician. Creating wonder in others was something he enjoyed, but no adult around him would entertain his ambition. With his humor in mind, he then considered being a professional clown. Perhaps if the city had been named Clown Town, he might have pursued it, but he ultimately dismissed clowning as just another one of his funny ideas.

Perhaps it was fate that put him in uniform, as there was nobody better suited to be the first responder to the traumatized boys he found. At first, he thought there was only the wailing baby. Then he saw the abandoned storybook on the back seat. Babies couldn't read. He listened more closely to the frozen night.

The sound of soft weeping was easy to pinpoint. The young boy was found crouched behind the roadside bushes. The child was obviously in shock, and possibly near hypothermia without a coat. Barnes slipped his insulated police jacket off

79

and draped it over the boy like a blanket. Thankfully the baby in the car was already well bundled and less exposed to the harsh winter elements. From the boy's position Barnes assumed he'd witnessed the execution of his parents, and he did his best to lure the boy away from view of their bodies.

The baby could not leave a statement beyond goo-goo and ga-ga, and the boy delivered precious few words in his shock. Those four words amounted to two statements. The first was his name, and he gave first name only. The second statement was his account of what occurred on the road to his mommy and daddy.

"Santa punished them."

Barnes wasn't wearing face paint or a red nose, but he might as well have been from the way Ricky reacted to him. The baby found his face delightful, laughing at every silly expression he made at him. It appeared the baby had cried himself out. The baby even reached up and twirled the end of his moustache with glee.

Barnes moved the baby seat from the station wagon to the back of his police cruiser. Barnes' face didn't cause laughter or joy in the boy as it did the baby, but the cop's soft features and sympathetic puppy dog eyes calmed him and won his trust. Perhaps this was due to his being the first adult to arrive after the tragedy. The rookie cop was easily accepted as his protector, for a limited time.

Once backup arrived on the scene, Barnes did his best to shield the boys from interrogation or contact with the other gruff officers. There really was nothing Billy could provide at this point that was necessary. His parents were dead, and Barnes soon received the reports on the radio that their killer had perished along with many of his brothers in uniform.

Due to the calming effect Barnes had on the children, he stayed awake with them all night at the police station. There was no family at home who would miss him for those extra hours he spent on the job.

The weight of this Christmas tragedy had a profound effect on the young man. The grief he saw in this boy who lost his parents made him not care to have kids. Especially for a man in his line of duty, where officers could die en masse based on one radio call. No way would he want his children to endure what these boys lived through. For his job, he would sacrifice his plans for a future family.

Barnes would never forget Billy and Ricky and would find himself wondering about them over the years. He hoped they were young enough that they could forget what they witnessed that Christmas Eve. He sure as hell couldn't.

There was no immediate family willing to take the boys in. Jim's brothers were not father material. The only living grandparent was certainly not fit for the job either. Grandpa had done enough harm to the boy already.

Billy and Ricky would never see their old home or Grandpa again. Their Christmas presents would remain unopened. His mother had been right, he would have loved his interactive toys very much.

The state shipped the boys where all the local castaways went. By Christmas night, Billy and Ricky would be sleeping in different wings of Saint Mary's Home for Orphaned Children. Officer Barnes accompanied Captain Richards on the ride there to provide additional comfort to the boys.

In what could only be deemed an unfortunate act of oversight, nobody ever saw the need to tell Billy that the man impersonating Santa Claus who killed his parents had died that night, mere minutes later. Nobody addressed the issue of what Santa Claus had done to his family. Billy continued to believe not only that Santa Claus had punished his parents and was still out there, but that it was all his fault for being naughty in the first place.

Adults assumed he was too young to process what he'd witnessed, but that was nothing but self-serving denial. Billy not only saw but understood everything that happened to his family, and he could never truly forget it.

This oversight would have catastrophic consequences for many, but for Billy most of all.

The town of Christmas Joy awoke to great tragedy on Christmas morning, 1971. The affected families were shattered on the most family centered day of the year. Christmas music was turned up louder to drown out the sound of wailing in many homes.

The Christmas Joy Tribune had a ghoulish headline rather than a holiday greeting on that all important day. Emblazoned atop the page was "Tragic Crime Spree On The Road". Not only was any mention of Santa absent, but so was the holiday the crimes occurred on. Christmas was not mentioned in the headline article once.

By dawn of Christmas morning, all the wreckage on the road had been removed. Thankfully, this occurred on the most traffic free night of the year. Left over on the asphalt were scorch marks, burned rubber, and patches of broken glass. None of these markers were left behind where the station wagon was found, but tacky splashes of blood remained on the frozen pavement, spilled by Billy's parents.

The town spirit might have been completely broken that Christmas, but for one pleasant holiday surprise. Perhaps this gift was sent from on high by the Christmas Star. Or maybe this gift was brought by Santa Claus himself.

In the wee hours of the morning, the gusty winds carried in some unexpected storm clouds that were not in the forecast. By dawn, the clouds began to unleash their icy cargo. Christmas Joy woke up to a surprise white Christmas.

This coverup was celestial. The blood stains on the road were concealed by a white blanket of snow, hiding the horror from view.

CHAPTER

Established in 1898, Saint Mary's Home for Orphaned Children was a towering two-story red brick building on the outskirts of Christmas Joy. An eight-foot-tall cross was mounted over the entrance, and an engraved wooden sign was erected in the yard outside. Over the years there would be renovations inside, including a baby wing and staff quarters added to the back of the building, but the cross and sign out front was never replaced, despite becoming heavily weathered.

Behind the building stood a wooden shed that was deceptively large as it opened into a wider space underground filled with yard tools, the electric panels, and water heater. The shed was an accident waiting to happen, and therefore off limits to the children.

Beyond the orphanage was a deep wooden expanse that stretched for miles, the worst place for an orphan to wander unaware. This would occur twice over the years, with no trace of the missing kids ever found. A few old timers claimed this was Wendigo country, and everyone knew a Wendigo's favorite feast was lost children. These ancient woods extended northeast until they became the Escalante Petrified Forest, the most legendarily cursed area of the state.

The Sisters of the Holy Cross operated the orphanage from its inception. Sister Bedelia expressed their mission thusly: "Saint Mary's Home for Orphaned Children was established to house, clothe, and feed innocent children who have been orphaned, of those abandoned by both parents through illness, poverty, or criminal enterprise. The Sisters will impart suitable education and lessons in morality and gospel, to best prepare these children to become worthwhile citizens in society, with great humility and devotion to Christ."

The orphanage was not always successful in its mission.

Setting up operation just before the turn of the twentieth century proved fortuitous. On May 1, 1900, the worst mining disaster in American history occurred in Scofield, Utah. An excessive amount of methane caused the initial explosion in Winter Quarters Number Four mine. Most Carbon County miners who perished died of deadly carbon monoxide poisoning. The recovered bodies would return to the ground soon after discovery, though not all bodies were found.

The number of dead from the Scofield mining disaster was estimated at nearly two-hundred and fifty. With so many shattered families, there was strain put on all the orphanages statewide. Saint Mary's Home for Orphaned Children welcomed many, reaching full capacity almost immediately. There would be further booms during the first and second

World Wars, requiring an additional wing. War was always the best business for orphaning children.

Saint Mary's was a godsend for generations of children. Many went on to secure honest livelihoods and become worthwhile members of society. A good number even stayed in Christmas Joy upon their release. Not so successful was their mission to keep them devoted to Christ. It was easy for many to lose faith after living through two World Wars.

In 1951, a new Order took over the orphanage with what could be described as a very firm grip. The Sisters of Persistent Devotion was an Order that originated in Santa Fe, New Mexico early that century before migrating north. Their control of the orphanage would hold for many decades. This Order's idea of charity was nothing like the Order that came before. Along with a new level of strictness, secrets and shame became a new norm for the young charges of the place. No child made it out unscathed.

The arrival of the Sisters of Persistent Devotion ushered in a Dark Age for Saint Mary's Home for Orphaned Children. A season of abuse and pain that for many children would haunt them for the rest of their lives. It was a season of punishment beyond imagination. And the rot did not just go all the way to the top; it started there.

This was the reign of Mother Superior.

Sister Margaret had some serious mother issues.

Back when she'd been Margaret Mayberry, living at home

with her parents and five siblings, her mother Margaret Mayberry had been her nemesis. This was entirely her mother's doing. What young girl didn't crave love and acceptance from her mother? She sure did. But mamma would never accept her, and Margaret believed she'd never heard those cherished words *I love you* from mamma's mouth once.

Growing up in Ogden, Utah had been a nightmare. Nobody in her family accepted her, and she became the object of her family's ire, taking the blame for every annoyance under the sun. Her father wasn't as antagonistic as the others, but he showed no interest in knowing her either. Half the time he wasn't around anyway, going between Ogden and Saratoga Springs where his other wife and family lived. They were the ones in the bigger, nicer house, whereas her family were squeezed into a ramshackle old farmhouse that sat on infertile soil.

She was a slender young girl on the shorter side who would grow into a slender young woman on the shorter side, and though bookish and reserved, most would describe her as pleasing to look at if not downright pretty. Her breasts were as slight as she was, which kept at least some boys at bay. Margaret Molehill had been a nickname she'd heard bandied about in middle school. So what, she didn't like boys much anyway, especially the immature ones.

Margaret's mother had a town nickname too, Mrs. Titsberry. She had the biggest breasts in town, awe inspiring mountains that preceded her everywhere she went. Her breasts brought her great pride, and she oft liked to call them two of the wonders of the world. Some of the cruelest shaming young Margaret received about her inadequate breast size came from her mother.

Breasts weren't the only thing huge about mamma. She weighed over five-hundred pounds, carrying it with much difficulty. Obesity was not just in her mother's genes, but her father's as well. He topped three-hundred-fifty pounds and would claim it was all muscle; it wasn't. Each of her siblings was oversized, all of them weighing over ten pounds at birth. They would top two-hundred pounds each when they entered their teens, and would have all added another hundred by graduation, if any of them had graduated.

Education was not looked upon favorably by the Mayberrys. When Margaret became the first member of her family to graduate high school, she was relentlessly shamed for it and went to her ceremony alone. As an added kicker, she was banished from home the day after graduation for thinking she was so smart.

While she did not judge her family for their size, aware that you could not help the DNA that was God given, she was judged harshly for hers. At birth, she weighed only five and a half pounds. She'd been a month and a half premature, the only child in her family to come out early. Perhaps she hadn't spent enough time in the oven to get her dough to fully rise. As for her father, she heard him deny paternity because she didn't carry the family resemblance. Her siblings called her Raisin, claiming she didn't spend enough time growing on the vine. She couldn't get them to understand that raisins were not the result of grapes not hanging long enough. Their willful ignorance frustrated her greatly.

It wasn't ignorance that annoyed her most about her family, it was their blatant hypocrisy. They acted holier than thou, but they did not practice what they preached, using the Good Book as nothing more than an excuse. They didn't even read the Bible because none of them could read. Her family's weekly attendance at church was abandoned in her teen years due to mamma's mobility issues and her church no longer having pews able to support her. Giving up church was something Margaret did not want to do, for the spiritual guidance she craved was absolute and all encompassing. Her attendance continued after her family stopped going. This only increased the division and animosity between them.

The Mayberrys were serious sinners, and it was plainly obvious to everyone. Her mother was a pharmaceutical addict, while her father was a proud alcoholic. Her siblings were all underage drinkers, and they also indulged in speed and pills, mixing them up. The drugs only amplified her family's anger and eagerness to fight. There were numerous arrests for drug possession, grand larceny, grand theft auto, battery, firearms violations, unwanted pregnancies, and sexual assault.

Despite their constant criminality, the Mayberrys claimed to be the most pious family in the land. There was no convincing them otherwise. Lord knows she'd tried. Meanwhile, they positioned their healthy, book reading, straight-A student daughter as the bad one.

Upon her banishment from home, Margaret had her life

direction decided. She wanted to become a nun and show her family who the pious one was – she would practice what she preached. She chose this rather than living as a consecrated virgin, as she wished for the order that a convent would provide.

What her future would not provide was male companionship. She would not take a man's surname in matrimony, but she would add Sister to her name in her service to Christ. There really was no dating for her during her high school years. Her sister Niecy teased her endlessly about her lack of a boyfriend. Niecy was knocked up at sixteen, and again at seventeen. Margaret saw her own independence from men to be a virtue.

She was not without desire for men, but she chose to suppress it to escape her family's dead-end world. If someone called her a control freak for her behavior, she would nod and agree.

As the history of the ultra-devout would attest, suppressing her sexual desires and adhering to abstinence would cause long term side effects and aberrations in her behavior. As she checked into convent school, she had no idea what changes were in store for her years and decades down the road. Along with love of God she was filled with optimism for the future and took pride in her purity. Becoming a nun was her avenue for making the world a better place.

Eager to leave her locale but not the state, Margaret set her sights on the city of Christmas Joy and the Order established there, the Sisters of Persistent Devotion. There was an age limit to join of twenty-three, but her heart was set, and patience was another of her many virtues. Her postulancy ended in 1970, and she became Sister Margaret.

Instead of residing in a convent, the Sisters of Persistent Devotion had a plan for her, and she was chosen for placement at Saint Mary's Home for Orphaned Children. Overseeing the children and helping in operations would be her manual labor. This was where she met Mother Superior.

Sister Margaret had some serious Mother issues.

Mother Superior tested her patience with every single exchange. There was no talking to the woman, only being talked down to by her. The old woman possessed no great wisdom that she could see, only the strictest adherence to morals and order with no other considerations whatsoever. Mother Superior was a byproduct of the Inquisition, and likely wished she could return there.

Sister Margaret was stuck living with her at the orphanage. Their rooms were right next to each other, so she was rarely ever away from her watchful eyes.

Mother Superior tested her relationship to God and faith in general. The old woman was a walking cloud of dark gas that caused depression and hopelessness. Sister Margaret was made to believe she could no longer contribute any good to the world, because Mother Superior would not allow it. This drab and dreary orphanage could be a warm place filled with hope and love, but nope, Mother Superior extinguished any chance of that right away. The Order might well call themselves the Sisters of Perpetual Discipline with Mother Superior around. That was the only doctrine she abided by.

Quite simply, Mother Superior was the most righteous stone-cold bitch she'd met since her mother. How could God be so cruel to subject her to this again?

This was another one of God's tests, she came to understand. At least this belief gave her the will to continue day-to-day. She would not let Mother Superior destroy her faith or deprogram her of her individuality like the other Sisters at the orphanage. Their personalities had been erased.

Sister Margaret had nobody to talk to other than the orphans, but they were far better conversationalists.

A year and a half into her time at Saint Mary's, Billy and his baby brother Ricky arrived. Brought in on Christmas day, 1971, they were a true gift, though it had been a living hell what had happened to the boys to bring them there.

In private, Captain Richards explained in tearful detail what happened to the boys' parents on Christmas Eve. The information about the Santa Claus suit the killer wore was shared, as he found it a necessary detail they needed to handle with care when the holidays came around. With relief he noted that other than a plain wreath on the front door, there were no Christmas decorations anywhere inside the orphanage.

"Santa Claus! Can you believe that son of a bitch?" Captain Richards groused with disgust and a shake of his heavy head. He caught himself as he remembered where he was. "Sorry, Sisters."

Mother Superior glared at him, and he crossed his arms as he turned away like a guilty child. The fear she struck in him, a lapsed Catholic, was real.

"Captain Richards, we do not appreciate your potty mouth," Mother Superior said sternly.

Captain Richards gulped, turned red, and felt a flush of dread. Even his testicles retreated up into his body to escape from her.

Mother Superior's first words to Billy that Christmas could not have been colder.

"We'll dip you for lice tomorrow. Now go to your room." Billy didn't even know where his room was.

Sister Margaret's heart went out to these boys, and she developed an intense, immediate bond with Billy. While she hoped her presence benefited all the children there, she wished to better the life of Billy most of all. He became more than a project for her because her feelings were involved.

This was Sister Margaret's first awakening to a deep, hidden maternal instinct. It was indulged with the passion and intensity of puppy love. Her eyes longed for Billy every moment, and she found ways to be around him more frequently.

Some might say she loved little Billy more than baby Jesus. She would likely agree.

She saw that Billy was withdrawn, observant, and always polite. He did not stand out in a crowd of kids, he never called attention to himself. His inquisitive nature had been tempered. When in the past he might have asked questions to satisfy his curiosities, now he just sat in contemplative silence.

Billy was the most behaved kid since the holy child, Sister Margaret thought, but she believed this was the result of hidden fear and distrust of adults. When you saw that most revered figure of Santa Claus, who was like a saint to children, murder your parents, then all bets were off. How could you trust an adult to protect you ever again?

The fact that so much hurt was contained within that meek, mannered, beautiful child, filled Sister Margaret with compassion and devotion to do everything she could to help him heal and grow into a healthy young man.

Billy was the reason God put her onto this life path of celibacy and service. She was to be his saint, his missing mother, his protector. As for his little brother Ricky, she loved him as she did any other child tucked in a crib, but he wasn't *special.* Billy she loved more than anyone she'd ever loved in her life.

She didn't know if Billy felt the same or had any special feelings for her. Emotions were rarely expressed by the boy. When a moment of cheer or animation did appear, her heart swelled.

For the first two years he was at Saint Mary's, Billy remained overly withdrawn, especially around Christmas. Growth and development were inevitable, and he learned structure and safety within the orphanage walls. Sister Margaret became hopeful that her motherly guidance aided in his progress.

The year Billy began to come out of his shell was 1974, when he was eight years old. This was also the year that his troubled phase began.

His problems increased as Christmas drew near.

December's heaviest snowfall occurred on the 15th. It began in the middle of the night as the town's inhabitants slept, and they awoke to elevated snow drifts.

The flakes continued to fall through the morning as classes began at Saint Mary's. Inches of snow sat atop the orphanage sign, which was typical for the month, but there were other remarkable changes from years past.

There was a collection of Christmas decorations visible on the front of the building, adding a colorful burst of holiday cheer. A Christmas wreath with red bows hung on each of the entrance doors, with fake snow painted around the borders of the glass – as though the whiteout outside wasn't enough. Multi-colored snowflakes cut by the kids from construction paper were taped inside all the first-floor windows. Most prominent was the life-sized wooden diorama of Santa Claus and four attentive reindeer erected before the building by the door.

For the children, Santa Claus was there to greet them every time they went in and out.

That morning, Billy sat in the classroom for the six- to nine-year-old children. His lesson brought frustration. This should have been a fun one, because it involved pictures. Billy liked to draw because it rewarded his creativity. There was a box of crayons on his desk; every child had their own pack to draw with.

The assignment was simple enough, draw your most vivid memory of Christmas. Each child was given a sheet of construction paper for their canvas. Everyone else had completed their assignment, and they were being called up individually to tape their artwork to the chalkboard. Billy scribbled feverishly on his paper, unsatisfied.

Sister Ellen, in full nun's habit, stood before the class with a smile. The thirty-five-year-old Sister had an easy smile which rarely left her face, and her gentle nature was useful for dealing with children of such young age.

"All right, now who's next?" Sister Ellen asked, a roll of masking tape in her hands.

Billy scribbled some more, traded his green crayon for a red one, and made a slash with it.

Sister Ellen's sight landed on Billy, hard at work. "Oh, yes. We haven't seen your drawing yet, have we?" She tilted her head quizzically.

Billy gave the red crayon another slash, and another, and another. If he heard her question, he gave no indication.

"Billy," Sister Ellen added to draw the boy's attention.

Billy drew some more.

"Billy!" Sister Ellen said with a stern rise in her voice. He didn't have to see her face to know that his friendly teacher had lost her smile. Billy looked up with a dumbfounded look on his face.

"Answer me," Sister Ellen added, although it wasn't an answer she sought, but rather his artwork.

Billy nodded and answered, "Okay."

"Let's go, Billy," Sister Ellen said, her smile returned. "Come on up here. Put your drawing up on the board with the others."

Billy carried his drawing to the front of the class.

"You put it in place, and I'll put the tape on it," Sister Ellen instructed.

Billy stepped up to the chalkboard and held his drawing up as Sister Ellen pulled pieces of tape off the roll. All the other drawings on display were crudely similar. Stick figure families stood by scribbled trees. A few had Santa Claus, easy to spot because he was the red one with a pointy hat.

A girl's shriek startled everyone. Margot had a hand over her mouth, her eyes wide above her fingers. When she removed her hand to speak, she pointed at the chalkboard.

"Sister, look!" A grimace of disgust stretched across Margot's face.

Sister Ellen looked at Billy's drawing. Her features sharpened, the cords in her strained neck popping out. The judgment in her eyes was harsh.

The children gaped at Billy's drawing with revulsion and horror. Alan covered his eyes, knowing he would have nightmares. Cindy began to sob, which caused runny snot to drip from her nostrils onto her desk.

"Billy, take that down!" Sister Ellen said in her sharpest tone. Her severity startled even her.

Billy looked at the teacher like a wounded doe. He knew he'd disappointed her very badly but didn't know why. He'd been the last one drawing, but that was because he was trying to make his artwork as vivid as he could.

"Young man, you go find Mother Superior and you show her what you've done," Sister Ellen said. She believed he was playing a prank on her, one more befitting the holiday of Halloween. Of Billy's traumatic past she had no knowledge.

Mother Superior and Sister Margaret were the only two with Captain Richards the day the boys were brought in. Only they knew his horrible history with Santa Claus. And Hell hath no fury like Mother Superior scorned, if the secret ever got out. Had Sister Ellen known Billy's tragic story, the reasoning behind his drawing would have been apparent, and her response more compassionate.

"March!" Sister Ellen shouted at him as he headed out, pinching the drawing painfully tight between his fingers. He also bit the inside of his lower lip in a nervous reaction. Sister Ellen had never shouted at him like that before. He wondered if he somehow deserved it. He tried to never be bad.

Billy's worry increased as he marched out to show Mother Superior what he'd done.

That woman scared the spit out of him.

CHAPTER 9

The drawing in Mother Superior's hand was an obscenity. Her scornful eyes took in every sordid detail.

The artwork depicted Santa Claus lying on the ground with his arms spread in a Christ on the cross pose. It was obvious he was dead because there were four swords sticking out of his body: one in his thigh, one in his stomach, one in his chest, and one in the center of his forehead. A pool of blood extended on each side of him.

What was next to dead Santa was even more graphic. A reindeer stood with its head chopped off and separated from the body, tongue hanging out. Blood squirted out and dripped from the gory neck wound into a crimson pool. A bloody axe was beneath the dead reindeer, and beside the weapon was the artist's signature, *Billy*. Behind this scene of double carnage was a Christmas tree with colored ornaments and a star on top.

Mother Superior saw this drawing as an affront to God, and an affront to her directly. That this drawing might be the result of the trauma he suffered when his parents were murdered by Santa Claus did not occur to her, because she had no imagination to see anything outside of her narrow, absolute assumptions. Nor did she have the compassion for such a belief. This drawing had been created for one reason and one reason only.

Billy was being a little asshole. That was a problem she intended to pinch.

Mother Superior thought Billy was a Pussyboy. From the day he was brought in with his whiny baby brother, she had him pegged and hated him deeply. The way he looked at you with those big blue eyes, wanting it, begging for it. She knew that look well, that was the way a street hooker looked at every man. Yep, Billy was a Pussyboy, all right.

Though foul language never issued forth from Mother Superior's lips, they dominated her thoughts. The endless reservoir of vulgarities that filled her head was so extreme they'd make a horny trucker on boner pills blush. She did not consider this sin because she was observing others and judging them. It seemed she had a Get Out Of Hell Free card for every one of her own transgressions against man and God. She believed she was beyond judgment, even from her beloved Lord and Savior.

Mother Superior had a sadistic God complex, and Saint Mary's Home for Orphaned Children was her kingdom. She was the Mad Queen.

When Captain Richards first brought the Chapman boys on Christmas, she did not believe his story of a homicidal Santa Claus. Her doubt she kept to herself. She didn't trust the word of any man who stopped going to church.

Mother Superior's view of law enforcement was low, seeing cops as little different from those they put behind bars. They were all vermin wallowing in the gutter. She'd read about the murders in the daily paper and there was no mention of a killer Santa Claus.

The captain was a liar, and nobody could convince her otherwise.

What Mother Superior could not deny was the boys' parents had been murdered on the road on Christmas Eve. What she disbelieved was that Billy could have seen it, let alone comprehended it. She couldn't recall a single thing that happened to her when she was five, no adult could, and her upbringing in Sicily had been a string of hardships including poverty, war, and sexual slavery.

Even if Billy did see something on the road, he would forget it in time. Five-year-olds were stupid, and she'd never met one that proved otherwise. If the boy did see something difficult, then that's exactly why he needed to toughen up. He would get no soft treatment from her. In fact, quite the opposite.

She had a plan for him which had been put in motion three years ago, due to the immediate deep hatred she felt for the boy. God put that hate into her guts for a reason, so she felt justified. With today's incident of acting out, it was time to crank her plans into higher gear. Boys everywhere were too soft these days. They even grew their hair out like they were *girls, Jesus fucking Christ!*

To fuel her acts of aggression, she evoked her favorite

biblical passage Ezekiel, 25:17 – "And I shall wreak great acts of vengeance with rebukes of fury, and they will know that I am the Lord when I lay My vengeance upon them."

Mother Superior believed that Billy drew this picture to challenge her. The gory images represented evil acts of evisceration he wanted to inflict upon all holy people. This picture was a threat in crayon, a vision that he wanted to deck the halls of the orphanage with Christmas carnage.

Challenge accepted, Pussyboy.

Billy had never been disciplined in class or given marching orders to see Mother Superior. He hadn't gotten into a fight or talked back or, God forbid, pulled a pigtail. All he'd done was follow the assignment. Granted, it hadn't been Santa and a reindeer dead on the road that night, so he was indulging in artistic license. So were the other students with drawings that included Santa Claus or flying reindeer or Jesus Christ beside the Christmas tree with a cookie. Apparently, Jesus was a fan of chocolate chip.

It made him sad that he upset Sister Ellen so much. It made him afraid of what Mother Superior's reaction would be. Sister Margaret was also in the office in a chair beside the desk. He didn't want to disappoint her either, but not because he was afraid of her.

Billy was so tense his legs were pinched together. He was fearful he might pee his pants if she spoke too harshly to him.

Mother Superior had no visible reaction to the drawing,

but she studied it intensely for some time. Sister Margaret leaned over a row of Jesus, Mary, and Joseph tchotchkes to give the drawing a look. She gasped and put a hand to her heart, which felt like it'd been socked hard.

Sister Margaret did not see an offensive drawing. What she saw was pain expressed in those doom-laden images. He was yearning to break free of his nightmare past, and this drawing was a cry for help.

Unfortunately, Mother Superior did not see it that way.

Mother Superior's habited head, which had the highest arch in the institution, shook in disappointment.

Billy stood rigidly with his hands clenched behind his back. His grip was painfully tight. Mother Superior stood behind her desk, and her rosaries tinkled in warning. Billy gulped and bit the inside of his lip again, the tender flesh there already raw and wounded.

At least Mother Superior wasn't crossing her arms. He'd seen her explode from anger before, and in that instance, she'd had her arms tightly crossed over her chest. That was the day that Tommy was caught chasing Rebecca around shaking the hot dog he'd kept from lunch in front of his pants. That image of Mother Superior, standing rigidly with her arms tightly crossed, had frightened him badly, and he hadn't been shaking his hot dog at anyone.

"Explain this, William," Mother Superior demanded.

Billy didn't know how to explain it. He'd followed the assignment as it'd been given. What he did know was he was in trouble and an apology was in order.

"I'm sorry, Mother Superior," Billy said softly in heartfelt apology.

"Are you?" Mother Superior snapped, and then followed, "I don't think so."

Billy's eyes opened wider with alarm. More trouble was coming.

"But you will be," Mother Superior continued. "You will learn what it is to be sorry."

As Mother Superior scolded Billy, Sister Margaret reached out to pick up Billy's picture. Studying the image closely, she looked beyond the violence and saw the child had a steady hand and artistic flourish. The coloring was beautiful. Even the reindeer was well proportioned. Billy could be a respected artist in the future if he applied himself.

Sister Margaret was wired to always see potential for Billy.

"Now go to your room and stay there until I tell you to come out," Mother Superior ordered.

"Yes, Mother Superior," Billy said with sadness. He unclenched his hands from behind his back. They were feeling numb after such an extended grip of tension. He closed the door behind him.

Sister Margaret thought Billy's drawing was the perfect illustration of the trauma he'd lived through and was still coping with. She shook her head at the grief the picture repre-sented. This was the proof she'd long been waiting for. When she spoke, Mother Superior's glare turned on her.

"Well, you finally have what you've been asking for, Mother Superior. Proof."

"Of what, Sister Margaret?" Mother Superior's question was a trap because she'd never asked Sister Margaret for proof of anything.

Sister Margaret looked up from the picture with pleading eyes. Mother Superior found her look pathetic, like a beggar, or a whore.

"Of what I've been saying," Sister Margaret clarified. "That it's all still inside him. All that terrible violence he saw. His drawing clearly shows that." She thought her theory was fool proof because she had evidence. There was no judgment of Billy in her tone. He was calling for their help. His drawing did not instill fear in her, nor should he deserve trouble for creating it.

"When did I ask for that?" Mother Superior inquired.

"The last time I told you what I thought..." Sister Margaret began but was not given a chance to finish.

"I am not interested in what you think," Mother Superior announced. "I thought you finally understood that."

Mother Superior's proclamation delivered a devastating blow to Sister Margaret right where it hurt most. Had she actually believed for a moment that Mother Superior might come to her senses and accept the truth in front of her face? When had facts mattered to her before? The very hope for understanding or compassion from Mother Superior had been a fallacy on her part.

Mother Superior continued. "As for the drawing, it shows exactly one thing. William is a little wretch who enjoys causing trouble for everyone around him."

How could Mother Superior say such a thing? Billy had never caused a single incident of trouble for any student or teacher before; of that she was certain. She stopped short of directly calling her out as a liar.

Sister Margaret lowered her head like an abused puppy. That terrible woman had the power to make her feel ashamed, and she hated not only Mother Superior for that, but herself as well.

"Simply because something unfortunate happened to his parents, which he knows nothing about, is no reason to allow him to run wild. He must be taught!"

Sister Margaret didn't care for Mother Superior raising her voice to scold her in the same voice she used against the children. She sharpened her own voice in response, almost like she was trying to teach a stubborn child who didn't want to learn.

"But the memory is still there, Mother Superior, waiting to come out."

"If it does, and if he's received proper training, he will know how to cope with it."

Sister Margaret saw the fundamental failure of Mother Superior's reasoning, because he wasn't receiving any proper training to cope with his trauma. What Billy needed was a therapist to talk with, instead he was getting Mother Superior's absolute denial. That was proper training for failure. Sister Margaret's persistent insistence that Billy needed a therapist had become a massive point of contention between them.

But she would continue to protest because that was the

right thing to do. The truth was meant to be spoken, and Mother Superior needed to hear it. There were no other Sisters who would dare speak to Mother Superior the way she was now.

"But if he keeps going on like this much longer it may be too late. It seems to get worse for him every Christmas." And that was to be expected because trauma, like Santa Claus, was a seasonal specter. Anniversaries loomed large as a day for reliving dread.

"Well, it won't go on any longer," Mother Superior stated with finality. "I'll take care of that child personally."

I'll get you, Pussyboy, Mother Superior thought. *Oh yes I will.*

Sister Margaret's spirits sank, and her eyes lowered. She was getting browbeaten, again, like always.

"He needs help, Mother Superior," Sister Margaret reiterated.

"He'll get it!" Mother Superior announced with an authoritative shout, and her eyes flashed a challenge – *keep pushing it, Sister.*

It was useless to argue further, Sister Margaret decided. She'd given her recommendation even though Mother Superior clearly didn't want to hear it. Mother Superior was on such a throne of superiority she thought her shit didn't stink. But she'd used the office bathroom after Mother Superior before, and she could swear on God's good grace that she stank to high heaven.

"Good day, Sister," Mother Superior announced, which

was her version of *get the fuck out of here*. She reached out for Billy's drawing.

Sister Margaret was hesitant to relinquish the evidence. If only she could take this drawing to a doctor or shrink, somebody who could give her useful insight and instruction.

Sister Margaret reluctantly handed Billy's drawing over, and then she rose from her chair.

"Good day, Mother Superior," Sister Margaret said with a nod of her head. She was eager to get out of Mother Superior's suffocating presence. Good thing her back was turned, so Mother Superior couldn't see her face flushed with upset. When she closed the door, she was more forceful than usual, the slam adding punctuation to her exit.

In the hallway, the startling truth landed before Sister Margaret, and she couldn't believe she hadn't seen the full picture before. That was because it was easy to excuse abusive behavior as something else, to feel less culpable or complicit in it. But now that the truth was revealed, she would not forget it. Time would tell whether she would be able to forgive it, or herself.

Her first two years at Saint Mary's, the orphanage had a firm No Christmas policy, resisting the modern traditions and iconography of Christmas promoted by department stores and soft drinks. She'd accepted the institution's policy and abided by it without argument. This was the practice in many parishes.

Over the past few years, that policy at Saint Mary's had changed. In December 1972, the first Christmas tree had been erected in the front room, and every child got to add a handmade decoration to it. The wreaths on the front door also became more elaborate, for the first time adorned with colorful ribbons and ornaments. Gift-giving was introduced, with each child receiving one gift from Santa Claus. In 1973, the children began to make arts and crafts to display throughout the orphanage, including the snowflakes for the windows.

December 1974 brought the introduction of Santa Claus to the orphanage's holiday display. The wooden Santa and reindeer diorama was put on display right outside the front door. Jolly old Saint Nick stood guard at the entrance to face every kid that walked in and out of the front door. He was ever present and unavoidable.

Mother Superior brought this Santa display to the orphanage without warning. The introduction of holiday decorations and modern Christmas traditions was all her doing. These indulgences of modern impulse were wholly unlike Mother Superior, who was otherwise as rigidly Old Testament as you could be in the twentieth century.

But something had changed. Billy had come into Saint Mary's custody.

Sister Margaret had at first questioned Mother Superior about the introduction of Christmas decorations and traditions within the orphanage.

"Get with the times, Sister Margaret," Mother Superior snapped, as though she were in any way modern. Sister Margaret knew the truth, that Mother Superior was far more medieval than that. The times she spoke of were her own, the Mother Superior Era. Her every edict was enforced as ancient law.

Even Mother Superior's title was suspect. Sister Margaret knew that in every other Catholic institution, Mother Superior would have been addressed as Reverend Mother or Your Reverence. The old woman's demand to be called Mother Superior seemed ego driven, because she believed she was superior to everyone.

Mother Superior was provoking Billy deliberately with these new Christmas traditions and decorations. Not in the service of *proper training*. This was being done out of cruelty, to bully and strike fear in the boy.

This was abuse in the guise of Santa Claus. Billy was being triggered, deliberately provoked like a zoo animal in a cage getting poked with a stick through the bars. And to what cruel purpose other than Mother Superior's own sadistic delight?

Sister Margaret had very little idea how much abuse actually occurred there. Sometimes, the habit was pulled over her eyes.

Someday, I'm going to make her pay, Sister Margaret thought.

CHAPTER  10

The day's heavy snowfall tapered off just before noon, and that afternoon the children were allowed to play in the fresh snow and build a snowman. Sister Sarah, who watched over the rambunctious little ones, had the snowshoes to supervise, though she kept close to the building. Her snow bunny days were long past.

The snowman with a gray felt hat and long winter scarf was taller than the tykes who made him. They named him Frosty.

Also keeping watch of the snow day activities was Santa Claus, in the form of the wooden effigy in perpetual holiday cheer.

From his second-floor window, Billy observed the children running in circles around the snowman and playing in the fresh snow he was denied.

Watching the other kids made him sad. He was still confused as to why he had to be confined to his room. Eventually, his window observation grew tiresome, so he moved to the bottom bunk.

Billy slouched forward with his head hung low, keeping uncomfortable company with his thoughts. He recognized that he was sadder this time of year, which made him dislike Christmas while all the other kids embraced it. This made him even lonelier.

Sister Margaret was right that unresolved trauma from his past was the culprit.

Billy did not sit around dwelling on the murders of his parents. His mind had erected a barrier to keep the most horrible roadside memories at bay. The barrier was porous, however, like a wall riddled with knot holes like his old wooden backyard fence.

Sometimes he would get a glimpse through those openings at unexpected moments, and a shocking image would replay in his head. Sometimes it was so brief he'd only see a hand wielding a weapon, or an up-close act of violence. In such cases, he might not even know what he was looking at. Other times his mind's eye would see a much longer act of harm inflicted upon his parents, and he would be horribly aware he was witnessing their murders. Then, he might have a night or two of vague nightmares.

These night and day terrors typically increased as Christmas approached, as would his fear that the same Santa Claus who took his parents was coming back for him. This was an understandable conclusion because nobody had told him that Santa was dead. The last he saw, Santa ran off into the night after butchering his parents (when in fact he ran into a police cruiser and his grave less than ten minutes later).

Mercifully, once the holidays were over, Billy's debilitating flashbacks would fade, at least until the calendar turned to December the following year.

A click, followed by the door opening, snapped Billy out of his melancholy. Sitting upright, he braced himself for Mother Superior. When he saw Sister Margaret, he was relieved. She was his favorite Sister.

Sister Margaret crossed the room toward him. There was a warm smile upon her face, and that was one of the reasons he liked her so much. There were far too few smiles within the orphanage, or his life. That she always had a smile for him made him feel special.

She was the one he had maternal feelings for.

This clandestine visit came at risk for Sister Margaret, as she hadn't cleared it with Mother Superior. But that superior hardhead thought she could control her like she could a wayward child, and that did not sit well with her at all. She was a Sister of the same Order, and her devotion meant something. So did her voice. Now she was going to use it. In this orphanage, she'd come to understand it was better to ask for forgiveness than permission, because permission would never be granted.

Sister Margaret believed Billy did not deserve punishment for his drawing today. And though Mother Superior had a problem with him, she wanted him to know that she did not. Her smile was offered with love and understanding.

"I think you've been locked away up here long enough. Why don't you come out and help us build our snowman?"

Billy looked up at her with disappointment. "I can't," he said, and hung his head back down.

The boy's dispirited look broke Sister Margaret's heart. She sat beside him on the bottom bunk. In a move that brought both comfort, Sister Margaret took Billy's hands into her own.

"Look Billy, Mother Superior only wants what's best for you. And I think what's best for you is to come out and play with the other children, okay?"

It was a bold plan of hers, to essentially break Billy out of confinement, but she believed she could get away with it. Mother Superior rarely left her office in the early afternoon. The old broad never deviated from routine, and this was the time of day she took her righteous shits. Plus, Mother Superior never went out in the snow with the children.

She knew better than Mother Superior that Billy needed normalcy, not isolation. Billy still looked uncertain, and she squeezed his hands reassuringly.

"Hmmm?" she added with a nod of encouragement.

Billy responded with a nod of agreement. "Yes."

"Okay," Sister Margaret said with delight, and she released his hands so she could stand. "Dress up warm first," she added. When she reached the door, she turned to him, beaming with pride, and then departed so he could have privacy to get dressed.

Sister Margaret believed she was doing the right thing for Billy. He'd been punished enough today. When he was joyful, she was joyful. When he hurt, she hurt harder. Little was she aware her gesture of goodwill to Billy was the start of a new skirmish in a long escalating war.

As was always the case with war, the blood that was shed would come from innocent children.

Though Mother Superior told Billy to stay in his room, Sister Margaret told him to come out. She was also an adult, and Billy believed it was his duty to follow the orders adults gave him. When he agreed to go down at Sister Margaret's insistence, he once again believed he was doing the right thing, trying to be a good boy, and doing what he was instructed to do.

Billy slipped into his wool-lined jacket. A thick mitten was stuck in each side pocket. He wrapped a striped scarf around his neck, and grabbed onto his stocking cap, which he'd wait to put on until he got outside. Dressed for the snow, he stepped out of his room and closed the door behind him.

Alone in the hallway, Billy heard what sounded like chirping. The corridors were cavernous and carried an echo. While he meant to head for the stairs, curiosity led him to follow the noise, first turning right. When he came to a three-way intersection, he stopped and listened closely.

The sound was now coming from the left, and along with chirping, he heard moaning. He wanted to see what kind of bird caused reactions like that. It was also a very excited bird from the sound of it, because it was chirping faster now.

Billy turned left. He was concerned that Mother Superior might spot him, but his curiosity was too strong. He didn't think he was doing anything deliberately bad, since all he wanted was a quick look. Regardless, he made a point not to make noise or call attention to himself.

This long corridor took him out of the front building into the back wing, where the staff and guest quarters were located. There was a rule that the children were not allowed to wander into this wing. This was new terrain for him.

The corridor led to another intersection. The last hall on the left was short and ended at a closed door. This room was the source of the noisy bird, only now he realized he had the sound wrong. It sounded like somebody was jumping up and down on a bed. Or some bodies, from the frequency of the squeaking mattress.

The door in the dark alcove drew Billy like a magnet. There was a large keyhole beneath the doorknob. He crouched and leaned forward to get a view inside the room.

It took a few seconds for his eye to adjust and understand what he was seeing. It was a mattress, bouncing up and down rapidly. There were legs writhing before him, bare and skinny legs that he recognized as belonging to a woman. And then there were hairy legs tangled with hers. It was a man and woman together on the mattress.

And they were NAKED!

He'd never seen adults undressed before, and he knew what he was seeing was forbidden. But now that he was seeing it, he couldn't stop looking if he tried. His eyeball moved as close to the keyhole as possible. Time and place were forgotten as his whole field of vision became flesh.

Positioned directly across from the foot of the bed, his view was graphic enough to make a pornographer proud. Because the equipment he was looking at was unfamiliar, he made comparisons in his head. The guy's pee-pee looked like a baseball bat with two hairy deflated balloons at the base. The guy's giant bat was sliding in and out of the girl's glove, which was hairy too, super hairy in fact. The bat was so thick it barely fit. Why the woman held a glove between her legs he didn't know, but this was a sport he wanted to learn more about, an adult sport for sure.

Billy started to feel hot, like the temperature had been cranked up. He was unaware his mouth was hanging open and his breathing was getting heavier.

The man and woman on the bed repositioned themselves, though his bat never fully left her glove. Now he could see their upper halves. The guy was unremarkable there. The woman, however, had two massive mounds on her chest with perky pink circles in the center.

Billy knew what those jiggling mounds were. Those were the woman's *boobies*. He liked the word boobies because it rhymed with *cooties* and made him giggle. He even imagined the sound they made – *Boing Boing Boing Boing!* Yep, he liked boobies just fine.

The couple were kissing a lot, but it was their bodies that kept him captivated. The guy kept squeezing her booby, running a finger in circles around the tip which was pointy like a balloon. She ran a hand over his bum-bum and squeezed. Was that some kind of spanking?

Now he became aware of a physical change in his own body. His pants were feeling tighter, but that was because his peter had grown in size. Along with the pressure there came a faint tingle, kind of like an itch, but pleasurable. He hoped his peter wouldn't go pee-pee in his pants in his excitement.

Billy didn't think he was doing anything wrong as he was snooping. Crouched before the keyhole, he'd forgotten all about going outside to play in the snow. There were only new sights and sensations.

Though he tried not to make noise during his journey, his footfalls in the hallway did produce some. Especially when they were on a creaky floor over someone's head. In her office, Mother Superior knew the children were outside, and nobody should have been traversing that corridor above at that time. Which meant one thing. Billy was on the move.

Unlike Billy, Mother Superior's black leather shoes, polished to perfection, could walk the orphanage floors producing only the faintest whispers. She knew exactly where to step to avoid every single creak in the boards. Nobody heard or saw her ascent to the second floor. These were her halls for haunting.

The moaning of the couple grew louder. The speed with which he was filling her glove increased. Her moans turned into cries, and her buckling increased under the guy, like she was struggling.

This carnal scene was an expression of pure pleasure, but it triggered something else in Billy, a recollection of something like this he'd seen before, a version of this that had gone bad with a man on top of a woman who also had big boobies.

The similar cries he remembered were his mother's, and who was the man who did something to her? It wasn't his father.

The keyhole was a very small opening, but that was enough to allow a diabolical memory through to interrupt his present.

Billy's sight was eclipsed by a vision.

He saw his mother lying on her back on the asphalt at night, her shirt torn open so her boobies jiggled as she cried out in fear.

Billy sat back rigidly with a gasp. Even with his eye removed from the keyhole, he was assaulted with another vision.

A red-gloved hand flicked up a switchblade, moonlight flashing off the sharp, slender blade.

Now he remembered who killed his mom. It was Santa Claus.

Billy jerked backward and a hand landed on his shoulder. Immediately he thought Santa Claus had a hold of him, but when he whipped his head around, he saw Mother Superior.

He was more afraid of the boogeyman in the hall than the one in his head.

That's when he felt the pain, a lancing burn from the front and back of his shoulder. She wasn't just pinching his shoulder. Her fingernails were so sharp they penetrated his jacket and shirt before piercing his flesh.

After one more painful squeeze that made him wince, Mother Superior let go of his shoulder. That's when he saw the thumb and index fingers of her right hand had longer fingernails that were cut to a sharp point, almost like claws. Mother Superior's claws were red with his blood.

Before he could react any further, he was stumbling backward as Mother Superior swatted him back into the wall with alarming strength.

When sinking her fingernails into Billy's tender flesh, Mother Superior could clearly hear sounds of sex behind the door. It was almost as if the fornicators cared not one whit for the commotion they caused. She glanced down and saw the reaction the boy had to what he'd seen.

Now the boy would have scars to remind him never to go spying through keyholes ever again. Her sharpened nails were her secret weapon used for decades to inflict suffering in children. The pinch was saved for those who needed to be punished, like the weaker ones. Like this deceitful, disrespectful boy.

Or like little Darla Cunningham back in 1962. She'd despised that blonde harlot who thought she was such hot shit, purely a projection on Mother Superior's part. Eventually the nurse became involved, and a full body inspection revealed sixty-six small lacerations all over her body. The scared girl would not reveal her tormentor, and Mother Superior suggested the injuries looked like rat bites. An exterminator was called in and Darla was subjected to rounds of agonizing rabies shots.

When Mother Superior threw Billy against the wall, it was an act of restraint on her part. Her real inclination at that moment was to pinch him again by the chubby tip of his penis. She wanted to pinch the head so hard the next time he took a leak he produced three streams.

With Billy out of her path, Mother Superior kicked open the door and charged into the room. She hadn't said a word when she caught Billy, because she was eager for the fornicators to be caught in the act.

Her pinching fingers were already wet in anticipation.

Kristy Wilde had just turned nineteen, but she still lived at home with her ailing mother Winnie. Her mother was extremely devout and had arranged for her doting daughter to work as a cook at the Catholic orphanage. At home, Kristy was the consummate good girl, so there was no bringing dates home to meet mamma.

Whenever Kristy was out of the house, it was tough to keep her clothes on. Sexual experiences were what she craved, and her appetite was insatiable.

Today was not the first time she brought a date to the orphanage for a tryst. An unlikely location for lust, but she knew there was a rarely used guest bedroom in the staff quarters reserved for visiting priests. The bed didn't have linens on it most of the time, but she and her dates didn't need to tuck in for the night. All they needed was a bouncy surface for half an hour, or ten minutes if he lacked control.

Her date today was Max, she hadn't bothered to ask his last name. Max was on the name tag he wore as a soda jerk at Noel's Place, the local greasy spoon. Max was her age, and it was obvious from his lingering looks he had the hots for her. It was easy enough to lure him into the back door of the orphanage for a secret liaison.

Kristy knew Mother Superior's routines well enough to believe they wouldn't be interrupted. The second-floor guest room was far from Mother Superior's first floor office. Max brought a joint along, but Kristy didn't want to risk lighting up inside and having Mother Superior smell it, so they smoked in Max's car first. She was positively blazing, and eager for action.

Three things caught Kristy by surprise in the vacant guest room. The first was the impact of the joint. They'd smoked the whole thing at Max's insistence, and she was higher than she'd ever been. The second surprise was the size of Max's joint. This slender guy was gifted with the biggest dick she'd ever encountered. Max also wielded his tool with the speed of a jackhammer.

The squeaking mattress should have concerned her, but she was in a delirious stoned stupor having the most incredible sex she'd had in her short horny life. Her moans of pleasure became cries of joy.

The final surprise was the door bursting open, kicked in by Mother Superior, who entered like a destructive force of nature.

"You filthy devils!"

The young couple froze mid-coitus, looking at Mother Superior with terror.

Mother Superior slammed the door behind her. Billy knew he was in big trouble for looking through the keyhole. But with the alarming commotion inside the room, he couldn't resist taking another peek.

Kristy wasn't concerned about covering herself up, her immediate worry was losing her job. How would her mother react?

Mother Superior saw the discarded clothes on the floor, and she picked up Max's pants, pulling his leather belt free of the loops. Then she folded it, holding the loose ends together.

Max knew right away what that gesture meant. His father had taken a belt to him in similar fashion all throughout his childhood. But this was a nun, she wouldn't do anything like that, right?

"You'll pay for this. Punishment!"

And punishment she delivered, with multiple strikes to their heads and faces. The strap split Max's lip and snapped his eye. He'd have a black eye later as a result, if not permanent eye damage.

"You devils! Take your punishment!"

The belt did worse to Kristy when Mother Superior released the buckle to maximize damage. "I'm sorry!" Kristy pleaded, and the buckle cracked one of her front teeth, then it tore out a chunk of her hair. Worse was what it tore out next, her right earring, which ripped right through her earlobe.

"Stop…" Kristy cried.

Mother Superior was only getting started, and she lowered her aim, going for their naughty bits.

"Take it! Take it! Take it!"

The belt snapped Kristy's breasts and ass. Max slid out of her, and the belt was turned against him.

"Devil! Sodomites!"

Mother Superior saw an opportunity before her. The looped belt was slid over the young man's neck and pulled tight, choking him.

She considered her sharpened index finger and put it to use inside the young man. His internal injuries would take months to heal.

"Take it, you sodomite!" accused Mother Sodomizer.

What Billy saw now, Mother Superior sexually abusing this young couple, he understood as punishment. To be naked with another was a bad thing, and it led to crying and pain. Santa would punish you for the same thing.

Billy had seen enough and rushed away from the door. He knew he was in trouble no matter what, and he decided to do what Sister Margaret had asked. He ran down the stairs to go help build a snowman.

Something was the matter with Billy from the moment he came outside, Sister Margaret thought. He avoided her and didn't say a word. Bypassing the snowman, he went to his brother's side. Ricky was using a toy shovel to scoop snow into a blue plastic pail with another four-year-old named Cameron. As Billy packed snow into a pail, he looked downright scared. What could have caused this worsening turn?

The front door burst open as Mother Superior charged outside. The wreath on the door flew out and almost fell off.

"William!" Mother Superior shrieked. Two young children saw the tempest of fury beside them and hurried inside in fear.

Sister Margaret was alarmed by what was in Mother Superior's hand, a folded leather belt, as if to deliver a beating. They didn't even use belts for corporal punishment here.

She was wracked with guilt, fearing her request for Billy to come play could result in blows to the boy.

Sister Margaret took a step forward to confront Mother Superior.

"Don't blame him, Mother Superior, I told him he could come out."

Mother Superior extended a hand at Sister Margaret in a stop gesture, while her eyes remained locked on Billy.

"Stay out of this, Sister Margaret!" Mother Superior lowered her hand. "William, come here."

Billy stood and slowly trudged through the snow toward Mother Superior.

Ricky was concerned by his brother's departure. "Billy, what's wrong?" Ricky asked. No reply was forthcoming.

Cameron thought he was a know-it-all smarty-pants and offered his assessment. "Your brother's a nutcase, that's what's wrong."

Cameron's name-calling made Ricky angry. Unlike Billy, Ricky fit in with the other scrappy boys his age just fine, and he would always be his brother's biggest defender.

"No, he's not!" Ricky shouted at Cameron, who's face he wanted to rub in the snow. "Take it back!"

"Boys!" Sister Margaret sternly said to keep the little ones from fighting. Billy was already in a heap of trouble, and she didn't want Mother Superior's ire to turn to his younger brother. She felt like she'd really messed things up today, all in her defense of Billy.

Billy stopped directly before Mother Superior, but he could not raise his head to meet her accusatory stare. Looking down was worse because he saw her sharpened fingernails were bloody.

"What did you see upstairs, William?" Mother Superior demanded.

"Nothing, Mother Superior." Billy looked up as he crossed his hands behind his back.

Mother Superior knew the boy was lying, because she'd gone behind the peephole and seen plenty more holes. But the boy likely did not know what he'd been looking at, perhaps unable to comprehend that tangle of nasty flesh.

"Do you know what they were doing?" Mother Superior asked.

"No, Mother Superior," he answered truthfully.

Sister Margaret realized there was more to this incident than she knew about. For now, she would listen, but if she raised that belt to Billy in front of his brother and other children, well, things might get physical between Sisters.

"Good. What they were doing was something very, very naughty. They thought they could do it without being caught.

But when we do something naughty, we are always caught. And then we are punished."

Billy didn't trust Mother Superior, but these words of hers he took as gospel. She was reinforcing all the things he learned on Christmas Eve, 1971. Grandpa, another old person, had taught him a similar lesson.

"Punishment is absolute," Mother Superior said, and then looked at Sister Margaret. "Punishment is necessary." She looked back at Billy. "Punishment is good."

Billy wasn't sure about that. There was nothing good about what happened to his mommy and daddy on the road that night. And there was nothing good about being moved into Saint Mary's Home for Orphaned Children, although he did like Sister Margaret a lot. Mother Superior also said punishment was necessary, which reinforced his sense that the punishment his family received had been their fault.

None of these points did he wish to argue with Mother Superior. It was his self-preservation instinct that told him to be good at this moment, at all costs. He knew the harm she could inflict. He'd witnessed it.

"Yes, Mother Superior," Billy said in agreement with her. He didn't have to like it.

Mother Superior leaned over him, giving added importance to her next words. "You left your room, William."

"Yes, Mother Superior."

Sister Margaret's heart broke as her favorite boy's spirit buckled. How she wanted to make Mother Superior pay. One day she would.

"Very, very naughty," Mother Superior issued her final judgment.

Sister Margaret gulped. Unfortunately, she knew what Mother Superior's punishment would be. It would be the same one she inflicted on all the naughty children.

Corporal punishment was always administered by Mother Superior. That was fine with the other Sisters, who did not care to deliver it. Punishment was one of the perks of Mother Superior's devotion. And her paddling arm was strong.

The practice was looked down upon by many orphanages due to the number of abused children taken in. That memo never made it to the Catholics, however, with some of the nation's most egregious abuses against youth flourishing within their institutions. Saint Mary's Home for Orphaned Children had a long sordid history in this department, going back to its inception.

The current state of discipline going on within Saint Mary's was but a fraction of what Mother Superior endured when she was a child at Saint Joseph's early in the century. Back then it was common for children to get thrown against the walls or onto the floor or over a wooden pew. You could get slapped, canned, or have your hair pulled out. It hadn't been uncommon for kids with sinful hands that touched their naughty parts to have their knuckles struck with a hard ruler, if not have their hands tied or shackled together. Kids were locked in dark closets as a form of solitary confinement or denied the use of the bathroom until they relieved themselves in front of others. In these enlightened 1970s, such practices were falling further out of favor, while she wished even crueler practices could be enacted.

When it came to delivering punishment, she wished she could conduct it in front of everyone, to maximize the recipient's shame and humiliation. Punishment had been regulated behind closed doors, but this gave her a chance to indulge in additional hidden cruelties. "Snitches get seconds," was a phrase she spouted like it was an eleventh Commandment. No brat ever snitched on her.

There was an institutional paddle that arrived sometime in the 1920s, nobody really knew anymore. Maybe the Pope left it under a pillow passing through town. This polished piece of wood with rounded edges was twenty-four inches long, three inches wide, and half an inch thick. There were twelve holes drilled through the paddle to maximize the pain it delivered, one hole for each of Jesus' apostles, making them complicit.

The traditional paddle would not be employed today. Mother Superior already had a leather belt in hand, and she intended to keep it for her own personal collection.

Mother Superior ordered Billy back into his room and closed the door. Then she ordered him to pull out the wooden chair from the desk. Next, she ordered him to pull down his pants, and his underpants too. Finally, he was ordered to lean over the chair.

"You will take your punishment without crying or complaint, is that understood?"

"Yes, Mother Superior."

Mother Superior struck his bottom with the belt. There was no holding back. All her rage at the ugly world and the terrible tykes who dared challenge her was channeled into every strike. She struck again and again.

Billy winced at every strike. He'd never been spanked on his bare bottom before, and never with such force. Tears sprang out from his eyes, but he did not cry. With each strike he let out an audible wince. He bit the inside of his lower lip until he tasted blood.

The lashes broke loose a memory inside his head, and he heard Grandpa.

The bad ones he punishes.

Each strike made Billy nauseous because the belt was sticky with something, and he could feel the leather peeling off his skin.

Mother Superior delivered twelve strikes, one for each Apostle. They were cheering her on in her head – *One, two, three, four! Pound that Pussyboy till he's sore!* The belt left welts, whereas the paddle would have delivered less damage. She took delight in his injury, and wanted his ass to still be sore when he woke up on Christmas morning. To guarantee he would, she pinched his reddened right cheek with her sharpened fingernails and tore through the skin.

Billy yelped at the pinch, there was just no helping himself. If his mother were still alive, she would have never let her treat him this way.

"Now go to bed, and stay there," Mother Superior ordered,

and she exited the room.

Billy was left ashamed and splayed out with his brutalized bare ass in the air. It was difficult to get his pants and underwear back up, and he cringed throughout the process. There would be blood stains on his underpants when he changed them the next day. When he laid down on the lower bunk, he was unable to lay on his back, so he rolled onto his side.

Billy knew Mother Superior had been very naughty.

Chapter  11

Outside the orphanage that night, every window was dark, indicating the whole building was asleep. For the first year in Saint Mary's history, there were Christmas lights wrapped around a pine tree in the front near the road, the only holiday lights in view on this edge of town. While the orphanage would never be considered a festive place, the lights did add some warmth to the scene, and seemed a long overdue cursory nod to the holiday obsession of the town.

It was not a completely silent night, however. Distressed moans and cries punctuated the darkness, emanating from one room upstairs.

Billy could not help the sounds he was making in his sleep. He was used to an occasional nightmare, but what he experienced tonight was worse than that. These were repressed memories resurfacing as night terrors.

This had been Billy's roughest day in years. His bottom ached badly, and he'd been offered no aspirin to numb the pain. One wrong shift on the mattress and he'd wake to the agony before drifting off again. There would be no easy slumber tonight.

Constantly gnawing on his mind like starving rats were the lessons taught by Grandpa and Santa Claus and Mother Superior, lessons about naughtiness and punishment.

Guilt constantly engulfed him. The punishment he received and was made to believe he deserved made him feel blameworthy. He prided himself on being a good boy all the time, and this perception that he was not made him feel culpable. He'd received his punishment from Mother Superior. Would he receive a second round of punishment when Santa Claus came for Christmas?

The true source of his night terrors was that scene through the keyhole. It was unsettling for most young children who accidentally saw what mommy and daddy were up to behind the bedroom door. For Billy, seeing what that boy and girl had been up to hit his psyche with the force of an earthquake. A fissure had opened in his mind like the earth splitting open, allowing deep, horrible, hidden memories to appear, out of order, out of context. The girl's breasts on the mattress became his mother's breasts on the asphalt. The girl's cries of pleasure became his mother's cries of terror.

Billy squirmed fitfully on the bottom bunk, the sweat on his face reflecting the pale moonlight that streamed through the curtains. He verbalized in his sleep.

"Uhh… no… don't…"

In the top bunk, Billy's bunk mate Alvin couldn't sleep with the commotion coming from below. Along with being noisy, Billy's tossing and turning was rocking the bunk bed frame.

Billy's legs kicked the mattress, as though he were trying to run away in his sleep. But there was no escaping the nightmare he'd endured three years ago. For the first time he was fully reliving it in his head.

He saw a red-gloved hand, Santa's hand, pull open the driver's door of their station wagon. Out tumbled his dad, his bloody face hitting the asphalt. His dad's eyes looked directly at him, but he didn't blink. Blood pumped from the extra holes in his head.

Billy kicked and whined harder on the bottom bunk. With his mom and dad dead on the road, he knew who Santa was going to punish next.

Santa was looking for him. Billy watched from the same roadside vantage point, in hiding behind the bushes. Even though three years had passed, he plugged right back into his terrified five-year-old self, paralyzed with fear.

"Where are you, ya little bastard!?"

Moonlight flashed off the upraised, bloody steel of Santa's switchblade like a twinkling Christmas tree topper.

"AAUUGHHHH!" Billy screamed as he was wrenched out of his Christmas nightmare. He sat upright, and then jumped out of bed wearing his long johns.

"Billy!" Alvin called out as Billy ran out of the room in flight mode. He knew Mother Superior wasn't going to like this one bit.

Billy fled down the hall. When he reached the top of the

stairs, he snapped out of his night terrors and grabbed the corner post of the railing to stop himself. One more blind step forward and he would have shot off the top of the stairs.

He needed a moment to collect his thoughts, but that's when the next shock dropped. A hand seized his right shoulder and squeezed, the shoulder that already hurt from the piercing pinch earlier. As he looked back, he was certain he would see the leering face of Santa Claus.

But Billy's fear had a new face. Mother Superior had a hold on him again. Like Santa Claus, there was no compassion, only violent rage.

Billy's epically bad day was about to get even worse.

A half dozen children in pajamas watched from outside Billy's doorway. None of them had seen this punishment before, and it terrified them. If there was a group consensus, it was *better him than us.*

Mother Superior and Sister Margaret were both in the room, dressed in their night clothes with long robes. In lieu of their habits, their hair was pulled back in buns. Unlike the other staff quarters, which were in the back wing, Mother Superior and Sister Margaret had their rooms in the front building, to make them better able to keep track of the children at night.

Mother Superior, hearing the running feet in the hallway, had been up in an instant, catching the boy in another act of disobedience she took personally.

A torn strip of bedsheet was tied around Billy's left wrist

and tied to the bedpost by Mother Superior, and she pulled tightly on the strap to ensure it was sufficiently secured. Billy's ankles and right wrist were tied to the other bedposts.

Billy struggled against the straps, near full blown panic. He felt so vulnerable, and if Santa Claus came in the middle of the night to inflict punishment, there would be no getting away.

"Please let me up! Please," Billy begged to whoever might help him.

With Billy struggling so hard against the straps binding him, Alvin looked down from the top bunk. The bunk beds were rocking so much he feared getting seasick.

Without a word, Mother Superior pushed Alvin's head by the face, forcing it back onto his pillow, and then pulled his blanket up over his head.

Billy's pleading eyes turned to the person he trusted most. "Sister Margaret."

Sister Margaret's heart broke for Billy. This punishment was far too cruel for any child. And this was happening to her favorite, the one she saw as a surrogate son. The guilt she felt was monumental, knowing her decision to call Billy out of his room today had led to this cruel punishment – make that abuse. She felt just as helpless, like she too had been strapped to the bedposts. She would have traded places with him if she could.

Mother Superior could see the sympathy for Billy in Sister Margaret's eyes, and it angered her. This Sister had feelings of favoritism for the biggest lying brat in the orphanage. Her future punishments for Billy would have to be shared with the Sister so they both paid.

"Leave him alone," Mother Superior snapped at Sister Margaret, and held her gaze for an extended moment fraught with tension and threat.

Mother Superior made a sharp turn toward the door, and the children gathered there scattered to their rooms as she charged out.

The punishment that filled the boy with terror filled Mother Superior with pride. This was a return to the old ways, the better ways. Punishment by bondage was a cherished pastime of yesteryear and never hurt anyone. She ignored the innumerable children who died through bondage in the past, their circulation cut off or their breathing, sometimes choking on vomit.

She couldn't help but think if she came back in the morning to find Billy unresponsive, she would be the victor in their eternal battle. Her actions were right no matter what.

"Help! Let me up!" Billy cried.

Sister Margaret stood an extended moment in the doorway looking at Billy. It took all her effort not to charge in and loosen the straps. Then she thought of Mother Superior's retribution if she found out and felt helpless to intervene.

She turned away from Billy, turning off the bedroom light before closing the door on her way out. Billy's cries for help continued behind her. To distract from her own heartbreak, she dwelled on her hatred of Mother Superior.

"Sister Margaret, help! Let me out of here! Please! I won't be naughty anymore!" Billy pleaded behind the bedroom door.

CHAPTER 12

The day after Billy's punishment, Sister Margaret made a secret plan to help him. Mother Superior had scolded her repeatedly, took away her voice, made her feel as helpless as the boy in bondage. Unable to sleep herself, she checked in on him every hour to ensure he was safe and breathing.

She was certain that Billy needed help to process the trauma of losing his parents, and no amount of Mother Superior's denial was going to change her mind about that. The help he needed was not something they could provide. They were Sisters, not psychologists. Faith itself was no fix. What was required was outside intervention.

There was no way she could whisk the boy out of the orphanage for a session with a shrink, but that didn't mean there wasn't a way to whisk one in. And she wouldn't have to wait long. There was a workable window coming the following week.

The Conception of Saint Mary Church held an evening service on the Winter Solstice, December 21st. It was a yearly tradition to take all the children to the service. Minutes before everyone was called to line up for the buses, Sister Margaret appeared in Mother Superior's office.

"Billy has a fever, and a terrible cold. He shouldn't attend the Christmas sermon tonight," Sister Margaret said rather convincingly. Lying was justified for she was on a mission of mercy.

"How do you know? The boy could be faking it." Mother Superior held nothing but suspicion for the boy and Sister Margaret.

"His temperature is 102.6," Sister Margaret answered, and held out a thermometer that gave mercurial proof. What Sister Margaret kept secret was she'd heated the thermometer herself in a bathroom sink.

"We have no Sister planning to stay behind to watch him."

"I will make that sacrifice tonight," Sister Margaret offered.

Mother Superior gave her an extended look of suspicion before she answered. "So be it."

Before her stunt with the thermometer, Sister Margaret visited Billy's room and asked if he was willing to stay behind as a gift for her, as she had her own special plans for him that evening. He enjoyed the idea of an evening alone with her. Plus, he'd been to that boring Christmas service two times before, and The Conception of Saint Mary Church was too cold for him, even chillier than the orphanage.

Sister Margaret had one request first. She asked Billy to lie in bed under the covers and fake sniffles and a cold if Mother Superior happened to stick her head in the door. Thankfully,

Mother Superior never showed. Likely the old woman wanted to avoid his germs.

Billy was excited to fool Mother Superior and get away from her for a few hours.

Dr. Elliot Stumpf was a bald and bespectacled child psychologist who was a towering professional in his field, if not in his height. He stood a stately 5'1" and had been compared to Mr. Monopoly more than once. His bushy moustache and round eyeglasses had something to do with that. He didn't mind this comparison because who didn't look up to the Monopoly man as an expert in his field?

Dr. Stumpf specialized in children recovering from trauma and abuse. Sister Margaret had done her research and chosen well, although he cost a pretty penny for his services. Most of her meager monthly income was required for his fee, but that was perfectly fine by her. This was her holiday gift for Billy. The boy's mental well-being was priceless.

The doctor charged an exorbitant amount for the late hour, making an out of office visit on the holiday week when his office was typically closed. It would have been easy for him to turn the session down, but his wife was far more miserly than he was, and she wouldn't let him pass up that fee.

Sister Margaret had given Elliot the history of the patient, and his curiosity was piqued. He remembered the terrible incident the boy survived with his brother, as every local psychologist did. They'd all dealt with survivors and their families in the wake of that great Christmas Eve tragedy three years ago. What he hadn't known was that the killer had been dressed as Santa Claus, a detail missing in the press that Sister Margaret divulged with great emphasis, having been told by the police chief himself, a reliable authority. He understood the coverup, and good thing too or every child in town would have needed his services.

Billy was a complex case study, but he had no doubts that his intervention could benefit the boy.

The hesitation Elliot had with this session was the location, within a Catholic orphanage. He hadn't stepped foot in a Catholic institution since he was ten years old, when he'd fallen prey to sexual abuse at the hands of Father O'Reilly at a private Catholic school in Phoenix, Arizona. His parents believed his claims about the priest, but the institution and state had no interest in investigating. Arizona's long standing clergy privilege laws ensured a successful coverup. It was better he didn't know that Father O'Reilly continued to destroy innocence to this day.

Elliot's parents pulled him out of the Catholic school and enrolled him in a non-religious private school. They also changed denominations and joined an Episcopal church. Over forty years, he'd been able to shed the weight of those oppressive memories.

Only he knew perhaps more than most that you just didn't forget. Those memories had to be contended with, or they were likely to manifest in myriad negative forms. He'd had the luxury of money and the support of an understanding family that believed in psychiatry. He became a child psychologist in part to cure himself.

Elliot was not prepared for the psychological shock he felt the moment he walked through the doors of Saint Mary's Home for Orphaned Children. His blood ran cold, and he knew that wasn't the result of the low thermostat. All the oppressive weight that had marred his childhood came back like a torrential downpour from roiling black clouds. He was soaked in dread, made to feel vulnerable to an institution that favored dogma and secrecy over mercy.

Thankfully, Sister Margaret was as easy to talk with in person as she'd been on the phone. Had she been of a severely rigid nature he likely would have turned this session down, regardless of his wife's vociferous demands. But the Sister paid up front and welcomed him warmly into a place that he innately found oppressive.

Billy was sitting at his desk when Sister Margaret introduced him to Dr. Stumpf. The boy wore a starched button up shirt tucked into his slacks. He'd dressed well because Sister Margaret told him he was going to meet a man who was very important.

"Billy, I'd like you to meet Dr. Stumpf."

"Hi, Billy. You can call me Elliot."

"Yes, Sir," Billy replied politely.

Elliot shook Billy's hand, and then told him a bit about who he was, that he was not a medical doctor, but one that liked to talk with special children, like him. Billy seemed open to talk with him, and he felt a kinship between them.

Sister Margaret had asked Dr. Stumpf beforehand whether she could sit in for the session, and he'd agreed so long as it didn't close Billy up to talking. Plus, she was the one paying his fee. Luckily, he took to the boy immediately, and even saw himself in Billy. This was a boy he truly wanted to help. Perhaps this late visit to this unpleasant place would reward them both.

After a brief chat to gain Billy's confidence, Elliot got to the meat of the matter.

"Billy, I'd like to talk with you about Christmas."

Billy nodded. Christmas was a subject he didn't like, but he would talk about it with this gentleman who perhaps due to his small stature and resemblance to Mr. Magoo put him at ease.

"What do you possibly need to know about Christmas?" Mother Superior sternly interjected from the open doorway.

Everyone was startled by the surprise guest. Dr. Stumpf bristled with irritation at the interruption, and he turned. The woman who filled the doorway appeared to be a nun of the strictest order. Her eyes pierced him like needles.

Sister Margaret was immediately fearful. She'd been caught, and as before, her transgression, her crossing of Mother Superior, would cause dire consequences for the boy she wished to protect. She'd been certain Mother Superior had gone to the service at The Conception of Saint Mary Church as was her yearly routine, but had she been outside to watch her board a bus and depart? She had not. Mother Superior had likely sniffed out her lie the moment it was issued from her lips.

Billy shared in Sister Margaret's fear of Mother Superior. He felt caught, guilty, and it was inevitable she would accuse him of being naughty. That seemed to be her only function in life. Always accusatory, looking for a reason to punish.

Despite his aversion to the woman, Dr. Stumpf offered a professional greeting. "Hi, I'm Dr. Elliot…"

"I do not care who you are," Mother Superior interrupted. "You have no business with this boy."

"Actually, I do have business. I'm a child psychologist, and my services have been paid for a session with Billy."

Sister Margaret closed her eyes, gulped, and caressed her rosaries. She knew deep down that this was going to go very, very bad.

"I called for no such services," Mother Superior snapped.

"I know that, Sister. Somebody else did."

"You do not call me Sister! I am Mother Superior!"

Mother Superior charged into the room a few steps. She had them all trapped.

Elliot's reaction to Mother Superior was to shrink back in his seat from her. The woman towered over him and carried the charge of an errant bolt of lightning. This was a woman of stricture more than scripture, the dreaded type of old school disciplinarian he'd dealt with before. Quite frankly, she struck terror in him, like encountering a specter from his past. Despite the cold indoors, he sprang into a nervous sweat, all too obvious as it glistened upon his forehead.

"I saw you touching this boy," Mother Superior declared.

This accusation alarmed Elliot to the highest degree. That

kind of talk could end his career.

"I shook the boy's hand when I arrived. That is all," Elliot clarified, repositioning the spectacles that'd begun to slip down due to the sweat on his nose.

"I should call the police," Mother Superior stated.

Alarmed, Sister Margaret interjected. "There's no need for that, Mother Superior. I paid and invited him."

Once again, Mother Superior silenced the opposition.

"You have no authority to bring a man into this sacred institution. One more word and I will escalate the punishment for you all."

Elliot's worry was eclipsed by anger. He was not a charge or staff of this orphanage, just a doctor here to help a problemed patient. These threats of punishment he did not have to put up with. He was no longer a victimized child in a Catholic school.

"There is no need to involve the police," Elliot said. "I was paid to be here, and I'm certain the court of law would agree my presence here is legal."

Those eyes of Mother Superior pierced him again and held him, pinned like a butterfly to a corkboard.

"You touched the boy for money. This is prostitution."

Sister Margaret's shock nearly paralyzed her. Since she'd been part of the cash transaction, was Mother Superior willing to risk her freedom too with a false charge of child prostitution? She had no faith in Mother Superior to do the right thing, so yes, it was entirely possible, and utterly diabolical.

Elliot's anger at the shrewish nun evaporated as fear

returned. This was his greatest nightmare. He was trapped in a Catholic institution where sexual secrets were used against the vulnerable, or anyone who questioned the church, no matter how corrupt their practices. This was an altogether different corruption than before, but no less destructive.

There was also great horror to think that he, a youthful victim of sexual assault in a Catholic institution, could be falsely accused of the same crime in the same place. The terror was so palpable it had a taste, bitter and metallic. Once again, he was being abused by a religious hypocrite.

"That is not true, and there are witnesses to the truth."

Elliot's desperate eyes turned to Sister Margaret, but she was looking down and shaking her head in the negative. Of course, she'd been told not to say one word, which meant no alibi, or the same fate could fall upon her. He could not count on Sister Margaret's help, even though she'd put him into this vulnerable position.

Elliot turned to Billy, and his heart broke. The boy shared his outright terror of Mother Superior. This was like looking into a mirror at his past self. No, he could not count on Billy to tell the truth of his corrupted keepers, just as he'd kept quiet on various abuses for some time before speaking out. In no way could he fault this boy for his complicit silence. He understood him all too well. And he could do nothing to help him.

As he considered the dark future for this boy, he'd lost sight of Mother Superior, and was caught completely by surprise as she seized hold of his tie and jerked him up off his seat. He looked right into her wicked face.

"Do you want to test me, little man?"

Elliot chose his next words very carefully, as he felt his life depended on them.

"No, Mother Superior."

A malicious grin touched the corners of Mother Superior's lips, and a glint of cruel triumph flashed in her eyes.

Before this terrifying encounter, he'd had no need to empty his bladder, but at that moment he let out a squirt of hot urine in his slacks. As a way of releasing fear, it was a fragrant one. Too bad he'd chosen his beige slacks tonight because the wet stain saturated the surface of his crotch.

And damn if Mother Superior didn't sniff his embarrassment out. Her nose twitched, she looked down, and her vicious grin flashed once more.

"Get out of here at once. And do not cross me."

As Mother Superior let the doctor's tie go, she stuck out her index finger and sliced it up the doctor's right cheek.

Shocked by the quick flash of pain on his face, Elliot got moving without saying a word. He didn't see that Billy was crying now, or that Sister Margaret refused to look at him. The session had ended before it'd really begun, but he was not relinquishing his fee.

Once the doctor had scurried out of the room, Mother Superior turned her accusatory gaze to Billy.

"Stop that crying. Sick boys should be in bed. Get under the covers now."

"Yes, Mother Superior." Billy did as he was told, even while fully dressed. Hesitation might get him tied to the bedposts again. If this was his punishment tonight, he would thank his lucky stars, as far away and dim as they were.

For Sister Margaret, Mother Superior had neither a word nor a look. The guilty Sister would not have seen her anyway, as her head hung low and her eyes focused on the scuffed, hardwood floor.

Mother Superior charged out of the room.

Elliot couldn't get out of the orphanage fast enough. Luckily the place seemed to be deserted tonight, as the stain on his pants embarrassed him. His bladder felt close to bursting, and he didn't know how long he could hold it. If he could make it outside, he could relieve himself in the bushes. He'd take some satisfaction if he could piss on this horrible place, but he didn't think he would make it in time.

Quickly retreating through a first-floor corridor, he spotted the Boy's Room, and pushed through the door.

The first urinal was reached just in time. He placed his free palm upon the wall to balance himself. His pulse was racing far too hard, and he was shaking.

Mother Superior had cut him as she released him, he was certain of it. Whatever weapon she'd been wielding went unseen, maybe a nail file or razor blade.

He heard his heavy breathing and urine splashing onto porcelain, but the sounds of the swinging door and soft foot-steps went unnoticed.

Elliot felt two points of piercing pain on the right side of his neck. He released the wall and his willie, and his stream veered from the urinal, splashing the wall.

Looking over his shoulder, he saw Mother Superior glowering with hate. He also saw the source of his pain; she had him in a piercing pinch. His reaction was pure terror.

Elliot was jerked back from the urinal and spun around. His urine stream spread over the tile floor, and over the front of Mother Superior's robe and rosaries. She released her pinch and looked down at the mess he'd made.

"You think you can baptize Mother Superior?"

"Hey, no, sorry…" Elliot stammered as he stumbled. His shoes slipped on the wet floor.

Mother Superior gave the doctor a sideways shove.

Elliot's legs tangled, and he pitched forward. His jaw smashed into the edge of the jutting porcelain sink, and he heard something crack. The impact busted the left lens of his eyeglasses before knocking them off his head. The broken spectacles landed on the tile floor. His blood dripped onto the lenses.

Dazed, Elliot's tongue explored the hole where a lower front tooth had been, only one sharp shard remaining. Blood spilled over his lip. He wondered what his wife would think, or if she would even believe him. He was getting his ass kicked by Mother Superior. The scarier thought was how much further the woman was willing to go.

From a psychological standpoint, Elliot understood exactly what Mother Superior was. She was a sadist.

And she was advancing toward him.

He quickly crawled back on the tile away from her reach. Something sharp punched into his palm as he propelled backward, and he saw the impalement was his broken tooth.

Suddenly a silver blur whipped his way, and he felt metal strike his left cheek. He had to wipe the blood out of his eyes with a sleeve. Even then, his world semi-blurred, he made out what she held.

Mother Superior was swinging a leather belt with a silver belt buckle.

Elliot pushed further backward, trying to make distance, and the next strike of the belt hit his thigh.

With alarm, he realized his floppy member still hung out of his fly. That's what she was aiming for. Mother Superior aimed to rip his dick off.

Elliot pushed back just in time to keep his cherished manhood unscathed. He shoved his dangling dingle back into his slacks, scraping his shaft on the sharp zipper.

"Take it!" Mother Superior sneered as she lashed out again. She saw the degree of terror she struck in the man. Her brute power filled her with righteousness, and a vicious grin appeared on her face.

Elliot scrambled up and bolted out of the bathroom with a cry of fear. His broken eyeglasses were left behind. The drive would be difficult without them but all he cared about was getting away.

Dr. Elliot Stumpf would have no problem keeping his promise to himself to never go into a Catholic institution again so long as he lived. This latest assault at the hands of another Catholic elder would go unreported.

Mother Superior's threat to involve the cops had been hollow, but the doctor believed it wholeheartedly. She never wanted to involve the authorities in affairs within the orphanage. This territory was not subject to their laws. She was the law maker here.

The truth which she had no problem overlooking was she had many terrible secrets she wished to keep hidden.

There was still payment due for the deceitfulness of Billy and Sister Margaret tonight. If Sister Margaret thought she could pull one over on her, well she was in for a shock. The shock treatment Mother Superior had in mind was not literal, and it would not be directed at Sister Margaret.

Billy would be the recipient, and Sister Margaret would have to watch him suffer.

Their punishment would come later when they were least expecting it. What better date was there than Christmas morning?

CHAPTER

Christmas Eve was a quiet night for Billy, and that was a holiday miracle of sorts. The memory of what happened three years ago that night stayed hidden in the deep, dark recesses of his mind, a lurking threat that would rear its hideous head another unwelcome time. This month had been hard enough for him, and he deserved this night of rest.

The silent night brought a fresh dusting of snow upon many icy layers as the rest of the kids at the orphanage barely slept, so excited were they for Santa's arrival. That included Ricky, who remained unaware of the tragic holiday legacy he was a part of. He shared fully in the communal Christmas excitement with the other kids. The date Billy dreaded Ricky anticipated with glee. At no time did Billy try to dissuade him of his joy.

The older kids knew Santa wasn't real, and most of the younger kids had been cued in as well, typically with accompanying tears of denial. Sure, Billy could agree with that, but that was *their* Santa. *His* Santa was real, and he was still out there somewhere, looking for bad people to punish. Not just children either; their parents were fair game too.

Most of the excitement the kids felt was due to the presents left under the Christmas tree downstairs. Every child received a gift, always addressed "From Santa". Each child also had a Christmas stocking pinned to the wall with their name written on top in cursive glitter ink, personally authored by Sister Ellen. Inside each stocking a candy cane and Christmas cookie had been placed. The anticipation for new toys and sweets kept the children restless the whole night.

The gift opening ceremony was a festive event, the closest to a party the children had all year. This was not a formal affair, as they were dressed in their pajamas, robes, socks, and slippers. They surrounded the lit Christmas tree, tearing into their presents with enthusiasm. Wrapping paper flew up in the air and toys were held up triumphantly. Balls flew and dollies danced. The excited chatter was at its absolute highest. At no other time of the year were the youngsters allowed to be this loud.

Sister Ellen and Mother Superior supervised the gift opening, the former with amusement, the latter with a scowl of disapproval.

"Fold that paper! I see nothing but greed where there should be gratitude."

Nobody was listening to Mother Superior; their cheer was too great. Wrapping paper continued to rip and get tossed all about.

Mother Superior shook her head with resentment. She

hadn't received any of this tawdry trash as a child, and she'd turned out just fine.

Yet all these new Christmas traditions in the orphanage over the past few years had been entirely her doing. This whole superficial spectacle was not for the enjoyment of all the kids, that was an unfortunate byproduct. These rituals had a darker intent, to cause hardship for one child alone. That was her Christmas gift to herself.

Mother Superior scanned the chaotic room, looking for the one child she wanted to find. Billy wasn't there.

Looking up the staircase, she saw Sister Margaret leading Billy reluctantly down the stairs by the shoulders. He remained dressed in long johns, which normally made him warm. Today, though, he felt a permanent chill he could not shake, like a low-grade fever. This was his seasonal flu of fear, arriving like clockwork on the calendar.

Sister Margaret and Billy passed a group of children sitting on the stairs playing with their presents. When they reached the bottom, she let him go and Mother Superior stepped before him.

Sister Margaret was suspicious of Mother Superior's behavior this morning, which made her keep a close eye on her. With the timid boy before her, Mother Superior evinced a grin, an entirely unsettling expression on a woman who prided herself on perpetual sternness, like her frown was carved in stone. Sister Margaret believed something bad was in store.

Standing before Mother Superior, Billy nervously clamped his hands behind his back.

"Are you ready to behave properly, William?"

"Yes, Mother Superior."

Mother Superior smiled, and the expression chilled him. Her smile was like that of a clown, painted on and not at all natural.

"Good," Mother Superior said, and put a hand behind him, guiding him forward. "Go find your present."

Mother Superior let Billy slip away to collect the last present under the tree. The "From Santa" tag had been carefully removed by Sister Margaret early that morning.

Mother Superior and Sister Margaret turned to watch Billy collect his present. He took the box to the sofa, sitting beside children with a doll, a toy plane, and a football. Unlike the others, Billy didn't tear the paper or make a mess of the packaging.

"We will have no more trouble with him," Mother Superior stated. "You will see how well my methods work."

Sister Margaret doubted that very much. Mother Superior's methods never corresponded with compassion, but with self-righteousness, and that would always be her failing. What she saw as failure Mother Superior would see as success.

"Of course he'll improve once Christmas is over," Sister Margaret stated. "He always does." She didn't want Mother Superior to take false credit for a positive change of behavior she played no part of.

"Well, it isn't over Sister Margaret."

Sister Margaret gave her a suspicious glance.

"We still have our annual Christmas visit from Santa Claus."

This caught Sister Margaret by surprise. The kids had already opened the presents Santa Claus left for them. And never before had a Santa Claus been allowed inside the orphanage.

"We've never had an annual visit from Santa Claus," Sister Margaret stated.

"This is the first. Isn't that special? William will sit on Santa Claus' lap and behave." All this she said while never taking her eyes off the boy, who was folding his wrapping paper before opening the taped plain box beneath.

Oh, you bitch. You diabolical Goddamn bitch, Sister Margaret thought. She gave Mother Superior a look of despair.

Mother Superior loved the look of defeat on Sister Margaret's face. Her grin returned.

"You'll see," Mother Superior insisted, and strutted away.

Sister Margaret looked back at the boy she loved, who was about to face a traumatic incident, and there was nothing she could do about it. Whatever joy he received from his present would be erased when he faced the man the gift supposedly came from.

Sister Margaret's new Christmas wish was that Mother Superior would die, sooner than later.

By late morning, the snowfall had increased, leaving a fresh six inches of snow. From inside Saint Mary's there came a boy's screams. These were sounds of terror and desperation, wholly inappropriate for the sacred holiday.

"No! No! No!"

A door into the main downstairs room burst open, and Mother Superior yanked Billy into the room. She had a piercing pinch on his left shoulder while her other hand was clamped onto his right arm. He struggled to get free from her grip, but he had no choice but to be guided where she was forcing him.

Billy was now dressed up. The children had been ordered to change into their finest attire, as though Santa needed to be approached formally like he was a priest.

Across the room, Santa Claus sat on a chair atop an elevated platform before the Christmas tree.

This Santa was employed through the holiday season at the Christmas Joy Mall. While this was not his ordinary gig, he didn't mind appearing for an hour as Mother Superior paid well.

This would be the first time the kids weren't prattling on to Santa about their greedy wants. Each child was simply to sit on his lap and give thanks for the present they'd received that morning. Easy money. To add personal joy to his having to work on the holiday, he spiked his morning glass of eggnog before coming into the orphanage.

All the children watched Billy's freakout silently. Ricky was most concerned, but also embarrassed. He personally loved to see Santa Claus, and to see his brother afraid of him just wasn't right.

Santa didn't like the look of this flailing boy one bit. He was used to bawling children, but they were usually many years younger than the one who was about to be forced upon him. Ginny, the little girl seated on Santa's lap, looked alarmed.

"Ginny, get out of the way!" Mother Superior shouted angrily.

With a hurt expression, Ginny leapt off Santa's lap just as Mother Superior arrived. Mother Superior spun Billy around, lifted him off the ground, and plopped him down onto Santa's lap. Santa Claus let out an *oomph* of discomfort. The boy wasn't light. How had the old woman done that so effortlessly?

"No!" Billy continued to cry, tears of fear cutting tracks down his face.

Mother Superior kept hold of Billy's wiggling shoulders and delivered her order right in his face.

"You will learn gratitude! Say thank you to Santa Claus!"

Mother Superior let Billy go, and Santa grabbed his arms to keep him in place. This was Billy's childhood nightmare seizing hold of him again, only this was not a dream. This was real.

"No! No!" Billy cried with even greater horror.

Sister Margaret watched her dear Billy suffer from across the room. Her feet remained firmly in place. She was aware this was a punishment for her too, for her ill-fated move to involve a psychologist. Deep down she'd known something cruel like this was coming.

"No! Let me go!"

Billy looked over his shoulder. Being this close with Santa

Claus cracked open that jagged fissure in his brain, allowing another memory to rise like a spring-loaded skeleton in a funhouse.

All Billy saw was his mother upon the road, her neck arched back. A switchblade in a red-gloved hand pressed against her neck, and then sliced deeply in. As her skin separated, blood was unleashed in a line before gushing out.

Billy slid off Santa's lap, and he dropped down to the floor. He wasn't going anywhere though, as Santa had a firm hold on his elbow.

"Let me go!" Billy screamed, and he threw a wide punch into Santa's face. Santa heard the crunch as his nose broke, and suddenly he didn't care about the pain because the chair shifted, the rear legs slipping off the platform. Santa Claus pitched backward.

Perhaps if he'd hit the Christmas tree his landing would have been cushioned, but instead his head hit the floor. The little sleighbells around his suit gave a pronounced jingle upon impact. For a moment he saw stars, then he saw the star atop the Christmas tree.

Mother Superior made a grunting motion forward when Billy's punch landed, like she was watching a knockout in a Heavyweight Championship. In private, she was a big fan of boxing and wrestling. They were where she learned most of her moves. That and a lot of good, hard practice.

Once free of Santa Claus, Billy sped past everyone for the staircase, running up as though Santa were hot on his heels in pursuit.

Sister Margaret nearly followed, but then caught herself. Ricky did move, though, launching up off the couch and running for the stairs after his brother.

"Billy! Billy!"

Sister Margaret swooped in to stop Ricky from following.

Santa Claus sat up without his hat. Blood streamed from both nostrils, saturating the white moustache and beard upon his face.

"What the fuck is wrong with that kid!?"

Santa put a gloved hand to his nose and winced. Yep, the little bastard broke his nose, all right. Merry fucking Christmas to him.

Only one gave Billy chase.

Mother Superior.

Billy burst into his bedroom and slammed the door. There was no lock, and he wasn't strong enough to move the dresser over. All he could do was cower and hide, crouching down and curling up in an empty corner, trying to make himself small.

It wasn't Mother Superior he feared, it was Santa Claus. Only now there was a slippage occurring, because both Santa Claus and Mother Superior lived by the same laws. They were all powerful and existed solely to punish the naughty, to punish him.

He imagined Mother Superior in a red suit instead of a robe, a Santa hat instead of a habit. Santa Superior, deliverer of punishment.

"I'm sorry," Billy said, wiping tears from his eyes. "I didn't mean to be naughty. Don't punish me. Please."

Through his sniffles and sobs he heard the resounding click of footsteps marching up the hallway. He looked up in slack-jawed terror as the door opened.

"William!"

Mother Superior filled the door frame. She did not enter, but just stood there, crossing her arms over her chest.

This was Mother Superior's most angry stance, the one no kid ever wanted to see. Now he understood why.

Mother Superior wasn't just covering her breasts. She was clutching them. Those sharp fingernails on each hand were piercing into her breasts, squeezing painfully hard. Only for Mother Superior, pain was her pleasure. Beneath her robe, she could secretly lay claim to the most scar-riddled tits on God's good earth. They brought her pride.

"Punish!"

The pain she felt was going to be shared. When she was through with him, he wouldn't be able to comfortably sit down until well into the new year.

CHAPTER

Sister Margaret was not granted her Christmas wish of 1974. Mother Superior did not keel over soon after the holiday. She was around for Christmas the next year, and the year after that, and before she knew it, they'd reached the next decade coexisting in friction. Thankfully, Sister Margaret had the patience of Job. Unlike her mother, who'd endured every malady from an early age on, Mother Superior never suffered any physical ailments, nor exhibited so much as a cold. It was as if the old crone was made of Teflon.

After the holiday decorations were taken down, Billy seemed to mellow out. Perhaps he'd learned his lesson after his punishment for punching Santa Claus. Only Sister Margaret didn't want to give credit to Mother Superior's abuse. The boy always got better after the holidays, when Santa Claus in his psyche was packed away in an unseen, dark closet like the seasonal decorations they now stored.

Sister Margaret's conflict with Mother Superior remained at a constant simmer, but she adapted to an uneasy silence.

The less she crossed swords with the authoritarian, the less Billy got cut. Perhaps nobody knew Mother Superior's routines better than she did, so she knew how to avoid her much of the time. As the years went by, Mother Superior sat on her ass in her office more, while there were always more duties to be done and children who needed Sister Margaret's attention.

And still, Mother Superior kept her needling ways sharp, and her oversight remained absolute. Like during the late winter of 1976 when Billy came down with the flu. He'd complained about the chill that no number of blankets could alleviate. The temperature inside the orphanage was kept at a crisp sixty-four degrees year-round with no deviations, a good temperature in the baby wing, but not suitable for the older kids.

That night of Billy's fever, Sister Margaret turned the temperature up one degree in the hopes that minor adjustment would aid in Billy's comfort and recovery. Thirty minutes later, Mother Superior barged into Sister Margaret's room and demanded to know if she'd turned the thermostat up. She feigned innocence, which brought an uncertain glare in return. Mother Superior departed with a huff, and she turned the thermostat off for the night. By morning, Sister Margaret could see her breath in bed.

Billy's fever did eventually break, but Mother Superior's coldness toward him never wavered.

When it came to subsequent Christmases, none reached the nadir of 1974. Though December always remained

Billy's darkest month, each year he displayed some degree of improvement. When Santa returned for a Christmas morning visit in 1975, Billy was polite and well behaved as he thanked Santa, though he was now too heavy to sit on Santa's lap.

Secretly, he still spent Christmas Eve in dread awaiting Santa's arrival. Though each passing year buried the memory of that tragic night in 1971 deeper, it could not be truly forgotten, only boxed away further from view until the seasonal light revealed it again.

The department store Santa did not return in 1975. To avoid outside lawsuits, it was decided the role of Santa should be kept in house, and Father O'Brien from The Conception of Saint Mary Church assumed the red suit and throne. He was ancient enough for the part.

To anyone other than Mother Superior, it was obvious that Billy was a consummate good boy, the most well-mannered in the orphanage. Most of the kids saw him as a goodie-two-shoes who never wavered from studious behavior. He never fell into the traps of delinquency most kids stumbled upon. No smoking, no swearing, no sneaking out for a kiss in the woods. Billy was determined to never be naughty.

There were occasional signs that convinced Sister Margaret that Billy's past was never too far from him. Sometimes this was evinced by the bags under his eyes and a morose attitude around the holidays. There were a few holiday nightmares that wrenched a scream out of him, but in each case, he could not clearly remember what caused him to make a commotion. If he did remember, he kept it secret from her.

An alarming Christmas Eve incident occurred in 1983, on his final holiday at the orphanage when he was seventeen. Billy didn't just let out a wrenching sob in the night, he punched a fist into the wall as he slept. Unlike every other nightmare, this time he did remember what caused his fist to react.

"I thought I saw Santa Claus. It was a dream."

"Looks more like a nightmare," Sister Margaret observed.

"Yeah, I guess it was," Billy admitted. She wiped the sweat from his brow, and couldn't help noticing how his hairless, muscular chest heaved before her, his hot breath heavy upon her face. He made her sweat too.

From the day Billy was brought into the orphanage, she found him a handsome young boy. Eventually he lost his buck teeth, his freckles faded, and he grew into the good looks he'd been blessed with. When he reached puberty, his voice dropped into a smooth baritone that felt like velvet caressing her ears. His brown hair lightened into a dark blonde. When those baby blue eyes of his looked at her with admiration, it made her heart burst. She saw him developing into one of those dashing male models that graced the covers of romance paperbacks on the racks at the five and dime, books whose spines she would never dare to crack.

A growth spurt following puberty turned Billy into the most fit young man in the orphanage, and he was often asked to do carpentry around the building. During the summer months he would work shirtless, and Sister Margaret would admire his development. Her eyes caressed his torso and musculature, which glistened in the summer sun.

Sometimes she wondered how strong his feelings were for her. Did he find her pretty? Were the gifts he left meant for her?

One of her duties was emptying the hampers in all the rooms. She was no stranger to the stains young men left behind that indicated temptations of the flesh, but the number of sticky socks Billy left behind was remarkable. They smelled so good to her, and she made a point to hand wash Billy's socks before tossing them into the washing machine. One time she collected a sock that was still wet and warm, which helped her conclude that he tasted as good as he smelled.

As she suspected, Billy did find Sister Margaret the prettiest woman in the orphanage, but he gave himself no leeway to express it. As was the case with all Catholic institutions, abstinence was hammered into the kids relentlessly until all forms of human intimacy filled them with shame. Fornication in practice and thought was to be viewed as a mortal sin, even when engaged with oneself.

The last thing Billy wanted to do was to end up on Santa's naughty list for playing with his naughty bits, so he abstained from sins of his flesh as much as he could. He was woefully unaware of the highly sexed nature of his father and grandfather, an increased desire aided by high testosterone levels that lurked in his loins, as well. He'd inherited the excessive drip of his pipe, and his socks became his preferred receptacle to collect it. His naivete was so great he believed he was being sneaky, and nobody could tell. Those gifts of seminal fluid to Sister Margaret were completely unintentional.

Billy did succumb to his natural desires a couple times a

week, typically when he was in bed in a state of half slumber. There was always a spare sock left under his covers to fill. Sometimes he dreamed of pretty nuns with their habits on, but their robes open so their breasts were exposed. And he wondered how hairy the glove between their legs was. To not wake his bunk mate, he learned to manipulate himself with the least number of digits and amount of movement possible. Sometimes one fingertip was all that was required.

Billy was highly susceptible to the most detrimental effects of the church's strict abstinence campaigns because he believed so stringently in them. As such campaigns were meant to produce shame in oneself, each time Billy ejaculated he was left feeling guilty and broken, like he failed himself, God, and Santa Claus. Shame followed him like a cloud and would take days to dissipate, until the cycle started again the next time he beat off.

For somebody who was an exemplary good guy, he'd been trained to wallow in self-hated and depression over his desires. He was unable to love himself in a healthy manner because he'd been taught that to love oneself was a sin.

When it came to his studies, Billy was top of his class. Only Billy's intelligence went higher than that. He was able to separate which subjects were secular, and which studies were influenced by religious dogma. While he excelled in his spiritual studies, he held heavy skepticism of Christianity due to the hypocrisy of those who preached it.

Billy preferred modern fantasy fiction, especially the futuristic, taking him to worlds and dimensions way beyond the drab walls of the orphanage. The universe and imagination were gifts meant to be explored.

Mother Superior more than anyone caused him to lose his faith. The woman considered herself holier than thou, but he knew better. Mother Superior was naughty deep down to her rotten core. He'd never met anyone so prideful or wrathful in his life, and he believed those traits made her a failure in her faith.

Not wanting to upset Sister Margaret, Billy kept his skepticism over religion to himself. When he finally set out on his own at age eighteen, he could defy the church as much as he wanted. Until then, he would keep his doubt unaired.

Billy believed he did not need to constantly refer to the bible to be a moral person. Good morals were innate within him before he ever read the Good Book or *The Night Before Christmas*. He tended to disagree with those who claimed they spoke for religion as though their every decree was a commandment. Like Mother Superior.

This hypocrisy he recognized on a greater scale in the early 1980s, when an actor supported by evangelicals took over the presidency. The Grand Old Party did not practice what they preached. Billy much preferred when the compassionate peanut farmer had been president.

The uneasy truce that existed within Saint Mary's Home for Orphaned Children ended in 1982. A national body count disrupted the delicate peace within the orphanage and nearly led to tragedy.

The incident could be classified as attempted murder.

The date was October 5, 1982, and the whole country was paralyzed in terror. Seven people had been killed the prior week around the Chicago area from cyanide-laced Tylenol capsules, and the Tylenol Terrorist, as the press called him or her, was still on the loose.

Riding that wave of abject fear that swept the nation in the wake of the Tylenol murders, Sister Margaret took it upon herself to inspect the orphanage for the painkiller and remove it from the building once the national recall was announced. She visited Billy in his room to ensure he had no pills in his possession.

His morbid curiosity was piqued, and she told him all she knew about the case, which led to a discussion about the day's headlines. Billy was a wonderful conversationalist, and she often spoke with him about the outside world at length, respecting his maturity level and engaging him in subjects like politics and social issues.

When Sister Margaret left Billy's room that afternoon, she encountered Mother Superior in the hallway, glaring at her accusingly.

"What were you doing in Billy's room?" Mother Superior demanded.

"I was checking for Tylenol. I'm removing it from the building."

"I did not ask you to do that," Mother Superior challenged her.

"I took it upon myself. There's been a national recall due to the murders."

Mother Superior gave her an extended look of disapproval. "You speak far too much to that boy."

Oh, he's not a boy anymore, believe me, Sister Margaret thought but was wise enough not to say.

"Not any more than I speak to the other kids."

"That is a lie. Your interest in that boy is obvious and improper."

Sister Margaret could not believe the accusation being lobbed at her, then she remembered what happened to Dr. Elliot Stumpf eight years ago. Mother Superior did not need proof. Her accusation would stand.

"I don't believe that is the case," Sister Margaret replied in a smaller voice.

"I do not want to see you in his room ever again. If I see you in there, I will have to request a relocation."

"What do you mean?" Sister Margaret asked with alarm.

"You will be relocated to another institution," Mother Superior clarified. "And you will never see that boy again."

The thought of being banished from Billy was too hurtful to comprehend. She didn't care about being separated from anyone else there, not even Ricky. Billy was her favorite, the one who made her excited to get out of bed every morning. He was her everything.

Suddenly she saw herself standing outside in the snow, looking through the windows at him, cut off from his life. How could she even live if that were the case?

Mother Superior liked the look of panic on Sister Margaret's face.

"Not once," Mother Superior reiterated, and then she whisked away.

That night, Mother Superior was startled when she came out of her bedroom at 8:25 p.m. to pass water before retiring for the night. For safety reasons, the lights in the corridors were always kept on for children who needed to use the bathroom at night. Tonight, the lights were off.

All except one.

Midway down the hallway, a single light flashed erratically, the one around the corner before the stairs to the first floor.

Mother Superior moved through the dark corridor toward the flashing light. The lights were individual bulbs screwed into frosted white wall sconces every fifteen feet, high enough to be out of reach to most of the children. The flashing light ahead was proof the switch hadn't been turned off.

When she reached the top the stairs, Mother Superior had a hard time looking at the flashing bulb. It occurred to her this could be a prank. If the bulb was unscrewed or loose in the socket, this flashing would be the result. As she moved to the sconce on the wall, she had no idea she wasn't alone.

A black cloaked figure was concealed in a pocket of shadows nearby. Suddenly, the figure was on the move, a silent phantom.

Mother Superior stood on her tip toes, reaching up to screw in the bulb. There was a soft push against her lower back, so gentle it could have been a gust of wind or the caress of spirit fingers. Whatever it was, it was enough to send

Mother Superior pitching forward off the top step. The bulb continued to flash as Mother Superior tumbled head over heels, cracking bones all the way down.

Sister Margaret loved those cracking sounds, but she couldn't stick around to savor them. She had to quickly get back to her room and slip her habit and robe off. When she ran back out moments later to respond to the screams, she was in her night clothes. Before the first responders arrived, Sister Margaret screwed the loose bulbs tightly into their sockets, returning light to the corridor.

Those breaks she'd heard were confirmation that Mother Superior was, like most women her age, a brittle bag of bones. There was one crack so pronounced it sounded like she may have broken her neck. That crack just might be her lucky break.

It was not.

Mother Superior could have easily perished in her mysterious fall that night, but Sister Margaret was not so lucky. Once Mother Superior was transported to the hospital, she was diagnosed with fourteen cracked and seven broken bones, mostly in her feet and legs. Her ankles and knees would never heal properly.

It was a relief to discover the old woman had physical vulnerabilities after all. At the same time, she worried that Mother Superior might be unkillable. Maybe she was Dracula. Just as Dracula never left his castle, Mother Superior never left the orphanage. When had Mother Superior arrived here anyway? Had she been lording over these halls since its inception, or even further back when the first vermin arrived?

Mother Superior returned to the orphanage in a wheel-chair, and it quickly became obvious she was going to spend the rest of her life in one. An unused downstairs classroom was turned into Mother Superior's new bedroom, and a new shower had to be constructed that she could use. Mother Superior would never go upstairs at the orphanage again.

Sister Margaret didn't believe she would have felt guilty if Mother Superior had died. There was no love between them, and she would never forgive her for the cruelty and abuse she subjected the children to. Especially her Billy.

Her goal had been to cripple Mother Superior to keep her first floor bound. In that aim she'd been wildly successful. Mother Superior could no longer enforce her order to keep her out of Billy's room. Now she could go visit Billy any time she wished for as long as she wanted, and she could collect his wet socks. Mother Superior would never know a thing about it.

No other woman was going to get between Sister Margaret and her man.

CHAPTER 15

Sister Margaret oversaw finding outside employment for the children once they reached eighteen years old, the age they shed childhood for adulthood and were set loose in the big bad world. Some were all too eager to turn down job assistance and split town, and she couldn't fault them for flight. In many instances she encouraged it.

With Billy, she took particular interest in setting him up with gainful employment in Christmas Joy. She wanted him as close as possible so she could see him on occasion. She would assist in his search for an apartment as well, and even put down a deposit out of her meager savings. He was worth it. The separation anxiety was going to be bad enough as it was.

Most of the time it was easy for Sister Margaret to find a collection of job openings within the Christmas Joy Mall. There were all manner of stores there looking for cashiers, salespeople, or kitchen help year-round. In Billy's case, there was added incentive.

If he was able to sustain a good job and put away savings,

by the time his brother Ricky reached the age of sixteen, he could be emancipated from the orphanage if Billy wanted to assume legal guardianship. That was a goal worth working toward.

For Billy, Sister Margaret bypassed the mall job openings. There was one place she felt would be a far better fit, and she made a call.

On April 10th, 1984, Billy's eighteenth birthday, Sister Margaret surprised him in his room with a large Angel food cake with red frosting roses on top. They each indulged in an oversized slice, as this was an occasion for being decadent together. His belongings were already packed, merely two suitcases of clothes, so he could enjoy his final day at Saint Mary's with reflection and rest.

The following day was departure day. He left in the morning after saying goodbye to Ricky, managing to give Mother Superior the slip. This was to be a day of joy and liberation, and she could only spoil that.

Ira's Toys wasn't located within the Christmas Joy Mall. That was the province of Toyland, and most would claim their stock was slim and overpriced. Ira's Toys was located on Main Street just a few blocks from the town square and municipal park. They were the biggest toy store in town, and possibly the state.

Most locals had forgotten that when Ira Grant first opened his store in 1947, it was called Ira's Sporting Goods. At the time, Ira believed sports would be the fad that would unite the country following two World Wars. That prediction was wrong. He was a shrewd enough businessman to recognize the explosion of television sets in American households, and he saw the product the boob tubes relentlessly sold to the American public - toys. On July 1, 1951, the struggling Ira's Sporting Goods shut its doors. On August 1, Ira's Toys had its grand opening, and they were a success from that day forward.

There was added benefit to having a toy store in a Christmas town. This was a place where Christmas never ended.

Near the back of the store, in the least trafficked section, there was a random collection of sporting supplies, long held relics from Ira Grant's days that the current owners had inherited. These were among the highest priced items for sale. With such hunting supplies as bows and arrows, these toys were for adult purchase only. Luckily, the only firearms for sale were of the toy variety for playing cowboy.

Ira's Toys was the first stop after Sister Margaret drove Billy away from the orphanage. She'd set up a meeting with the store's manager, Mr. Terrance Sims. They spoke in one of the aisles that Mr. Sims was straightening up while customers browsed around them. Their talk was punctuated with jingling from the cash registers up front.

She'd dealt with Mr. Sims in the past when she shopped for toys for the orphans. To ensure the orphanage chose Ira's Toys over Toyland at the mall, he applied a ten percent discount to each order, a church discount he always boasted with pride as though that was a ticket to get him through the pearly gates.

Mr. Sims was a decent fellow, though she found him to

be a bit of a phony. With his endlessly jovial nature and *aww shucks* manner, he reminded her of Gomer Pyle, to whom he shared more than a passing resemblance. Yet sometimes she saw that façade slip, like a mask with a loose strap. She didn't believe he was aware how easily his mask slipped, revealing his insincerity. Then he resembled a smarmy used car salesman more than a toy merchant. Regardless, she found him suitable to be Billy's employer.

Sister Margaret also thought Billy would blossom within a business that catered to children and their joy. She'd seen how well he interacted with kids at the orphanage, talking with them instead of talking down to them. Little ones trusted him easily. This was the sort of work environment that would be beneficial to his psychological well-being.

Or so she thought.

She asked Billy to wait nearby while she spoke to Mr. Sims first before calling him over. He nodded and waited for his introduction.

Much to Sister Margaret's surprise, Mr. Sims did not seem receptive to her offer for help, even though Sharon, a cashier up front, had confirmed they were looking to fill a full-time position. There was even a Help Wanted sign in the front window.

"Please, Mr. Sims. Every store in town has turned us down," Sister Margaret all but pleaded. This was a fib, Ira's Toys was their first stop, but she felt justified if the result was for the benefit of Billy. "There must be some job you can give this boy. He just turned eighteen, and…"

Mr. Sims cut her off.

"I'm sorry, Sister, but I only have one job open, and I need a man for that, not a boy. It's in the stockroom, hauling crates. It's just not a job for a kid."

The kids Sister Margaret brought in the past tended to be good workers, but not physically built. The kind of man he pictured for the job, like the men in his favorite band The Village People, was the type he also desired.

"Why I suppose not," Sister Margaret replied.

"Sorry I couldn't help."

"Well, you wouldn't expect some kid to haul heavy crates all day long, would you?"

"Glad you understand," Mr. Sims added and began to turn away from her.

Sister Margaret looked over Mr. Sims' shoulder and beckoned for Billy to step forward.

"Oh, here's Billy now!" Sister Margaret announced. "Maybe you'd like to meet him, Mr. Sims."

"That's not necessary," Mr. Sims replied as he turned further away from her, still resisting her offer.

"Billy? Billy, meet Mr. Sims."

When Mr. Sims turned around, his eyes were low. First, he saw legs as massive as tree trunks. Sister Margaret's kid had the legs of a linebacker, and they were stuffed within the tightest blue jeans he'd ever seen, like they'd been painted upon his meaty thighs.

His curiosity piqued, Mr. Sims' eyes crawled up Billy's body. As he reached the top of his jeans, he saw the biggest mooseknuckle in his life. A brown leather belt hugged his jeans to his hips. Looking further up, he saw Billy's blue button up work shirt, the top few buttons unfastened to reveal the white tank top underneath. His short sleeves were rolled up nearly to his shoulders, revealing his impressive musculature.

Finally, Mr. Sims saw Billy's face, which was so ridiculously handsome and innocent looking he likely had no idea how fucking hot he was. Topping it off was a sly grin that made you want to be his slave or master or both.

No way was Mr. Sims going to let this gorgeous Adonis get away. No interview was necessary.

"Oh. Well, umm, uh..." Mr. Sims stammered. He was literally tongue tied with lust. "I'm always happy to help the church, Sister. He starts Monday morning, nine o'clock sharp."

Billy looked at Sister Margaret with joy, because he could see his employment filled her with pride. Although he was a bit worried for her now, suspecting she'd told a lie about the other businesses in town. He didn't want her to be naughty on his behalf.

"Oh, thank you Mr. Sims," Sister Margaret said with genuine gratitude and shook his hand. She could tell from his grip that his pulse was racing.

Mr. Sims hoped Sister Margaret and Billy would quickly depart before they could notice how excited he was.

Billy took pride in his job at Ira's Toys. This was his first experience with gainful employment, and he wanted to excel. He thanked Sister Margaret often for her foresight to match him to the perfect job.

Being part of a team comprised of many generations and backgrounds awakened him to a variety of new people. Even better than the camaraderie were the smiles, an endless number from excited children. Billy beamed his winning grin at everyone and received a wealth of smiles in return.

He really wasn't aware of how appealing he was, the envy of every woman and man. Meanwhile, children were drawn to him like he was a big puppy dog, a 6"3' puppy dog.

Once, he even received a kiss while on the job. The young mother was a bombshell, looking like she'd stepped right out of an episode of *Charlie's Angels*. She and her young daughter were looking up at the top shelf, which held a selection of teddy bears. Neither mother nor daughter could reach them, but the girl was trying with her arms upraised.

Billy stepped up to assist, grabbed the girl by the waist, and raised her effortlessly to the top shelf, where she retrieved her teddy bear of choice. The girl's landing was as gentle as her lifting. The mother flashed an appreciative smile, but her daughter was far more demonstrative in her admiration. She threw an arm around his neck and planted a big wet smack-aroo that smelled of bubblegum on his cheek.

Billy's job performance was exemplary. His timecard was the most perfectly stamped in the racks, clocked in and out to the exact minute, every shift. His meal breaks were timed with the same precision. A packed lunchbox was brought to save money and time with his meals: a homemade hoagie, yogurt, fruit, nuts. His meals were as wholesome as he was.

There was no formal dress code at Ira's Toys. However, Billy's position as stockboy required him to wear a long beige coat over his clothing. Mr. Sims insisted it would be helpful to protect his attire and keep buttons or belt buckles from getting caught on boxes. The manager always wore dark dress slacks and a white button up shirt topped with a bow tie that changed color every day of the week.

Billy got along with his co-workers just fine and thought they were all hard workers, well, everyone except for Andy, the thirty-year-old inventory supervisor. Andy wore his title with authority, even though he wasn't one of the managers.

Andy often sat at his desk in the stockroom when there was plenty of hard work to be done. This became obvious on his first day, when a shipment of massive boxes containing self-assemble playground sets had been delivered. These boxes were so big Billy could barely get his arms around them. Meanwhile, Andy just sat back with his shoes kicked up on his desk, browsing a girlie magazine. Billy saw a bare boob inside the pages and made sure he didn't look that closely again.

Andy took a moment away from ogling centerfolds to peek over the magazine at Billy. There were still more boxes to move, and he nodded at them with impatience.

Billy thought that was an entirely unnecessary gesture, as he was just taking a moment to catch his breath. The next box was seized. He didn't need to be told twice.

Any time a toy was observed out of place, he'd return it to its rightful shelf. If the coloring books were askew in their racks, he couldn't just walk past without straightening them first. He knew Mr. Sims appreciated his thoroughness because he was often spotted watching him with a smile and a nod.

In his second month there, Billy was awarded Employee of the Month. Andy never warmed up to him, though. One day as he and Andy ate lunch together in the stockroom – Andy at his desk, Billy on the floor – Andy griped that he'd worked for Mr. Sims for nearly ten years and had never once been named Employee of the Month. As Andy said this, he pulled a bottle of Scotch and two paper cups from his desk.

Despite Andy's urging, Billy refused to take so much as a sip. Not only was this breaking work policy for drinking on the job, but he was also three years shy of legal drinking age. So far, he hadn't tasted so much as a sip of alcohol in his life.

What a pussy, Andy thought. If the kid wasn't going to indulge, that left more for him.

Billy reached into his sack lunch and withdrew a milk carton, his wholesome drink of choice. Andy watched with bemusement as Billy tore into the carton and drank, thinking Billy was a big baby who wanted to guzzle from his mommy's tit.

Shocked by Andy's delinquency, Billy thought it was no wonder the inventory supervisor had never received an award for his performance at work.

Directly after being hired at Ira's Toys, Sister Margaret took Billy to the apartment she'd secured for him. The building was nondescript, a collection of low-income studio apartments in a horseshoe formation. Other orphans had been relocated there in the past, so Sister Margaret had no trouble securing Billy a unit. He was the only person whose rent she paid, for a few months at least.

Billy's studio didn't provide much in the way of square footage, and the wood panel walls offered inadequate insulation, but he absolutely loved the privacy. This was the first time he'd had his own place, four walls that held his own kingdom. No crying kids to wake him up at night, no Mother Superior to barge in unannounced. Even better was the uncovered walkway that led to his own door. He didn't have to share indoor hallways that may have reminded him of Saint Mary's Home for Orphaned Children. He was an adult now.

His freedom allowed him to explore the town at greater length, and he often ate out or at the park, which allowed him to people watch. Talking to others he didn't do often, as he was too shy to start conversations.

The Quad Cinemas was the premiere movie theatre in Christmas Joy, and that's where Billy saw his first R-rated film during his first weekend on his own. On Saturday night, he blindly bought a ticket to the movie that all the teenagers stood in line for, *Friday the 13th: The Final Chapter.*

With no knowledge of the prior chapters in the series, Billy took his seat with a Coke, buttered popcorn, and Red Vines. The film that unspooled shocked him from the first reel to the last with its constant stream of profanities, skinny dipping, teenage copulation, pot smoking, porno watching, shower scenes, boobies, and brutal, bloody murders. The audience screamed and he joined them.

The damage the axe wielding killer delivered to nubile young flesh was horrifying. He'd never known movies could show such explicit sex and violence. Multiple times he became sick to his stomach, and during one window-shattering scare, he threw his Red Vines into the air with fright. Still, the communal party atmosphere was palpable, and he enjoyed engaging in this ritual of youth.

No wonder Mother Superior had spoken about R-rated films as though they were evil. Was it naughty to watch movies like these? He didn't think so, because he was of age and not breaking any rules to see them. Sex comedies also held great allure, and that summer's release *Bachelor Party* was like an instruction manual. This was the raunchiest film he'd ever seen, with enough bouncing boobies to make him dizzy.

Cinema became Billy's window into how the world really operated, the modern world that the church wished to hide and deny. It took a few pay checks for him to buy a VCR to go with his modest television. There was a video store located a few blocks from his apartment named Ma & Pa's Video Palace. Here he could rent all the forbidden films he'd heard of, and many more he hadn't.

Ma & Pa's Video Palace had a back room behind a beaded curtain that was labeled Adults Only. It took over a month before he had the courage to pass through those beads. This was Billy's first step into the world of pornography. The VHS boxes on display showed explicit sex acts that made the

R-rated movies he watched look tame in comparison. Even though he felt embarrassed to rent these tapes, he did so anyway, and quickly became a porn connoisseur.

Pornography became Billy's first bona fide addiction. He would rent a new smut film every night, sometimes more than one. The store didn't mind since he became their most steady customer.

None of these tapes brought back memories of the violent sex acts he'd witnessed as a child, on the road and in the orphanage. The sex in these films did not end with screaming, but with squeals and grunts of pleasure.

The films were incredibly instructional on how to touch himself, giving him different techniques for jerking off he'd never considered before.

No longer did he need to hide under the covers in the dark keeping movement to a minimum. Now he could lie spread-eagle atop the covers with the lights on and look at himself, comparing himself to the men on the screen. Having always wondered before if he measured up to other men, now he could say with confidence that he did.

Along with his inhibitions, his socks were retired from the process. Now he could let that excessive drip of his flow as it may. Without his socks as a catcher, he could let his fluid fly, excessive amounts that launched an incredible distance. Moaning was another new freedom to give voice to his pleasure.

Masturbation became Billy's second addiction.

There was a side effect more terrible than rubbing his dick

raw, and that was shame. While he was quick to distance himself from the strictures of the church, the abstinence campaigns he'd been hammered with for years kept a cruel hold in the back of his mind, making him feel naughty for his excessive enjoyment of his flesh. This created occasional bouts of depression and self-loathing. He experienced confusion on whether he was naughty or nice.

Pornography gave Billy explicit lessons on how to mate with a woman, but they offered scant information on how to talk to them first. Incredibly shy, he let his desires remain secret. There was even a beautiful young woman he'd developed an interest in at work.

Billy had a crush on Pamela, the brunette salesgirl.

CHAPTER  16

It was the Monday after Thanksgiving when Billy found himself restocking toys alongside Pamela. The stock had been heavily depleted over the holiday weekend, and Mr. Sims wanted the shelves packed with product. There were flirtatious looks and banter between them, but Billy wouldn't go beyond that.

Pamela was flirting hard, had been for some time with him. Normally she liked authoritative, older men. Billy was three years her junior, but his reserved, innocent act made him seem even younger, like a fourth grader experiencing his first crush. Or was it really an act?

Perhaps his upbringing at the orphanage had something to do with his inexperience. Billy was a closed book who revealed very little about his personal life or past. He also refrained from asking personal questions of her. She wished he would ask to get to know her better.

Pamela had no qualms about dating another employee. She'd done it before. Last year, soon after she'd started working at Ira's Toys, she'd gone on a few dates with Andy. Dates was a kind way of describing those few awkward fumblings in his car, where his intensity of passion lasted all of two minutes. Her rides with Andy ended soon after.

Andy wasn't really her type anyway because she was taller than he was, and she preferred her men to tower over her. She also liked smooth talkers who paid her many compliments. She'd probably have shagged Mr. Sims if he'd been interested and asked nicely enough, but he was gay and had a partner.

Oh God, was Billy gay? Considering the lingering looks she sometimes caught him making at her, she didn't think he was queer.

Physically, Billy was totally her type. She appreciated his curves as much as he admired hers. He could probably pick her up and break her in half, and she thought that was hot. He was a himbo, but that was fine because she could be his bimbo.

They were currently stocking packages of toy Wild Bill Hickok Handcuffs beneath a shelf of Jabba the Hut Action Playsets.

"I like handcuffs," Pamela commented and flashed Billy a coquettish smile. "They're yours, look." She pointed at the cowboy's name on the package. "Wild Billy."

Billy blushed, and he lowered his head, giving him a better view of her tight sweater clinging to her heaving breasts. His blush turned brighter as he looked down at the floor.

Pamela leaned in to place more packages on the shelf, letting her breast rest upon his hulking bicep. She hoped he noticed.

Billy definitely felt her press against his muscle, and another muscle responded. He resisted the urge to move away from her. The truth was, he liked the pressure she was putting on him. This was the first time a woman's breast had been laid upon him, and it was thrilling. It was as warm and pillowy as he'd always imagined.

For months he'd felt an attraction to Pamela, but he didn't know how to express it. Only part of his hesitation had to do with his shy nature. Shame of succumbing to his sexual urges continued to prevent him from acting upon his desires, though he no longer feared the judgment of God in such matters. He was holding onto his virginity not in service of Christ, but of Santa Claus. The result was the same. He was afraid to fuck.

During today's shift he'd been building up his bravery to ask Pamela out, although he didn't know where to ask her out to. The question nagged whether it was appropriate to ask a co-worker for a date, or if he could be fired for doing so. How terrible it would be if he lost the job Sister Margaret had been so proud to secure for him.

Just as he was getting the nerve to ask, Mr. Sims walked up behind them, carrying a squeaky eight-foot ladder in one hand and a rolled vinyl banner in the other. Pamela pushed Billy off, hoping Mr. Sims hadn't seen their point of contact.

"Pamela, can you hold this end?" Mr. Sims asked as he extended the loose end of the banner to her.

"Sure, Mr. Sims," Pamela responded, and she held the side with both hands. Mr. Sims stepped away to unwind the ten-foot-long banner. Billy stepped back with a smile to see what the banner would reveal.

Two giant words were revealed on the left, MERRY CHRISTMAS, and three other words on the right, HAPPY NEW YEAR. In the center was a giant holy wreath, and within that was the jolly painted face of Santa Claus.

The smile dissolved from Billy's face, and a frown materialized in its place.

Santa's smile was so sweet, his cheeks and nose so rosy with mirth, it seemed he was mocking Billy, laughing at him. Behind that smile, Santa knew his secrets.

Billy shuddered with dread. Did Santa know he'd been up most of the night jerking off and spraying the walls? Good thing Pamela and Mr. Sims were admiring the banner, otherwise they would have seen him shuddering.

"I love this banner," Mr. Sims said and nodded. "We can put it up after lunch. Today we're going to start decorating for Christmas!"

"How fun, I love decorating!" Pamela squealed with excitement.

Billy's mood sank further at the job to come. He'd known the time was coming, the holiday season that swept in a mental fog of fear and darkness. In December, it was harder to breathe, and he couldn't fault the drop in temperature for that. Now he was employed by a business that would see its biggest boom in sales in December.

Only now did he take note of the song playing over the store's loudspeakers, "The Warm Side of the Door." Listening to the lyrics, he realized he was hearing his first Christmas song of the season.

"There'll be thunder and lightning, but we're safe and sound, and I won't need no more on the warm side of the door."

Billy wasn't so sure of that. There were always orphans like him left out in the storm for the holidays, left out on the cold side of the door.

"There's always people who love you, that will kiss you and hug you, and it's always Christmas on the warm side of the door."

Such was the abundant optimism of Christmas music, but he heard the bitter notes others chose to ignore. Some people didn't want it to always be Christmas. Perhaps he preferred the cold side of the door after all.

It would take effort to not let his holiday hesitation hamper his job performance. Most of the toys that would delight the town's children on Christmas morning would be toys that he stocked, processed in his workshop.

He didn't recognize, in that respect, he resembled Santa Claus. At least not yet.

When Mr. Sims said they were going to decorate for Christmas, Billy imagined the orphanage during the holidays, with a Christmas tree, some lights, wreaths, and paper snowflakes. Ira's Toys was altogether different. Mr. Sims turned the store into a Christmas winter wonderland. There was likely more Christmas kitsch per square foot inside the toy store than the mall or anywhere in town.

Mr. Sims wanted to make his store the primary destination for youngsters during the holidays. As a shrewd salesman, he knew how to bleed his customers' wallets dry.

In charge of the decorating was Mrs. Randall, Mr. Sims' forty-eight-year-old assistant manager. She performed every duty, from cashiering to decorating, with great flair and fanfare. Her voice was sharp and pronounced, as if she were the world's oldest cheerleader. Her good cheer endeared her to most everyone, and Billy liked her a lot.

There was a motherly quality to Mrs. Randall that Billy found comforting. She was a real mother, with a thirteen-year-old son named Chad who dropped into the store on occasion. Billy thought Chad and his brother Ricky could be good friends if they were to hang out together. Mrs. Randall was a mother to everyone, including Mr. Sims, who was quite aware his success was due in part to her tireless efforts. Sims certainly didn't have the style or wherewithal to spearhead the holiday decorating.

"When we're done, kids will think they've been marooned on the Island of Misfit Toys!" Mrs. Randall announced to the crew with excitement.

She wasn't kidding, and they accomplished that lofty goal. The decorating process took all week.

On Tuesday morning, a window painter arrived, and it took him three days to complete his holiday scene. To one side of the front door, HAPPY HOLIDAYS was painted in massive green letters decorated with ornaments, atop an illustrated snowbank. On the other side of the door was a whole Christmas town covered in snow, with cartoon animals decorating a Christmas tree. Why those animals were rabbits and mice nobody knew. The artwork covered every square foot of the windows, obscuring the view inside. Strings of multicolored Christmas lights lined the front windows and door.

Inside Ira's Toys, the Christmas village was literal. A large quadrant at the front of the store was roped off for the massive display that included a fully decorated Christmas tree, fake snow drifts, and animatronic elves that nodded and turned their mechanical heads and limbs. One waving elf sat upon a rocking horse. Nutcrackers of varying sizes were lined up like a choir. There was even a massive red sleigh draped with sleighbells and garland. A rather impressive holiday prop, but kind of a waste of space, Billy thought.

Also taking up considerable space was a long table with a miniature Christmas village in the center, surrounded by train tracks for a motorized toy locomotive that traveled in an endless circle. Assembling the train and its tracks with Mrs. Randall made Billy sad, as he felt nostalgic longing for a childhood he'd been denied. The orphanage never had a display like this, nor would they have allowed such a noisy, motorized distraction.

The honking train brought Mrs. Randall a ridiculous amount of glee, and any time the locomotive passed beside her she'd loudly announce, "Choo-choo-choo!" He was glad he mostly worked in the stockroom because that toy train was noisy and honked an awful lot. He felt sympathy for the cashiers that had to listen to it chugging all day long, all month long.

Hanging high over the register counters was the banner featuring Santa Claus, keeping an eye out for those who might shoplift or think of being naughty. Billy had to get into the habit of not looking toward the ceiling during his shift.

The store had become an oppressive environment for him, so chock full of Christmas decorations it was suffocating. No longer did he look forward to going to work. With the turning of the season, he now dreaded clocking in.

The daily supply of smiles and good cheer he typically carried became forced, if he could achieve them at all. He hoped nobody noticed his change of disposition, but everyone did.

His seasonal depression hit as the final calendar page turned to December. This was a difficult month to watch television. Since the moment Santa was ushered in at the end of the Macy's Thanksgiving Day Parade (a broadcast he studiously avoided), ol' jolly Saint Nick had a habit of popping up during every commercial break with bellowing laughter. Less television viewing and more video cassette rentals were the cure. His porn intake increased, as did his masturbation sessions, and that led to more shame. He hated feeling this way but couldn't find a way out of it.

Guilt was a trap that kept him in a dark cage. How long until he responded with rage? That was a predictable reaction for a trapped animal.

His loneliness was exacerbated by the season, as it was for

so many others. Plus, this was his first holiday season living by himself. He increasingly missed being around Ricky, and he missed his deep conversations with Sister Margaret.

The first week of December he spoke to Ricky and Sister Margaret by phone. It did a world of good to hear their voices. When they inquired how he was doing, he assured them everything was fine though everything clearly was not. Could they sense the falsity of his claim? They wanted to see him before Christmas if possible, and he agreed that would be great if he could get the time off work. Mr. Sims would likely have him working overtime all month.

To some degree he didn't want to see them, because it might be obvious that he was in his dark place once again. His seasonal doom and gloom had followed him like a dark cloud from the orphanage to the center of the city.

The staff of Ira's Toys were his family now. They were friendly if not outright friends. He'd had numerous illuminating conversations with Mrs. Randall over the months, as she assumed the void left by Sister Margaret. But this friendship didn't extend beyond work hours, as Mrs. Randall had her son Chad who needed her attention.

Pamela, however, remained someone he wanted to get to know better. It took over a week since Mr. Sims blocked him from asking her out on a date with his Christmas decorating announcement to gain the nerve to ask her out again.

The first Wednesday in December, Billy arrived at work fifteen minutes early and lingered around the time clock, waiting for Pamela to come in for her opening shift. She walked in three minutes before her start time, looking so pretty in a soft blue fuzzy sweater and a long pastel skirt. The smile she had for him was huge, as if she were as excited to see him as he was to see her.

Once she was clocked in, and only because there was nobody else around, Billy made his move. His approach was hesitant, his voice jittery, hands clasped together before him. Basically, he couldn't have appeared more nervous if he tried. She found his shyness endearing.

"Pamela, hi, would you like, like to go out with me on Sunday to... to get an ice cream cone?" So went Billy's first time asking a girl out, and it was one of the most nerve-wracking questions he'd ever asked. Before his approach, he'd checked the employee schedule and found Sunday was the only day in the coming week they both had off work.

Pamela was glad Billy had finally mustered up the courage to ask her out, though his date of choice seemed juvenile. It was also impractical.

"There's supposed to be a snowstorm this weekend. You want to get ice cream when it's snowing?" Pamela asked.

Billy had checked the work schedule, but he hadn't checked the forecast. And she was right, his suggestion had been silly and ill-informed.

"Oh, I guess not," Billy said with a lowered head and dejected look upon his face. "How foolish, forget I asked."

"But hot chocolate would be nice," Pamela replied quickly, perhaps desperately. It'd taken this long to secure his interest and she didn't want to lose him now.

Billy's forlorn look turned hopeful.

"Yeah, hot chocolate. That would be great. Would Sunday afternoon be good?"

From his choice of time, it seemed to her he was more interested in getting a drink rather than some of her sugar. But she would give him some time. His inexperience had some appeal because that made her his tutor.

"Sunday afternoon is good," Pamela confirmed.

"I like The Coffee Bar, do you know it?"

The Coffee Bar was Billy's favorite because the shop was refreshingly free of seasonal decorations. And they'd had a poster advertising hot chocolate in their front window since Thanksgiving.

"Oh, yes. They're good."

"Great!" Billy said, perhaps a bit too enthusiastically. "Hot chocolate on Sunday. I'll see you then."

"You'll see me all week too," Pamela corrected him with a coquettish grin.

Billy blushed and grinned back. "Yeah, I guess I will."

As Pamela and Billy headed to the front of the store to get their daily duties, they were unaware their conversation had been overheard.

Andy had been ready to push out through the Employees Only door when he heard Billy and Pamela's voices on the other side. He paused to listen, and his patience was rewarded with their plans for an off-work drink. Some lame date at a coffee bar. It was a surprise that immature dumb fuck hadn't asked her to the neighborhood Kool-Aid stand.

The thought of Billy moving in on the girl he'd been inside of ticked him off. Pamela was into quantity, not quality, so it was no wonder she'd go on a date with any swinging dick in her vicinity.

It wasn't Andy's style to silently stew in anger. It was time he turned up the heat on Billy.

About an hour after securing his date with Pamela, Billy pushed out through the Employees Only door. He came to an abrupt stop, filling the open doorway.

Pamela was standing at the nearest shelf, positioning a Daffy Duck doll inside a Porky Pig ride-on toy car. His eyes traveled down her body and back up, a grin of gratitude upon his face. It was hard to believe a woman so pretty had agreed to go on a date with him. He wondered if she'd agreed out of pity more than mutual attraction.

Pamela looked up from Daffy and saw Billy watching her. The smile she returned was so big and bright, he found it overwhelming to look at. Suddenly self-conscious, he withdrew back into the stockroom.

Turning, Billy found himself face-to-face with Andy. Hands on his hips and head at an irritated tilt, Andy looked angry.

"Just what the fuck do you think you're doing?" Andy snapped.

Billy had no idea what he could have done to draw such ire. The foul language Andy employed made him extremely uncomfortable. Mr. Sims didn't talk like that, and he suspected Andy made a point not to use such language around the head manager. Curse words were *naughty*.

"I... you shouldn't talk like that," Billy stammered.

"Oh!" Andy said with mock offense. "Well, excuse me, Ann Landers. You know, what is it with you lately, Billy?"

Andy's questions were confirmation that he was not as good at hiding his seasonal doldrums as he thought. Still, he didn't deserve this reaction. So far as he knew, his job performance was satisfactory. He was punctual for every shift, and he certainly never drank alcohol or looked at porno magazines on the job, bad behavior that Andy indulged with regularity.

"Nothing," Billy said, though not convincingly. Telling untruths was not his strong suit.

"I'm going to level with you. When you came here a couple of months ago you were an all right kid. But all of a sudden you got this fucking attitude problem." Andy said this while fully aware he was serving the attitude in this confrontation. Shaking Billy up was his aim. "Getting snappy with me all the time. You're staring off into space like some moon goon."

When Billy replied, it came out as a scared whine, giving Andy the satisfaction of getting deep under his skin. Like sharpened fingernails.

"Will you just... just leave me alone?"

"When I leave you alone, asshole, none of your fucking work gets done," Andy spit out.

Billy wasn't going to raise his voice like Andy, but he was

being pushed too hard, and he would give voice to that fact. That was the freedom of being an adult. At no time would he have ever responded this way to Mother Superior at the orphanage. He was learning to stand up for himself.

"Look, I don't care about my fucking work."

Billy felt relief in saying that dirty word, *fuck*. A word he'd never spoken before, though he was getting used to it lately from its excessive presence in the pornos he watched nightly.

Andy's response was a grin that made Billy feel fearful and guilty, the way Mother Superior used to make him feel.

"Oh, is that so, wise ass?"

Now Billy worried that his speaking up might cost him his job. Sister Margaret would be so disappointed in him.

"Sims is going to hear about this, you sonofabitch," Andy threatened.

Billy thought Andy might be bluffing. The reason Andy was inventory supervisor and not assistant manager was he wasn't manager material. Mr. Sims knew it, and Andy resented him for that. He'd seen Mr. Sims get short in temper with Andy before. Meanwhile, he'd only received compliments and satisfactory looks from the boss.

"Look, just leave me alone." Billy headed out while he still had the courage to walk away.

Alone in the stockroom, Andy nodded with a grin. The kid had run off with his tail tucked between his legs. Exactly the reaction he wanted to see; a cowardly retreat was a bully's favorite snack.

As for Pamela, it'd been too long since they'd last been

intimately entwined. Even if she was no longer interested in him, he believed he could force her into doing whatever he wanted.

When Billy stormed out of the stockroom, Pamela was no longer there. Hopefully she'd been far away before Andy unleashed his stream of profanities at him.

It wasn't Pamela he wanted to find now, as she also made him nervous, though in an excited way. Mrs. Randall was always a beacon of cheer, and hearing her bellowing laughter would do him some good. He even heard it now as he passed through an aisle of toys, only she didn't sound the same. This bellowing laughter was deep.

With growing concern, he realized he wasn't hearing Mrs. Randall at all.

Billy stepped out of the toy aisle and came to a stop so abrupt, had anyone seen him they would have thought he walked into an invisible wall.

Sitting across the store in the sleigh was Santa Claus, waving at children.

"Merry Christmas, everyone! Ho-ho-ho-ho! Merry Christmas!"

Even though Santa Claus wasn't looking his way, he knew Santa was there for him, to deliver punishment for being naughty. He'd just uttered the F-word for the first time in his life. Immediately he promised himself he would never utter that bad word ever again.

That was a promise he kept.

Santa Claus turned his head, spotted Billy, and waved.

"Merry Christmas!" Santa bellowed.

The shock delivered by Santa's greeting was calamitous, rocking him so hard a memory was jogged loose, rising to the surface like dangerous gas released from a fissure in the earth created by an earthquake.

Billy saw the Santa Claus that hunted him on the road on Christmas Eve, 1971. His view was from down low, as he hid behind the bushes and weeds.

"*Where are you, ya little bastard!?*" Santa called out.

Then he saw the flash of moonlight on the switchblade in Santa's hand. The blade dripped blood, his mother's blood.

Billy recoiled backward and collided with a tall bin full of large, rubber bouncing balls. Both Billy and the bin overturned. The balls bounced on the floor, but Billy's ass did not. He was stunned, but at least he was back inside Ira's Toys. The date was not Christmas Eve. That ghastly vision had departed.

The commotion drew Pamela out from behind her register. Alarmed, she rushed to Billy's side and grabbed ahold of his arm. He flinched at her touch.

"Pamela," he said breathlessly.

"Are you all right, Billy?" she asked. He appeared frightened and had broken into a cold sweat. His hand was clammy to the touch.

"Yeah, yeah," Billy said shakily. "I… uh…" he mumbled.

"You don't look so good," Pamela said with genuine concern.

"No, I'm fine, really. I..." Billy was unable to finish his thought.

Pamela helped Billy up off the floor, holding his arm. As he rose, he accidentally kicked one of the loose rubber balls.

"Don't worry about this stuff. I'll straighten it up for you, okay?"

Billy straightened his stock coat as he gained his bearings, providing no acknowledgment to what she'd said.

"Are you sure you're all right, Billy?"

Billy shoved his hands into his coat pockets to conceal the fact that they were shaking. He saw Santa Claus across the store, but he was waving at a young girl by the door. Santa was not here to deliver punishment for his naughtiness. At least not yet.

This Santa was just somebody hired by Mr. Sims to entertain kids and boost sales for the holiday season. Still, he'd been horribly rattled. It was better to get away from Santa until he was over the shock.

"Yeah, I... never felt better in my life."

Billy headed for the stockroom without a thank you for Pamela's assistance, leaving her to clean up his mess. She watched him go with concern, and hoped he was feeling better for their date on Sunday.

Santa Claus had seen the employee fall across the store, but he was unaware his presence had caused the man's collapse. He also didn't recognize the young man as the kid who'd knocked him out of his chair while playing Santa Claus at Saint Mary's Home for Orphaned Children ten years ago.

He might have quit on the spot if he had. That bucktoothed boy was much bigger now, and it looked like he could put some serious hurt on whoever he wanted.

CHAPTER 17

Billy did get into Pamela's cleavage during their date on Sunday, just not in the way he intended.

The snowstorm in the forecast barely materialized, offering nothing more than a light dusting. Billy and Pamela met at The Coffee Bar at 2 p.m. and took a table for two. Their conversation was awkward at first, with his basic questions about her family skirted around. That was the last thing she wanted to talk about on a date. He had little to add in this department, as his time at the orphanage was an off-limits topic.

Thankfully, the radio inside the store caught Pamela's attention and got her gabbing excitedly about pop music, her favorite subject. When Billy started working at Ira's Toys, Pamela was obsessed with Cyndi Lauper and sang "Girls Just Wanna Have Fun" incessantly. It might have been annoying if she weren't so darned cute.

Cyndi Lauper had been forgotten by December. When "Like A Virgin" came on over the radio, Pamela knew every lyric and sang along, and then gushed her unending devotion to Madonna, whom she styled herself after. Like the pop princesses of her time, Pamela positively sparkled with color in her clothing and makeup.

Billy knew nothing of popular music or style, and Pamela literally gasped when he admitted he'd never watched MTV. At Pamela's insistence, he agreed he would check the channel out. Personally, he didn't care for his first sampling of Madonna, but he wasn't going to say so and dampen her enthusiasm. He certainly didn't know what to talk about, but he could nod and smile just fine.

Following The Coffee Bar, Pamela suggested they walk the block that would take them to the Christmas Market at the city park. The market was in full swing with numerous local vendors hawking their holiday wares. Pamela made the first move, reaching for his hand. His hand flinched at first, then he clamped onto hers and they walked through the market.

Billy could hardly believe it. He was walking hand in hand with the prettiest woman in the park, one who drew every man's attention. Today she wore a wool jacket meant for fashion and not inclement weather, as it was cut low, exposing half a foot of flesh beneath her neck. To guard against the chill, she wore a pink scarf. Lucky snowflakes drifted into her exposed cleavage. He wanted to melt there too.

He was hoping she expressed interest in a garment of clothing or jewelry so he could buy it for her, price permitting. She made more per hour at the store than he did.

He never got his chance.

They came into view of the elevated gazebo that was the

center point of the park, encircled by garlands and lights. Upon a throne inside the gazebo was Santa Claus, welcoming a long line of children waiting impatiently to climb the steps and sit on his lap. The tyke currently seated there reacted to his fuzzy face with wails for his mommy.

Santa looked up from the bawling, snot-nosed brat with a grimace of irritation, and his eyes locked on Billy's as he was passing by.

Billy jerked to a halt, yanking Pamela to a stop. Seeing how ghostly white he appeared, she was alarmed he might have another fainting fit like in the store that week.

The angered look on Santa's face was familiar because this was his childhood Santa returned. Suddenly it was night. The gazebo was gone, and his Santa stood in the middle of the road. Billy watched him from behind the roadside branches again. The switchblade in Santa's gloved hand flashed with moonlight. Blood dripped from the blade, while more blood pulsed out of his mother's gaping, slit throat.

"Billy?"

Billy seized on the woman's concerned voice calling his name, which was not a part of how this flashback went. With the quickness of a blink, Billy was back in the city park. Now he heard that alarmed voice much louder, right beside him.

"Billy! That hurts!"

Pamela had no idea what had overcome Billy to stop him in his tracks and fill him with horror. His grip on her hand remained, and his pressure increased to a painful degree.

"Let go!"

Pamela's shouts drew the attention of the children in line to see Santa, along with their parents.

Billy released Pamela's hand and spun to face her, removing Santa from his field of vision. Relief flooded her as blood rushed through her hand again. Then Billy lurched forward and vomited his hot chocolate onto her chest. Her scarf only caught some of the splash. Most of it ran down into her cleavage.

Pamela's initial reaction was shock, and then disgust. This was, no doubt, the most disastrous date she'd ever been on. Everyone at the Christmas Market had witnessed her getting puked on.

"Gross me out!" Pamela shouted. She saw the line of children laughing at her. So was Santa Claus.

"He barfed on her boobies!" one red-nosed brat brayed as he pointed at them.

"I'm sorry," Billy said, his nausea apparent in his watery voice. Pamela feared he might barf on her boobies again and she took a fearful step back.

"I'm… I'm not feeling well. I have to go."

Billy ran out of the park without offering any help to clean Pamela up.

Aghast at the situation and soaking in Billy's sick, Pamela carefully unwrapped the scarf around her neck and used it to dry her chest as best she could. For a second time Billy had left a mess for her to clean up. Tears of embarrassment cut cold tracks down her cheeks.

When Billy saw Pamela at work next on Tuesday morning, she asked with concern how he was feeling. His assurances that he was fine relieved her some, as catching a seasonal flu would ruin her holiday season.

The humiliation of that date would be much harder for her to shed. The snickering of kids and townsfolk who'd witnessed the incident would be cruel, as bitter as the bile Billy ejected onto her chest. No matter how relieved she was that he was better, or how much she'd liked him before, there would be no more dates between them. No going out in public with him either. Kissing the mouth that barfed on her? *Gag me with a spoon!* Kissing Billy would never happen.

Nobody at work knew about the embarrassing incident at the park, at least not yet. She knew all too well how easily gossip spread among social circles in town, having engaged in plenty of it herself. At some point, the staff would hear about it and laugh, and she'd have to deny everything. The phrase *Barf me out!* would have to be retired from her Valley Girl vernacular.

For Billy, he still held illusions that Pamela might go out with him again. His attraction to her had not diminished in the least. For now, he would keep some distance until he was over his embarrassment. In his fantasies he continued to imagine being intimate with her.

Billy would touch Pamela again, though in ways he never could have imagined.

On Saturday December 15th, Sister Margaret visited Ira's Toys, surprising Billy on the job. This Christmas shopping trip was her yearly duty to gather gifts for the orphans. She would be buying a gift for Ricky today, and she could use Billy's help for recommendations. Part of her reason to get him employed there was her ability to visit him on the job.

Only now, from the moment she'd taken a step back into the store she realized how foolish, short sighted, and, well, selfish her actions had been.

Sister Margaret saw Santa Claus sitting in his sleigh. There were no children demanding his attention. Santa waved at her.

The wave she returned was hesitant.

What a fool she'd been to get Billy employment at a business that had a seasonal Santa on the premises. If her decision contributed to his depression, she wouldn't be able to forgive herself.

Sister Margaret crossed herself before proceeding further.

Scanning the store, she didn't see Billy anywhere, so she approached Mrs. Randall at the cash register, whom she'd known for many years.

"Is Billy working today?"

"Oh yeah! He's probably in the stockroom. You go right on back, Sister," Mrs. Randall announced loudly.

"Thank you, Mrs. Randall."

Excited to see her Billy, she headed back toward the Employees Only door and entered the stockroom. The thrill she felt was akin to a girl venturing into the boy's locker room on a dare. Might she find Billy putting on his uniform?

Billy and Mr. Sims were working together when Sister Margaret entered the stockroom. Both men were delighted to see her, but Billy was the one she hugged.

"Is it okay if Billy helps me select toys for the orphans, Mr. Sims?" Sister Margaret asked meekly.

"Why of course! Billy's the best boy you've ever brought to work for us, Sister."

Mr. Sims' compliment brought a blush to Billy's face. Despite his size, with this look he did in fact resemble a boy, a very big one.

Billy assisted Sister Margaret for over an hour, during which they engaged in small talk. Toys were the main topic for the day. She carefully observed his body language to gauge his well-being. Though he was doing his best to hide it, she could tell his spirits were low. At no time did Billy look at the Santa Claus working in the store. It was as if he wore blinders that removed Santa from his sight. That was likely a wise safety mechanism, she thought.

Sister Margaret's choice of date for this shopping trip was deliberate. Exactly ten years ago, Billy had endured one of his roughest days at the orphanage. At her insistence, he'd strayed from his room, been punished severely by Mother Superior, and then tied to his bedposts for the night. Just watching Billy endure such hardships had been traumatic for her and made this a dark anniversary for them both. It was her belief he might be carrying that weight as well, and she wished to alleviate some of his burden.

Before she left, Sister Margaret told Billy she would call

him again on Christmas Eve, the day she would be most worried for him.

When Sister Margaret departed she felt as guilty and culpable as that day ten years ago when she told Billy to leave his room, and it led him to misery. It was as though she'd poured a circle of gasoline around Billy and left a roman candle sparking in his hand.

Sunday December 16 was the date Billy had his dream about Pamela, which was remarkable for a few reasons. For one, it was the most vividly sexual dream he'd ever had, so detailed it played out like the pornographic videocassettes he rented with regularity.

A week had passed since his failed date, but his affection toward Pamela had only grown in that time. He couldn't call it a first date because a second date had not been scheduled, at least not yet.

Billy answered a knocking at his door and Pamela was outside, smiling at him. Words were not exchanged as he let her inside, and she began to undress him. He undressed her, in turn. Soon they were both upon his bed, atop the covers. They laid together in a pool of light, the room around them dark.

Their limbs intertwined, and their hands explored the landscapes of each other's bodies. Billy squeezed her breast, amazed at how supple it was. It was so fun to fondle he never wanted to stop. His other hand slid down her belly and explored the fuzzy heat between her legs. Her hands explored him the same way, caressing his furry muscle butt and the peach fuzz over his taint. While it tickled, this was a sensation he didn't want to stop. Her other hand slid over his hard chest.

They moaned and groaned and sometimes laughed at a pleasurable sensation. This verbal expression was made manifest, and Billy moaned in his sleep.

Pamela marveled at the size of Billy's erection, and then she pulled him in for a deep kiss, his stiffness pressing up against her belly. That was too much sensation for him to bear, and he prematurely erupted, spraying her face. Pamela gasped and squealed with ecstasy, and he loved the affirmation.

Billy had achieved his orgasm hands free, without any digital stimulation.

Pamela looked over his sweaty shoulder and let out a blood-curdling scream. Billy looked back. A red-gloved hand shot out of the dark, holding a bloody switchblade knife. He didn't need to see any more of the attacker to know who this was.

Santa was here, and they were being naughty.

The switchblade punched into Billy's side beneath the armpit. With savage strength, Santa carved the blade down through his torso, opening his body with a rush of blood.

Billy cried out in his dream and real life, and the sound wrenched him out of his bloody wet nightmare.

"No!" Billy launched out of bed to get away from a threat that wasn't there. He backed up into a corner, shaking and sweating. Unaware he'd ejaculated in his sleep he mistook the substance dripping from his chin for blood.

Billy slid down into a crouch in the dark corner, shrinking

away from a threat that never went away, no matter the season. The pressure to not be naughty was a constant burden.

He saw that he was alone. The dream remained potent in his head, including the passion that preceded Santa's attack. Now those lustful thoughts of Pamela darkened. Those thoughts were bad, because those urges were bad, and Pamela was bad for putting those urges into him.

It was easier to misplace the blame onto her than accept his own shame. By extension, maybe those pornographic movies were also to blame for illustrating such naughtiness in explicit detail, giving him ideas, lustful ideas.

The degrees of this nightmare and his guilt were too heavy a burden to hold onto any longer. They'd already reduced him to this weak and broken victim cowering in the corner in the middle of the night, just as he had in his room in the orphanage, waiting for Mother Superior to burst through the door to punish him.

Punishment is good, Mother Superior echoed in his head.

Billy wrapped his arms around his upraised knees, curling up tight. He banged his head back against the wood paneling a couple times, trying to knock those terrible memories out of his head. Tears filled his eyes and spilled over.

"I wanna be good," Billy pleaded to a higher power, whether it was Santa, Mother Superior, or God he couldn't say.

In his memory, he remembered cowering in the orphanage like this after punching Santa Claus, and he remembered how he had begged that day.

"I didn't mean to be naughty. I'm sorry," Young Billy wept.

"Don't punish me," Adult Billy pleaded.

"Don't punish me, please," Young Billy begged.

If he didn't want to be punished and suffer in this debilitating fear, then that was up to him and him alone. It was his choice to be good or not.

It was easier to blame his urges than wrench free the claws of the shame-based abstinence campaigns that sunk into his flesh like Mother Superior's sharpened fingernails. That shame shifted from himself into blame onto others. It was others' fault for turning him on, tempting him, whether it was a co-worker who wore her sweaters too tight and showed off her cleavage, or the owners of the video store for renting those dirty video tapes, or the pornographers who put those obscene images on film in the first place. All of society was conspiring to make him naughty and cause him punishment.

Well, he would show them all.

From this point on, he would make major changes. He'd no longer seek a date with a co-worker or go beyond the beaded curtain into the Adults Only section at Ma & Pa's Video Palace. Nor would he masturbate. All that oppressive guilt he carried could be shed if he simply did not succumb to the temptations of his own flesh. Until he was married, he would not engage in any sexual activity whatsoever. Or even think such naughty thoughts.

With Billy's new mission of strict morality set, he quickly grew resentful of everyone else who could live and love freely without the shackles of shame he continually kept fastening to himself. Everyone noticed his demeanor worsen further.

Part of his resentment was the thought that his strict morality and chastity made him better than everyone else. They were weak while he was strong. They were wrong while he was right.

The abstinence campaigns instilled into him were creating the exact behavior they were designed for – total repression of natural sexual thought. He was a radicalized pressure cooker, and sooner than later it would cause him to explode. Instead of a joyful explosion of passion, it would be a violent explosion of rage.

CHAPTER 18

Inside Ira's Toys, it was the calm before the storm, though on that date of December 24, there were no storms in the forecast. A foot of snow had fallen over the prior week, so a white Christmas was guaranteed.

Mr. Sims and Mrs. Randall arrived early to set up for the most important shopping day of the year. Every Christmas Eve, to reward his staff for a season of great sales, he would close the store one hour early for a holiday party for employees and loved ones. This was always a binge-worthy affair, as Mr. Sims provided a bevy of sweets, party food, and strong drinks.

Mr. Sims and Mrs. Randall took pride in these parties and had a reputation for getting more than a little wild. The singing could get quite loud as inhibitions were shed. Alcohol played a major part in that.

As for their loved ones, they did not plan to attend this year. Mrs. Randall's son Chad had been to the parties in the past, and often ended up embarrassed by his mother's drunken antics. One year she got up atop a register counter to shake her fanny as she sang Christmas carols out of tune.

Far worse was the year she tried to ride a nodding animatronic reindeer like it was a mechanical bull. The reindeer didn't like that, shot a burst of sparks out of its mechanical asshole, and never went back on again. Chad was so embarrassed he wanted to crawl into a dark place out of sight, like maybe his mother's womb.

Chad was now thirteen and old enough to complain he didn't want to go. At the age where he didn't need a babysitter, he preferred an evening of privacy where he could spank it to a dog-eared Hustler magazine found in a neighborhood dumpster and take secret sips of his mother's booze stash. She drank too much to notice, he believed.

As for Mr. Sims' partner Terrance, he'd been on the wagon for over a decade, and he avoided shindigs where hard liquor flowed freely.

Soon after the store opened, Mr. Sims inspected a G.I. Joe Playset that was returned the day before due to a missing piece. Overturning the box, over a dozen plastic pieces fell onto the counter with folded directions which appeared to be written in Japanese. How was he to make sense of what piece was missing? It wasn't worth the hassle.

Mrs. Randall sauntered up on the other side of the counter wearing a shit-eating grin. That meant one thing, she'd already eaten a helping of crap and wanted to share the serving.

"Christmas Eve. Only one more day and this Christmas crap is history," Mr. Sims said.

"I hate to ruin your party mood, Mr. Sims, but a teensy problem has arisen personnel-wise."

Mr. Sims stuffed the plastic pieces back into the box, so he could tape it up and donate it to the church later with other returned but defective toys.

"Well, do something about it, solution-wise."

"It ain't that simple, Mr. Sims. I just got a call from one of the employees. It seems he went ice skating last night and broke his ankle. He'll be out for the remainder of the season."

"Lucky him. Call the temp agency and get a replacement. Do I have to think of everything around here?"

"Well then think of this," Mrs. Randall challenged, and the shit-eating grin remained on her smug face. "The agency's only got women. This job requires a person of the male persuasion." Mrs. Randall pointed at the sleigh.

Mr. Sims saw the sleigh was empty and understood what she was getting at.

That news tasted like shit all right. Santa Claus was absent on the day he was needed most. If they could not fill that sleigh quickly, Ira's Toys would be known as the toy store that ruined Christmas.

"Oh," Mr. Sims said.

"A fat jolly one," Mrs. Randall added. "Are you receiving me?"

"Oh, oh no," Mr. Sims said. He understood what she was getting at now. Not only was their star for the day absent, but she was implying he should get into the suit. Was she calling him fat?

"Ho-ho-ho, ha!" Mrs. Randall said teasingly. Sims could fit the store's suit, and he was the most age-appropriate for the role.

Billy was the only other name she entertained, but he was too young to play Santa. Also, he hadn't appeared to be his usual friendly self for weeks now, ever since the day he fell over into the ball display. She'd worked with enough people over the years to know that some reacted to the holidays with depression. This was Billy's first Christmas at the store, so that might well be the case with him. While he still got his work done, his genial side seemed to be on vacation. A gruff Santa that made kids cry would defeat the purpose.

Mr. Sims realized he needed to be part of the solution, and fast. There was already a half dozen children in the store eager to see the day's star attraction.

Within the stockroom, Billy was unpacking new products and checking them against the inventory count on his clipboard. There was plenty of work to keep him occupied throughout his shift, as the day following Christmas would require a hard restocking of the store.

Billy welcomed the work distraction. It was his heaviest day of the year, and with his job, he didn't have the luxury to hide at home under the covers until the date passed. At least busy work kept his mind off that terrible minefield of memories.

The shift wasn't without its difficulties, namely Andy, who'd been hounding him since the moment he clocked in.

The inventory check was both of their jobs, and there were boxes everywhere that needed unpacking. It didn't appear Andy was going to lift a finger to assist. At only 10:35 a.m., Andy was kicked back in his chair with his feet propped up on the desk, drinking from a can of Pepsi spiked with tequila.

"You pull another disappearing act like yesterday, Billy, and I'm going to go straight to Sims," Andy threatened.

Billy didn't take his eyes off his clipboard as he answered. "I didn't disappear yesterday."

"You constantly disappear, you just don't see it. You shut down as you stand around daydreaming. Or maybe you're up all night having wet dreams about Pamela."

Billy had to wonder whether Andy might be right. Was he falling into a stupor while on the job? If so, why was Andy the only one who harped about it? He didn't want to give credence to Andy's crude comment, and he had his own judgment to pass.

"I'm not the one who reads those dirty magazines on the job," Billy said, and he gave Andy a look that his secret was no longer safe with him.

Andy glared at Billy with beady eyes, and Billy turned back to his work.

"I don't think you realize this, but I'm giving you a break. That's a hell of a lot more than he'll do. Sims is nobody's friend. Remember that."

Andy got great satisfaction out of pressuring Billy and putting him down. Now he realized it might be time to get into Sims' head and get Billy fired.

The door pushed open, and Mr. Sims marched into the stockroom. Andy slid his shoes off the desktop and put his soda down, hoping Mr. Sims wouldn't smell the alcohol in the can.

"Ah, Mr. Sims," Andy announced.

Mr. Sims was all smiles, but they weren't for Andy. The boss marched up to Billy. Andy's face soured at being ignored.

"Billy boy, how are you?" Mr. Sims asked and gave Billy a friendly pat on the arm. "I've been meaning to come around and see how you're enjoying yourself."

Billy was surprised by his boss' good natured visit, which was in complete contrast to the negative picture Andy had just painted of him. Of them both.

"Well, everything okay?" Mr. Sims added with a wide smile, the kind he usually employed when selling something to customers.

Billy realized Mr. Sims' smile deserved one in return, and his face brightened. "Uh, yeah, yes, fine. Everything's fine, Mr. Sims."

Mr. Sims nodded with satisfaction. "Good. Good boy." Billy liked hearing that because that was how he modeled himself. The all-American good boy, totally righteous, beyond reproach.

Mr. Sims lifted and dropped his hands in a helpless gesture. "Ah, listen Bill, the reason I dropped by. I got a little problem maybe you could help me with. I mean if you like."

Andy looked ticked off by Mr. Sims' request, but nobody noticed. Why wasn't he being asked to help instead, since he had seniority?

"Of course, Mr. Sims. Anything you want. You just tell me what it is, and I'll be glad to help out."

And Billy meant it too. He liked Mr. Sims and wanted to help him in any way possible. Unless the boss asked him to do something bad like rob a bank, punch an elderly woman on the sidewalk, or pull a pigtail.

That kind of behavior was naughty.

Mr. Sims nodded with appreciation. "Good. Good boy. Thank you."

Billy's smile was genuine, and as automatic as a dog told he was a good boy. If he'd had a tail, it would be wagging.

"That's very good. Very realistic," Mr. Sims said, nodding with a smile of satisfaction. He stood just outside the stockroom door, Mrs. Randall at his side. She appeared just as delighted as he was.

"Isn't it, Mrs. Randall?"

"He's definitely fat and jolly," she agreed.

Mr. Sims and Mrs. Randall looked over Billy's shoulders from behind. They all observed his reflection in a tall mirror on the wall used by customers trying on the year-round supply of Halloween costumes. The supervisors admired Billy with glee.

Billy stared at his reflection with dread, although were anyone looking directly at his eyes, they might have claimed they were glazed over. His jaw was hanging slack, but nobody noticed behind the bushy white moustache and beard he wore.

His reflection was unrecognizable to him because who he saw was Santa Claus. Though he'd simply slipped on wool pants, an oversized jacket, red gloves, fake facial hair, and a stocking cap, the illusion was complete, and uncanny.

Mrs. Randall had called him fat and jolly, yet Billy was neither. Billy had no large gut, but his broad shoulders and muscles helped fill in the rest of the suit. A thick black belt was cinched high upon his waist. Small jingle bells circled the white fur cuffs of his jacket. The long white hair of his wig was attached to the moustache and beard with an elastic string. The tall black Santa boots seemed perfectly sized, as though he were meant to wear them.

Santa had never looked stronger.

Mr. Sims placed his hands upon Billy's shoulders and gave him a reassuring squeeze.

"Take a closer look at yourself in the mirror, Billy."

Good thing Mr. Sims ended his statement with his name, to remind him who he was. The vision of Santa in the mirror did not summon any flashbacks, at least not yet. He was Billy, and he was at Ira's Toys. It was Christmas Eve, 1984. The reason he was dressed like this was because it was his job.

Billy could have said no. But he'd made a promise to his boss to do whatever task he asked. The request was difficult for him, more than Mr. Sims could have imagined, but he didn't want to break his promise. A broken promise would be naughty.

So long as he remembered who he was, where he was, and what his job entailed, he believed he could get through the day. When he returned to work the day after Christmas, the red suit would be packed away until next December.

"And just remember, be jolly," Mr. Sims reminded him. "Lots of ho-ho-ho. And try not to scare the little bastards. Sometimes they cry their heads off. I guess they think the old guy's scary. Silly, isn't it?"

Billy knew all about those kids who found Santa scary. He looked deep into his own eyes in his reflection. So far, he could still recognize himself.

"Yeah. Silly," Billy said softly, trying to convince himself.

A line of children stood between stanchions from the sleigh to the front door of the store. Like Santa's lap, the line was for kids only. Their mothers watched from the other side of Santa's sleigh, supervising from a distance this rite of passage. Mr. Sims sauntered up beside the squadron of mothers to observe Billy's performance.

The children waited with remarkable patience, expecting their good behavior would be rewarded in Santa's gift giving. Well, all of them except for Dillon, who kept flicking boogers at the animatronic elves beyond the ropes. A few of his snot rockets landed. He also wiped a booger in the long hair of the girl in line before him.

God help him if Santa saw him being snotty and naughty.

Sitting on Billy's lap was a young girl wearing a plaid dress. She wasn't sitting so much as trying to squirm away. She looked like she might start bawling her eyes out. Not a good look in front of the boss.

"Stop it. Please stop it," Billy said softly to the girl, whose restlessness only increased. One red-gloved hand held her side, while the other clenched her thigh tightly. The distressed girl looked like she might try to launch off his lap at any moment. "What's the matter with you? Please stop it."

The scared girl began to whine loudly, and her legs kicked the air, eager to escape.

"Stop it. Stop kicking," Billy ordered the girl. Her struggle didn't cease.

Mr. Sims observed the child's disturbance with concern. A few of the mothers were more observant of how Santa filled his suit. This new Santa was giving them hot flashes. One mother in a low-cut dress ran a finger down her sweaty cleavage.

Mr. Sims was having a similar reaction. There was really nothing Billy could do on the job that he would criticize. Hell, the big boss man wanted to hop on Santa's lap, tell him he'd been very, very naughty, and offer his bottom for punishment.

Billy could not tolerate the girl's disobedience any longer. The girl should have been showing him gratitude.

"Do you have any idea what you're doing? You're being naughty," Billy said with authority. This was Santa's edict, but in his voice, he also heard Grandpa, who'd taught him a similar lesson.

"You're being naughty right on Santa's lap. I don't bring toys to naughty children."

The girl hadn't answered his original question of what she wanted for Christmas, but this threat of withholding toys caused her to ease her struggling a bit. Now she was listening.

While she feared Santa, the idea of no toys on Christmas was much more terrifying.

"I punish them. Severely. Now do you want to be naughty or nice?"

In deepening terror, the girl clutched her hands in front of her face.

"That's right. Stop it. Or I'll have to punish you," Santa hissed at her.

The girl stopped squirming. The tears that had threatened to fall had suddenly dried up.

The other children and their parents were too far away to hear the threat. What they saw were the results. This girl who'd been frightened to sit on Santa's lap was now well behaved.

The girl's mother nodded in appreciation. "He sure knows how to handle kids," she said aloud, and wished he were handling her instead.

"He's great, isn't he?" the woman nearest her replied, hoping Santa would pay her a late-night visit and sample her cookie.

Mr. Sims nodded and thought it might be time to give Billy a raise. That might help keep him around longer.

Santa's message had been delivered, and he handed the girl a candy cane. Once the girl hopped off his lap, she ran over to her mother. "Mommy," the girl whined as she clutched her mom's leg tightly.

The store phone rang atop the desk in the stockroom.

Andy was incensed he had to do the entire inventory

count alone, a massive workload, while Billy got to sit on his ass all day in a padded sleigh. He'd confronted Mr. Sims before Billy slipped into the Santa suit and said he wanted to do it, but the boss laughed off his suggestion.

"You can't play Santa. Maybe one of his elves," Mr. Sims snickered.

Andy's nose crinkled and his lips pursed, and it took all his self-control not to sock Mr. Sims in his kisser.

Andy sauntered his way to the phone. "I'm coming, I'm coming! Christ! Keep your head on!" There was nobody around to hear him bitch, but he liked the sound of his own whining. The clipboard was slammed onto the desk before he grabbed the receiver.

"Ira's Toys stockroom, Andy speaking."

The woman's voice on the line was so soft he had a hard time understanding who she was asking for.

"Who?"

"I'm looking for Billy Chapman, who works in the stockroom," Sister Margaret replied on the line.

A grin spread on Andy's face. "No, no, Billy don't work back here no more." He pulled out the chair to take a seat.

"Can you tell me where he does work now?" Sister Margaret asked with concern.

"Sure, sure. I can tell you his new job." Andy kicked his shoes up onto the desk with satisfaction, bully satisfaction. While he'd asked to don the suit earlier, the fact that Billy now wore it would be a source of bullying for him.

"Ho-ho-ho. He's playing Santy Claus for a bunch of

snot-nosed kids." He cackled like that was a shameful thing.

The store Santa Claus, Sister Margaret thought with dread. There was no more to say to the crass man on the line. The phone receiver was removed from her ear and lowered back into its cradle.

She could hardly think. She could hardly blink. Sitting behind Mother Superior's desk, she experienced a low-level shock that brought an intense wave of emotion.

No, not her Billy. He could not be Santa Claus. That was not healthy for him, not at all. And how were they to know that? No one at Ira's Toys knew how he'd suffered as a child, exactly thirteen years ago to the day. How could they? Nobody ever told them.

She never told them.

Guilt landed like an anvil upon her head. So much of Billy's predicament was her fault. It was her effort that got him the job in a store that had a seasonal Santa Claus on the premises. It stood to reason that employees had to fill that suit. And her Billy was a big man.

The ignorance she'd exhibited astounded her. Could she ever forgive herself? Would Billy?

She'd inadvertently put Billy into that Santa suit. What could she do to help him now? She thought of Captain Richards, who brought Billy to her in the first place.

It was just after 4 p.m. Captain Richards' number was on file in their rolodex, on a card she'd filled out on Christmas, 1971. She hoped the number was still current. It was, but it was his recording she received. The message she left was vague, but she said it was urgent she speak with him right away.

Her following call was to the police station, and they informed her he took Christmas Eve off every year. She understood his reasoning for that.

What Sister Margaret didn't know was Captain Richards was four and a half miles away, drinking his dark anniversary memories away with the hardest proof rot gut they served at The Kickstand, a dive biker bar on the edge of town. He would stumble out drunk and drooling just after 8 p.m. that night and pass out in the front seat of his car until he was woken up after 2 a.m., marinating in the piss he'd unleashed in his pants.

Three hundred sixty-four days of the year he didn't touch alcohol and was the most capable captain the town could hope to have. Christmas Eve was the date this did not apply. Captain Richards would be useless to himself and the entire town tonight when they needed him most.

It wasn't until just after 6 p.m. when Sister Margaret came up with another plan. Perhaps she could sneak out and drive to Ira's Toys and be Billy's savior. Why, she'd even stay at his bedside overnight if he needed her to.

Sister Margaret didn't own a car, nor did she have cash on her for a taxi. The solution she arrived at was not ideal, but it was the only one she had.

She would have to steal Sister Ellen's car. This did not seem like a sin to her, because she was doing it to save Billy.

CHAPTER 19

Just as the sun went down that evening, a freezing wind brought in heavy storm clouds that carried a cargo of snow. This had not been in the forecast. A similar miscalculation had occurred exactly thirteen years ago.

Ira's Toys was the brightest business on the block with the Christmas lights that lined the windows and dotted the wreath on the door. The painted windows kept hidden from public view the festivities inside. At 7 p.m., the closed sign was put into the window one hour early.

On the other side of the doors, Mr. Sims used his key to lock the deadbolt.

"Seven o'clock. It's over! Time to get shit-faced! Ah-hahaha!" Mr. Sims announced loudly, giving voice to his Christmas fatigue.

A cheer erupted from the dozen employees gathered after hours for the Christmas party. There was no gift giving except for the party itself, Mr. Sims' gift to his dedicated team.

During the past half hour, as customers slowed to a

trickle, Mrs. Randall and the other employees helped to bring out the ice buckets, chips, dips, nuts, and napkins, spreading them on the long empty checkout counters. With the doors locked, Mr. Sims pulled out three bottles of wine, a bottle of whiskey, and an extra-large bottle of vodka.

The music over the loudspeakers was changed to more danceable pop music, which got Pamela shaking her shoulders to the beat. Andy and Mrs. Randall arrived from the back carrying refreshments. A small toy Santa danced in Andy's free hand.

"Merry Christmas, Helen! How about a cheap thrill?" Andy asked in a high-pitched doll voice. The rest of the staff were about to get their drink on, but Andy had been taking shots since before noon. Already three sheets to the wind, he hoped the others would get drunk fast, so they didn't notice.

Mr. Sims broke the seal of the whiskey bottle, unscrewed the cap, poured a shot into his plastic cup, and downed the drink with gusto.

The staff was gathered around the checkout counters except for Billy, who observed from the seat of Santa's sleigh. The party antics were of little interest to him. Partying was not something he was accustomed to.

Though all the children had departed, Billy remained in full costume, the wig and beard upon his head. One question had him completely preoccupied.

Who am I?

Ever since he'd put on the suit and seen Santa looking

back at him in his reflection, his mind was clouded with confusion. It'd been easy enough to adapt to the work, which wasn't all that hard.

After he scared that first crying girl into submission, he began to like his job. With every child he inquired whether they were naughty or nice. All of them said they were nice, but inevitably some of them were lying about it. Those he suspected of lying he gave his speech about punishment. The same spiel he received from Grandpa on this day in 1971 he preached throughout the day like it was gospel.

He could relate to Grandpa much more now. There was satisfaction in striking fear of Santa into kids.

As the day went on, a curious thing happened. Billy lost the fear and apprehension that plagued him throughout the holiday season. Most of that anxiety was due to the ever-heavy presence of Santa Claus, who was always watching and eager to pass judgment. But today he was Santa Claus, he'd seen so in the mirror. The alleviation of this fear had a monumentally freeing effect upon him.

Along with his loss of fear came a sense of confidence. He felt as if he was finally able to take a deep breath of fresh air after being confined within a dusty closet for years.

In his own skin, he felt vulnerable, guilty, and afraid. In Santa's suit, he felt all powerful.

Billy snapped out of his deep introspection as somebody stepped up to him. It was Pamela, and she wore a welcoming smile.

"Hey, Santa Claus. Come join the party!" She had finally

warmed up to him again. She'd always been into men in uniforms, and this suit made Billy appear older.

She didn't ask for Billy, she asked for Santa Claus. This he took as further confirmation of who he was. The name fit the suit and his job position, and by extension, his identity.

Billy stood without a word and stepped out of the sleigh. Pamela led him to the refreshment counters and his co-workers. He pulled the beard down, so it held underneath his chin.

"Santa Claus! Come on over here," Mr. Sims declared. Being addressed as Santa by his boss made Billy's illusion solidify further.

Billy and Pamela stopped at the end of the aisle, and Mr. Sims handed a plastic cup with red wine to each of them.

"There you go," Mr. Sims said. Pamela responded to the wine with exuberance. Billy responded with a grimace. Although Santa was ancient, Billy was not, and he remained aware he wasn't of legal age to consume alcohol.

Mr. Sims was asking him to do something that was naughty. And he knew better.

"I've never had this before," Billy said to let Mr. Sims know he was not a drinker. Outside his view, a few employees including Andy snickered at Billy's inexperience.

Already spinning from two quickly downed shots of whiskey, Mr. Sims didn't notice Billy's hesitation. "Stick with me, kid. By the time this party's over, you'll think you really are Santa Claus!"

Billy turned his uncertain gaze to Pamela. She gave him

a nod to assure him it was okay to take a drink, taking a sip herself.

Now Pamela was doing the same thing as Mr. Sims, encouraging him to be bad.

Billy tentatively brought the cup up to his lips and tipped it back. The wine touched his lips but went no further. He feigned his first drink.

Everyone seemed fooled, and they paid less attention as he followed his first non-sip with another, selling the illusion that he was drinking.

Mr. Sims and Mrs. Randall broke into song. "We wish you a merry Christmas, we wish you a merry Christmas…" Mrs. Randall waved a plastic fork like a conductor's wand in one hand while trying to balance her drink in the other.

Everyone joined in the song, except for Billy. Though he knew the words, he was feeling in no way merry or bright, and he couldn't lie about it. He mouthed the words silently, selling another illusion.

Did he really wish them a merry Christmas, or did he wish for them to get the punishment they deserved?

Standing on the other side of Pamela was Andy, and he wasn't singing at all. Instead, he was whispering into her ear. His grin was slick, and whatever he told her made her smile. He nodded toward the back of the store, lifted a mistletoe, and gave it a jiggle.

Billy knew what that mistletoe was for, and it made him jealous.

Whatever Andy was saying convinced Pamela to take his

hand, and he led her away up an aisle toward the stockroom.

Billy's eyes narrowed into condemnatory slits.

"Good tidings to you, wherever you are. We wish you a merry Christmas and a happy New Year," the staff sang with jubilance.

Billy was about to follow the absconding couple, but Mrs. Randall caught his attention.

"Cheers!" she announced and began a toast. This was another first for Billy, and he toasted the others with a cup that remained just as full of wine as when it was first poured.

By 8 p.m., the unexpected clouds over Christmas Joy had unloaded most of their cargo, and only a smattering of snowflakes drifted in the air.

The party continued inside Ira's Toys, although a few employees had trickled out after a few drinks. Billy was among those that remained. The same cup of room temperature wine remained in his hand. Nobody questioned him about this or tried to pour him another.

Much of the time he was talking with Mrs. Randall, or more correctly, she was talking at him. The woman grew louder the more she drank, but she was loud when she wasn't drinking too. Mrs. Randall was so unlike the Sisters at the orphanage, and so unlike his mother had been. It was refreshing to see a woman so animated and unreserved, but it was exhausting to stay on her level.

Even with such distractions, his mind wandered to his

mother and father frequently, as was the case every year on this night. The loss felt as heavy and profound now as it had back in the early 1970s. That was the kind of grief that never really went away. Though he thought of losing them, he did not consider the how. He lost them on the road he often told himself, a terrible accident.

This Christmas Eve work celebration was the first adult party he'd attended, where the goal of most of the attendees was getting shamefully drunk. Because he wasn't used to party etiquette, he didn't know how long he was supposed to stay. Did he need to be excused by the boss first? Over half the employees had departed already. Pamela was still here, somewhere in the back with Andy.

The truth was, he didn't want to take off the Santa suit yet. It wasn't just that it felt cozy, like a comfort blanket on a cold winter's night. The suit simply felt... *right*. Like it was tailored for him. Even the boots were perfectly sized.

Mrs. Randall went to refill her drink and got to gabbing with Mr. Sims, rather loudly. Without anyone paying attention to him, Billy wandered back to where Andy led Pamela. Looking down the aisle he saw them standing before the door to the stockroom, passionately making out. These were no modest pecks on the lips. It appeared they were devouring each other.

Unaware of the history between Pamela and Andy, Billy assumed he was taking advantage of her. What was worse was she'd been drinking, and perhaps unable to make clear decisions for herself. What stopped him from marching over to pull Andy off her was the degree to which she was enjoying it.

His resentment grew, towards them both, and towards the naughty world. He was the good boy. Why were the sinful ones rewarded, while the most righteous one was left wanting?

His contempt for his co-workers grew, with their partying ways and bad behavior – drinking on the job, profanity, lustful actions in the aisles. From his rising position of moral superiority, the loose and immoral ways of his peers sickened him.

With a growing surge of moralism, he was basically fighting the tides against himself. This rising wave of harsh judgment of others and the anger it summoned was wholly unlike the young man who had distanced himself from the church and their teachings. Now he was acting more akin to the extremely devout.

He was thinking like Mother Superior, deliverer of punishment. He was Santa Superior. That kind of power tripping was addictive.

Which version of himself would rise to the surface, and which one would be drowned? Was there anyone who could throw him a life vest to keep him afloat? Somebody sober enough to remind him who he was?

Mr. Sims staggered his way. Good thing there wasn't a drink in his hand because every drop would have spilled. When Mr. Sims came to a stop, he grabbed Billy's arm with both hands to retain his balance.

"Hey! Hey Santa Claus! Whatcha' doin'?" Mr. Sims slurred, then let go of Billy's arm. He stepped back to lean against the register counter, which helped to keep him upright.

"I was thinking about my parents," Billy admitted.

Mr. Sims clapped loudly, then slapped Billy on his shoulder. "Oh good! Good! That's fine. A boy should think about his parents at Christmas," he barely managed to say in a coherent manner.

"They're dead," Billy said softly, his eyes not on his boss but on his bitter past.

Mr. Sims covered his face with shame. "Oh, I'm sorry." His embarrassment quickly turned to exuberance. "Hey Santa! You better sober up. You got a long night ahead of you!" This Mr. Sims followed with a gale of laughter.

Billy was genuinely confused. "Huh?"

"Well, you remember what Santa Claus does on Christmas Eve, dontcha?"

Once again, Mr. Sims had confirmed that he was Santa. That name felt right to him. And he did know what Santa Claus did on Christmas Eve because Grandpa taught him well.

All the naughty ones, he punishes.

"Yeah. Yeah, I know what he does," Billy replied.

"Better get started!" Mr. Sims got a case of the spins, and he put a hand to his dizzy head as he repeated himself. "Ah, you better get started."

You better get started with the punishment, was how Billy heard him.

Mr. Sims glanced around the store.

"Fuckin' party's dead anyway." Mr. Sims slapped Billy in the arm. *"Go get 'em, Santa! Go get 'em."*

Mr. Sims lost interest in his drinking buddy and wandered off.

Mr. Sims' order echoed in his head. Go get 'em, Santa!

Billy looked to the side down the aisle. Andy and Pamela were no longer kissing, but he was sweettalking her and nodding at the Employees Only door. Whatever he said worked because she led him by the hand toward it. He put a hand on her back as she led him into the stockroom.

An animatronic Santa beside Billy nodded his head up and down. Santa instinctively knew who was being naughty and who was being nice.

It took Andy some time to get Pamela alone in the stockroom. Luckily, he got to suck face with her plenty first to loosen her up. His intentions were not pure, but Pamela wasn't pure, either. His own nickname for her was Easy Pam. Perhaps he'd start calling her that to his drinking buddies after tonight.

It was all too easy to seduce her, especially after she'd had a few drinks. All he had to do was tell her how much she resembled Madonna. Like most women, she was a sucker for a compliment. Hopefully she'd be a swallower for one too.

The overhead fluorescent lights were off, but a few spotlights and the strings of Christmas lights that ringed the stockroom and shelves were still blinking. Pamela was unnerved by the darker room, which was not quite so welcoming with so many pockets of shadow. You really needed more light to safely maneuver through without tripping over a box or bicycle.

She'd enjoyed making out with Andy again, though she was reluctant to take it further than that. Andy was lacking when it came to intimacy. He had little stamina and cared only about his own pleasure.

He'd told her he had a special Christmas gift for her but wanted to present it to her in private. What girl didn't want a nice present?

"If you got me a present, Andy, I don't see why you just don't bring it out there where everybody can see it."

Andy chuckled. The surprise he had was for her only, and it was currently hidden behind his zipper. He tenderly took her hand.

"Pammy, this particular present isn't for everybody to see. It's something I've been wanting to give you for a long time."

This revelation brought a smile to her face, which happened every time a man made her feel special.

"Come on, it's right back there." Andy pointed at one of the dark aisles.

Pamela was hesitant. Andy raised the mistletoe again and shook it. Some mistletoe to get into her camel toe. "Hey, trust me, huh?" He leaned in and gave her a kiss. "You're gonna love it." So would he when she had a hand or mouthful of his present. Nobody could claim he wasn't giving for the holiday.

"Come on," Andy said and gave her hand a tug. As he led her forward, she didn't see him slowly unzip his pants.

It wasn't Pamela absconding with another man that angered Billy, but rather his overwhelming judgment of them being naughty and his growing desire to mete out punishment. How else were they to learn if they weren't punished?

He was a one-man Moral Majority, and he felt it was his business what consenting adults did behind closed doors.

Billy was watching.

At a checkout counter, Mrs. Randall and Mr. Sims joined in drunken disharmony on a popular carol from the early 1970s, one with a local history.

"Santa's watching, Santa's creeping. Now you're nodding, now you're sleeping. Were you good for mom and dad? Santa knows if you've been bad."

Billy took the lyrics of "Santa's Watching" to be about him specifically. They were reminding him what his purpose was tonight. He set his cup of wine on a counter. There was no longer any need to sell the illusion.

He stepped into the aisle, away from his caroling co-workers. His eyes were strained on the door ahead, as though he were trying to see through it. That was one of Santa's special talents. He was all-seeing.

Billy was creeping.

"Ooooh, Santa's watching, Santa's waiting. Christmas Eve is slowly fading…"

There was a drunken lull in the song as both carolers struggled to remember the words. When Mrs. Randall jumped back in, she was chuckling. She may have been wasted, but she was a cheerful drunk.

"Can you hear him in the night? Close the doors, turn out the lights."

Reaching the door, Billy slowly pushed it open with a red-gloved hand. The singing continued behind him.

"Too late now, 'cause Santa's here!"

Billy stepped into the stockroom.

As the swinging door settled closed behind him, Billy let his eyes adjust to the low lighting. He knew the stockroom as well as his own apartment, maybe better, and the Christmas lights were twinkling to guide him. There was nobody visible, but he heard Pamela's voice.

"Hey, stop it."

Billy crept toward the far aisle, as quiet as a mouse.

Pamela issued a stream of protestations. "Come on, don't do that. Uh-uh, no. Come on, let's go back now."

From the sound of it, Andy was being naughty. Billy really wanted to punish him. Every shift Andy did something that would put him on Santa's naughty list.

"Andy, stop it! Please Andy, no!" Pamela exclaimed forcefully. "Come on, let's go back."

Billy turned left, and they came into view.

Between stacks of boxes at the end of the aisle, Andy and Pamela were in an embrace. This was no tender hug. Andy's hands were clamped on Pamela's sides tightly, holding her in place. His face was buried in her neck, kissing her desperately. His lips were trying to work lower into her cleavage.

Yes, Andy was being bad. But he wasn't the only one.

Despite her protestations, Pamela had a hand on the bulging crotch of his jeans.

"Don't, no!" Pamela exclaimed in protest though her body language said *please, continue*. At least that's how Santa saw it.

Andy squeezed her breasts through her low-cut blouse. She was playing hard to get into, and he was tired of waiting. He was also too drunk to give a fuck.

Gripping her shirt tightly, he ripped it open so hard all the buttons flew off, revealing her bare breasts.

Pamela couldn't believe this was happening to her. What her mind focused on were the sounds, the buttons hitting boxes and tinkling upon the tile floor. Breaking the silence was Andy's lurid snickering. That awful laugh outraged her.

Pamela slapped Andy's face hard. The chuckle was knocked out of his mouth.

Billy took one step forward, prepared to interfere, but sudden fear and uncertainty stopped him, making him feel helpless. A tear ran down his face.

Andy rubbed his reddened cheek. Well, if she wanted to play with pain, he could deliver it back. And he would enjoy it.

"You goddamn little bitch," Andy hissed through gritted teeth, and he lunged forward, seizing Pamela by her arms. He shoved her back onto large boxes of stock and quickly followed, mounting her. While holding her arms down over her head, he buried his face in her breasts.

Suddenly gasping for air with the weight of Andy upon her, she squealed and managed to get one word out, the simplest word that men like Andy refused to heed.

"No."

What Billy was witnessing was a sexual assault, the third one in his lifetime. The last one was seen through a keyhole at the orphanage, with Mother Superior as the assaulter. The first one had been on the road thirteen years ago on this night. This scene repelled him back, and he was stopped as his back jammed against the wooden support of the stock shelves.

Shock slammed into him. There was absolutely no sight worse for him to witness than this. Especially tonight.

Suddenly, Billy's mind was filled with his mother screaming *"No!"* from the front seat of the station wagon. As quickly as it appeared, the vision cut off, and he saw Pamela's assault again.

Pamela let out a shriek. Though Andy was turned on by the sound of women crying and protesting, he needed her silent. He clamped a hand over her mouth. His mouth took in her right nipple and sucked hard. If she didn't stop her squirming, he would bite it.

Billy trembled and sweat ran down his face along with helpless tears, both saturating the beard hanging from his chin. Now he remembered what made his mother scream in fear that night on the cold country road. Then he saw it, another clear flash of memory, just as he saw it outside the side window that awful night.

A gun rising in Santa's hand, the gun that would kill his father.

To fully score with Pamela, Andy needed access. Her mouth and arm were released so he could yank her skirt up and panties down. This wasn't easy with the way she was struggling.

Pamela released another cry, louder than before. "No!" It occurred to her nobody up front was likely to hear her through their soused sing-along. Doom enveloped her as she resigned herself to this terrible fate.

Billy was besieged with a flood of flashbacks in quick succession. Each one more horrible than the last. Through it all, he heard Pamela's despairing squeals as Andy roughly forced himself inside her.

The gun in Santa's hand firing.

The windshield shattering with a web of cracks.

His mother screaming in the passenger seat with horror.

Young Billy running from the car toward cover on the side of the road.

Santa searching for him while screaming, *Where are you, ya little bastard?*

The driver's door opening, his dad falling out onto the road with his face in bloody ruins.

His mother squealing in terror as Santa wrenched her out of the car.

His mother struggling on the hard asphalt with Santa atop her.

His mother's blouse ripping wide open, revealing her breasts.

Santa punching his mother senseless.

Unbeknownst to Billy, he was biting the inside of his lips so hard they bled, and he swallowed the blood. The flashbacks continued their graphic retelling of his traumatic history.

The switchblade clicking open in Santa's hand.

Moonlight glinting off the upheld blade.

Santa's maniacal eyes looking down.

The switchblade carving an arc downward.

His mother's neck separating as the switchblade slowly sliced through it.

Upon that most awful memory, Billy's mind separated from his sanity. He'd lived in fear of this incident for too long, worrying every day and judging every action by whether Santa Claus would punish him for it. A flood of guilt accompanied this terror, because both his flashback and the assault before him had helpless women with their breasts bared, and these visions aroused him.

The next flashback rocked him.

Santa laughing maniacally after committing murder.

In the guise of Santa, his fear evaporated. He wasn't that frightened boy fleeing in terror. He was wearing Santa's suit, Santa's cap upon his head, which he thought of as a crown. All day long, young kids sat upon his lap and called him Santa while he scared the fear of punishment into them. That was a satisfying way to feel. It sure beat him being the frightened one.

He was Santa, Mr. Sims had said so himself. His boss had asked him if he knew what Santa Claus did on Christmas Eve. Why yes, he did know, because his next flashback showed him.

The switchblade dripping with fresh blood.

Santa's job was to punish the naughty. And that punishment was murder.

A voice echoed in his head.

Punishment is absolute. Punishment is necessary. Punishment is good.

Mother Superior's mantra and Santa's mission were identical. He often saw the two combined as one: Santa Superior.

It was his job to deliver punishment tonight, all across town.

His radicalization was complete. The years of unresolved trauma of his parents' deaths mixed with the soul-breaking Catholic guilt built through years of religious trauma, abuse, and abstinence indoctrination proved to be a lethal cocktail. Not for him, but for those in his vicinity, those in his judgmental sight.

He'd gone from a God complex to a Santa complex. He knew the Ten Commandments but didn't care. God's Law meant nothing to him now. Santa's Law was all that mattered. Even God could be naughty if Santa deemed it so.

The white beard and hat were a mask eclipsing his identity, even to himself. This mask tethered him to the holiday, and made him the holiday legend, the Christmas myth. The illusion fed his delusion that he was the holiday avenger. Billy's Santa suit now took on the equivalence of an Executioner's hood, or a Ku Klux Klan robe, or a Nazi uniform. They were all costumes for self-righteous murderers.

This had long been his destiny. He'd been such a good boy for so long, there was nobody else pure enough to become Santa. Santa Superior was no more because he saw himself standing above Mother Superior in judgment. She'd been naughty too, very, very naughty. Mother Superior abused children. She abused him.

He was Santa Billy now. The realization brought a grin to his face.

At the moment he lost his sanity, his personality split into two. A segment of Billy remained. This was Young Billy, running to the side of the road to hide. Young Billy would always be peering through those prickly, icy bushes, a horrified witness to Santa's menacing rampage. In truth, he'd never left this vulnerable spot since the night of the original crime. Barely concealed in hiding, he couldn't shout out, or even cry, lest the tears turn to jagged ice upon his cheeks.

"You're a little tease, huh?" Andy seethed as Pamela struggled. He really didn't understand why she couldn't just hold still and enjoy it.

These words brought Billy back to where he was inside Ira's Toys. He witnessed what was happening before him, the assault. Yet he didn't see it the same anymore.

Tonight, Andy had taken his bad behavior to a new level. It was obvious that he was stinking drunk and forcing Pamela into fornication.

But Pamela had been drinking on the job, and she'd encouraged underage alcohol consumption. Plus, she'd made moves on Andy, kissing him passionately, leading him into the stockroom, squeezing his crotch. And if all that weren't enough, she wasn't even wearing a bra!

Yes, she was most definitely being naughty.

As he thought of Pamela's sexual transgressions and

witnessed her violation, he was getting excited inside Santa's slacks. As with every other hypocritical religious moralist eager to cast damnations, he'd developed a misogynist mindset, seeing women in charge of their sexuality as immoral whores deserving of punishment. Women were guilty for turning him on. His credo could now be *Abstinence Or Die*. The Catholic Church had force fed these beliefs to him for years, and he'd spit them out before, but tonight he swallowed the poison entirely.

There were personal vendettas in play in his mission tonight. His Santa was not just unleashing patriarchal violence upon younger generations to reinforce repressive, old-fashioned mores. Billy's Santa aimed to punish his peers and older generations for the systemic violence they visited upon him as a ward of an uncaring state and abusive religious institution.

The town had failed Billy. He was shamed if he spoke out about his parents' deaths, because the truth was an uncomfortable reminder of events the town wanted to not just forget, but erase. Mass murder by a Santa Claus on a public road was not good for business in the holiday paradise of Christmas Joy.

The entire town had done him wrong. Christmas Joy had been very naughty.

Christmas Eve was well underway, and he had a lot of work to accomplish before dawn. He had a Naughty List, and he would be judge, jury, and executioner.

Santa Billy stepped forward to deliver punishment.

CHAPTER

Santa's Naughty List existed in his mind, appearing as a scroll of ancient parchment. The first name appeared on the list, written in cursive with classic flourish as though penned with a quill. The name appeared in red since the ink was blood.

The first name was Andy.

Andy was about thirty seconds away from nutting – it was incredible he'd lasted over two minutes – but he would not get his Christmas wish. There was a roar of rage over his shoulder.

"Naughty!"

Andy's shoulder was seized, and he was wrenched back off Pamela. His feet were barely upon the floor again when a second hand grabbed ahold of him, and he was quickly spun to face his attacker.

Andy saw Santa Claus.

His vision was a blur as he was shoved backward. The back of his head slammed against a wooden ladder mounted on the wall. There was a crack, whether from the ladder or his cranium he wasn't sure.

With Andy's weight removed, Pamela pulled up her legs protectively and scooted back atop the boxes until her back was against a stock shelf. She felt vulnerable and exposed, grabbing the sides of her buttonless blouse to hold them closed.

Santa Billy considered removing his wide leather belt to use against Andy. He knew from personal experience how a belt was used for punishment. Only the punishment he had in mind for Andy went way beyond paddling his bare bottom until it was rosy red.

A string of blinking Christmas lights lining the wall caught Santa Billy's attention. The lights were celebratory, but so was this occasion, his first Christmas Eve punishment spree.

Santa Billy grabbed the cord of lights and looped them around Andy's neck. After yanking the twinkling noose tightly, Santa Billy wrapped the cord around his right hand. His short inventory supervisor was lifted off the ground.

As Pamela watched Andy get assaulted, she felt a twinge of satisfaction and then concern. If Billy kept this up much longer, he might hurt Andy badly.

Andy's eyes bulged in shock. He'd been in the throes of passion, and the next moment he was in the throes of impending death. His grunts of joy were now desperate gasps for air.

Andy's instinctual response should have been fighting back, but his booze-soaked brain couldn't even comprehend how to catch his next breath. One of the bulbs pinched between the cord and his neck shattered, and the shards sank into his flesh. The rest of the lights on the cord continued to merrily twinkle.

Santa Billy was sweating, less from the physical exertion than from pure excitement. He was doing it, he was *punishing!*

It felt good to live up to his full potential. There was nothing and no one that he feared. This was his reward for being so good that nobody else on Earth could be Santa other than him. He had the strength and the power. His heart was racing, and his blood was pumping hard. He was also erect and excited to the point where he was wet.

Andy's legs kicked, hanging a foot over the floor. His shoes tried to find a surface but could only hit boxes. His eyes bulged harder as pressure built within his cranium, like his brain was filling with blood. Santa's blurry face was all he saw, while a dim realization occurred that the stupid young stockboy was doing this to him. As for why, he didn't understand that at all.

Desperate gasps added vocals to the murder jingle coming from the silver bells that ringed the cuffs of Santa Billy's jacket. Soon those gasps became a wheeze and then no sound came from Andy at all. This murder jingle had lost its soloist.

To ensure punishment was complete, Santa Billy let Andy dangle longer, like the world's biggest tree ornament. Blood from the bulb piercing Andy's neck ran around the cord and spilled onto the floor. Though he'd been raging hard just a minute ago, Andy's dick had shriveled into nothing more than a button poking out of his open pants, like a timid mouse peeking its snout out of a hole in the wall.

Satisfied that Andy's punishment was complete, Santa Billy

released the cord and his cargo. Andy dropped to his knees like an altar boy in prayer, only his time for asking forgiveness was over. He fell forward onto his face. The string of lights fell back against the wall and kept twinkling with one less bulb.

Whimpering drew Santa Billy's attention. Pamela sat defensively in the corner between the wall and stock shelves, weeping in distress. That wasn't necessary anymore. Andy would never rape her again.

"I had to punish him, Pamela."

Pamela quivered under his intense stare. She'd been mad at Andy, yeah, but she didn't want him dead. This wasn't just grody, it was grody to the max!

"Don't… please…" Pamela whined.

Santa Billy was perplexed by her reaction. She should have been thanking him for saving her.

"He deserved it."

A red-gloved hand extended forward to stroke Pamela's tousled hair. She recoiled from his touch.

"Don't touch me! Get away!" Pamela cried, and she smacked his hand away. This action caused her ruined blouse to fall open, revealing her heaving breasts. Sitting there so fully exposed, she didn't even try to cover herself up, like a good girl should. She was tempting him.

Naughty.

She was asking for punishment.

The name Pamela appeared next on Santa's Naughty List in red letters.

"Oh God, you're crazy," Pamela whined.

She was wrong about that because he was greater than God. He was Santa.

"Stop it, Pamela."

"You bastard! You're crazy! Get the hell away from me!" Pamela cried out, and then she surprised him as she leapt forward off the boxes, beating him with both of her arms. Why, she hadn't fought like this when Andy was assaulting her. That meant she *liked it*.

Santa Billy seized Pamela by her forearms, shoving her back into the stock shelves.

Pamela was momentarily stunned. She thought this was bogus. Totally. Her co-worker had turned into a freakazoid!

Santa Billy had Pamela cornered. Andy could not get away from him, and neither would she. Once someone's name was on his list, they were his. Her punishment needed to be different, however. Punishment was like snowflakes, no two would be exactly alike.

Santa Billy grabbed a box cutter with its razor blade extended from a nearby stock shelf.

"You shouldn't talk like that. It's naughty."

Pamela tried to make a run for it, but all she did was run right into Santa Billy's grip. He held her in place by her shoulder.

"Punishment is necessary, Pamela. It is GOOD!"

To prove his point, he used the point of the box cutter, punching it hard into her stomach. Pamela's eyes bulged open with agonized disbelief. Her right hand gripped his baggy left sleeve, holding on for dear life. Tears streamed down her face, at least they would escape if she could not.

He opened Pamela like he opened his stock boxes, cutting up in a straight line. The blade continued between her breasts. This would never have happened if she'd just worn a bra. Hot blood rushed down her belly. She heard that terrible murder jingle from the bells on his sleeves, but this was far worse because the murder was hers.

Pamela shook her head as she looked up at her killer. Only she looked through him, at the life she would be denied. She'd never hear "Like A Virgin" again. She'd never watch MTV again. The last thing she saw before her world turned off was the glowing face of her savior, her Material Girl.

Santa's sleeve was released as Pamela collapsed onto the bloody floor. With her stomach opened wide, her punctured, stinking intestines oozed out, proving this material girl was made of shit and offal like everyone else.

Upon Pamela's death, Santa Billy orgasmed in his pants, hands free. His fluid ran down his leg and joined the blood on the cold concrete floor.

This was Santa Billy's reward for delivering good punishment. He wore a grin of satisfaction and pride.

Watching these executions unfold with horror was Young Billy, peeking through the roadside branches. This terrible scene in the stockroom mimicked the one he'd witnessed on the road in 1971. First the man was murdered, and then the woman with her boobs bared. It made no difference that the man sexually assaulting this woman was a bad man. Murder was messy and disturbing no matter the recipient.

Two murders were all he'd witnessed thirteen years ago.

That would not be the case tonight. Young Billy could only watch helplessly as this new sinister Saint Nick continued his reign of Yuletide terror.

Santa Billy retracted the blade into the box cutter and pocketed the tool into his jacket. He did not remain empty handed for long.

A curved claw hammer was retrieved from another stock shelf.

The Christmas party was deemed a success by the party hosts. It was also the last Christmas party Ira's Toys would ever have.

Success was judged by the number of shots slammed, the number of Christmas songs sung, and the number of laughs shared. Mr. Sims and Mrs. Randall had lost count of all those numbers.

They'd been a legitimate power couple for over a decade, and likely more prosperous because there was no sexual tension between them. They had no offspring together, but the success of Ira's Toys was the fruit of their labors. It helped that consumerism seemed to be one of the defining characteristics of the decade.

The year of 1984 was the most profitable in the store's history, so they partied harder than ever in celebration. Mr. Sims' drunken mind spun to Billy and how well he fit in the role of Santa, soothing the noisy brats into submission. Perhaps he'd make Billy the store Santa all season next year.

After Mr. Sims left Billy's side, he found Mrs. Randall

singing a Christmas tune while doing a jig and waving an empty wine bottle around. When it came to the yearly Christmas party, they always drank each other under the table, or in their case, under the register counter. Tonight, they nearly drank the place dry.

By the time they were the last two employees left up front, Mr. Sims was so soused he thought he was hearing things. There was a loud thump from the back that vaguely caught his attention. His head cocked.

"Did you hear sumpfin?" Mr. Sims slurred.

Mrs. Randall was pinning on a gaudy pillbox hat with plastic holly on the wide brim.

"I don't hear anything, Mr. Sims. It must've been your imagination."

He figured she was right and shrugged it off. A minute later, he heard something else. It sounded like a scream.

"I heard something, by God." Mr. Sims wandered off toward the back of the store, his curiosity leading him away. Mrs. Randall only had interest in getting her holiday hat pinned on right. In her inebriated state, she kept pinning her fingers instead.

Mr. Sims encountered no one on his way to the stockroom. He pushed the Employees Only door open.

The stockroom was darker than the rest of the store, but that made no difference. Nobody knew the layout better, even in the dark. It was silent back here, until he heard soft jingling. He stopped his forward advance to listen more closely. Now it was silent again.

"Sims, you're drunk. You're hearing things." He laughed at himself because he was a silly drunk. Once again, he heard those jingle bells, and they were closer. Somebody was back here ringing their bell, or getting their bell rung. He was eager to see who it was and what holiday mischief they were up to.

"Yoo-hoo!" Mr. Sims called out and slowly turned. He nearly toppled like a top at the end of its spin.

There was a sudden blur of red moving through the dark, stopping directly before him, wrenching an audible gasp out of him.

It was Santa Claus. Even as pickled as he was, he recognized his stockboy Billy.

Santa Billy's arm swung up, and what he held was the curved claw hammer. Santa had turned diabolical.

Mr. Sims let out a scream. In that, he didn't slur. He also felt a flash of betrayal because he'd given Billy a job, welcomed him into his store, and treated him like family.

He saw a quick blur of downward movement. The last sound he heard after the crunch of his skull caving in was the splat of his blood and brains against the stock boxes.

What Mr. Sims was too newly dead to hear was Santa's edict that came after.

"That's what happens when Santa punishes you. That's what I do to you when you're naughty."

Once her pillbox hat was pinned into place, albeit a bit crookedly, Mrs. Randall reached for her cup and found it empty.

There was still wine in a few open bottles, but she didn't need any more. She'd already taken many sips beyond her cut off point.

At some point soon, she'd have to get home. Getting a DUI or a ride was not a concern, as she lived less than half a mile away and walked to work daily. Nobody else here was sober enough to drive her home anyway.

It dawned on her that she was alone in the front of the store. Were she and Mr. Sims the last hold outs? It didn't matter, as it was rather peaceful in this near empty toy wonderland on Christmas Eve. The busy season was now behind them, and all these decorations that were her pride and joy would be packed away for the next eleven months.

The store was quiet with the Christmas music off, but it was not entirely silent. The animatronic decorations had much to say as their motors hummed and gears whirred while they nodded and waved. The holiday locomotive chugged past beside her.

Her thoughts turned to her son, who was holding down the house tonight. Chad liked to stay up late, and no doubt he'd be up watching R-rated movies on HBO or stealing sips from her alcohol stash. He had no idea she was very aware of his covert drinking. So long as he was staying in and keeping out of outside trouble, she didn't think some adult movies or beverages were all that bad for him.

Hopefully she could get Chad into bed quickly when she got home so she could put out his Christmas presents for the morning. It was time to say good night here.

Where was Mr. Sims anyway? He'd been gone for about five minutes.

"Mr. Sims?" she called out, and her voice echoed. She had the kind of booming voice you could hear anywhere in the store. He didn't reply.

"Oh Mr. Si-immmms!"

He had to hear that, or he was dead drunk, she thought jokingly.

"Mr. Sims!" she shouted one more time. There was a response of sorts, just not the kind she expected.

The overhead fluorescent lights turned off, while the decorative circuits remained on. The store looked like a Christmas wonderland at night. Strands of colored lights lining the walls and shelves continued to twinkle. The jolly automatons continued their dancing. The Christmas tree sparkled before the painted front windows. A small headlight lit the circular path of the toy locomotive.

The look of the store, with so much piercing color decorating the darkness, she found breathtaking.

"Ooo. Mr. Sims! Come out here and see this! It's lovely!"

This image of Christmas lights in the dark brought her a deep nostalgia for the holidays of her youth. Those memories were less clear year by year and shared the same quality of flashing bursts of color in the dark.

As enchanting as the store appeared, her isolation within it was a tad unsettling.

"Mr. Sims?" she called out as she made her way to the back. The Christmas lights along the shelves guided her. It was noticeably quieter toward the rear of the store, away from the chugging train and animatronics.

Stopping before the Employees Only door, she pushed it cautiously open a crack. It looked much the same on the other side, with the overhead lights off and the Christmas lights on.

"Mr. Sims, are you hiding in there?"

She stepped through the doorway into the stockroom.

In the back she heard a soft jingling of bells. She only took a couple of steps before locating Mr. Sims ahead. At first, she thought he was passed out, but that was not the case. Her wide grin twisted down into a grimace of disgust. Her scream sounded strange to her, almost unrecognizable.

Mr. Sims wasn't dead drunk; he was stone-cold dead. Only he wasn't cold yet. Collapsed atop a pile of semi-crushed cardboard boxes, his eyes were open, but his eyelids drooped like he was only half-awake. The claw end of a steel hammer was buried deep in his dented forehead. Blood ran in rivulets from the wound. There were soft chunks creeping down his face that she assumed were his leaking brains.

Mrs. Randall knew this carnage was no accident, no matter how drunk and clumsy Mr. Sims was. His was an untimely death.

And who committed this brutal murder? The killer was likely in the back with her. Again, she heard soft jingling bells, but could not place them in the stockroom.

Mrs. Randall backstepped through the door. Beside the time clock, she momentarily froze.

"Oh, oh God! Ooooooooh, shit!"

Being quiet was the wisest move, but she couldn't help herself. She'd just lost her best friend in the most horrible way. Plus, she was highly intoxicated, which impaired her self-control.

A deep voice replied from the other side of the door.

"You shouldn't have said that. It's naughty."

She knew that voice. It was Billy. Only he wasn't himself today, not in his attitude or appearance. Today he was Santa Claus.

Just like Mr. Sims, she felt a twinge of betrayal. She genuinely liked Billy, so much so that she wished her own son Chad would grow up to be like him. They'd had deep conversations together, and she'd received nothing but hard work and good will from the young man.

Only Billy's demeanor had changed over the holiday season for the worse. No matter what Billy's grievances were, Mr. Sims did not deserve to be dead on the other side of that door.

And he said she'd been naughty for what she said. Did he mean *Oh God,* her taking the Lord's name in vain, or did he mean *shit,* a profanity? She usually swore like a sailor – though never around children, except her own – and Billy never protested her language before.

That's because his statement didn't come from Billy. It came from Santa Claus. And this Santa was a strong young man with an angry streak.

Those doors before her could burst open at any moment.

She bolted for the front doors, not once looking back as

she maneuvered through the dark. Her hope for escape evaporated as she rushed through a register aisle and came upon the entrance.

The front doors were locked. Of course they were, she'd watched Mr. Sims lock the deadbolt with his key after letting each employee out.

She did not have the key. If she planned to get out the front door, she had to go back to the stockroom to lift the keys off Mr. Sims' corpse. If she ducked out the back, she'd find herself in a long, dark alley, and the thought of being further away from people and safety made her dismiss that option.

She had to venture back into the killing zone to secure the key and her exit. She saw the phone next to a register, partly obscured by the party supplies. With no Santa in sight, she rushed to the phone, shoving a near empty bottle of wine out of the way to access it.

Now that she was in survival mode, she was able to operate without screaming or hysterics. Her finger shook as she dialed a number and heard the line ringing.

As she waited for an answer, she realized she'd called her home number by accident, though maybe that was better. It'd calm her to hear Chad's voice, giving her greater focus to do whatever it took to survive. She'd tell him to call the police and let them know she was in mortal danger. It was also her chance to tell him she loved him. If he answered that was.

Why wasn't her son answering the phone? The line just kept ringing.

"Answer," she said in a panic under her breath.

The next ring cut off partway through as she heard the click of the other line picking up.

"Thank God," Mrs. Randall said with relief. It was her boy.

A sudden downward blur appeared before her and WHAMMM! The entire sales counter shook as the fire axe chopped deep into it. A shiny red ribbon was tied around the handle beneath the blade. This was the safety axe that was mounted above the emergency fire hose in back. Safety was no longer the tool's purpose.

Mrs. Randall's heart skipped, and a startled shriek escaped her.

Santa Billy leered at her over the handle. The bastard was grinning. He was enjoying this late-night delivery of terror.

The receiver remained against Mrs. Randall's ear, but her son wasn't on the line. She traced the phone cord and saw it was split in two by the axe.

There was another phone in back.

"You said a naughty thing. Don't worry, Santa will punish you."

"You're not Santa!" Mrs. Randall shouted and studied his reaction. His insane leer remained.

Santa Billy pulled on the handle of the axe, but the blade was wedged within the counter.

Mrs. Randall saw her chance, and she threw the phone receiver as she took off. The receiver struck Santa Billy in the face, turning his head to the side. Yanking harder on the axe handle, he wrenched the blade out of the counter, and turned to look within the store.

Mrs. Randall was nowhere in sight. There was movement on all sides as the locomotive chugged, Christmas mascots waved, and lights twinkled.

Santa Billy stepped into the store with killer confidence, emboldened by the weighty weapon in his hands. The tool was now meant for execution, and he knew just how to handle it. He remembered how the killer in that movie handled an axe on Friday the 13th, punishing teenagers who transgressed with naughty behavior. Perhaps Jason should have been wearing a Santa suit, too.

Mrs. Randall wasn't out of Santa Billy's sight for long, but it was enough time to slip away. Just an inch over five foot tall, she moved at a crouch, making herself smaller. She heard the counter crack further as the axe was freed from it, and she stopped soon after. From her low, limited vantage point, she wanted to keep track of where he was. He had advantages over her, namely his strength and weapon, but if she was tracking him while she stayed hidden, she felt that gave her an edge to survive this ordeal.

Santa Billy slowly proceeded up the second toy aisle on the left of the store. His black Santa boots made not a sound upon the floor. He thought they were magic boots designed for silence to better catch the naughty ones. While his boots were silent, his voice was not.

"Twas the night before Christmas, and all through the house..."

This isn't a house; it's a toy store! Mrs. Randall wanted to shout. He was taunting her, as was typically the case with bullies and moralizers. If Billy had been this way before, she'd never have become friends with him. As she spotted him creeping through the aisle in her direction, she couldn't help wondering what happened to turn Billy into a cold-blooded murderer, and she feared for the other employees. Could some of them also be dead like Mr. Sims?

Much as she loved her job, she didn't want to die there. Fighting back would be required, because she had to get home to her son and deliver the Christmas presents hiding in her closet.

"Not a creature was stirring…" Santa Billy recited, and that was true, there was no movement at all within this aisle. Only he didn't need movement to spot his target. Through the open shelving, he could see into the left aisle, spotting the top of Mrs. Randall's holly adorned pillbox hat sitting low.

He knew right where she was hiding, crouched at the end of the final aisle. Her punishment for profanity and drinking on the job was coming, just one line of the verse away. The thrill of this hunt excited him greatly. Despite spilling so many fluids in the stockroom minutes ago, he was still leaving a trail. He believed his balls were as deep as Santa's sack.

"Not even a mouse."

After hoisting the axe high and creeping to the end of the aisle, Santa Billy charged around the shelving and swung his axe down.

The blade pulverized the pillbox hat as it cleaved through, crushing the stack of boxes the hat rested upon.

A tall stack of unpacked stock boxes in the corner teetered

forward and toppled against Santa Billy's back, sending him sprawling face first onto the floor. The ribbon adorned axe handle launched out of his hands, and the tool slid to a stop on the tile, out of his reach.

Mrs. Randall leapt from behind the boxes, maneuvering around Santa Billy before he could regain his senses. Retrieving the weapon, she ran out of his reach just as a red-gloved hand grabbed for her ankles.

She could have raised the axe and ended him right there, but inflicting violence was not the solution she had in mind. Simple escape was.

Her bold move gave her hope that she might make it out after all, albeit without her favorite Christmas hat. No longer did she need to venture into the stockroom to dig the keys out of Sims' pocket. One hefty swing of the axe at the front windows was all that was needed to get to the other side, where people walked the sidewalk and cars cruised the street. There would be others who could intervene and save her. Perhaps she would just keep running until she reached her front door and saw her son, and then call for help.

She didn't look back as she heard boxes kicked out of the way and her stalker's roar of frustration.

When she reached the exit, she prepared to swing the axe but hesitated when she saw the metal bar handles across the doors. She didn't want that barrier getting in the way of her swing, so she turned to face the enormous plate glass windows. The heavy axe was hoisted over her head.

"No!"

Mrs. Randall instinctively turned back at the exclamation, and she saw Santa Billy was armed again. He was back at the toy aisles, but that didn't lessen his threat. He held a bow and arrow, which he'd retrieved from the sporting goods shelves, aiming with the bowstring pulled back.

There wasn't a moment to waste, so Mrs. Randall turned to the front window. How foolish she'd been to get distracted for even those few seconds.

She heard a whoosh behind her and jerked in place as a sudden fire in her back traveled through her stomach. The axe fell out of her grip, and she spun in a half circle, facing her killer. Looking down, she saw the tip of the arrow dripping with her blood sticking out through her blouse, the fabric turning red as it was saturated.

Mrs. Randall's eyes looked up at Santa Billy with shock and betrayal. Her eyes pleaded for mercy, but she would not be receiving that gift from Santa this year.

The piercing arrow was less than a half inch beneath her heart, sparing that vital organ. Less fortunate was her spine, which had been shattered as the arrow ripped through it. Suddenly unable to support her weight, she felt like she was made of rubber, slowly folding down onto the ground, and collapsing into a Christmas display. A bank of artificial snow cushioned her fall. A mechanical toy Santa Claus curtsied above her, nodding his head in greeting.

The last thought to flicker through Mrs. Randall's mind was for her son Chad, as she imagined him standing with the phone, confused as to why her call for help had been cut off.

Chad's mother's lifeline had been cut as well.

Santa Billy was the last person alive inside Ira's Toys. His co-workers had been punished: Andy, Pamela, Mr. Sims, and Mrs. Randall. He'd liked them all except for Andy, but they'd been naughty. There would be no sympathy for those he punished. He knew their punishment was good, whether they knew it or not. Punishment was absolute, as were their deaths.

There was no longer any need to stay within Ira's Toys. The clock was ticking, and he had more punishment to deliver. Mother Superior was on his Naughty List, written in the largest red letters on the parchment. Hers was not the only name, however. There were others between Ira's Toys and Saint Mary's Home for Orphaned Children who'd been bad. He'd get to them whether they had a chimney or not. When Santa was coming for you, he would find you. Those were the rules on Christmas Eve, all worked in his favor.

The bow and arrow had been effective in punishing Mrs. Randall, but it was not practical for use all night. The bow was dropped on the floor. He passed through a register aisle and came upon the fallen axe. There was no better tool for punishment that he could think of, and he picked it up. Mother Superior would soon find out how much more effective it was than a leather belt.

Had Mrs. Randall made it back into the stockroom to fish Mr. Sims' keys from his pockets, she would have found them empty. Santa Billy had the foresight to pocket the boss' keys after punishing him. While he could have exited the store as Mrs. Randall intended, with one swing of the axe, it was wiser if he didn't call attention to himself. Santa Claus walking around on Christmas Eve was bound to attract the eyes of everyone as it was.

Not even God could save those who got in his way tonight.

He unlocked the deadbolt and then dropped the keys. They were of no use to him now. The moment Santa Billy stepped outside into the freshly fallen snow, Christmas Joy was doomed.

He was a teetering boulder atop a hill, tipping off and rolling a destructive path through town, annihilating everyone and everything in his path. All they could do was assess the damage when it was over and realize it was all their fault. They could have long ago set up the safeguards that kept that boulder in place. Instead, they pushed him off the edge.

Santa Billy stepped into the freshly fallen snow, the axe hanging at his side. The door swung closed behind him.

Young Billy watched Santa Billy exit the store. All he could do was observe helplessly from behind the roadside bushes as his original trauma played out before him again and again.

Seven minutes after Santa Billy exited Ira's Toys, a visitor arrived. The front door slowly pushed open, and Sister Margaret cautiously leaned her head inside. The interior was dark, though merrily lit, and it took a moment for her eyes to adjust to the gloom.

"Hello? Is anybody here?" she called out.

The sign in the window said the store was closed, but a

closed store didn't leave their door unlocked. She'd gotten there as fast as she could, although it appeared not fast enough.

Sister Ellen didn't do her final rounds of checking that lights were out until nearly 8:30 p.m.; normally she did so an hour earlier. Wrapping the Christmas gifts for placement under the tree in the early morning was the source of the delay, and she'd been helping her, wrapping as fast as she could. As if Billy's life depended on it.

As Sister Ellen made her rounds, Sister Margaret snuck into her room and snatched her car keys. Immediately she fled, and perhaps too fast because she forgot to bring a jacket on this exceptionally chilly winter's night. The speed with which she shot into town was highly unsafe, and way beyond the legal limit. Thank God she wasn't stopped by the cops. In her haste she'd also forgotten her wallet and driver's license, which somehow concerned her more than stealing a car.

Seeing nobody in the front of the store, she wondered if the employees were in the back. Perhaps it was an oversight that the door was open. If she didn't find Billy here, she'd make his apartment her next stop.

Cautiously, Sister Margaret stepped further inside, letting the door swing closed behind her.

"Billy? Are you in here?" she called out again and looked around. As she turned, a body came into view.

It was Mrs. Randall, speared through the center with a long arrow. The artificial snowbank she rested in was as saturated red as a cherry snow cone.

Sister Margaret let out a full-throated scream, and looking

up from the body, she saw a shelf of nutcracker soldiers screaming back at her, their wooden mouths open wide.

If she ventured further in, would she find Billy numbered among the dead? If that was the case, she would look for the nearest sharp implement and stab herself in the heart.

It was highly likely her Billy was responsible for Mrs. Randall's death, but that did not make her fear him. In no way could she imagine Billy lifting a hand to hurt her.

But he had put on that Santa suit. And maybe he couldn't help himself anymore.

Using the Christmas lights to guide her, she ventured further into the store. The damage to the register counter confirmed that a struggle had occurred. The phone was off the hook and the cord was cut, preventing her from calling the cops.

She worked her way to the stockroom. Upon stepping through she discovered Mr. Sims. More of his brains had escaped, clinging to his face like jelly. Moments later she found the body of a salesgirl whose name she didn't know, her bloody breasts exposed above her pile of guts on the floor. Next to her was another dead man whose eyes bulged grotesquely within their sockets. In fact, every victim had their eyes open in disbelief.

Had Billy been the last thing they saw?

None of the victims back here elicited a scream out of her. Billy's absence further confirmed to her he was responsible for these horrible murders.

And she was at fault. It was her hope that before the police found him, she would, so she could apologize. And kiss his cheek one last time before he was arrested.

There was a phone on the desk that appeared operational. As she started toward it, she slipped in something slick. Looking down, she expected to find blood on the floor.

It wasn't blood. The goo appeared shiny and whiteish. Due to low light, she crouched to get a better look at the substance. Hovering over it, she recognized the smell, and felt a pelvic thrill that was positively electric.

After dabbing a finger in the sticky fluid, she gave it a taste. This was from Billy. Oh, how she missed his delicious socks! She couldn't leave a drop of him behind.

Before she dialed the police to report the murders, she made a meal of the gift Billy left her. Once she hung up, she discovered there was a shiny trail Billy left behind that went all the way through the store. This had to be purposeful, a trail left just for her to lead her to him.

Sister Margaret continued to eat on her way out, getting down on all fours to lick the trail like a starving person licking their plate clean. She didn't get back up until the windows lit up with the emergency lights of the first responders.

Chapter

It was about a ten-mile trek from Ira's Toys to Saint Mary's Home for Orphaned Children. Santa's sleigh was out of commission this year, nor did he have wheels. If Santa Billy were to make a straight line there by foot, he could arrive soon after midnight. There might be snow upon the ground, but his big black boots were up for the trek.

Making a beeline for the orphanage was not his intention. He had an important stop to make along the way. There were two names on the list before Mother Superior's. Both naughty individuals could be found in the same place.

While it was wise to keep off heavily trafficked streets, the stop he needed to make was located on Holly Lane, a busy road lined with shops and eateries. In his favor, Santa Billy was travelling the streets on the quietest night of the year, where tradition was to be behind closed doors after nightfall. You didn't want Santa to catch you out after dark.

There were a few pedestrians who passed Santa Billy on the snowy sidewalks. They would express mirth at seeing

Santa walking the streets on his big night but smiles dissolved once the axe at his side was spotted. Santa Billy was given a wide berth, and some changed their direction to get distance from him. Good thing the two that jaywalked across the street behind him weren't noticed. Jaywalking was most definitely naughty. Instead of a citation, they would have received dismemberment.

When he reached his destination, the businesses on the block were closed for the holiday, except one. It was lit up like a beacon with bright windows and flashing lights around the marquee mounted on the awning.

Santa Billy pushed open the door to Ma & Pa's Video Palace and stepped inside. A bell on the door jingled to herald his arrival.

The new names on his Naughty List were *Ma & Pa,* written in red just like they appeared on the store's signage. All of Billy's interactions with the senior couple who ran the store had always been cordial, and the way they interacted on a personal basis with each customer made them adored elders of the community.

His view of Ma and Pa had changed drastically over the past two weeks, as he radically transformed from a genteel young man with sexual curiosities to a morally uptight executioner for abstinence.

Ma and Pa operated their business in accordance with the law. It was legal to rent pornography to adults, and indeed the store owners were careful to card any customer of questionable age who wanted to rent R or X-rated tapes. Never had they forced Billy to rent dirty movies, but they provided them, causing him to get turned on and pleasure himself, sometimes all night long. Ma and Pa tempted him to be bad.

That made Ma and Pa naughty, and they deserved punishment. On his moral crusade, instead of testifying at Congressional hearings or picketing with a placard against films he deemed obscene, his axe would cast lethal judgment.

The interior of the video store was decorated with Christmas lights and garland. There was a Christmas tree, but instead of ornaments hung on the branches, there were empty clamshell video cassette boxes for films like *Private Benjamin, Meatballs, Grease,* and *Halloween II* – not very Christmas-like in Santa Billy's holier than thou opinion.

Coming up with more reasons to justify cold-blooded murder, he thought the store should have been closed in observance of the holiday. His holiday. There were rules. Ma and Pa should have been at home under the covers of their bed awaiting Santa's arrival.

There were two people he saw within the store. One was Ma, sitting behind the far register counter, impossible to miss in her candy cane striped shirt. The other person was a customer, a middle-aged man browsing movies in the Action aisle.

Ma adjusted the spectacles on her nose as she strained to see Santa across the store. Her initial delight at Santa's visit was eclipsed by her curiosity as to who was in the suit. He was also carrying something large with a long handle that looked like a snow shovel.

"Is that Billy Chapman?" Ma asked over the counter.

"No," he replied because he was Santa now. The name Billy Chapman didn't ring a jingle bell in his brain.

Santa Billy walked up the center aisle toward the counter. Movement to his side drew his attention. The lone customer turned away from the Action section and stepped through the beaded curtain for another kind of action movie.

Santa Billy knew what naughty business that customer was going to do once he rented one of those dirty films. He now found it imperative to stop the naughty ones before they were bad. Punishment would precede the sin.

Changing course, Santa Billy turned into the Action aisle on his way to the Adults Only section.

As he turned into the side aisle, Ma's near-sighted eyes clarified what he was carrying. It wasn't a shovel after all. It was an axe.

Ma slipped through the door behind the counter into the office as Santa Billy parted the beaded curtain with his axe and stepped through.

In the office, Pa was pouring two glasses of homemade Glogg, a drink that'd been a holiday tradition during his upbringing in Denmark. As he was savoring the tangy scent of the drink's heavy spices, Ma arrived.

"Billy Chapman's back. He's dressed as Santa Claus."

Pa nodded with satisfaction. "I was wondering where he'd been lately. He bring presents?"

"He brought an axe."

Pa's eyes widened behind his spectacles. Through the wall, they clearly heard a shout from the Adults Only section.

"Naughty!"

A blood curdling scream followed. Pa was so startled that Glogg sloshed out of the Christmas mug onto his shirt. Ma put a hand to her heart.

Pa quickly placed the mug on the desk and retrieved a wooden baseball bat stashed in the corner.

"Call the police," Pa said and charged out of the office.

"Wait!" Ma shouted and followed.

The store appeared empty.

"Wait here," Pa said, and Ma thought that was a wise idea. She was an unarmed seventy-one-year-old woman and ill-equipped to confront a violent customer. Granted, her husband was four years her senior and little more than a bundle of brittle sticks in slacks and a candy cane striped shirt. Pa also had an overabundance of bravado, aided in part by the Glogg he'd been drinking for over an hour.

Pa pushed through the beaded curtain, leaving his wife behind. The first thing he saw was the man on the floor, crawling away from him. A few dozen explicit video boxes had fallen off the shelves in the struggle. There was a massive gaping wound directly between the man's legs. Blood flooded out with such ferocity Pa knew there would be no saving him.

The dying man was in civilian clothes, not a Santa suit. So where was Billy Chapman?

The Adults Only section was arranged in an L-shape, and that's when Pa saw Billy suited up as Santa step out from around the corner. Also visible was the blood-dripping weapon used on the customer. Ma had been correct about that too.

Pa cocked the bat for a swing.

"Put the weapon down, Billy. You don't want to do this."

Within the store, Ma was too paralyzed with fear to call the police. The beaded curtain before her was still, and it was quiet on the other side.

Then she heard that word again, and recognized Billy's voice. "Naughty!"

Following the word was a thump, and then more agonizing silence.

"Pa?" Ma called out with worry.

Could she find the bravery to peek through the beads? She didn't have to find out, because the beads parted as a bloody hand reached through them, Pa no longer holding the bat as he emerged. He was looking at her with wide eyes. There was a chasm of gore between them, going down through his upper jaw. Blood rushed out of his grievous facial axe wound.

Pa gurgled as he tried to pronounce "Ma", but all that came out was a watery "aaah". His extended hand clenched her candy cane blouse, and he yanked her down to her knees as he collapsed.

"Pa!" Ma screamed as she struggled to wrench free from his death grip. Her blouse tore as she achieved release, and she backed up in horror.

The beaded curtain was swinging again. Billy was in the store with her, but she couldn't see him anywhere.

Nearly breathless with fear, she forced herself to steadily back up toward the front. The shelves that made up the aisles were five and a half feet tall, and Billy was taller than that.

Which meant he was crouched in hiding somewhere. She continued her slow retreat, passing the Action aisle.

Ma came upon the movie decorated Christmas tree. She was afraid Santa Billy was hiding on the other side, and she held her breath as she passed it. Santa wasn't there.

When Ma reached the Horror section, she looked down the row and saw her path was clear to the center aisle. From there, she'd be a few strides from the front door.

Ma slipped into the Horror aisle. At 5'3", she didn't have to duck to keep out of sight. As her speed increased, so did her sorrow. She was leaving Pa behind. The hurt would break her heart literally and lethally.

As the center aisle got closer, Ma believed her husband's killer was right behind her, and she looked back. The aisle remained empty. When she looked ahead, the aisle was clear before her.

Video boxes flew off the shelves to Ma's left. *Friday the 13th, Prom Night,* and *Funeral Home* were among the titles she saw flying, and then she spotted the axe carving a sideways arc within them. The blade punched deep into her stomach. Her hands clutched the handle as she lowered to the floor in agony.

This was no longer Christmas Eve; this was Christmas the 13th. Her funeral home was real, she would be checking in shortly.

Santa Billy issued his judgment from the parallel Action aisle.

"It's naughty to rent those movies. Think of the children."

Those movies he dared not speak of now were the same ones he'd been the most avid consumer of before becoming a murderous moralist. As if to underline his hypocrisy, he was the one who left jism on the floor of the porno section tonight.

Murder was his morality now. And his aphrodisiac.

In the national wake of tonight's killings, Women Against Pornography would release graphic police photographs of the pornography strewn crime scene and claim that obscene movies were responsible for the murders.

CHAPTER

Ten carolers were gathered in chorus formation on a snowy lawn on Winterbottom Avenue. The house chosen had the most Christmas lights strung up in the windows.

The group were bundled in thick winter jackets to keep them toasty as they sang, the notes lingering as mist before them. Their song was "Christmas Fever."

"On this eve when saints and angels sing among us, holly hung just right and faces bright with Christmas fever. Happy eve of happy day, candles burning, tables full, drawers of spilling wrapping paper, closets stuffed with down and wool…"

This song was wordy and sung at a fast clip, making it the most taxing tune in tonight's repertoire. But it was no problem for Carol, leader of this mobile chorus, who supplied the cocaine many of them were on. Carol saw herself as the Snow Queen, and she'd done so many lines throughout the night she bounced in place during the song as though it carried the beat of a Go-Go's tune. Her massive perm bounced with her.

Though the lights were on inside the house and the curtains were parted, none of the home's residents made their presence known to the carolers. A lit-up plastic Santa Claus on the lawn was their audience. The guys deemed this a disappointment, as they all wanted to get a glimpse of the jingle booty inside.

This was the house of Denise Delaney, 1971's Little Miss Christmas Cutie crown holder. Now at eighteen-years-old, she was Christmas Joy's teen queen of wet dreams.

Denise's reputation as a bombshell began the night of that sensational beauty pageant, with locals repeating her catch phrases "jingle booty" and "my booty is a cutie" to this day. She loved the attention she got. Every school hallway or store aisle was treated like a runway. What girl didn't want to be the desired center of attention?

Once Denise reached puberty and started to fill out – bodaciously many boys would say – her popularity grew. Some girls didn't like how much attention Denise attracted, pretty much all the attention in every room she entered, but she was in no way a mean girl and she made it easy for everyone to like her. Adults were the ones who appeared most uncomfortable with her flaunting her sexuality. Teachers wanted to scold her for her provocative attitude and attire, but her mother encouraged her to be herself.

It was a surprise to no one that Denise grew into an exhibitionist. Denise loved to dance, and she loved rock and roll, especially wild and sexy rockers like Robert Plant, Mick Jagger, and Iggy Pop. Around the age of sixteen, she began to regularly dance in the front windows, and soon the dances turned to stripteases.

Sometimes the windows would be open so she could interact with admirers through the screens.

"Hey boys," Denise would call out. "Want a dance?"

Inevitably, they would nod yes.

If she liked the guy watching a lot, she'd give him the choice of an encore and ask, "Got any requests?"

One day she asked one of the high school football team's star players if he had a request as she danced with her blouse unbuttoned, giving an occasional flash as she gyrated.

"A boob!" the star player shouted, showing his maturity level was far less developed than his physique.

Denise let the blouse slip off her shoulders.

"How about two?" she asked and gave them a shake.

The footballer was so appreciative he thanked Denise from the field when he played his next winning game.

Occasionally her admirers left gifts on her porch, mostly dollars or phone numbers. There were more than a few Polaroids of random ding-dongs. She was flattered by them.

When 1984 arrived, her taste in rock and roll was growing heavier, and her favorite band became Motley Crue. That January, Motley Crue released the single "Looks That Kill", and it quickly became her favorite song for stripping. Little did she know she was so hot that her looks could kill, and she'd killed more than once.

Denise had a nemesis, and that was Mrs. Crabbe who lived in the house directly across the street. The elderly woman made it known every time she saw her that she did not approve of rock and roll music or dancing. While Mrs. Crabbe acted all offended and righteous, Denise thought she was just super crabby, because the woman yelled at her husband often, and he was a very mellow guy.

Mrs. Crabbe thought the teenager killed her husband. A few months before his death, he moved his favorite rocking chair across the living room to the front window. One unfortunate afternoon she found him dead of a heart attack in his rocker. This didn't surprise her terribly, as he was in his early eighties and already had three heart bypass surgeries.

What wasn't normal about his death was his open fly, or his peter hanging out of his pants. Looking through the front window, Mrs. Crabbe witnessed Denise dancing topless in her front window. Only then she understood why he'd moved his chair there, and why he'd been spending increasingly long hours street watching.

Mr. Crabbe died with a smile on his face.

Mrs. Crabbe became Denise's arch enemy, shaming and screaming at her every time she saw her, accusing her of mortal sin.

"You're going to hell, you harpy!" Mrs. Crabbe once shouted as Denise was walking home from school carrying her schoolbooks.

"It's just dance," Denise replied in her defense. "It's an art form."

Mrs. Crabbe pointed a crooked finger at Denise's crotch.

"I saw your cooter! It didn't even have hair!"

Denise shook her head. Why was this woman so hung up on her grooming?

"You're a weirdo," Denise said before hurrying into her house.

This outraged Mrs. Crabbe even more. During her rages, the old woman's hateful, broken heart grew weaker.

One early evening three months after her husband's death, Mrs. Crabbe saw the greatest outrage of her harried life. Denise was dancing in her front window topless, and a red lamp had been added to the routine, giving her a devilish hue. Watching from the sidewalk were two stunned Mormon missionaries. Denise shimmied out of her panties and danced fully nude in the window. Once again – Oh horrors! – she was fully shaved. One of the missionaries shoved a hand into his pants.

Mrs. Crabbe's ticker gave out and she croaked in the same spot as her husband. Denise's hot body had killed both Mr. and Mrs. Crabbe, one in pleasure and one in outrage.

While Denise enjoyed dancing for admirers, she didn't see herself as promiscuous. Dates were infrequent, and when she did go out with a guy it wasn't for long. As for going all the way, she had no issues with that. She wanted to try on guys the way she tried on clothes. You had to put them on you to see if they fit. And she always used protection.

For the past few weeks, she'd been dating Tommy, a nineteen-year-old she'd met at Merry Records & Tapes, the town's music store and teenage cruising spot. Not only was he blonde and fit, but he carried a bad boy edge. You might find him having a tailgate party in a stadium parking lot outside a Rush concert, something he admitted to doing every time they toured. She first spotted Tommy browsing the heavy metal section and wearing a Motley Crue T-shirt with the sleeves cut off.

Oh yes, she definitely wanted to dance naked for him.

Three weeks later they had yet to tire of each other. This Christmas Eve was a special night for them. Her parents were gone until the 26th, visiting Grandma for the holiday, and Grandma didn't like Denise much. Though they were gone, she was committed to watching her seven-year-old sister Cindy. Grandma didn't like children of any age.

Once Cindy went to bed, Denise snuck Tommy inside and took him down to the basement. This was the recreational room of the house, containing a pool table and stereo system that played records and cassettes. Tacky flea market oil paintings adorned the wood panel walls.

She was eager to get her stocking stuffed tonight. They were sprawled upon the pool table, a perfect place to score. Tommy, without his shirt, was on top of Denise, without her pants. As they made out, his hand kept slipping through the side of her panties, but she wasn't shedding them yet. His focus shifted to getting her shirt off.

Though there was no dancing, there was still music, a live chorus of carolers outside. The repetitious singsong was getting on Tommy's nerves. He didn't like any music without an electric guitar.

"Shit. I can't concentrate with that racket. Hold on."

Tommy removed himself from Denise, as difficult as that was, so he could step to the stereo. He pressed play on the cassette player, starting a sexy holiday tune called "Christmas Blues".

Tommy slid back on top of Denise and began to open the snap buttons of her blouse. She grinned and giggled, as she quite liked to be unwrapped by him.

The soulful crooner heightened the mood. They could no longer hear the carolers outside.

Once all the buttons were unsnapped, Tommy tenderly opened her blouse, revealing her heaving breasts. He leaned down to kiss her mouth, then lowered to kiss her neck, and then lowered to kiss her supple…

"Denise?" a young girl's voice called out. "Denise!" came the voice again, closer than before.

Cindy arrived at the top of the carpeted basement staircase. The young girl wore a sleeping gown and carried a stuffed Santa doll. The pool table was out of her view from the top of the stairs.

"I wanna stay up and see Santa Claus!" Cindy shouted.

Tommy sat up, allowing Denise to rise onto her elbows.

"Cindy, go back to bed right this minute," Denise said sternly.

"But I can't sleep!" Cindy shouted, and then she started down, each stair creaking.

"Holy shit, she's coming down," Tommy said and slid off Denise. She fumbled with her blouse, trying to snap it closed in a hurry.

"Cindy, ummm, don't come down here!"

Cindy came to a stop eight steps from the top. If she advanced two more steps, the pool table would come into view.

"We're... we're doing our homework!" Denise shouted, and then realized she'd snuck Tommy into the house after sending Cindy to bed.

"Who's there!?" Cindy asked, and another stair creaked. "Is it Santa!?"

"No! Just a friend! Cindy, if you don't go back to bed, Santa won't come!"

Tommy leaned into Denise's ear and spoke softly.

"He's not the only one."

Denise bit her lip and rolled her eyes, trying not to laugh.

"He won't?" Cindy asked, once again at a stop.

Tommy couldn't contain his passion any longer and he leaned in, kissing Denise on the side of the neck.

"No! You're being bad Cindy, now go back to bed!"

"Well, okay," Cindy replied. The stairs creaked again, but she was heading away.

Denise listened closely to ensure Cindy was departing.

"Back to our studies," Tommy suggested.

Denise smirked as he opened her shirt again. Tommy peeled the garment off her shoulders, tossing it onto the floor.

"Two ball in the corner pocket," Tommy said, and Denise giggled.

She purred as she laid back on the pool table. Tommy topped her again, pressing his entire body against her as they tongue wrestled. She wrapped her bare legs around his tight jeans and found the denim too course on her tender thighs. This time she would undress him, and her hands traveled down to unzip his pants.

Through the sexy background music and the moans of her man, Denise heard a steady jingling. This sound she recognized.

It was Puddy-Tat, her old tabby.

"Oh, shit," Denise said with exasperation.

"What now?" Tommy asked with growing frustration while kissing her neck.

"Sorry, Tommy. I gotta go upstairs for a minute."

"What for?"

"The cat wants to come inside," Denise said.

Tommy couldn't believe he was getting cock blocked first by carolers, then a kid, then a cat.

"How do you know?" Tommy asked.

"I heard her collar jingling at the door."

Resigned to another delay, Tommy rolled off Denise so she could get to her feet. Her top was left on the floor, but she did slip into her denim Lee cut off shorts, which were cut nearly as high as her panties. They were so tight on her ass, she struggled to get them buttoned. Shorts secured, she leaned forward and gave Tommy a brief parting kiss. Then she bounced up the stairs, and Tommy had to admit he enjoyed watching her go.

Tommy wandered to the stereo and turned it up louder. When Denise came back, he wanted no further jingling interruptions. The lyrics to the song caught his attention.

"And I'm trying to be jolly good golly, but I got the blues, I got the blues, I got the Christmas blues."

If Denise delayed their tryst much longer, he was going to get a case of Christmas blue balls.

Denise bounded up the stairs and her breasts bounced freely. If Cindy was being a good girl, she'd be back upstairs in bed by now.

There was no more singing outside. The carolers had departed in a van decorated with Christmas lights inside the windows.

Another jingle came from the porch, prompting Denise to call, "I'm coming!".

Two slender panes of glass ran parallel to the front door, both lined with Christmas lights. The decorations blocked some of the view through the windows, but not all.

Denise approached a window just as Santa Billy passed on the sidewalk outside.

Looking at the Christmas lights of the house, Santa Billy saw a topless young woman prancing in full view inside.

Topless Bimbo appeared next on his mental Naughty List. He had a gift for her tonight, a gift of hard punishment, the kind that would leave him and his axe wet.

When she reached the door, she unlocked and pulled it wide open. Freezing wind caressed her skin like icy fingers, and her nipples hardened fast. Though she'd just heard the jingle of her cat's collar, Puddy wasn't waiting on the welcome mat like usual.

"Puddy. You out there?"

Puddy neither replied nor showed herself.

"Puddeee! Kitty, kitty, kitty!"

Puddy usually responded with haste to her voice, but not tonight.

"Where'd she go?"

The night outside was still. Just a minute ago she'd heard a chorus of carolers and jingling. Now, nothing. The quiet was disquieting.

The cold was refreshing at first, but now she felt chilly. Only this was a deeper chill, like someone had walked over her winter grave.

Denise let out a huff and she could see the frost of her breath. Her Puddy was out of time.

"Okay, you're on your own until morning. Merry Christmas."

Just as she started to close the door,, she heard a jingle, followed by a startling flash of incoming movement. Puddy-Tat darted through the shrinking opening into the house, much to Denise's surprise. Her eyes followed the cat's movement inside.

"There you are, you bad kitty!"

There was another jingle behind her through the open door, along with more incoming movement.

Denise spun around as Santa Billy bounded up off the steps onto the porch, lifting his axe.

"Punish!" Santa Billy shouted.

Denise released a startled shriek, then slammed the door and backed up before it occurred to her to lock it.

The axe smashed into the laminated wood door, one side of the double-headed blade tearing all the way through. The cheap door cracked down the center from the impact. The axe was wrenched out of the wood, and the door splintered inward as Santa Billy charged inside.

Denise backed up in the foyer and bumped into a standing plant. Though rarely modest, she crossed her arms over her bare breasts.

Santa Billy stood in attack mode, both hands gripping the handle of the axe, appearing like a wild animal ready to charge.

Denise felt too weak to scream. When she spoke, her words were timid.

"Who, who are you?"

Though she saw he was dressed as Santa, she had no illusion he was the real thing. What she didn't comprehend was that he believed it wholeheartedly.

This intruder didn't answer her, but his eyes narrowed in anger. Well, she could be angry too, because this nutcase had just ruined the door and invaded her house. He was also leering lustfully at her.

"You better get out of here! My boyfriend is right downstairs!"

She wasn't lying about that, but in her panic, she'd backed up into the living room. The side staircase to the basement was cut off by this axe-wielding stranger. Tommy was a tough guy, and he could protect her from this man. But he was downstairs, and he'd turned the music up as she left. The only other witness was a stuffed deer head with enormous antlers mounted on the wall, a rather ghoulish family heirloom passed down to her father by his father.

"You've been doing something naughty. Both of you."

"Get out!" Denise shouted and hoped Tommy would come up to investigate.

"You have to be punished!"

Santa Billy lunged at her. Denise spun and ran further into the living room, past the Christmas tree, and stopped at the far wall beside the crackling fireplace where stockings hung from the mantle. Panic had blindly driven her into a dead end. She pressed her back against the wall.

Santa Billy stopped across the room from his prey. With terrifying strength, he lifted the axe above his head and threw it, the heavy tool spinning before chopping into the wood paneling a few inches from Denise's face. Her terrified eyes looked at the protruding blade and she understood how close she'd come to death. This guy fully intended to kill her.

If she was going to get away, she had to make a bold move to escape. The doorway to the dining room was on her left. If she could get there she could get to the kitchen and back door, or she could grab a knife.

Blocking her path was a recliner and coffee table. She was going to have to scramble over the recliner to escape. She leapt into action, grabbing the back of the chair as she got a foot onto the seat.

Two gloved hands seized Denise by the waist and lifted her up. She clenched the back of the chair, but he held her tighter. Cries were unleashed, as her only hope now was that Tommy would hear her and race up to her rescue. She kicked and flailed so hard her attacker dropped her on the floor.

Stunned and weeping, Denise crawled across the carpet, heading for the basement staircase. Suddenly she was crawling on air as she was wrenched up off the floor.

Santa Billy threw his struggling victim over his shoulder, constricting her breath and reducing her cries as he lurched across the room.

Watching this horrible scene of cruelty unfold was Young Billy, shivering in equal parts terror and cold. All the violent acts he watched his other half commit in that red suit were appalling, yet it was somehow worse when it was happening to a woman in a state of undress. These attacks were too reminiscent of the needlessly cruel death of his mother. Didn't his Santa half see that?

Young Billy considered shouting for him to stop, stop this madness. Doing that, however, would give up his hiding spot, and then Santa would punish him too. He didn't dare make a peep, though he was unsure he would be heard if he spoke. It was as though Santa Billy and Young Billy existed in different hemispheres.

This was in fact the truth of his split mind on this night.

Something ahead caught Santa Billy's attention, a new form of punishment since his axe was not in hand.

Denise kept kicking and crying. There was nothing else she could think to do. This crazy young guy was so strong she could not match him in a struggle of strength. Would

Tommy hear her? Suddenly, an all-new terror revealed itself, scaring her greater than any fears for her own safety.

Cindy was upstairs, and she could be hearing all of this. It was doubtful she'd fallen asleep so quickly after being sent back to bed. Likely the girl was listening in wait of Santa's arrival. What if the curious girl wandered down the stairs right now? What chance did Cindy stand against this maniac?

Protecting Cindy became her top concern. The best way to protect her sister was to stay quiet and keep from drawing her downstairs. That meant she couldn't call for Tommy either.

The force of Santa's assault was so rough she whimpered. Her ribs felt as if they might crack as he lifted her torso off his shoulder, raising her high in the air. Unable to see behind her, she didn't understand what was coming, and perhaps it was better she didn't, because she would have screamed upon sight.

"Punish! Punish!" Santa Billy shouted.

Denise was jabbed twice in the lower back by two sharp points, one on each side. With great horror she realized those points belonged to the antlers of the stuffed deer head mounted high up on the wall.

"Punish!" Santa Billy roared and pushed Denise back.

The frontal horns slid into Denise's bare back. With her skin no longer providing resistance, the antlers tore easily through her tender insides.

Denise was horribly aware of what was happening to her. She could see the eyes of her murderer and they were cold and cruel. With the impaling antlers growing in thickness inside her, the agony was beyond anything she could have ever imagined.

As this was her death, she wanted to scream her lungs out. Only she wouldn't. She would endure this suffering in silence in the hopes that Cindy would stay upstairs in bed. To achieve this, she bit her tongue.

The antlers were almost all the way through her, but Santa Billy didn't think her punishment was complete. The young woman was still too pretty, too intact, too much of a turn on. Obviously, she hadn't fully learned her lesson.

Santa Billy pushed Denise back harder on the antlers.

She could feel the popping of organs, the snapping of cartilage. The temptation to scream was so great she bit the tip of her tongue off. Blood spilled out from her lips, and she began to choke on it.

The skin of Denise's stomach stretched out in two points from her belly. With another shove, the antlers tore out. With those bloody protrusions of bone extending from her stomach, she was finally less appealing to Santa Billy. The naughty young woman could never be bad again. Her punishment was complete.

As Denise's vision departed, she thought of Cindy asleep in bed, eagerly awaiting Santa Claus, as she'd done herself many years ago at the same age.

Denise went limp but her body remained on her antler perch, much like a rag doll would. The well mounted deer head was able to withstand all one-hundred and two pounds of her. The blood that spilled from her mouth ran down between her breasts.

Admiring his handiwork, Santa Billy believed he was far more moral than his victim. He was covered in an excited sweat.

Santa Billy stepped away from his horrifying holiday decoration. Now he had to punish the guy who'd been bad with her.

Tommy sank a trick shot into a side pocket and stood back from the pool table with his cue. He'd been waiting for Denise for five minutes, maybe ten. She'd gone up to let in the darn cat, but maybe she had to deal with her little sister as well. Tuck her into bed and tell her Santa stories or something.

He couldn't hear anything upstairs with the stereo blasting. The song playing now was especially loud, a pop dance number called "Merry Christmas, Baby".

"Hey, Denise! What are you doing?"

No reply was forthcoming. He decided to head up and check on her, placing his cue on the pool table. Though Denise had pranced upstairs without a shirt on, he didn't want to run into little Cindy that way, so he grabbed his discarded T-shirt and slipped it on. He traipsed up the carpeted stairs without his shoes or socks. Along the way, he heard a brief jingling and a meow above, confirmation that the cat had been let indoors.

The moment he reached the second floor, the carpet turned cold under his feet, and he quickly saw why.

The front door was destroyed, the outdoors exposed. Freezing wind blew inside, lowering the temperature by many degrees. Puddy-Tat, sitting to the side of the door next to the radiator, appeared unharmed. The cat meowed a warning that trouble was afoot.

"Holy shit," Tommy said, surprised he hadn't heard this commotion. Granted, he'd been next to the speakers of a stereo downstairs and high on grass. He was a walking stupor when in party mode.

Now he wondered whether Denise was all right, and her little sister as well.

"Denise? Where are you?" Tommy called out as he carefully ventured through the foyer toward the living room. He regretted not putting on his shoes, because the carpet was not only cold, but host to many wooden splinters from the destroyed door.

"Denise? Are you okay?"

As he stepped into the living room, the Christmas tree drew his attention, and then the fireplace with its flickering flames. What he saw next brought him to a stop.

Stuck in the wall across the room was a massive double-bladed axe. No doubt this was the tool that'd taken down the door. His worry for Denise was genuine, and yet he had a hard time believing this odd scene was for real.

"If this is some kind of joke, I'm gonna kill her."

Tommy stepped backward and felt a warm drop land on his bare forearm. A second drop landed on his hand. He saw the drops were blood. With alarm, he began to turn, and his shoulder bumped something fleshy. Slowly, he looked over his shoulder, his eyes rising upward.

Denise was dead, impaled on the front antlers of the deer head above him. Blood ran down her legs, dripping into pools onto the carpet. Her eyes were open but unblinking, her final expression of terror frozen upon her face.

Never had Tommy experienced a shock of this magnitude. Somehow, he'd felt incapable of being frightened, but reality revealed an unforeseen weakness. Frozen in place, he let loose a startled scream of fear.

A red-gloved hand gripped Tommy's shoulder from behind and wrenched him back, throwing him across the room. Tommy tucked into a somersault and rolled before the fireplace. After grabbing a fireplace poker, he turned to see Denise's killer.

Santa Claus was facing off with him. He knew Santa didn't really exist. Whoever was in the suit was a stranger, a rather impressively built stranger unfortunately. Luckily, Santa was empty handed, while he had a lengthy steel poker. It was time to make this costumed creep pay for what he did to Denise.

Tommy swung the poker, but his target moved out of range. With his second swing, the poker hit Santa's stomach. Santa Billy fell back into the recliner and tumbled over the tipping chair, spilling him against the wrought iron railing of the basement staircase. Santa Billy rose to his feet, unsteady.

Tommy's next swing struck Santa Billy in the face so hard he thought he heard something crack. Another strike to the head sent Santa Billy backward over the railing, hitting the stairs with his head, tumbling to an immovable heap at the bottom landing.

Tommy could thank his lucky Christmas star, but he didn't believe in such things. He'd done what needed to be done, and it was only a shame he'd been too late to save Denise from this maniac. The thought occurred that this Santa could be a jilted ex-boyfriend who returned to spoil Denise's holiday.

Turning away from the railing, he saw the ribboned handle of the axe stuck in the wall. He considered relinquishing his fireplace poker for this more lethal weapon in case the guy regained consciousness. The phone on the coffee table caught his attention instead.

Tommy set the fireplace poker down to grab the receiver and dial an operator. His heart was pounding so hard he found it difficult to catch his breath. The house was silent, except for his labored breathing. Where was that little girl anyway? Had she suffered a similar fate at the hands of this killer Kris Kringle?

There was a click on the line as his call was answered. Thankfully his voice did not fail him; in fact, he sounded remarkably firm and measured in his words.

"Operator, I need the police."

The response was a jingle-jingle behind him, and then he was flying backward again, landing right before the Christmas tree. He felt the jab of tree branches against his back and neck.

A hollow voice spoke on the fallen phone receiver, asking if anyone was there. Santa Billy sought the phone cord and yanked it out of the wall.

Tommy saw the axe wedged in the wall behind this crazy guy, and the fireplace poker was out of reach. There were no suitable weapons around him.

Santa Billy lunged with the telephone cord, looping it around Tommy's neck. With his victim in a makeshift noose, he hoisted him up.

Tommy was a scrappy young man with a short fuse, the first to throw a punch at a bar, ball game, or barbecue. Having that physical advantage gave him absolute confidence that had never faltered, until now. This was the first time he felt outmatched. The way this Santa freak was holding him up and choking him with the phone cord had him afraid he could end up, like Denise, hung by the chimney with care.

These thoughts raced through his mind as he was thrown back into the Christmas tree, feeling those sharp jabs of branches and pine needles to his back and neck again. This time, some of the needles stuck. Then he was turned and smashed into the mantle, and that hurt his back much more. It was getting more difficult to breathe by the second. That was because the cord was being lifted again, and Tommy's bare feet left the carpet.

Luckily, Tommy knew how to fight dirty if he had to. He kicked upward into Santa's balls.

That was the correct release button, and the strangling phone cord was dropped. Tommy's feet hit the carpet as air was drawn into his lungs. His weakened legs didn't support him, and he fell onto the floor on his face, gasping for air. Each breath seared his throat.

Santa grabbed the back of his shirt and hauled him up. The shirt tore off his torso, and he again dropped to the carpet. His next attempt to rise was met with fists to the small of his back, sending him back down. A black boot kicked into his stomach, knocking what little air he had out of him. He was being abused like an unwanted doll by an ungrateful brat on Christmas morning.

Gloved hands grabbed Tommy under his arms and hauled him up. His feet scrambled to find purchase on the carpet, but he was on the rush forward, with no control over where he was being carried.

Tommy thought another toss into the Christmas tree was coming, but he headed instead toward a large plate glass window with the curtains parted. He closed his eyes a second before he hit.

"Punish!" was the last thing Tommy heard before he heard glass shattering.

Tommy was heaved through the living room window. The cold outside was just as cutting as the broken glass. For a few seconds as he was airborne, he thought he was flying like an angel. Within seconds of landing on the snowy lawn, he was an angel, not that he believed in angels, heaven, or the holy ghost. Such religious platitudes would be delivered excessively by his family at his funeral, whether he'd believed in them or not.

Santa Billy admired his handiwork outside the window. His punishment created a lawn decoration for the neighbors to behold. The body would also be a warning sign of what would happen to them if they too were naughty.

He crossed back through the room to wrench his axe out of the wall. In lieu of a sack of presents, he would carry sharp steel.

He'd been banged up in his fight with the young man, bleeding from a tear in his scalp acquired from either the fire poker or his tumble down the stairs. Regardless, this unexpected detour was a success. How could he just walk past the house with those tits waving in his face? Their punishment was necessary. Two more names had been added to his Naughty List, Topless Bimbo and Topless Bimbo Boy Toy.

He slowly made his way through the living room toward the front door, the jingling from his outfit adding music to his exit. A voice stopped him in his tracks.

"Santa Claus!" Cindy exclaimed from the bottom of the stairs, holding her Santa Claus doll.

Santa Billy turned to the girl. She looked young, around his age when he first met Santa Claus. The adults in this house had been very naughty, and he needed to know if she was too. His Naughty List unfurled again, awaiting another name written in blood.

Cindy had no fear of Santa. It was almost as if she didn't see the axe hanging down at his side. Santa was a mystical figure to her, and she stepped right up to him.

"I knew you'd come," Cindy said excitedly. "Did you bring me a present?"

Cindy wore an expectant smile.

Santa Billy thought, like Grandpa, that everyone was naughty, no matter their age or upbringing. The only one who was truly good was Santa, which meant his Naughty List contained the names of every person in the world.

Santa Billy leaned forward, his sweaty face lowering toward her.

"Have you been good, or have you been naughty?"

"Good!" Cindy said without hesitation, believing it wholeheartedly.

Suspicion eclipsed Santa Billy's face and he leaned in. He was looking for any telltale sign that she was lying, like a random twitch or a dubious blink. As he was able to see through walls in determining behavior, he was a master at discerning tells and fibs. In this way he could see through skin. If there was an inkling of dishonesty in her he would sense it and chop it out. He desperately wanted her to be bad.

"You haven't done anything naughty?"

As he spoke, his free hand slipped into his jacket pocket, where a second weapon was in wait, just in case the axe wasn't enough punishment for her. She was bad, bad to the bone, he just knew it.

Cindy shook her head, a smug smile on her freckled face.

"No, Santa Claus!"

The hand slipped out of his jacket pocket holding the box cutter he used to open Pamela at Ira's Toys. He extended the razor, still messy with Pamela's blood.

"Are you sure?" Santa Billy asked. This was her last chance to be honest with him before she got cut.

Cindy nodded with a buck-toothed grin.

Young Billy watched from the side of the road, holding

his breath, tears running down his face. This confrontation between Santa and the girl was too much like his youthful confrontation with Santa, an incident he was still trapped in thirteen years later.

Santa Billy caught not a whiff of dishonesty in the girl. Perhaps she was telling the truth, and this wasn't a lie. This girl was good, for this year at least. His Naughty List rolled back up and was tucked out of sight in his mind. He lowered down to her level to look eye-to-eye and saw only innocence and goodness.

Since this girl was nice, he had to give her a present. He extended the box cutter to her, the deadly tool passed from his red gloves to her little hand. Clutching the box cutter, Cindy gave Santa a quizzical look. Weren't Santa's presents supposed to be wrapped or have a bow? Still, the girl's response was polite.

"Thank you, Santa Claus."

Santa Billy responded with a wide smile. He felt genuine joy to meet another nice person, there were so few of them in the world these days. Perhaps she might make a good Mrs. Claus someday.

Santa Billy stood and sauntered off on his merry mission, his axe hanging at his side. The cat named Puddy meowed at him as he crossed through the foyer. A loose broken board was kicked out of the door frame as he exited the house.

Cindy was a rather imaginative girl, certainly more so than most kids her age. She hadn't had a wink of sleep all night, as she'd been too excited waiting for Santa. She'd been absolutely certain she'd see him tonight, and she was right. To occupy herself, she'd played a game to bide her time.

She'd heard the commotion downstairs, but all that noise she attributed to her imagination. Also, those sounds were muffled because she'd been playing in the closet with the doors closed.

Receiving the box cutter was puzzling at first because at no time that season had she told Santa Claus what she wanted. Yet right here on Christmas Eve, Santa had arrived with the toy she'd been hoping for. Not a doll, a dress, or an Easy-Bake Oven. Her interests were less gourmet and more ghoulish.

Cindy wanted surgical equipment for Christmas.

Before she went back upstairs, Cindy called out into the house. "Denise! I got my wish from Santa Claus!" As she climbed the stairs back to her bedroom, she fiddled with the sliding button on the side of the box cutter and saw how to change the length of the blade.

Once she was back in her room, she kept the lights off and went into the closet, closing the door behind her. She had the closet light on to operate her hidden laboratory.

A square of thick cardboard was the operating table. Her much-abused Barbie doll – the twelfth one she'd owned; her dollies always came to an unfortunate end – was pinned down by two long rusty nails she found long ago in the gutter. One nail pierced Barbie through her neck, the other through her pelvis, pinning her down. Sometimes these nails were used to give Barbie shots in painful looking places, like her eyes or the bottoms of her feet. Barbie's clothes had been shed; they would only get in the way of her operation.

For some time, she'd been wanting a blade sturdy enough to play advanced games with her dolls, games like Autopsy and Amputation. This box cutter was even more exciting than a scalpel because the blade was bigger. Dolls were her training ground until she graduated to worms and bugs and then stray animals.

Cindy's Santa doll was set nearby to watch the operation.

Cindy extended the blade and sliced Barbie up the middle. Had she more time to talk with Santa Claus tonight, they could have swapped tips on the best forms of punishment.

When the police combed the crime scene later, they would find Cindy's ghastly tableau in the closet, but attribute its existence to Billy. Cindy had little compassion for her sister, but she enjoyed putting on an act and fooling everyone. She was a great liar and possessed an extraordinarily naughty side. It was no wonder she and Santa Billy hit it off.

The police never found the box cutter, as she'd hidden it well.

Santa Billy's first impulse about the girl had been correct. She was very, very bad.

Cindy was the only survivor of the night's massacre that Santa Billy let go.

After exiting Denise's house, Santa Billy cut through the yard in a southeast direction. His boots crunched through the snow and over broken glass as he passed the body he ejected through the window. There were two grievous injuries upon the naughty boy, each one a life-ender. A butcher knife sized shard of glass stuck out from the center of his face. This piece had punched into his brain as he went through the window. After landing on his back on the lawn, another massive section of the shattered window fell from above and planted deep into his stomach. This jagged pane of glass was about the size of Poe's Pendulum.

As Santa Billy rejoined the sidewalk, he had a direction in mind. He would continue along the residential streets before crossing over two hills that would deliver him to the road out of town that led to the orphanage.

His path to the outskirts of town would take him through the most affluent neighborhood of Christmas Joy, though he'd be crossing a few back yards and hopping a few fences to get there. Soon, Santa would be visiting Candy Cane Lane.

CHAPTER

The police lights atop the Ford Bronco were off as it patrolled a residential street at 11 p.m. Officers Murphy and Miller had just left Candy Cane Lane, which was still merry and bright but nearly empty of foot traffic at this hour. They scanned the dark yards of the homes around them.

Neither officer was happy to be on this late-night hunt. Officer Miller had been scheduled to get off work at 10 p.m., but the call from Ira's Toys had come in during his final hour and every officer on shift was suddenly given overtime. His wife was going to bitch up a storm when he finally got home and say his work ruined her holiday once again.

His partner behind the wheel, Murphy, had no significant other to nag at him, and while he wasn't scheduled tonight, he was okay with coming in, more for the money than the thrill of the manhunt. Murphy wanted an easy shift of cruising and hoped other cops found this killer Santa first.

Every officer in town had been called in to deal with tonight's unfolding crisis, except for Captain Richards.

Nobody could reach him. Most officers believed he left town and would not return until tomorrow, right as his city suffered the greatest crisis in its history and needed him most.

"Can you believe this? Christmas Eve, and we got orders to pick up Santa Claus," Murphy griped. "Hey Miller, what do you think the captain would say if we brought in the real one?"

"I say we bring them all in, every Santa in town," Miller responded and chuckled. "Let them do a line-up." Neither officer seemed to grasp the gravity of the situation, but neither had been at Ira's Toys to see the carnage firsthand.

As they turned the corner onto another residential street, something ahead caught their attention.

"Hey! Look!" Murphy said with urgency.

There was a two-story house on the right with Christmas lights lining the rooftop. An extendable metal ladder leaned against the front of the house. Santa Claus was climbing off the ladder into an opened, darkened second floor window. Santa disappeared beyond the white curtains.

The driveway was empty, allowing Murphy to pull right up to the house. The officers bolted for the door, grabbing their firearms.

There was no time for knocking. Santa Claus was already in the house. A home invasion was in progress.

Murphy grabbed the doorknob and found it locked. Murphy's boot was the key, and he kicked the door open.

A woman named Elizabeth was on the couch snacking on a bowl of air popped Orville Redenbacher popcorn as she watched a rerun of *Perry Como's Christmas in New York* on ABC. Her favorite crooner was singing while dressed as a Salvation Army Santa when the front door burst inward. Two uniformed officers charged in with guns out. Popcorn spilled in her lap as she jumped, and she shrank back into the cushions in fear.

"What are you doing?!"

The officers gave her little more than a cursory glance, then Miller nodded at the staircase. He led the charge upstairs.

The popcorn bowl overturned as Elizabeth leapt up off the sofa.

"What do you think you're doing!?"

She joined the charge to the second floor.

"What in the goddamn hell is going on!?"

The officers reached the top and entered a hallway with closed doors on each side. Miller went to the first door on the left, Murphy following close behind.

Inside the darkened bedroom, a six-year-old girl slept deeply with visions of sugar plums and candy canes and Christmas taffy dancing in her head. A little sugar junky, this was her favorite holiday, and she'd gone to sleep wondering what Santa would bring her this year to satisfy her sweet tooth.

As she dreamed, she didn't see Santa Claus enter the room and lean over her, his red-gloved hand reaching down.

The door swung inward, and a hand reached inside to flip the light switch. Miller and Murphy charged inside with their guns leading them.

Santa Claus froze while hunched over the girl, who sat up with wondrous excitement to see him.

"Hold it! Stop right there!" Miller shouted.

Startled, Santa Claus stood quickly upright.

Overeager to be the hero, Murphy fired.

A 9mm slug tore into little Betsy's face, right between the eyes.

Elizabeth screamed so hard behind the officers she would be spitting blood later.

Angela looked back at her ruined Cabbage Patch Doll that sat on a shelf above her headboard. It didn't occur to her how close to death she'd come. Betsy had been a gift from Santa last Christmas and was her best friend. Now Betsy had a smoking hole in her pinched face.

Angela pouted. "Betsy!"

"Hands up!" Murphy screamed, confident this Santa was their suspect.

Santa Claus raised his hands and the bells on his cuffs jingled.

Angela took a longer look at Santa Claus and recognized him.

"Daddy," Angela said with wonder. She had no idea her daddy was also Santa Claus. How cool was that?

"Daddy?" Miller asked incredulous. He pulled his gun up off its target, and Murphy followed his lead.

Thurston pulled the beard down off his face.

"Yeah, daddy," Thurston said indignantly, and sat on the edge of the bed. Angela threw her arms around him.

"Can I have a new Cabbage Patch Doll?" Angela asked hopefully.

Miller gave Murphy a look that they were in for a whole heap of shit. This was obviously not the eighteen-year-old suspect they were looking for. There was no crime in commission here. They were the home invaders, barging in without a warning or warrant. For this family, their Christmas was ruined.

Murphy and Miller need not have worried. In the expansive aftermath of the night's murder spree, the family was thankful to be among the survivors, and a quick settlement would be reached to ensure their silence on the near fatal slip. The incident would never make it into the newspaper.

Very soon, Angela would have a whole shelf of brand-new Cabbage Patch Dolls.

The star attraction on Candy Cane Lane, a life-sized Nativity scene erected on the expansive front lawn of the Pennington mansion, had a star above it. This star was of the electric variety and erected upon a high pole. That this display rested at the end of a cul-de-sac made the scene even more of a spectacle and holiday destination.

Near the edge of the lawn was a three-sided hut with an arched roof, constructed with a wood frame and straw walls. Inside this hut was the manger that held baby Jesus upon a bed of straw. On each side of the manger were Mary and Joseph, hunched among blocks of hay.

Outside the hut stood the three wise men holding their ceremonial gifts, and around them lounged a calf, a goat, and two sheep. The life-sized animals had once been alive but were now stuffed. The same could not be said of the human figures. As the Penningtons made their fortune with a chain of furniture stores, mannequins were easy to employ for the display. Some thought the baby Jesus looked too realistic, with wide glass eyes that never blinked.

Before the Nativity scene stood a mailbox for the public to leave monetary donations that went to the church.

The carolers that left Winterbottom Avenue made Candy Cane Lane their final destination to sing before the holy scene. It was the same every year, and this tradition in the past had reaped rewards, which included everything from home baked cookies to Pennington Outlet gift certificates to a crisp $100 bill for each caroler. Mr. and Mrs. Pennington would watch from their front window where their ornate Christmas tree was displayed, the glitziest tree in town.

Normally the carolers were done by 10 p.m., but they'd been partying hard tonight, doing lines in the van throughout the evening. As it was after 11 p.m., all the holiday sightseers were in for the night. The Pennington's front curtains were open, displaying the tree in all its glory – this year it flashed as bright as a casino sign – but the old couple were not in the window to watch the show this late.

The carolers' audience were the mannequins and taxidermy animals, but that didn't dampen the enthusiasm of their performance. If anything, they were louder in hopes of drawing the homeowners to the windows. They wanted gifts, especially if it was cold hard cash to buy more blow.

Though this was their last stop of the night, Carol was still revved up. As the group launched into their second song, Carol bounced her way behind the others and slipped away a few steps. From her winter jacket she brought out her compact mirror and a rather generous baggie of coke. With the mirror clear of narcotics, she could see the reflection of somebody standing behind her. The reflection was of Santa Claus, and he didn't look jolly.

The Snow Queen turned with a white powdery nose. Santa Billy stood before her with a disapproving look, his weapon held behind his back.

As it was Christmas Eve, goodwill toward men and all that, she offered to share.

"Want a line, Santa?"

Santa Billy had an offering of his own, his axe.

"Naughty!"

Before Carol had a chance to react, the axe buried deep into her forehead and was wrenched out. The compact dropped and the mirror shattered on the frozen sidewalk, blood raining down upon the shards.

Carol pushed back through her singing friends with her head spraying blood, flinging the open baggie and dusting the carolers with cocaine, a narcotic snowfall.

The singing was replaced by screams. Carol stumbled ahead of the group until she slipped in the snow and collided with Mary inside the Nativity scene, falling spread-eagle over the virgin mother of Christ as she twitched in her death throess.

Santa Billy charged into the chorus who were covered in drugs.

"Punish! Punish!"

His first wide swing took down three carolers in rapid succession, opening their stomachs and spilling their bowels.

The screams grew and a few of the guys tried to fight back, revved up with narcotic bravado. None were a match against Santa Billy. The Penningtons arrived in their pajamas at the front window to see what the commotion was about. What they saw made them close the curtains and turn off the Christmas tree before calling the police.

Two young women in high heels took each other's hands as they fled. Hysterical, they slipped in the snow and pulled each other down. Santa Billy ensured they never got back up. Provocative attire like high heels was bad and warranted punishment, so their feet were chopped off first.

There were nine new names on his Naughty List, Coke Fiend #1 - #9, but he'd counted ten carolers when he arrived. Perhaps one got away, he thought, and remembered nobody could escape from Santa Claus. That's when he noticed the kneeling young woman praying with her eyes closed and head down. She'd been mistaken for a mannequin at first, but mannequins didn't invoke Christ's name with pleas for salvation.

Prayer would offer no protection from punishment, and the axe amputated her steepled hands before chopping into her bowed head.

As he left the scene, Santa Billy deposited a human heart into the church donations mailbox.

By the time the cops arrived ten minutes later – it was a rather busy night for the law in town – Santa Billy was gone. The Nativity scene was a blasphemy. Ten carolers were spread around in thirty pieces. Santa Billy was giving the coroners a gift of human body puzzles. Who didn't want a good puzzle for Christmas?

While much of the Nativity scene was destroyed – mannequins overturned, even the stuffed cow was tipped – the baby Jesus remained in his upright manger. Instead of a bed of straw, the manger was filled with entrails. An intestine sagged over baby Jesus' face. The infant savior looked like he was sucking on it like a candy cane. Maybe he was. It was a night of dark Christmas miracles.

Scrawled in large bloody letters on the sidewalk before the Nativity scene was NAUGHTY.

The following year, the anti-drug group D.A.R.E. would use sickening crime scene photos to accompany their new Christmas campaign slogan – *D.A.R.E. To Say No To Drugs… Or Santa Will Get YOU!*

Once he ventured beyond the affluent neighborhood, Santa Billy reached a rarely travelled service road that accessed the power plant, water treatment center, and little else. With no traffic in sight, Billy ambled along the shoulder traveling southeast.

The road would curve ahead as it circled the town's perimeter. He needed to detour off this street and traverse a couple snowy hills to reach the road that would take him to Saint Mary's Home for Orphaned Children.

The axe was the only belonging he carried with him. The tool was weighty, but he didn't notice. It was necessary. He needed a tool for punishment.

Despite the desolation of the area, Santa Billy heard an engine behind him, and he looked back from the shoulder of the road. A police cruiser in the distance was speeding his way. The rotating lights were on, but the siren was silent.

Santa Billy ducked behind a clump of bushes. He watched the police cruiser pass, the taillights retreating.

Santa Billy thought nobody saw him there, but he was wrong.

Crouched in hiding behind the bushes on Santa Billy's right was Young Billy, only ten feet away. Young Billy tried not to move or make a peep, afraid if his Santa side saw him, he would be punished with that axe that had ended so many lives tonight.

It occurred to Young Billy he was in the perfect position to tell his Santa side to stop this madness. If he begged and cried, would his other half see the error and terror of his ways, or find compassion and stop? It was unlikely.

For thirteen years, Young Billy had been trapped in this most vulnerable position of his past, and he didn't dare vacate his hiding spot, not yet. What chance did he have against his fully grown, armed, maniac side? None, really.

For now, Young Billy tried to wish himself invisible.

Soon enough, Santa Billy vacated his hiding spot without

seeing his innocent side at his side. Crossing the street, he began climbing the snowy hill that would take him to his destination.

As Santa Billy disappeared into the old growth woods, he believed his path would be clear of people until he reached the road out of town.

This assumption was incorrect. There would be punishment along the way.

Doug and Jay were up for an adventure tonight. Or at least a good ride. Jay was thirteen and Doug was one year older. They were a grade separate from each other but best buddies regardless.

They met a year and a half earlier at a local Al-Anon meeting and hit it off immediately. They understood each other's woes, as they both had alcoholic parents. Once they bonded like brothers, it was easier to tolerate their horrible home lives knowing they were not alone.

Tonight's adventure was taken without their parents' consent, not that they would notice or care. A mix of pills and booze would keep Doug's mother unconscious until morning, so he was able to swipe her keys and take her car out, as he regularly did.

The car was needed to carry their cargo, two Flexible Flyer sleds. After parking on the side of the road in a bank of shadows, they hiked up the hill with their sleds, eager to take advantage of the fresh snowfall.

There was an illicit thrill to tonight's festivities, as they'd committed a few crimes to get to this place, but they realized there was worse trouble they could be getting into. Most others their age were looking to score their first beer, but alcohol held no allure for them. Booze was the bane of their daily existence.

The hill was a popular riding spot for locals, with a well-worn track between the banks of trees that drew thrill-seekers on the weekends. Tonight, they had the hill to themselves, or so they thought. When they reached the top, they marveled at the untouched path that was theirs for the taking.

"Wow! Look at this hill. Virgin, man," Doug said excitedly.

"Only kind you'll ever get," Jay teased him.

"I'm going down first," Doug said, placing his sled in position and taking a seat. His ears picked up a sound that seemed entirely out of place up here, a jingling bell. Had he imagined it?

Jay saw his friend sitting silent, looking off into the distance.

"Go on. What's the matter? You afraid?" Jay asked.

"Shut up a second," Doug said, looking around cautiously between the trees. Once again, he heard a jingle. Did Jay not hear it too?

"Are you having a religious experience?" Jay asked jokingly.

"Somebody else is out there."

Because Doug spoke with such conviction, Jay scanned the woods. He knew his friend well enough to know he was not fooling around. The quiet desolation of this dark night started to unnerve him. All he heard was the breeze through the naked trees.

"Who'd be out here this time of night on Christmas Eve?" Jay asked. "Go on," he encouraged.

"Be quiet for a minute. I feel like somebody's watching us." Doug was suddenly worried it was the cops closing in, coming for the kid who stole his mom's car.

"Like who? Santa's little elves?" Jay asked, perhaps a bit too loudly, as he could hear the echo of his voice in the night.

"Well, maybe it was my imagination," Doug admitted. He didn't hear any more of that mysterious jingling.

"Yeah, it's a pretty big one," Jay said, hoping humor would ease his nerves. "Now ride your sled, or I'll go first."

"I'm going. Watch this." Doug got in push off position, and hesitated. Tree branches ahead on the left waved severely, and as he turned that way, he was struck in the face with an incoming snowball. As Jay's jaw dropped, a snowball hit his face as well.

Two seventeen-year-old high schoolers jumped out from behind a tree and gloated.

Doug and Jay knew who they were, the most notorious high school bullies in town, so cowardly they hung outside the middle school regularly to pick on kids years younger than they were. The kind of bullies who couldn't pick on others their own size.

"Well, if it isn't Bob and Mac," Jay said as he wiped snow off his reddened face.

Bob was the bigger of the two, a blockheaded farm boy in a wool lined denim jacket who made livestock look smart by comparison. Behind him stood Mac, a skinny pretty boy in a stocking cap.

"Scared you girls!" Bob laughed.

Jay gave his hands an exaggerated shake. "Ooo, good one. I almost pissed my pants. Now why don't you guys get the fuck out of the way?" Jay was still at an age where saying fuck brought an illicit thrill. He also wasn't one to take the teasing of bullies quietly. The bullying he received at home from his father was more than enough.

Doug gulped. He also dealt with a heavy degree of bullying at home. If only he could tell Jay to be quiet and not provoke these idiots. In the event he had to fight or flee, he got up off his sled.

Bob stepped up to Jay with a lopsided grin, stopping right in his face. Now Jay felt apprehension and believed he just might receive a black eye for Christmas.

"Glad to, little man. But we're going to go sledding." Bob's eyes drifted down to the sleds Jay and Doug brought with them.

Jay caught his drift. "That's the plan, huh? You guys are gonna take our sleds."

"Yeah," Bob replied snidely.

"You guys are great. You know, I want to grow up to be just like you. Ugly and very stupid."

Despite his nervousness, Doug couldn't help but chuckle. His best friend was fearless, and he'd never seen anyone stand up to Bob so boldly. He couldn't help but be impressed.

Glancing back at Doug, Jay grinned at his friend's admiration. At the same moment, Bob looked at Mac, who licked his lips in malicious anticipation.

"Is that so, pansy?" Bob asked.

"Look who's talking," Jay said fearlessly.

Bob delivered a hard fist to Jay's gut. Jay bent over and realized his prediction was wrong. He didn't get a black eye for Christmas, but maybe a cracked rib.

Taking his cue from Bob, Mac rushed forward and gave Doug a shove in the chest. Doug stumbled back and his shoe hit the sled, causing him to fall backward over it. Mac dropped down and sat on Doug's stomach. Doug could handle the humiliation and Mac's weight – thankfully he wasn't as heavy as his bully buddy – but what he couldn't stand was the rattling flatulence Mac let loose on his stomach. Not only did he hear it loud and clear, but he could also feel it like rapid-fire finger flicking on his tummy. The wafting hot stink of Mac's freshly served butt biscuits made him want to hurl.

Bob wasn't finished with Jay yet, grabbing his right arm and pinning it painfully behind his back while taking him into a headlock from behind.

"You want to take that back, fuckface?" Bob seethed, and Jay could smell the bully's rotten beer breath. Just like his father. What a loser.

"Drop dead," Jay said through his constricted throat.

"I said take it back!" Bob whined and twisted Jay's arm harder.

"All right! All right! I'm sorry!" Jay repeated in defeat,

then he was thrown down into the snow. With newfound urgency he scrambled up and away.

"Now get out of here!" Bob shouted, and Jay took off. Mac got up reluctantly, letting Doug take off after Jay. The sleds were left behind, but Doug and Jay would live to sled another day. Never would they come back to this slope, however.

"Go! Go!" Bob shouted as the younger boys disappeared into the trees.

"Get lost, turds!" Mac said and followed with a high-pitched snicker.

"We got them little pansies, huh? Now we got new sleds for Christmas," Bob bragged.

"Uh-huh," Mac replied with pride.

"All right, let's go. You go first," Bob said with a pat to Mac's back.

"Okay," Mac replied excitedly and took a seat on a sled. About to kick off, he hesitated as he heard the jingle of a bell somewhere close.

"Hey, what if I hit a tree?" Mac asked apprehensively.

"Just go," Bob said with irritation.

Mac pushed the sled off and gained momentum as he shot down the steep slope. This wasn't his first time down this incline, and he easily maneuvered between bushes and trees. He howled with excitement.

Somebody else watched Mac's rapid descent down the hill, peering through bushes on the side of the slope. He'd seen everything these two had done. They were very naughty.

Mac's sled took a small, successful jump and then slowed

to a stop at the clearing at the bottom. Mac dismounted the sled and waved up at Bob.

"Okay, Bobby! Bring it right in here, man!"

Bob waved down as he responded. "That's beautiful! All right! Now watch this!"

Pushing off on his sled, Bob let loose a cry of excitement, enjoying the echo. His arms raised in victory.

Eager to come in faster than Mac, Bob pushed at the snow and hollered louder. As he came upon a stand of bushes, a huge figure in red leapt out in his path. Even with bouncing, unsteady sight, he knew he was looking at Santa Claus.

"Naughty!" Santa Billy shouted. He held out an axe.

Instinctively, Bob threw his hands up before his face and screamed. This was the first time he'd screamed in fear, and it would also be the last.

Santa Billy swung the axe in a horizontal arc.

Mac became alarmed when Bob's hollering abruptly cut off. Had his friend fallen off the sled? When the sled came into view through the trees, he saw his friend on board. It was strange though how he was hunched over like he was touching his shoes.

Mac craned his neck to get a better look at the incoming sled.

Something was seriously wrong. Bob was missing his head. Bob's neck stump sprayed blood like a broken sprinkler. The sled slid to a stop right before him.

"Oh, God!" Mac cried out, and then started screaming.

Additional movement on the slope caught Mac's attention.

Bob's head rolled down the slope, coming to a stop near Mac's boots. Bob's eyes remained open, almost looking right at him.

"Oh, my God!" Mac exclaimed with delirious horror.

Bob's headless torso slowly tipped off the sled onto the snow. His neck stump hit the ground remarkably close to his head, as if in a failed attempt at reattachment.

Mac's screams shattered the silent night, so high-pitched that owls took flight and foxes hid. He caught more movement up the slope.

Santa Billy was walking down the hill toward him, his axe dripping Bob's hot blood. Mac continued screaming, and he made no move to escape as the threat approached. He fell to his knees before Bob's murderer.

"Punish!"

Mac's screaming ceased when his lopped off head hit the snow. Mac's head stopped rolling when it knocked into the noggin of his buddy.

CHAPTER

By 2 a.m., December 25th, the police count of the dead stood at sixteen. The bodies of Ma, Pa, and their final porno patron wouldn't be discovered until the first customers pushed through the unlocked door in the morning. Unfortunately, that family had three children in tow eager to rent Looney Tunes. What they found was not G-rated.

The decapitated bodies of Bob and Mac wouldn't be discovered until just after noon on Christmas day, when another family with kids arrived to sled the hill. By this time, not all their bodies remained. Wildlife in the area had been gifted a fresh buffet for the holiday. It took three days for Bob's head to be recovered, as it'd been moved to a nearby cave and chewed on by, well, nobody knew for sure.

Officer Olly Barnes had worked on Christmas Eve, clocking out before nightfall. When called back in for this mandatory shift, Barnes hurried in without complaint. Once he learned the situation and who the suspect was, he felt an overwhelming responsibility to find Billy. Not to shoot or arrest, but to apologize.

Much like Sister Margaret, Officer Barnes felt great responsibility for Billy, even though he'd only been part of his life for one night. But what a consequential night that was.

Thirteen years ago, he rescued Billy and Ricky on the side of the road, shielding them from their dead parents. After staying up all night watching the boys, he'd helped deliver them to Saint Mary's Home for Orphaned Children on Christmas day. From then on, he never interacted with them, even though he thought of them often, especially around Christmas.

The horror of what happened on Christmas Eve 1971 turned him away from pursing a family at the time, and that conviction never wavered. At thirty-seven years old, he'd avoided any long-term relationships, never lived with a woman, and always wore protection when he did engage in a brief fling. He didn't want any accidents that would call him daddy.

The years had not been kind to him. He'd developed the paunch of a beer belly, premature wrinkles to his face caused by the stress of his job, and a widening bald spot under his fuzzy winter hat. The funny face that had been his hallmark as a young man had turned sad, a clown with a permanent frown.

Though he thought of those orphaned boys often, he never made a point to visit them or have any additional positive effect on their lives. And now look what everyone had to deal with. The whole town was guilty in failing those boys. All the institutions intended to protect them had broken down due to negligence, stubbornness, or apathy, a conveyor belt that went to a garbage can, or a grave.

Could he have done more to set Billy on the correct path in life? Absolutely he could have, but he didn't, and now all he could do was swallow his guilt and hope he didn't choke on it.

Around 1:20 a.m. he stopped at a gas station to grab his second cup of coffee of the night, and then continued the manhunt. It was 2:07 a.m. when he spotted Captain Richards' car parked in the near empty parking lot of The Kickstand.

Barnes pulled into the lot silently with his rotating lights on. The bar sign was on, but the closed sign was up. He didn't think Richards could still be inside, and as he pulled up beside the captain's car, he saw a figure behind the wheel.

In the event Richards was sleeping it off, Barnes turned on his siren just long enough to let out a startling whoop. The slumped figure didn't move.

With growing concern, Barnes got out of his car and drew his gun as he approached the driver's door. The limited light of the parking lot revealed little inside Richards' car, but it didn't look like he was breathing.

Barnes realized he might be about to discover the latest victim of tonight's rampage. After looking around to ensure Billy Chapman wasn't closing in, Barnes grabbed the door handle. It was unlocked, and the door opened.

The smell and scene inside the car assaulted his senses, causing him to recoil.

Captain Richards' mouth hung open, vomit crusted on his chin and shirt. From the look and smell of it, his dinner had been peanuts. Even worse was the urine saturating his pants. From the severe wetness, the captain must have relieved himself quite recently.

Thankfully, the captain was breathing. Snoring, in fact.

What repulsed Barnes most was the captain's abject failure tonight. Once again, a citywide crisis had gripped Christmas Joy, even worse than what happened in 1971. And here was the chief guardian of the town, covered in his own sick, completely checked out and ineffectual.

They should have all known this could happen again. They should have been ready. Once again guilt washed over him because he hadn't predicted it himself.

Maybe they all deserved Billy's wrath.

"Richards, wake up," Barnes said disgustedly, holstering his gun.

Richards was not roused from his blackout.

"Captain Richards!" Barnes shouted and gave the horn a blast.

Richards snored and drooled in response.

Barnes walked back to his car and got his lukewarm cup of coffee. He peeled the lid off as he carried it to the captain's car and threw the beverage in his face.

This was how Captain Richards woke to the worst day of his life.

As news of the murders got out, fear and gossip fell over Christmas Joy like a blizzard. A high number of citizens had their sleep interrupted by the startling ring of their phones, followed by devastating news. There were no reports of unrest on the 11:00 p.m. local news broadcast, but word was already traveling around at that hour.

Once the populace heard of the killer Santa Claus on the prowl, most locked their doors and bolted their windows. Many homes turned off their outside Christmas lights and indoor Christmas trees. Others lit their fireplaces to block Santa's preferred entrance with flames.

While most wanted to hide from Santa tonight, there were a few who wanted to hunt for him. One of the rashest reactions came from Mrs. Randall's son. Immediately after being notified by the cops at his front door about the murder of his mother, Chad charged outdoors without a coat to hunt Billy down. The police had to restrain him, as it was past curfew, and he was now a ward of the state until they could find a relative to assume custody.

One vigilante did hit the streets, and if there were a betting pool, everyone would have placed their money on Dolores Cliff of Mistletoe Farms, the plant nursery that still thrived on the edge of town. She wasn't going on the hunt for sport. Her thirst for vengeance was personal.

At 1:28 a.m. she received the call that her twenty-six-year-old nephew Thomas had been killed that night. His pieces were mixed with the other nine carolers in that naughty Nativity scene on Candy Cane Lane.

Speaking with a loose-lipped cop, she learned that the suspect was Billy Chapman. His name and tragic story she already knew, as she was the type who knew where all the town's skeletons were buried. The weapon used was a double-bladed fire axe. The Penningtons witnessed it taking apart her nephew outside their window.

Her living quarters were located behind Mistletoe Farms, so she was able to easily gather her supplies inside the nursery. The costume Billy wore was also revealed to her; there would be no coverup this time on the killer's attire. Too many people had seen him on the streets. Finally, she learned Billy was travelling by foot, making him rather easy to spot.

It was 3:41 a.m. when Dolores stepped outside of Mistletoe Farms with the only three supplies she needed. The first was a metal folding chair she set out on the shoulder of the road, facing into town. The second item was slung around her neck, a pair of binoculars she usually used for bird watching. Her final and most important item was placed across her lap, the double-bladed tree chopping axe that long ago gave her the nickname of Lezzy Borden.

She knew Billy had grown up at the orphanage that was just a few miles further on this road. Many disillusioned young people held resentment for the home they came from, just like she did. Her suspicion that Billy was making his way back to the orphanage was not shared with her friend in law enforcement. She wanted to take Billy down herself the way he took down her nephew.

Good thing she had focus and patience because she had a while to wait.

Had Santa Billy headed straight for the orphanage after punishing the bullies who stole the sleds, he might have made it there by 3 a.m. However, he'd committed twenty-two murders in four hours, so it was time to give his axe-swinging arms a rest. Murder was a sport. Good thing he was built for the job.

Passing an outcropping of rock that created a snowless patch on the ground, Billy ducked under the overhang and found much of the breeze was blocked underneath. Less than one minute later he was in a deep sleep. The thick wool Santa suit kept him toasty. Visions of viscera danced in his head.

When Billy awoke to a growl and rustling in the foliage, it was still fully dark out. Christmas Eve was not yet over, to his relief. He slid out from his cubby hole and went down the hill.

While he thought just a few minutes had passed, he was out for over four hours. His arms were well rested; he could double the amount of punishment now.

Santa Billy crossed two modest hills, taking it slowly so as not to slip down a slope. It took nearly an hour before he worked his way out of the old growth cover and found himself back on level ground. That's when he noticed a subtle softening of the darkness. He'd slept for some time after all and felt regret he'd lost so much of the night. Christmas morning was going to dawn soon.

There was one more name on his Naughty List, written in extra-large letters: MOTHER SUPERIOR.

It didn't matter if the sun was blazing at high noon, his Christmas Eve mission would not be complete until the final punishment was delivered.

Ten minutes later, the street out of town revealed itself in the distance. Not a single car passed in the time it took him to reach the asphalt.

Dolores Cliff had no problem staying awake until dawn. Her resolve was strong, and her desire for justice absolute. In the distance, she spotted a dark shape moving along the road. She raised the binoculars and focused the lenses.

Santa Claus was walking her way with the sun rising behind him. He was carrying something, the same tool resting across her lap.

"Keep coming, asshole."

As Santa Billy closed the distance, Dolores stood from her chair and sauntered onto the street. One minute later, they stood six feet apart.

With the sun rising on the horizon, Santa Billy and Lezzy Borden faced off in the center of the road with near identical weapons. Her axe was clean and hung down beside her denim jeans. His axe was crusted with dried blood and hung down beside his fuzzy red pant legs.

"You killed my nephew Thomas," Dolores said.

"He was punished."

Dolores' rage grew. "He was a good kid!"

"He was naughty!"

"You've been naughty, fucker."

Dolores wasn't going to give Santa Billy the privilege of

striking first. She swung horizontally. Santa Billy shifted back just out of reach, and then he was swinging down at Dolores. She shifted to her right.

Santa Billy's axe struck the cold asphalt, chipping the blade.

Dolores had more to teach Billy before she killed him. "Santa's good. You're a fucking psycho."

"You're naughty!"

Dolores lunged as she took her next swing. This time the blade got close enough to slice Santa Billy through his beard. Miraculously, the hair piece remained hooked to his head, losing only a few strands.

Santa Billy's follow-up swing also got closer, striking the binoculars hanging around Dolores' neck. The strap broke, and the binoculars flew, breaking when they hit the road.

Dolores was glad it was her binoculars hitting the road and not her head, but it was too close for comfort. Her next move needed to be unpredictable.

"Maybe you didn't get the memo at the orphanage, but you should know not to mess with Lezzy Borden. Fuck with me, you get forty whacks."

Santa Billy's eyes narrowed in judgment.

"You shouldn't say dirty words like…"

Santa Billy didn't finish because Dolores lunged again. Her next swing wasn't aimed at Billy, but at his weapon. Her blade struck the ribboned handle and knocked the weapon out of his hands. The axe clattered on the asphalt directly between them, acquiring a chip to the other blade.

This was her chance to strike while he was unarmed. She

swung straight down at him. That's when he caught her by surprise.

The axe came to an abrupt stop, clenched in Santa Billy's right hand. He'd grabbed the incoming blade, and she could see the steel embedded in his hand through the glove. What her swing didn't do was lop his hand in two. His strength and submission to pain startled her.

Santa Billy shoved the axe in his grip forward. The other blade bounced against her face as it deepened the wound on his hand. A three-inch gash was left beside Dolores' nose. The force was enough to chip the bone. She was momentarily stunned, believing the injury to be worse than it was.

Santa Billy yanked the axe handle out of Dolores' hands. As she wiped away blood that spilled into her eye, Santa Billy grabbed the second axe off the asphalt. He raised both and swung them down simultaneously.

The blades cleaved deep into Dolores' collarbone on each side of her neck. She dropped to her knees, and by the time the blades were wrenched out, she'd already passed out from the pain. Santa Billy didn't let her indifference get in the way of her punishment.

Later, the coroner would confirm that Lezzy Borden died by forty whacks.

While the prior victims were left where they perished, Dolores was hidden from view, dragged out of the street, and dropped behind some shrubbery before Mistletoe Farms. A blood trail would lead right to her, but most cars speeding by would not notice it.

On the final leg of his journey, Santa Billy followed the road to the orphanage, ducking off the side whenever a car approached. There would be few cars passing on this holy morning of judgment.

Santa Billy had a final present of punishment to deliver.

CHAPTER  25

Sister Margaret went through the longest, most restless night of her life that Christmas Eve. After giving her statement to the police at Ira's Toys, she didn't want to hang around that sanguine scene any longer. She asked if Captain Richards was in and they assured her he was not, which seemed strange. More than most, she'd seen how heavily Billy's story affected him. An officer informed her they would call her in to speak with the captain later.

She also wished to flee this cop heavy scene before they asked if her car was hers.

Knowing her Billy was walking the cold streets some-where, she randomly drove around town in search of him. While she'd followed Jesus her whole life, this was the first time she'd gone cruising for a man at night.

There was one close call. She drove down Winterbottom Avenue past Denise's house five minutes before Santa Billy walked the same street.

Driving in circles made her dizzy, exacerbated by the

unusually late hour. Going back to the orphanage was not an option. In no way would she abandon Billy in his hour of greatest need. Hers as well, as this hunt was leading her into a crisis of faith.

And what would Mother Superior have to say about all this? She really didn't care anymore. She only cared for Billy. Even God would have to ride in the back seat.

Her best bet would be to wait for Billy where he was most likely to return, his apartment building.

When Sister Margaret came upon Billy's building, she discovered a police car parked outside. That was to be expected. Parking across the street from the officer, she could tell he was sleeping behind the wheel. That was good. If she saw Billy coming up the street, she could run to him first and warn him the cops were waiting. She could use her car as his getaway car. Sister Ellen's car, she remembered.

Despite her state of extreme concern for Billy, she had a hard time staying awake. There were no stimulants she engaged in, not even caffeine.

It grew colder throughout the night, and she didn't have a coat. The car was idled sporadically to blast the heat. Once turned off, she would doze off until she awoke shuddering in the cold. The only warmth she received was from her memories of Billy.

It was 4:47 a.m. when a knock on the side window awoke her with a start. Her hopes that Billy had come back were dashed when she saw the officer from across the street shining a flashlight at her. She unrolled her window, suddenly afraid he was going to tell her the search was over, and they had Billy in custody, or on cold ice.

"Yes, Officer?"

"Captain Richards is at the station now if you want to see him."

"Oh, thank you."

Sister Margaret's priorities changed, because it was better if she could convince Captain Richards that Billy wasn't bad. Billy needed their help and compassion.

Her earlier romanticized notions of escape with Billy were jettisoned as foolish and selfish. The best thing she could do for Billy was spare him from execution by cop. She had to get them to understand.

Once at the station, the officer at the front desk informed her Captain Richards was extremely busy, and she'd have to wait. The waiting area was one long wooden bench against a brick wall. At least it was warmer inside the station than the car. It didn't take long for her to fall asleep with a hard plank for her pillow.

Each time the entrance door opened, she awoke with worry and looked to see if they were leading Billy inside in handcuffs. As the minutes became hours, she wondered if Captain Richards was going to bother to talk to her at all.

Who took nuns in society seriously, really? They were a laughingstock to anyone outside of the diocese ever since that television show *The Flying Nun*. They were the butt of jokes, not credible women to be believed. And they were ridiculed. Rather than take her warnings seriously, they would dismiss her as a superstitious shrew. Could she blame them, when there were women like Mother Superior in high positions giving her kind a bad name?

Regardless, it was her duty to warn the community and lay out exactly what was happening and why. She had all the information on what made the killer tick. There was no mystery if you looked at the events that led Billy from a traumatized young boy to a delusional murderer. It was no surprise his break would occur on Christmas Eve. This was all telegraphed if anyone cared to look at the graph.

Sister Margaret saw herself like the doctor in that suspense movie, chasing his escaped mental patient around on Halloween night, a film she'd caught a few years ago on television. In her immaculate nun's habit, her discreet scruples, and her persistent crusade, she appeared like that determined psychiatrist in his flowing trench coat on the hunt for a dangerous young man. Could she really be the savior of Billy? Would anyone bother to listen to her story or take her seriously? Mother Superior certainly never had, not once.

And what exactly was she going to do if she came face-to-face with Billy now? Before the past twenty-four hours, she would have approached him with zero fear. Only now, Billy might no longer reside inside his head. He was Santa Claus now. Santa was an ancient being carrying the weight of centuries of sin. A sin-eater. A diet like that inevitably made the eater sick.

Although she'd always been firmly in Billy's corner, his most vocal defender for thirteen years, might he equate her with the sins of the orphanage and deem her one of the naughty ones in need of punishment?

Punishment is good, Mother Superior liked to say regularly. Billy had adopted her abuse as gospel, well, Santa had. Mother Superior had radicalized Billy and done everything but put the axe in his hands. That old bitch was totally responsible for this woefully lost young man and his trail of carnage. And she would make it her mission to speak of that every chance she got.

Her time at the orphanage under Mother Superior's rule was over. There was no going back after this, after the dead bodies she'd seen at Ira's Toys. Innocent victims who would not be going home to their families for Christmas. They did not deserve to be punished. Billy had never deserved to be punished either at the orphanage.

Why hadn't Mother Superior broken her cursed neck when she took that tumble down the stairs? That alone was proof there was no God, not anymore. Mother Superior would tie baby Jesus to the bedposts if she could.

If she faced Billy now, and found him unreachable, what could she do about it? She wasn't a nun with a gun, nor would she accept a firearm if offered one. She'd likely shoot herself by accident. And if she did have a weapon, could she truly use it upon him, the one who she savored?

Maybe she deserved to be struck down because she failed him. She could have snuffed out that old bitch Mother Superior for good long ago, and while that might have put her behind bars, she could sleep easy at night knowing she'd saved all the kids at the orphanage, Billy most of all. He could never have a normal life again.

It was 7:58 a.m. when Captain Richards appeared before the bench. She was dozing again, and he touched her hand to rouse her. He looked as exhausted as she did, with the additional baggage of a hangover.

After Richards was brought back to the station in the back of Barnes' car – the captain smelled far too ripe to sit up front – he washed himself in the bathroom sink at the station. Thankfully, he had a change of clothes stashed there, and some mouthwash as well.

"Oh, Captain Richards, I'm sorry. I must have fallen asleep. Any news?"

"All bad, Sister," Richards said, and repeated. "All bad."

Hearing that made her fear the worst, and she worried the next thing he would say was Billy was dead. Richards sat on the bench beside her and leaned his heavy head back on the bricks. His cranium felt full of bricks.

"Sixteen murders," Richards said, holding back from adding *so far.*

Sister Margaret's hands covered her mouth. So many lives lost because of her Billy. She would love him no matter what.

"He's been eluding my men all night. The kid may be nuts, but he's not stupid."

"No, he's not stupid," Sister Margaret said with a bit of offense at the captain's choice of words. Billy was a victim. He deserved their compassion. "In fact, everything he's been doing has a kind of logic to it, once you understand what he's gone through."

"There ought to be a way to predict his next move,"

Captain Richards said while aware his own ability to predict was hampered by his hangover.

"He believes he's Santa Claus now."

"Where would Santa Claus go on Christmas day? At least, where does Billy think he'd go?"

Sister Margaret hadn't looked at the situation from this angle even once, and suddenly the answer appeared quite clear to her. She sat forward as the revelation landed.

"Oh, my Lord."

She'd thought little of the orphanage she'd fled from like a fugitive. The institution had been pushed to the back of her mind. But Saint Mary's was likely at the forefront of Billy's mind, if she understood his mission.

Billy thought punishment was good, a concept that had been beaten into him by Mother Superior. Billy was heading to the orphanage to punish her.

Sister Margaret had to admit if she'd been in Billy's Santa shoes, Mother Superior would be at the top of her Naughty List too.

The gift giving at Saint Mary's Home for Orphaned Children began promptly at 8 a.m., and the race to the tree was practically a stampede. Mother Superior thought they would tip her wheelchair as they charged, the ungrateful brats, every last one of them.

Sister Ellen passed out the presents since Sister Margaret hadn't arrived downstairs yet. Mother Superior just sat in her chair and barked orders. Before coming down, Sister Ellen knocked on Sister Margaret's door to wake her, but she did not open the door. She wasn't aware her keys and car were gone with the Sister.

Mother Superior thought the children looked barbaric the way they were tearing into their presents, completely uncivilized. They were wild animals in need of corralling.

"I want that paper folded and stacked, not tossed about! And I want each one of you to write a nice thank you to Santa for his visit later."

The kids continued to tear into their boxes like cheetahs chomping bones to get to the marrow. This she thought as she watched excitement starved children embracing their toys and dolls with joy and love.

"Are you listening!?"

The children continued to ignore her edicts.

Among the excited throng, though acting more civilized, was fourteen-year-old Ricky. He felt indifferent about Santa's visit that morning, but he would play along to not spoil the delight of the little ones. Ricky was excited for the day, as later he expected a phone call from his brother.

Mother Superior was always critical of the children's behavior on Christmas morning. And where was Sister Margaret to help control this stampeding herd? Her least favorite Sister had better get downstairs before Santa arrived. Or else!

Part of the problem was the Santa story, which made children believe they should be given presents if they were good. When she was young, you were good because you'd be punished if you weren't.

Lips pursed in disapproval as her head shook in disgust, she made her decision. This would be the last year Santa Claus would visit Saint Mary's Home for Orphaned Children. Billy wasn't around anymore anyway to be tormented by Santa's visit. No gaudy tree either, or obnoxious blinking lights, or ugly jagged snowflakes taped to the windows.

Next year, Mother Superior was cancelling Christmas.

Little Rebecca was only six years old, but that morning she was feeling maternal. Minutes ago, she met her new best friend, Olivia, a girl doll with curly blonde hair that she thought was a cutie-patootie. She loved Olivia right away and wanted to teach her everything she knew.

Not only was Rebecca assuming a motherly role, but also Mother Superior's position. She'd wandered unseen into Mother Superior's office, which was connected to the rear of the main room. Once inside, she took a seat behind the desk and showed Olivia how to use the telephone. Rebecca had only used the telephone a few times, but she found them magical and wanted to share that magic with her new best friend.

After picking up the receiver, Rebecca play-dialed her favorite person in the world, Olivia Newton-John. She'd even named her doll after her. After introducing her doll to her imaginary friend, she held the receiver to Olivia's ear for a bit, until she was jealous that they were talking to each other more than her.

"You better say goodbye now. Mother Superior wants us to write a note to Santa Claus," Rebecca told Olivia, and she set the receiver down before jumping off the chair. Rebecca returned to the main room without anyone knowing she'd been gone.

Rebecca thought she was adept at using the telephone when in fact she was not. The receiver had been put down not into its cradle, but upon the desktop, where it would soon begin to beep a busy signal. Nobody would hear it through the excited chatter in the main room.

No one would ever discover who was responsible for taking the phone off the hook at that critical moment.

Captain Richards called the orphanage again. He'd called a half dozen times already, receiving a busy signal each time.

The receiver was slammed back into the cradle and Richards crossed to the front counter, leaning an elbow upon it. Sister Margaret paced back and forth with worry on the other side.

"Is that the only line out there, Sister?" Richards asked.

"I'm afraid so."

"It's still busy."

"I can't imagine who'd be on the phone so long," Sister Margaret replied. Mother Superior never used the telephone, she was not that modern. That left Sister Ellen, who had good reason to tie up the line that morning, to report her stolen car.

"We can't wait any longer," Richards said with resolve, and marched over to the coat bar, where his police jacket hung on a hangar. "I'm going down to the dispatcher, and then you and I are going out to the orphanage together."

Sister Margaret thought that was a workable plan. If anyone was going to catch Billy, she believed it'd be Captain Richards, whose legacy would be judged by his role today in stopping this crisis. She wanted to be there with him when he found Billy.

"Sister?" Richards said and motioned for her to follow him to the dispatch room. She'd be leaving Sister Ellen's car behind to ride with him. If Richards pulled a gun on Billy, she would jump in the line of fire to save her man.

CHAPTER

After finding Captain Richards unconscious in his car, Officer Barnes took him to the station even though he asked to go home. Barnes was so furious he could barely talk, but he did say this.

"Sixteen dead tonight. While you drank and slept!"

Taking Richards to the station would be humiliating to the captain, but it was deserved. Other officers could clean him off, sober him up, and get him back to work, while he had to clean the mess Richards left on his back seat.

Barnes then patrolled the streets until dawn. The light would make the search easier, and he believed they would find Billy soon. He felt this in his bones, and believed he was going to be the one to find him.

Barnes wasn't afraid of Billy, even with the mind-boggling body count he'd left behind. The young man had killed ten people at once. Had anyone even fought back? They had no idea if he was injured at this point. Santa Billy had what amounted to a mythical amount of strength.

And yet he had only sympathy and understanding for him, because he still saw him as Young Billy, hiding behind those roadside bushes. He knew what Billy needed more than anyone, a helping hand and understanding. He did not want to approach him as a cop with his finger on the trigger, but as a peace officer extending a helping hand.

The police radio crackled, and Captain Richards' voice came through.

"I need the nearest available officer to go out to the orphanage right away. The Santa Claus killer may be on the way there now. Responding officers are ordered to shoot to kill if necessary!"

The captain's order had devolved into an angry shout, and Barnes suspected he was overcompensating in the wake of his embarrassment.

Patrolling the back roads on the outskirts of town, he believed he was the closest to the orphanage, though heading in the wrong direction. He turned his vehicle around on the slushy roadside gravel and hit the gas.

Richards' order had just grown the target on the subject, who was likely not going to get out of this day alive, if any other cop found him.

"This is Barnes. I'll be at the orphanage in five minutes max," he replied into the mic.

He didn't know if he'd be able to shoot Billy, as he wanted to get him the help he needed. Every other available option would be exhausted before resorting to hot lead.

● ● ●

The front door of the orphanage opened as Sister Ellen let the eager kids outside to play in the freshly fallen snow, most carrying their Christmas gifts with them. Ricky was among them.

Sister Ellen would usually stand outside with the kids to supervise, but Sister Margaret had yet to come downstairs. Maybe she was oversleeping, or perhaps she wasn't feeling well. If it wasn't such a chaotic morning, she'd head upstairs to give her another wake-up call and check on her well-being.

"If any of you get wet or start to feel cold, come back inside," she called from the doorway, relieved to see the children bundling up in their coats and hats.

Sister Ellen remained inside. She could keep an eye on the outside from the warm side of the door.

Because she hadn't gone out to supervise, Sister Ellen didn't see her empty parking spot beside the building.

She also missed sight of Santa Claus as he approached the orphanage, his black boots crunching in the snow as he stepped onto the property.

The children were so preoccupied playing with new toys, packing and throwing snowballs, and patching up the snowman whose eyes had fallen out that they didn't see the adult stranger approaching. Ronald, packing a fresh snowball, turned to the road and was the first to spot him.

"Wow," Ronald said, watching the man of the hour

approach. A snowball struck Ronald on the arm, and he whipped his head around.

"Cut it out! Can't you see who's coming?"

The snowball thrower turned with Ronald. All the kids stopped playing when they looked the same way. Wonder spread across their faces.

Santa Claus had arrived, and he was making his way toward the children.

Out of everyone's view, Officer Barnes turned his car onto the road at high speed, though his sirens and rotating lights were off. He didn't want to give declaration of his arrival, giving Billy time to flee.

Barnes was relieved to see the orphanage ahead, and he was correct that he was the first responding officer on the scene, an echo of 1971. He peered through the windshield, hoping to find a tranquil scene. There was a group of children playing in the yard, but he didn't see a Sister supervising them. That seemed careless.

Barnes grabbed the mic. "This is Officer Barnes, I'm approaching the orphanage now. Everything looks okay, there's a bunch of kids playing in the yard."

Through the windshield, he saw Santa Claus step out from around the tall Christmas tree, thirty feet from the children and heading their way.

"Holy shit!" Barnes shouted. The mic dropped as he hit the gas and then skidded to a stop on the side of the road. He threw open the door and rushed to the fence around the yard while unholstering his weapon. Being a quick draw had not been part of his plan with Billy, but his timing was diabolical, just seconds too late to get in front of him. At this point, he had no choice.

"Hold it! Stop right there!"

Santa Claus kept walking toward the children, who were approaching him as a group. Including Ricky.

"I said stop! Put your hands up! Do not approach those children!"

Santa's hands remained out of sight in front of him. Barnes couldn't see if he was carrying his axe, but he had to assume he was armed.

"I said stop or I'll shoot!" Barnes repeated, his arms braced upon the fence, his firearm aimed at Santa's back. He didn't want to do this, but the suspect was disobeying his order.

Although Santa wasn't responding to him, he hoped the children might.

"Get out of there kids! Get away from him!"

Ronald led the other kids forward and extended a hand to Santa Claus.

Santa Claus stopped and leaned toward the boy.

In Barnes' mind, he could see the axe about to swing down into that innocent child, and as much sympathy as he had for Billy, he could not let that happen.

Barnes fired three times in rapid succession. Three blooms of blood erupted high upon Santa's back. Santa jerked on his feet with each shot, and then he slowly fell forward, landing face first in the snow.

The children stood momentarily silent, in a state of shock,

none more so than Ronald, who wore Santa's blood on his face and jacket.

Over Ronald's shoulder, Ricky looked on in horror. This was the first time he'd witnessed bloody murder, or so he thought. As the date was Christmas, now he would be haunted by a holiday murder like his brother.

Blood saturated the snow, the stain extending from each side of Santa's back. Santa was turning into a blood snow angel.

While he had to protect the children, Barnes despaired at the tragic scene he caused. These young ones would be traumatized for life. So would he. He'd just shot somebody he truly wanted to protect in the back. Even if given a hero's accolades, he would forever deem himself a failure over this devastating outcome.

Sister Ellen, panicked by the gunfire, burst through the entrance door. Immediately she saw Santa collapsed on the snow and knew where those gunshots had landed.

"Oh my God," Sister Ellen said in shock, and instinctively clutched the crucifix around her neck, grasping for forgiveness for taking the Lord's name in vain. "Children! Inside! Hurry!"

As the children began to cry, they turned to Sister Ellen and did as they were told. All except Ricky, who stood over the body of Santa Claus with morbid curiosity.

"Ricky! Come away from there!" Sister Ellen shouted.

Ricky obeyed, the last to return. She ushered him inside and locked the entrance door behind him.

With the scene clear, Barnes hopped the fence and approached the body of Santa in the yard. He kept his gun out, as he knew Billy was a strong young man, perfectly capable of withstanding three shots.

The scene wasn't as clear as he thought. As he checked the body in the snow, Barnes was observed by somebody watching from the stand of trees on the other side of the orphanage. Barnes couldn't hear his pronouncement.

"Naughty."

Sister Margaret sat in the passenger seat beside Captain Richards as he drove them toward the orphanage.

The dispatcher's voice burst forth from the police radio. "The man dressed as Santa Claus was shot and killed at Saint Mary's Home, ambulance is on the way."

With a burst of static, the announcement ended, and Sister Margaret closed her eyes. It felt like her world had collapsed with the delivery of that grim transmission, the one thing she feared most, harm coming to her Billy. She would never see him, smell him, or taste him again. She didn't think she could live with a hunger that deep.

Sister Margaret's tears began to spill. Richards looked over and saw the devastation on her face. He understood it. This woman had cared for Billy since he was five. It would be like losing a child for her.

"I'm sorry, Sister. But at least it's all over."

The dispatcher's voice came over the radio again, and his tone was altogether different. "Uh Captain, we've got a problem here. The description of the dead man, it's all wrong."

Sister Margaret's eyes opened with hope as Richards snagged the mic.

"What do you mean all wrong?" Richards snapped back.

"Barnes says the guy's about sixty, under six feet tall."

Sister Margaret gave Richards an incredulous look. "My God. It's Father O'Brien! He was our Santa this year!" She left unsaid that he was their Santa every year for over a decade. She also had this ghoulish thought, *better Father O'Brien than Billy.*

"The kid we're looking for is eighteen!" Richards shouted into the mic.

"Barnes warned the guy to stop, Captain. He wouldn't respond," the dispatcher replied.

Sister Margaret responded, although only Captain Richards heard her.

"Of course not, he's hard of hearing! He couldn't hear it," Sister Margaret said, her thoughts a storm of conflicting emotions.

"You tell Barnes to stay at the orphanage," Richards ordered into the mic. "The killer may still be on his way there!"

"Ten four."

As awful as the news was about Father O'Brien, Sister Margaret desperately held onto some hope.

"We've got to help him. We've just got to!"

Richards nodded and increased their speed. He wanted no more dead bodies today, not even the killer.

If Billy Chapman survived Christmas, Sister Margaret would count her blessings. If not, then God was dead to her.

● ● ●

The two paramedics got Father O'Brien's body into the back of the ambulance as quickly as possible. While Barnes confirmed to the responders that the crime scene was clear, he could not confirm it would stay that way for long. To conceal his car, Barnes moved it behind the orphanage.

Once the rear doors of the ambulance were closed, the paramedics hurried back to their seats and peeled away. Barnes watched them depart through the glass front door, framed through the center of a lit Christmas wreath.

Left behind in the yard was a massive blood stain in the snow, which was a distressing sight, but he didn't want to call attention to himself shoveling it away right now. Barnes backed up from the door, and when he turned, he was faced with Mother Superior, who glared at him.

"I don't understand how you could have mistaken Father O'Brien for the murderer in the first place. He was dressed as a Santa Claus."

Barnes looked down with shame. Father O'Brien's death was entirely his fault. He could blame Captain Richards for ordering him to shoot on sight, but there could have been a different outcome if he hadn't reacted so impulsively. He was guilty of *shoot first, ask questions later.* Good thing he wasn't Catholic. After shooting a priest he wouldn't be able to live with the guilt.

"Captain Richards can explain everything when he gets here, ma'am. I'm sorry for what happened, but there is a killer on the way here."

Maybe the gravity of what he said finally sank into that stubborn head of hers, because her tone changed. She looked back at the room full of children, who'd been ordered to sit in prayer and silence as the body cleanup commenced. While words were verboten, their sobbing was constant.

"The children. No harm must come to the children, do you understand?"

"That's why I'm here, Sister."

"I am Mother Superior!" she announced sternly. "And so far all you've done is harm."

Barnes lowered his head again. This shrew knew how to draw blood. He suspected she liked the taste.

"I'm sorry. I'm going to check out the grounds. In the meantime, you make sure everyone stays locked up inside. Don't let anybody come in unless you know exactly who it is."

"No one is going to get in who doesn't belong here!" Mother Superior barked back.

Barnes knew her combative behavior would make it harder to protect her, but he'd done his best to warn her of the threat. If she'd seen some of the bodies left behind, as he had at the Nativity scene, she'd get off her high and mighty throne and work with him instead of against him. Only Barnes had kept one piece of the story from her, and that had been in error.

Mother Superior had been told time and again a killer Santa Claus was on the way, but Barnes never told her who was wearing the suit. Had she known, she'd have understood Santa's mission was entirely personal.

Santa wasn't coming for the children. He was coming for her.

$$\spadesuit \quad \spadesuit \quad \spadesuit$$

Barnes drew his gun as he stepped outside Saint Mary's. He planned to walk the perimeter of the building and look for any signs of disturbance before heading back inside. It was preferable to confront Billy outside before he got into the building.

After any officer involved shooting that left somebody dead, the officer was relieved of duty until the investigation was complete. This was only a formality, as no officer on the force had ever been kept from coming back. Every shooting was justified on the books whether it was morally justifiable or not.

A few minutes after the shooting, he'd talked to Captain Richards on the radio, saying he would turn in his gun as soon as the next officers arrived. Richards' reaction was a surprise. He told Barnes not to relinquish his firearm or his post. Even though he'd already killed one man by accident – a priest who jigged his way into the afterlife in a hail of friendly fire – Richards wanted him to remain. He was already on the scene and knew the score, more than most officers. Plus, if Barnes turned out the hero and brought Billy in, the outrage of the accidental death would soften for him.

Barnes was thankful for this opportunity. No other officer knew Billy like he did, and he still felt sympathy for him. Nobody would be harder on Barnes for the death of Father

O'Brien than he would be himself. But collateral damage was a part of the job.

The next time he faced Billy, he promised himself he would not fire impulsively, and he'd give him a chance to surrender with no further bloodshed.

Barnes turned the corner of the building with his gun pointed at the ground. No accidents.

The children sat in grim silence around the tree. Ricky had his hand on Ronald's back, consoling him after wiping the blood off his face. Ronald's blood-stained jacket and hat had been removed.

Sister Ellen came down the stairs and went to Mother Superior, who faced the door at the front of the room.

"Did you wake Sister Margaret?" Mother Superior asked.

"She wasn't there. It doesn't look like her bed was slept in last night," Sister Ellen replied.

Mother Superior's brow furrowed with suspicion.

"We will have to tell the police when they come back."

Although there was a murder spree in progress, Mother Superior believed Sister Margaret's absence was due to her own nefarious doings. She'd lost all trust in Sister Margaret ever since she'd taken her crippling tumble down the stairs.

If only Sister Margaret had been riddled with bullets instead of Father O'Brien. That incompetent cop remained out there waving his gun around, so there was still hope.

"Poor things. They're scared to death," Sister Ellen

observed. Mother Superior failed to notice as she watched the door and fantasized about Sister Margaret's demise. Sister Ellen tapped her on the shoulder.

"Oh," Mother Superior said, coming out of her haunted head, and turned her wheelchair around. "Yes, they need something to keep their minds off it." Mother Superior observed the children, waving one up.

"Richard."

Nobody called Ricky by that name except for Mother Superior, but he knew not to challenge her about it. The old woman scared him a great deal. He'd seen firsthand how she'd treated his brother. Ricky stepped forward.

"Yes, Mother Superior."

"Will you please get my pitch pipe? Thank you," Mother Superior asked with a pinched smile, the kind that Billy never saw once in his years there.

Ricky went to a desk behind Mother Superior, checking inside the drawer. Mother Superior looked up at Sister Ellen.

"Such a good boy. Not anything like his older brother William."

Ricky heard Mother Superior's diss of his brother as he rummaged, and he disliked the old woman even more.

"Children, listen to me," Mother Superior said, and looked around to make sure she had everyone's attention. "I know that you're very upset, and I understand. But I want you to stop that moping. We're going to sing."

Ricky arrived beside Mother Superior and handed her the pitch pipe before returning to Ronald.

"Thank you," Mother Superior said. Sister Ellen sat on the corner of the sofa, as there were no other seats available.

"Ready, Sister?"

Sister Ellen nodded. Mother Superior blew into the pipe until she found her pitch.

"'Deck the Hall.' And a-one, and a-two, and a-three."

With her gnarled fingers swaying to the notes, Mother Superior led the room into song.

"Deck the halls with boughs of holly, *fa la la la la, la la, la la...*"

Denial was always Mother Superior's solution to everything. With the news shared by Officer Barnes, she should have been looking for ways to protect the building while sending the children up to their rooms to hide. But she foolishly thought nobody would dare challenge her.

Soft singing could be heard inside as Barnes circled the building. So long as he heard fa la la la las instead of screaming, he would know the kids were safe behind locked doors.

Reaching the back of the building, he hurried around the corner with his gun ready, and saw only desolation. He headed for the back door. Grabbing the knob, he gave it a shake, and was relieved to find it firmly locked. Frozen shut by the feel of it.

Drifting in the winter breeze, he heard "Don we now our gay apparel, fa la la la la..." Approaching the next corner, he made an aggressive move around it. There was no one in sight.

That's when he noticed another noise, a soft squeaking. Barnes turned and discovered the source.

The door to the utility shed was cracked open. The persistent breeze had the door swinging back and forth by a few inches, the door's rusty hinges squeaking.

The shed had to be investigated. Billy could have broken in, leaving the door unlatched. There was a chance he was hiding inside now.

Barnes stepped cautiously toward the shed. As he reached it, the door whipped all the way open, banging on the inside wall.

Barnes leapt beside the door with his back against the wall, and then he spun into the open doorway with his gun aimed.

The shed interior was empty. There was no floor inside, just a stone staircase that led downstairs to an open doorway.

He would have to go down to investigate. There was no light fixture upstairs, so he left the door open for illumination for his descent. His boots crunched on grit. It appeared the steps had never been swept in the century of their existence. No longer could he hear the seasonal singsong from inside the orphanage, and his hearing sharpened.

Reaching the bottom, he aimed into the dark doorway. Looking into the long cavern with cracked cement walls, he regretted not bringing a flashlight. It was too late to go back to his car for one now. There was one small high window that let through a modest shaft of dimmed sunlight, but every corner of the room was cloaked in impenetrable darkness.

"Is anybody there?" Barnes called out. There was no reply, not even a mouse.

Barnes gave his eyes a moment to adjust to the low light, then he stepped into the basement. The water heater took up much of the interior, located directly in the center. To explore the room, he would have to walk all the way around it. Whether from nerves or the humid interior from the radiating heater, he broke into a clammy sweat.

Each turn around the massive water heater was tense, but when he reached the third side, he began to suspect the basement was empty, the open door above the result of wear, storm damage, or negligence.

The water heater suddenly squealed and rattled, a hair-raising fright that made Barnes spin and nearly discharge his firearm again. When he saw the scream was from shaking pipes, he laughed it off and lowered his weapon, completing his journey back to the door.

His sweating was worse in the wake of the fright, and he unzipped his jacket as he walked back up the dirty staircase. Just as he reached the top landing and faint singing filled the air again, Santa Billy lunged into the open doorway, his axe rising beside him.

Officer Barnes gasped and raised his gun. He could shoot Billy in the face right now. But he didn't.

"Billy, stop!"

Much to his surprise, Santa Billy stopped.

The next few seconds were critical. Barnes desperately wished to prevent Billy from becoming his second execution of the day.

"You don't have to do this. I don't want to shoot you. Lower your weapon."

Santa Billy glared at him suspiciously, unmoving.

"I'll lower my weapon too. See?"

Barnes lowered the barrel of his gun. The axe followed suit, lowering at Santa Billy's side.

"Good. Good," Barnes said. "I know you, you and your brother Ricky. Maybe you remember me?"

Santa Billy had a quizzical look on his face, his curiosity piqued.

"I found you and your brother, thirteen years ago, on Christmas Eve. I found you on the side of the road. You were hiding."

Santa Billy's brow furrowed as he looked back into the past. Searching for a face.

"I spent that night with you boys. I brought you here."

Santa Billy looked uncertain, lost in his memories.

Young Billy watched this confrontation unfold as he hid behind the roadside bushes. He recognized Barnes as the officer who treated him so well during his hour of greatest need.

"Your brother is inside, right now. He doesn't want to see you hurt. Neither do I," Barnes said sincerely.

Santa Billy's features softened. Barnes was certain he was getting through to him.

"I understand what you've gone through. I want to see you get the help you need. Let me help you."

To fully gain Santa Billy's trust, he let his right hand slide off his gun, and he extended a helping hand. Foolish? Perhaps, but this was something he had to do in penance for shooting Father O'Brien.

Weeping profusely and wanting to be rescued from his roadside hiding spot again, Young Billy reached for Barnes' hand. Young Billy went unseen by Barnes as Santa Billy held the cop's attention.

With a quick flash of movement, Santa Billy swung the axe down, severing Barnes' right hand at the wrist. The hand did not tumble down the stairs, as it remained connected by one dangling ribbon of skin.

In his surprise and agony, Barnes lost hold of his gun. The firearm bounced down the stairs behind him.

Young Billy reacted with horror to the severed hand hanging before him, the wrist squirting blood. He tried to reach for it, but the hand spun around on its string of skin just out of reach.

Barnes looked for any spark of compassion in Santa Billy's face and saw none.

"Billy, don't do this. It's not too late," Barnes pleaded.

Santa Billy's expression was one of pure judgment.

"Naughty."

"No, please…" Barnes begged.

"I saw you kill Santa. You're a Santa killer."

"No… Billy…"

"I'm not Billy."

Barnes' last hope for reasoning was dashed.

"Punish!"

Barnes raised his remaining hand defensively and the axe swung beneath it, burying deep into Barnes' stomach. Barnes' breath and consciousness were knocked out of him, and when Santa Billy wrenched the axe out of his guts, his body tumbled down the stone stairs and crumpled at the bottom landing, his intestines oozing out.

Despite the severity of his injuries, it would take twenty-six minutes for Barnes to perish on the freezing stone basement floor. His body was discovered three minutes later.

CHAPTER

"Oh come let us adore him.

Oh come let us adore him.

Oh come let us adore him, Christ the Lord."

The strains of "Oh Come All Ye Faithful" sung by young voices could be heard outside as Santa Billy approached the orphanage. Ricky's voice was somewhere within the cacophony, not that he remembered his brother now. Mother Superior was the only face he saw. He even saw her face upon the snowman in the yard.

His weapon still dripping with Barnes' warm blood, Santa Billy swung his axe, decapitating the snowman – Mother Superior – with one swipe.

A practice run.

He hated to be back at this cursed place that held such bad feelings for him, but his visit would be brief. The punishment inside would not take long. Then he could head back to the

North Pole and go into hibernation until next Christmas Eve.

His identification as Santa Claus was absolute.

Once the children reached the end of the song, Mother Superior spoke up.

"See? Don't you feel better now?"

"Yes, Mother Superior," the children answered in unison, the ones who weren't too shell-shocked.

"I knew you would. All right, let's try 'Jingle Bells.'"

Andrew, a boy of six with bowl cut hair, looked toward the front door with disinterest. His sleepy eyes perked up.

A red-suited man was stepping up outside the door.

"I want no hold outs this time," Mother Superior announced sternly. "Now sing."

Mother Superior and Sister Ellen started into the song, and the children joined in. There was one holdout, Andrew. A smile spread over Andrew's face as he recognized Santa Claus outside. He'd just seen Santa gunned down in the yard, but that one must have been an impostor, while this Santa at the door was real.

Andrew stood up and stepped past Mother Superior.

"Andrew, where do you think you're going?" Mother Superior asked. "We need altos."

A red-gloved hand grabbed the outside handle and found it locked. That was okay, because Andrew arrived on the other side, opening the door for Santa.

Mother Superior looked over her shoulder. Panic gripped her.

"No! Don't!" Mother Superior exclaimed, and quickly turned her wheelchair around.

But it was too late. Santa Billy stepped inside, one hand planted on Andrew's shoulder, his other hand behind his back. The door slowly closed behind them but did not latch.

Mother Superior knew who this was, and it wasn't Santa. *He needs more punishment* was her first thought after recognizing Billy.

Sister Ellen understood the gravity of this situation and froze, not only her body, but her will. If Santa Billy was to walk up to her, she would be completely unable to move away.

The gloomy children turned, delighted by a real live Santa Claus inside the orphanage. A few believed it was a Christmas miracle that he'd come back to life. No child was frightened by him. In fact, they teemed forward as a group to get closer.

"It's Santa!" little Chrissy announced, and she skipped ahead of the others. In her hand was a Rubik's Cube, her present from Santa that morning.

Santa Billy stepped further into the room with a hand on Andrew's shoulder.

Chrissy bypassed Mother Superior on her way to Santa.

"Chrissy! Stay away! Stay away from him!"

Chrissy came to a stop and gave Mother Superior a sassy look.

"But Mother Superior, it's Santa Claus," Chrissy lisped through her missing front teeth.

"Chrissy, stay away from him," Mother Superior repeated. She had completely lost control of the children. It was as if they didn't hear her. After the trauma of that morning, the children were reaching for a fantasy to make them feel better.

Mother Superior never understood the true needs of children.

"Hi, Santa," Chrissy said, looking up with wonder.

Santa Billy came to a stop with his arm around Andrew, who wore a goonish grin on his face.

Mother Superior leaned forward in her wheelchair, reaching an arm out.

"Chrissy, come here. I mean it!"

The urgency of her order finally got Chrissy to break away from Santa and move to her side. Mother Superior's other arm went out.

"Andrew, come here."

Reluctantly, Andrew slipped out of Santa's grip and stepped to the other side of Mother Superior.

Now that Santa had stopped, a grin of recognition spread across Ricky's face. Santa's beard was down beneath his chin, revealing who it was.

"Billy," Ricky said excitedly.

Santa Billy gave no recognition of his name or his brother. Ricky could tell something was wrong with him, noting a strange glint in his eyes. There was also a line of dried blood on the side of his face. Ricky's smile faltered.

Santa Billy and Mother Superior were positioned face-to-face, and he towered over her. They were mortal enemies in their final showdown. Only one would be leaving alive, of that they were both sure.

Santa Billy saw the name at the top of his Naughty List, written in the largest letters – MOTHER SUPERIOR.

This old woman was the source of his greatest suffering in life. She'd abused him for over a decade. She treated him with derision at the best of times, and cruelty during the worst. His needs had been ignored. His already malleable mind had been filled with shame and harmful indoctrination cloaked as religion. She'd subjected him to Santa shock therapy every Christmas, reinforcing the holiday as the day of the year he dreaded most. Her belt had torn the tender skin of his seat. Her hands had tied him to the bedposts, leaving him in terrified agony all night. Her fingernails pierced his skin and soft tissue, drawing blood and leaving scars. She had punished him hard, relentlessly, inventing grievances that only applied to him to inflict more physical pain.

The reason for all this he now saw with extreme clarity. She was a sadist. A sexual sadist, in fact. He remembered how she'd pinched her own nipples with her sharpened fingernails in his doorway after he decked Santa Claus. Her rapturous pleasure led directly to his victimization and pain. She got off on her abuse.

Even her moniker was a deceit, she was a mother to no one. She was Sadist Superior.

And now it was time to punish her.

What Mother Superior saw was a man with violence in his eyes, though she didn't see that she'd planted those seeds and helped them grow sour fruit. In this fight she was greatly unmatched. All she could use to stop Santa were her words.

"There is no Santa Claus."

Santa Billy thought that was an odd statement for her to make, because she'd been responsible for bringing Santa Claus into the orphanage every Christmas morning. Now she wanted to convince him otherwise?

Santa Billy took another step toward Mother Superior.

"There is no Santa Claus!" Mother Superior pronounced more forcefully, pushing Andrew and Chrissy further back behind her.

The young kids were mortified by Mother Superior's pronouncements. They'd already seen Santa Claus killed today, and now she was saying he didn't exist. Their illusions were being crushed like a boot stomping on delicate Christmas ornaments.

Santa Billy knew Mother Superior was lying through her rotten teeth. There was a Santa Claus, and he was standing right before her. What other evidence did she need?

"Naughty," Santa Billy said.

Ricky looked at his brother with greater confusion. His brother barely sounded like himself, and he wasn't acting like himself either.

"There is no Santa Claus!" Mother Superior repeated like a skipping record.

"Naughty!" Santa Billy said, and finally revealed the blood-streaked axe from behind his back. Mother Superior looked up as the chipped weapon was raised in the air.

The front door burst open as Captain Richards charged inside with Sister Margaret behind him. Richards' firearm was out and raised in a flash.

"Billy!" Sister Margaret shouted, and her beloved Billy looked back.

"Put it down, Billy!" Captain Richards shouted. "Don't make me do this!"

Billy saw the gun aimed at him, but he believed he was Santa, and therefore invincible. This was the moment he'd been heading toward, delivering this last punishment, then his grand mission would be complete.

But looking at all the naughty boys and girls before him, he knew it never would be. There really were no good kids anymore. These guilty brats deserved punishment too. Especially that older kid who'd called him Billy. That kid looked especially naughty.

Mother Superior's next shout turned Santa Billy's attention back to her.

"There is no Santa Claus!"

Two furies faced Mother Superior at that moment. Behind Santa Billy, Sister Margaret glared at her. After tormenting the boy with Santa Claus shock treatment for so many years, Sister Margaret thought her audacity was abominable. That frail old woman in the wheelchair had let power poison her head, turning her into a modern disciple of the Inquisition. Everyone suffered in the vicinity of this callous, evil woman, and the innocent little children suffered most of all.

Young Billy, forever observing from his roadside hiding spot, finally broke his vocal paralysis. He shouted out like he'd never shouted before. *"Billy! It's me, Billy! Over here!"*

Santa Billy's head cocked, hearing something.

"I'm right here!" Young Billy shouted and jumped up behind the roadside bushes.

Santa Billy heard a young voice he recognized, a voice that soothed him. He tried to listen harder. He bit the inside of his lower lip so hard he took a chunk out of it, digesting the scrap with his blood.

Young Billy reached out over the bushes, straining forward. *"Take my hand!"* He knew if he reached himself, Billy would be all better.

Santa Billy couldn't fully understand his younger voice because somebody else was shouting over it, a desperate voice coming from behind him.

"Do it," Sister Margaret insisted, wanting to see Mother Superior's punishment herself. Needing to see it. "Do it!"

Sister Margaret understood Billy a whole lot better now. They had the same Christmas wish. Her message got through to Santa Billy and he remembered his mission.

This new voice Santa Billy also trusted. Her advice to him had always been sound.

"Punish! Punish!" Sister Margaret screamed in encouragement.

Santa Billy raised the axe over his shoulder.

"Naughty!" Santa Billy shouted.

Mother Superior closed her eyes, afraid to look her judgment in the face.

Two gunshots rang out, causing many young ones to scream. Sister Margaret and Sister Ellen shrieked as well. The slugs tore into Santa Billy's back, one bullet searing through his heart.

The axe dropped to the floor behind Santa Billy before he fell forward. His left hand reached out, seizing Mother Superior's brittle arm and spinning her wheelchair around as he collapsed.

None of the children were hit by shrapnel, but Ricky received a spray of blood to his face as his brother's chest erupted before him. Some of the spatter got into his mouth, which had been hanging open in shock.

Captain Richards slowly lowered his firearm as whisps of smoke rose from the barrel. There would be no more firing necessary.

Santa Billy's hand let go of Mother Superior's arm as he rolled onto his ruined back.

At that moment, Ricky was paralyzed with shock. It became difficult for him to breathe, as if he'd forgotten how. His mind could not comprehend the execution of his brother directly in front of him.

Sister Margaret approached Billy, crouching down at his side. He was still conscious. His expression was equal parts pain and confusion. She slipped a hand under his head, cradling it. He looked up at her. If this was his last vision, then she wanted him to see her, the Sister who loved him more than life itself.

His head turned to look at the frightened children piled on the sofa. One girl's tears saturated the teddy bear held under her nose.

"You're safe now. Santa Claus is gone," Santa Billy said with relief.

Santa Billy was looking toward the kids on the sofa, but all he really saw was Young Billy. They were finally reunited. In his vision, Adult Billy was laying on his back on that road thirteen years ago, no longer in the Santa suit. Young Billy ran out of his hiding spot behind the bushes, joining him at his side. Young Billy took Adult Billy's hand and squeezed tightly. They were together again. He knew who he was.

He was Billy Chapman, the perfect little boy of Jim and Ellie Chapman and older brother of Ricky. He was the boy who had looked at the illustrated *The Night Before Christmas* with absolute wonder with his brother at his side and his parents in the front seat of the car. There was no longer any need to fear Santa Claus because Santa Claus was dead.

"I love you," Young Billy said. "I love you too," Adult Billy replied.

Young Billy leaned over to take himself into a loving embrace, and they ended their existence together as one.

Sister Margaret felt Billy expire in her arms, and her tears saturated his Santa suit. Her beautiful perfect boy was dead, while this monster Mother Superior lived on. The world was an abomination. God was dead. She suddenly understood the allure of torching a church.

Sister Margaret looked up at Mother Superior with hatred. Mother Superior jerked back with a start, and at that moment she knew deep down that Sister Margaret was responsible for her crippling fall. She was sure of it. And she would punish her for it. Oh yes, she would.

"This is all your fault!" Sister Margaret screamed.

Mother Superior couldn't argue with that because she felt this *was* her fault. She believed she hadn't punished Billy enough.

Sister Margaret leaned over and kissed Billy on the lips. This was the most intimate kiss she'd ever had with a man. She could smell the smoke that discharged from the gun, and the precious blood he was spilling, but there was something more potent. A smell she liked. Her favorite smell in the world!

Sister Margaret shifted on her knees and unbuckled the thick leather belt of Billy's Santa suit.

"Sister Margaret, just what do you think you're doing?" Mother Superior asked with alarm.

With the belt loosened, Sister Margaret slid a hand down his pants and found them pleasantly moist inside. Why, it was as satisfying as sticking her fist into a nest of honey!

Pulling her hand out of Billy's pants, her fingers were slick with his jizz.

"It's Billy's gift, for me!"

To the mind-boggling shock of everyone in the room, Sister Margaret stuck her dripping fingers into her mouth and pulled them out clean.

"Stop it!" Mother Superior shouted. "Stop it you filthy whore!"

Sister Margaret grabbed the waist of Billy's pants to yank them down.

"There's more! There's so much more!" Sister Margaret shouted like the most strung out junky in the world who just found the mother load.

Mother Superior grabbed the Rubik's Cube out of Chrissy's hand and threw it. She had to do something because this out-of-control nun was about to rape a corpse.

The hard plastic toy hit Sister Margaret in the face, turning her attention to the thrower.

"You're sick!" Mother Superior scolded her.

Sister Margaret snapped out of her grief induced mania and remembered where she was. The children were looking at her with shock. Sister Ellen fainted and collapsed off the end of the sofa. Captain Richards was frozen in horror by Sister Margaret's transgression.

Sister Margaret stood up, feeling like she had a scarlet letter on her forehead – maybe she deserved it. With shame, she ran through the room toward the back, eager to throw herself upon her bed and cry forever. She suddenly stopped and turned around.

"I'm going to kill you, Mother Superior," Sister Margaret stated with chilling authority, then she ran out of the room.

An uncomfortable silence gripped the scene. Many children sniffled and wept, but nobody was bawling anymore. Captain Richards couldn't say a thing, because his alcohol sour stomach was threatening to empty itself at any moment. He didn't want to worsen this cleanup by barfing all over the crime scene. Necrophilia before a Christmas tree had not been on his Bingo card that morning, no siree.

Mother Superior saw herself like one of the champion wrestlers she watched frequently on TV, standing victorious in the center of the ring with an arm raised in triumph. It was a struggle for her not to smile because she was filled with glee at bringing an end to that terrible boy for good. She felt so righteous it was intoxicating.

Ricky was the one who saw the subtle upward twinge of Mother Superior's lips. He saw she was *happy* about this, the death of his brother. He could see right through her, and she was filled with malice. She'd always been indifferent with him, but she'd been ice cold to Billy. Everyone saw it, everyone knew it, but everyone was so fearful of her they dared not speak out.

Mother Superior's wandering eyes caught Ricky's gaze. He was glaring at her. She cracked a smile, and he saw it.

Ricky knew a word that described a woman like Mother Superior. He'd learned it from his brother.

Ricky's eyes narrowed into slits. When he spoke, he could taste his brother's blood on his lips.

"Naughty."

Author's Acknowledgments

Nobody can build a Christmas village alone. I'd like to recognize those who helped bring this book to life.

Thank you to editor Jeffrey Fenner and to Kevin Mangold, my trusted team who helped me trim this tree and drape the tinsel.

Thank you to Anthony Masi for recommending me to tackle this novelization. The Beyond Killer mastermind is really unleashing the killers with these books, and for that we are all grateful.

A bow to Michael Hickey, whose original SLAYRIDE screenplay was such a bold and thoughtfully rendered take on the slasher film. A story this great is timeless.

To the artists and talent who brought the film to life in 1984, a toast of eggnog to you all. Critics may have declared it the most reviled and despised film of the decade, but audiences and history have made it an enduring Christmas classic.

Credit must also be extended to songwriter Morgan Ames

for the original songs that give SILENT NIGHT, DEADLY NIGHT such delicious flavor. Play this film's album at your next Christmas party and shake your jingle booty.

Finally, thank you to Co-Executive Producers Scott Schneid and Dennis Whitehead for letting me pilot this sleigh, and for being so brave to allow me to bring such a naughty take on this story. They brought this killer Santa to life in 1984, and now they have done it again in 2023. This is a gift for us all.

Now let's go frolic in the snow, but please play nice.

Or Santa Claus will punish you!

About the Author

Armando Muñoz's debut novel, *Hoarder*, was hailed by Fangoria magazine as *"dynamite - a sickening, imaginative shocker."* His second novel, *Turkey Day*, marked his foray into the holiday horror subgenre and earned praise from master storyteller Clive Barker, who declared himself *"a new fan"* of Armando's work. He followed it up with the sequel, *Turkey Kitchen*, in 2021.

In 2022, Armando wrote *My Bloody Valentine*, the epic tie-in novel to the 1981 classic slasher film. In December 2023, he released the First Edition hardcover of *Silent Night, Deadly Night*, and in 2024 he continued his horrifying takeover of the holiday calendar with tie-in novelizations for *Happy Birthday To Me* (released in May 2024), *Basket Case* (released in October 2024), and *Black Christmas* (released in December 2024).

Armando is currently compiling his first collection of short Gothic fiction.

For more fantastic fiction, author events,
exclusive excerpts, competitions, limited editions and more

VISIT OUR WEBSITE
titanbooks.com

LIKE US ON FACEBOOK
facebook.com/titanbooks

FOLLOW US ON TWITTER AND INSTAGRAM
@TitanBooks

EMAIL US
readerfeedback@titanemail.com